Translated from the Original Shark

A Year of Words
by Briane Pagel

Golden Fleece Press

PO Box 1464,

Centreville, VA 20122

www.goldenfleecepress.com

Special discounts are available on quantity purchases by corporations, associations, and others. For details, contact the publisher at the address above.

Print ISBN 13: 978-1-942195-68-9

Pdf ISBN 13: 978-1-942195-69-6

Printed in the United States of America

First Edition

10 9 8 7 6 5 4 3 2 1

For Rich Cemka

Thanks for everythig.
I'm sorry I didn't know you sooner.

Editor's Note:
There are two ways to read this book. You can read all of the stories and then the end notes, or each story and its associated note. Either way, don't skip the end notes! They're an important part of the story.

Also, we encourage you to personalize this book. We've left white spaces on the pages for you to put in your thoughts, or add a drawing, or even write out a grocery list.

365: No Souls Will Burn in the Sky Tonight

When you see stars, you see...

History?

No, that's not right.

Energy?

No, that's not right, either.

Giant balls of plasma forging in their hearts elements that make up everything, spitting them out into cold dead space hoping that someday they will find another another and become...

Closer, but let's tone it down.

Let's look instead at something real.

When you see the street below, you see...

A dim haze of people who all have some place to go.

And you have no place to go.

And you have no place, too? Go.

Go away from the rail. Go away from the edge. Go away to the door. Spring to the door, swing it open, sling yourself into the stairwell, taking the stairs two two at a time, flying, almost, almost flying, down down your hurdler's stride, like the stairs are years off your life which of course they are not.

You always liked the hurdles.

Because it was a metaphor not because I was good at it.

It felt when you were going over them you were accomplishing something.

The lobby burst, burst across, slowing for the revolving door but not too much

No, it's good: we see you straining, see the brass bar and airtight seal of the entryway slowing you against your will.

Like a metaphor.

Ah, metaphor as simile!

Other runs, sprints: headlong down the orchard's grassy hill. To the waiting cab 40 minutes before the wedding (20 minutes later than it should have been).

The choir concert.

That was a fall.

Then the time at 2 a.m. as the ambulance was loaded. Let's not mention it.

We just did.

Time moves again. Rush out. Grab her.

It does not matter who. You simply need an anchor.

Grab! Her!

You tell her.

You: tell! Her!

Tell her

This is what I should have done.

And hold her like you are afraid of falling into the sky to be sucked into the stars and reassembled as someone else, but also afraid that you will not do that, too.

364: Times That Feel Like My Real Life/Times That Do Not.

Times that feel like my real life include the time at 12:40 a.m. (that's 40 minutes after midnight which is a.m. not p.m.) when a guy left this message on my cell phone:

> *Hey*

(this guy said)

> *Hey, I am just calling to let you know that we have the same phone number, except for the area code. I haven't gotten any calls for you. I thought you'd want to know.*

That's what he said. That much is true.

That much, or rather T_____H_____I_____S
much,
Is not.
I think about punctuation a lot, actually, like I did there, inventing new punctuation but Keira says it's not so much new as it is just taking other punctuation and making it look different.

"You just stretched it out," she'd say of where I talked about what is not true.

"Like taffy," she did not say. That part is true.

Keira still feels like my real life. Keira feels like the part of life I left behind, the part where I was real and she was real. She would walk ahead of me to the bus stop from our apartments, and I would see her every day for three years (well, two years and 11 months and 1 day) and never said anything to her but "Hey," a time or two, both of us with ear buds hanging out of our hoods, coffees and smartphones hanging out of our hands.
Then we got jobs in the same place, her on Four, me on Eleven which sounds like I was more important than her but really our jobs were equally important.
I first re-saw her when I was in the breakroom on Five, where everybody ate, and I was doodling a Reverse. It looked like this:

<>

And what it meant was that you were to go back and read the previous discrete set of words again for emphasis before going on. It works like this:

> *I have been getting weird phone calls in the night that make me think of you. I don't think I can go on without you<> come back home I love you, Keira.*

363: I Write Fan Fiction for People That Don't Know I'm a Fan.

Lisa is this girl.

She works in the mill, just like Dani.

Dani is this other girl.

They both do different jobs at the mill. Lisa's job is more manual labor, more heavy lifting, more pickup-truck owning, though Lisa doesn't own a pickup truck. You'd guess she does, but you'd be wrong, she doesn't.

Dani's job is paperwork. Dani always has paperwork, stuffed into her purse as she leaves, underneath the gym bag on her front passenger car seat next to the empty paper coffee cups. Both the paperwork and the gym bag have a fine dusting of pollen on them, undisturbed over the last few months of summer and fall.

Let's say they were going to a costume party, for Hallowe'en, Lisa and Dani, to a party to celebrate drinking and adults getting to dress weird forgetting that once this night was 12 hours of cowering in fear lest a headless demon ghost knock on your door and drag your spirit off to Hell to free its own for a night of blood lust.

Or something.

Would Lisa ask Dani to give her a lift? To the party? In hopes that Dani would maybe then on the ride home feel tired, and feel a connection to Lisa, who would be dressed as Wonder Woman for the night, or maybe as a sexy witch, and when they were at Lisa's sidewalk up to the duplex where she rented half from Mr. Forrester, Dani would look at Lisa in the orangey yardlight glow and Lisa would say Dani could come in and stay over if she wants and Dani would look at Lisa and would know what that meant, and then would nod almost as if nobody could see her nod but Lisa could see her nod.

The next day, they would call in sick to work and go walking around and look at the leaves that were all over the sidewalk, leaves needing raking and bagging and transporting off to wherever the city took them—*to the dump?*—one of them would ask and they would both think that was funny.

362: Happy Happy

There was a pink bunny. The authorities put it in the report. There were lots of balloons. Maybe a band, with a tuba, people said, later, to the cops, firefighters, paramedics, low-ranking government officials, self-important reporters, and onlookers with no official status but with badges who rushed in late to where they were not needed.

It was a party!

If you made a list of things you believe most unlikely to happen to a neighborhood in your life, that night would be on the list. It was so out of the expected, which says a lot for the world: a night of sheer happiness (featuring the aforementioned bunnies, probably-band, etc.) is so unexpected that when it happened we treated it like an earthquake. It was on CNN for three weeks afterward with Cynthia Sharner ("Happiness Expert, author") opining it was a mass hallucination.

But it wasn't. People were there. People lived it. Some of the streamers were still on the trees when the television cameras arrived, late, and anyway, if you hallucinate that you are happy is that any different than actually *being* happy?

That's what I used to argue with my sister:

> **"What's the difference between thinking you're feeling an emotion, and feeling an emotion?" I asked her, when she said she thought she was in love with the man she wouldn't marry anyway.**

"There's a difference," she said, and moved away with him to Florida but never married him, telling us she didn't *love* him or if she did she wasn't sure it was *love love*, unsure of the difference between states of emotion.

> **I was there that night. I can tell you I'm not exactly sure how much of the fun was just me thinking this is a lot of fun, how much was people like me and me too thinking boy I should've brought my phone to get pictures of this to put it on my blog because that was what we thought was fun before that night, but I can tell you even with not being sure what was real (the pink bunny, the hamburgers) we were not just happy, but we were happy happy.**

361:

"Do not worry if you cannot dance... no woman has ever stopped loving a man simply because he could not dance."

-- Marie Curie

He wondered if the poster was real.

She moved slowly through the crowd by the kitchen.

He wondered whose house this was.

She wanted to see what the poster of Marie Curie *said*.

He wondered how everybody else knew about the party.

She didn't have a beer in her hand, had set down her $3 cup 10 minutes after coming in, had left Kaitlyn by the guy pretending to be a DJ.

He wondered how he had heard about the party?

It didn't seem, as he stood there, that he had heard about the party, that someone could have told him about the party and he would have gone home from his classes, blown off his homework, showered, changed his shirt into the t-shirt with the obscure band name on it from his hometown, in hopes that some girl would ask him about it, and he could say he'd known the band, had sometimes filled in on rhythm guitar for them, no he wasn't a musician…

His beer was warm.

The guys playing beer pong annoyed her.

That was crazy, right? Someone had told him about the party.

Or had he simply been walking home from the Rec, seen the party, come and paid his $3 and gotten his cup, stood in the corner while guys played beer pong, looking for someone from his classes, his building, somewhere?

She saw him, standing there, looking a little flushed, staring at the poster of Marie Curie, too.

He felt dizzy, staring at the poster of Marie Curie.

His shirt looked on him like he couldn't let it go, like he was still homesick and wished he'd gone to work in his dad's garage instead of going off to college, like maybe he might not be back next semester.

The quote couldn't be real.

She tapped him on the shoulder.

After all, it was Einstein who'd said all the stuff about dancing.

He looked startled.

"I think it was Einstein who talked about dancing," she said.

He was right, of course.

360: D Is for Drums.

If God created everything then God created drums, right?

And drumsticks?

And mothers who don't like drums?

And sons who want to be drummers in rock bands, too, one could suppose.

The thing is, who wants to be the drummer in a band? Is the drummer ever anyone? Phil Collins I suppose is someone and that guy Keith Moon was someone until he was dead, because when you are dead you aren't someone anymore, is what I believe, and what Grandpa believed, too, because that's what he said to me that time that he had to take me to the doctor. Mom had to work that day. She had no more sick time and nobody had seen Dad for a year or two, maybe, although sometimes he still sent a check.

Grandpa was Dad's dad. I knew Grandpa felt bad about Dad leaving us because he told me so, driving to the doctor's office that day, my Egg McMuffin in my lap and him holding a cup of coffee he kept blowing into.

"Your dad…" he said, and shook his head. "I should've whipped that kid more," he finally said. An ambulance went by us, and Grandpa hadn't pulled over for it like I knew he should.

I was tapping my Egg McMuffin with my fingers, drumming a rhythm from a song I'd seen in a video on Youtube. I was trying not to feel like throwing up. Nobody knew why I kept feeling that way.

"Nerves," Grandpa'd said. But Mom had simply gone to do the dishes.

The ambulance turned off its lights before it turned left to the hospital, where we were going, too.

"Guy's dead," Grandpa said. "Now, he's nothing anymore. They don't have to hurry for dead guys." Later on, he'd explain to me what he meant by "nothing anymore." We'd be standing in the music store, the one over behind Denny's, and he'd be picking out the drum set he was buying for me.

"When your body stops, everything stops," he told me. "So if you want to do something, you do it now and don't worry what your mother says."

359: Pirates of the…

…South Pacific! Long waves curling over sandy shores on islands in the middle of vast seas, a large wooden ship at bay, while on the shore bonfires roar to Heaven, their ravenous maws tearing into the logs in a metaphor for how the men, and two women who have earned equal pay, today poured onto His Majesty's fleet's flagship vessel, teeth in a grimace, swords held high: chopping, slicing, pushing overboard any seaman daringly stupid enough to challenge them.

One of the women, the one who first suggested to the other that they become pirates, here, and now, rather than what they were doing there (and then) stares at the stars. "You could never see the stars in *Chicago*," she says.

"Yeah, but is it wrong, though?" the other one, the one who'd thought this idea was crazy, says to the first. She flops down on the sand, ignoring the men shouting and demanding native women bring them more wine.

"The killing, you mean?"

"Well, no." The hesitant one embarrassingly realizes even though she herself that day took a cutlass and lopped a kid's head clean off, a kid who must've been 15, and some of his blood was still on her pants, even though *that*, she wasn't *in fact* talking about *the killing* being wrong. "I mean the messing around with what's already *happened*," she explains.

Her friend, whose name, now, is *Lil*, that's what she wants to be called, asks: "How do you think we can mess around with what already happened?" It's something she's been thinking about, too, and she has her own answers for it.

Lil's friend, who still uses her old name of Diane, but maybe will change it, says "Because we *are*. The machine…"

They both think about the machine that brought them here, sitting there in its limbo.

"If it already happened," Lil tells Diane, "Then we can't change it."

Does that mean, Diane wonders, *I have always killed that kid? And it has always not bothered me?*

"If you're uncomfortable with it, we could always go to a different now," Lil offers.

Diane says she'll think about it.

358: Wind

Before I tell the story: Did you say *wind* or did you say <u>wind</u> when you read the title?

I'd like to know…

…if you said wind, like a breeze ruffling the VFW Post's American flag while you're walking in the Fourth of July parade wearing your "Sunderman Ins" t-ball shirt, squinting into the sun to see Mom and Dad on the curb with your little sisters, helping catch candy thrown off the back of cars by someone related to the Mayor.

…or if you said wind, like a wind-up toy robot with a shiny metal body and two little claw-like feet that carefully placed themselves in front of each other, walking across the coffee table while cartoons played and Mom slept upstairs, because she worked third-shift and couldn't be woken 'til two.

I'd like to know, which it was.

Maybe you and I think alike. Maybe we don't. But even if we think alike I need to know more about how we think alike.

It's not enough, you see, to say we both read wind the same way. We have to mean the same things when we read the same things.

What if *your wind* is

A breeze blowing salt into your face as you stand on the shore of the Atlantic ocean wondering why it's so cold and gray, how anything wondrous could live in there?

A tornado?

Flying a kite with your dad just after the separation, and you were too old for it but didn't tell him?

How will we ever connect? You and I, I mean?

What if your <u>wind</u> is:
What you do to a clock because you have to get up even on Saturdays?

Cranking a Jack-In-The-Box for a baby sitting in a chair eating Cheerios?

How you end things like *let's wind this up*?

The way you misspelt whined in a text to your boyfriend and didn't bother correcting it?

I don't think I could live with that. With any of those.

Too risky.

You're an unknown quantity, sitting there, reading this.

Too many variables. Too many misunderstandings. Things have to be just right.

I'm keeping the story.

357: I Am One of the Lucky Ones.

There are never any superheroes around when you need them.

There are cowboys around, and astronauts, and princesses and ballerinas. Even ballerina princesses! This is because kids, who are still free to dream, dream of becoming cowboys, etc., and so if even 1% of 1% of 1% of... you get the picture... grow up to be their dreams, that's more than enough astronaut princess ballerinas.

There was a kid, one kid, once, who told his parents "When I grow up, I want to be a superhero." His parents laughed and told their friends at cocktail parties about this. Each friend who heard the story reacted one of two ways:

Some, the mean ones, thought why're you always talking about that kid?

Others drove home in near-silence wondering why they had never dreamt of becoming superheroes.

That kid didn't care about their reactions.

Every day he exercised, because he knew superheroes had to be strong.

In school, he paid attention, asking lots of questions, because he knew superheroes had to be smart.

Around other people, he was always polite and helpful, because you know why.

He kept his eyes peeled for fires, bank robberies, giant robots tromping cities. He didn't see any of these things, but that didn't stop him from looking.

On prom night, he was staring up at the stars, outside the party, when his date asked him what he was looking for.

"Shooting stars," he said. He was lying. He had been imagining where his satellite secret hideout would orbit, but the lie was okay because superheroes need a secret identity.

How this story ends depends on you.

If you are one of those people who, upon reading this, wondered why you didn't dream of being a superhero, and who really wants this guy to become a superhero, then he became a superhero.

If you are one of those people who'd've changed the subject at that cocktail party, then the kid grew up to be a C.P.A. and you still live in a world without superheroes.

Lucky you.

I'm being sarcastic. I don't think you're lucky, at all.

356: CHOMP!

By *shark*(translated from the original)

Swim

Swim

Scent scent scent

swimswimswimswimmmmmmmm

Gone.

Swim

Swimming.swim

Scent

Splash

Splashsplashscentsplash

swimswimswimswimswim

Swimswim

Lunge!

Gnash!

...

Gone.

Light?

Something?

Swim
                down
                            down
                                      down

                                                Turn
Up
Up
Swim

SPLASH!

BREAK

THROUGH!

What?

What?

So...

Thin!

SPLASH.

Water.

Water.

Circle.
Swim.
Swim.

What?

Swim.
Circle.
                    <hunger>
Swim
Swimswimswimswimswimswimswimswim

                    <hunger>
Swim
Swim
                    <hunger hunger>
Scent
SCENT

                                                            Splashing splash

Swim
            Swim
                Swim
                        Swim   Splashing splash
                    Swim Scent Swim
                                    Swim   Splashing splash
                                        Screams! Splashing splash

                                            Screams loud screams
                                                            What?
                                                    Light, round?
            <hunger hunger hunger>
                                            Splashing splash screams
                                    Swim bite gnash bite screams
                                    Splashing screams bite swim

                                                            Gone.

                                                    Light, round?

                                            Stuck swim swim swim
                                                            Free
                                    Swim
                        Swim
    <hunger hunger hunger hunger hunger>

CHOMP!(cont.)

                                        Swim
                                Swim
                        Swim
                Swim
Swim
Swim
                        <hunger hunger hunger hunger hunger hunger>

Swim
Swimming swimming swim
Swim

Scent
                        <hunger hunger hunger hunger hunger hunger hunger>

Swim
Fast fast fast fast fast

BITE!
BITE!
CHOMP!
BLOOD! BONE! MEAT! BITE! CHOMP! EAT!
EAT
EAT
EAT
EAT
BLOOD!

                                YAY!
                        <full>
Swim
Swim
Hmm
                        Hmm

Scent

                        <full>
                                Swim
                        Swim swim swim swim swim swim swim swim
                                                S   L   O   W
                                                        Swim
                                                        Circle
                                                        Swim
                                                        <careful>

                                                        JUMP!

                                                    Thin
                                              <nowater>
                                                   Light.
                                                  Round.
                                                  Bright
                                              <Beautiful>
                                                  Round
                                                  Bright
                                                   Light
                                              SPLASH.
                                                   Swim
                                                   Circle
                                                   Swim
                                                  Circle.

                                              <careful>

                                              JUMP!

                                                   Light
                                                  Bright
                                                  Round
                                              <beautiful>
                                              More lights
                                                 Smaller
                                              <beautifuls>
                                                  Lights!

                                              SPLASH!

                                                   Swim
                                              <careful>
                                                   Swim
                                                   Circle
                                              <careful>
                                              JUMP!
Sounds.   Lights light
        Rumbles.   Big Small
Sounds   Rumbles.   <beautiful>
     Sounds Rumbles.
        Sounds Rumbles.
           Sounds Rumbles.
              Sounds Rumbles.
                 Sounds Rumbles.
                    Sounds Rumbles.
                       Sounds Rumbles.
                          Sounds Rumbles.
                             Sounds Rumbles.
                                Crack! SWIM!

                                Swim Sounds Rumbles

CHOMP!(cont.)

                                                          Swim Sounds Rumbles
                                                  Crack! Crack!
                                          Swim Sounds Rumbles
                                  Crack! Crack!

                          Zinnnnngggggggg!
                    Swim Swim   Sounds Rumbles
              Crack!

              Zingggggggg!
        Swim Swim Swim   Sounds Rumbles
Swim Swim Swim   Sounds Rumbles
Swim
Swim
Swim   Sounds
Swim

                        D
                        E
                        E
                        P

Swim
Swim
Quiet.
Swim
Circle
Quiet.

Swim   <beautiful>
              <sad>
Swim   Sounds
                                                                  <beautiful>
              <sad>
                                      Sounds
Swim
Circle   <beautiful>
              <hunger>
Swim
Swim
        Swim swim   Sounds
                        <careful>   Swim   D
                                                              E
                                                              E
                                                              P

Swim Swim Swimming Swim Swim Circle Swim

<careful>

Circle Swim

<careful>

JUMP!

Light! Lights!

<beautiful>

Sounds Rumbles.   Screams!

Sounds Rumbles.

SPLASH

Sounds Rumbles.   Swim

Circle

Swim

<careful>

<beautiful>

Sounds Rumbles.

<beautiful>

JUMP!

Crack!

Zing!

<ouch>

S w i m,,,

Can't.

355: Knowledge.

On the ice planet of *[the name is unpronounceable to humans because we do not use ice-crystal vibrations to speak, the way they do, so don't worry about the name]* the ice people have built a life for themselves despite the fact that the temperature of the planet is always absolute zero.

They're not much for science, on *[never mind the name, remember? Focus]*, or art, or politics, or sports. It is hard to move, what with (nearly) all molecular motion having stopped.

Instead, they talk, by vibrating, at various resonances, certain portions of their bodies. Their bodies are hard to fathom. Some say they look like icicles. Others say like rocks. A small group maintains the people of *[seriously are you still worried about the name? Fine, call it Grrzzk]* look like crystalline sea urchins only with far finer bristles, so fine they appear to be fuzzy but the bristles are superstrong and would not break no matter how much you tried to pet them. Nor would they be fluffy. They would be beautiful, though.

All those people are wrong, guessing, or both, as is anyone else who tells you anything about *[*sigh* Grrzzk]*. Nobody has ever seen, been to, or learned anything about *[I can't do it]*, other than the one thing we know about them, which is how they talk, and the other thing we know about them, which is what they talk about.

We know those because their conversations reach us and we hear them in our dreams.

The songs of the *[I am just going to have to insist that we be serious about this and not make up any more words this isn't Star Trek okay?]*-ians are beautiful, hundreds, thousands, millions of harmonies interlaced as these peaceful, long-lived beings spend the eons in conversation with each other, blessing us in our sleep with their graceful constructions.

For years, we did not know what *[…]* they sung of, but our best minds and most powerful computers have finally broken the code, and now we know: they are singing about which of them has supposedly slept with others of them.

354: Grasshopper, Leaving.

When winter ended the ants broke the news: the grasshopper would have to leave.

By the weekend, they said. The grasshopper expected this. It'd heard them last night, voting to kick it out and resolving that next winter they wouldn't let it in, but the grasshopper didn't care (much) because they were just ants, after all.

The grasshopper assured them it would leave by Friday, much to their relief, for the ants were not sure what they would have done if the grasshopper had resisted.

On Friday, only one ant came to see the grasshopper off. That ant—the grasshopper didn't know its name, didn't know if it *had* a name—brought the grasshopper a gift bag, which the grasshopper was going to wave off, magnanimously, but which he accepted after noticing there were no leaves on the trees yet, and the grass was still the dead brown stuff from last year. Technically, it might be spring, but he suddenly felt the ants were being a little hasty, here. So he took the bag.

You can't come back next year, the ants had warned, and the ant at the entrance to the hill now reminded the grasshopper, told it to better start preparing now.

The grasshopper said it wouldn't need to, and told the ant of his plan, to head south—the sun on his left, each morning—until he reached a land where it was always summer. No snow, no cold winds, things didn't die each year.

The ant was skeptical such a place could exist. It wondered why there wouldn't be winter *there,* when it was everywhere else. Neither bug knew science; the grasshopper had heard of *the South* from a butterfly it had spent a weekend with once.

The grasshopper shrugged. It didn't matter if the ant believed. What else could the grasshopper do? It hopped away, waving good-bye over its thorax.

The ant turned away, thinking to itself that if *the South* existed, it was probably full of birds. That is how ants think.

The grasshopper, for its part, never even wondered about the birds. Grasshoppers don't wonder.

353: 5 Chickens.

Five chickens are waiting.

It is a cloudy day. No wind. No traffic on the highway not far away. It is as though the five chickens are the only things left living in the world.

Perhaps they are.

None of the five chickens worry they are alone, alive. None of them worries they are not, though, either. For one thing, none of the chickens is really sure what "alive" means, and if they are it.

Each chicken worries the other chickens are smarter than it. Each chicken is sure that at least one other chicken has a grudge against it. Each chicken secretly has a grudge against one other chicken.

Sometimes, as now, four chickens gather and the one left behind wonders what the gathering is about. At the same time, the four in the group wonder why the fifth does not join them.

Each time it is a different set of four chickens. Today's combination is not the same as the one yesterday, the day before. It does not matter, even to the chickens, which four chickens gather. Whichever chickens gather, they wonder about the fifth and whichever chicken on a particular occasion is the loner thinks black thoughts about life and then forgets them quickly, what with all the distractions the world offers.

Today, there are fewer distractions. Moments ago, four chickens gathered near the fence, glancing sidewise at the fifth, who tried to pretend she was not disturbed by being the odd one out.

Now, the fifth wonders: should she join the others?

The four wonder: why does the fifth not join them?

None of the chickens talk, this time.

The fifth chicken takes One. Two. Three. Three steps towards the others.

All five chickens pause, wondering.

The four chickens glance around nervously.

The fifth chicken has a foot raised. That foot could go either way. Forward. Or backward.

Only a few steps separate the fifth chicken from the group.

If chickens could pray, each chicken would have been praying for guidance.

Chickens can't pray.

They can't.

They will have to figure this one out on their own.

352: 100,000,000 Angels Singing.

It would be difficult, Jesus knew, to get the 100,000,000 angels altogether and all singing on cue, but it was also, Jesus knew, going to be worth it.

Jesus knew those things not because he was omniscient but because he had tried getting the angels organized before. Angels disliked being bossed around, even by him. Jesus was not the kind of guy to pull rank, even when he should. Sometimes, he would politely ask an angel to do something (deliver a message to someone or intervene after an earthquake and save two small children who would be found after 8 days, something like that) and the angel would respond with:

"Yeah, when I get to it."

Jesus would feel like showing his stigmata and saying *You know, when I say* "would you mind" *I am just being polite, that was an order...* but He would instead turn the other cheek, which was kind of his thing. The Holy Ghost kept saying, at his performance reviews, that he needed to be more stern. Jesus always promised to try.

Most of the 100,000,000 were here now, milling around the cloud. Most of the 100,000,000 had forgotten to bring their sheet music and Jesus figured they probably hadn't practiced, either.

"Guys," he said. Angels aren't really *guys* but whatever, "Guys, can we get this rehearsal going? I feel like the apocalypse deserves our best effort."

The angels kept joking, pushing each other around, talking about the last night's game. Jesus raised his voice. "We *are* on a schedule, after all," glaring at the nearest 75,000 or so angels.

"What's this for, anyway?" said one angel, near him. Jesus rubbed his beard, explained again: golden ladder, four horsemen, flames falling from the sky.

"Your song is supposed to echo around the firmament," Jesus said, taking the conductor's podium. 3,200 angels elbowed their neighbor and made jokes about things that were *firmaments* along the lines of *that's what she said* but it was really a joke particular to angels and you wouldn't really get it.

Jesus got it, but he didn't find it funny.

351: Here There Be Dragons.

People say dragons are a myth. But dragons exist. They are just disguised. Dragons are good at disguising themselves.

Every tree, every bear, every crossing guard might be a dragon. You never know.

Pymn is a dragon. He is 3,057 years old. Every year, on his birthday, he picks a new disguise so he can go on living and not be hunted down by men, who fear dragons (for good reason).

Today is Pymn's birthday. He has spent the year as a horse, roaming the west. Now, he will choose what to be next year. He stands looking up at the full moon.

What shall it be? Pymn wonders. He has been a boulder, sitting calmly for a year. He has been an elderly factory worker. He has been a tarantula. He was a housecat living with a woman who never suspected his nature, who still mourns her missing companion.

A voice whispers inside him: *What good to live if you are not a dragon?*

He has thought this before. Many times. Now, here, under the full moon on the plateau, the thought lingers. He misses his scales. He misses breathing fire, his wings. He misses people fleeing in terror. He misses *Pymn*.

There are cities, full of millions of men. There are jets with missiles. There is radar. He will never make it. They will hunt him without stop.

What good is living if you are not a dragon?

He remembers sunlight dappling the forest as he hopped along the trail as a jackrabbit. He remembers the ocean's cool depths when he spent a year as a whale. He remembers a backyard cookout when he was a fat man with a bald spot, in 1973.

What good…

Pymn takes off his horse disguise.

It has been a long time since he unfurled his wings in the moonlight. It feels right.

He roars. He shoots flame. He thrashes his tail.

The voice in his head is as quiet as the night is wide.

I will be myself for a year, Pymn thinks, *And see how that goes.*

350: Everything is a Love Story.

Two particles cling to each other. Love.

Peanut butter + jelly. Love.

Love is like gravity.

So why is Bernard alone?

Why is he in that cab, staring out the window at a world in love, love that eludes him?

He can't avoid other elemental forces. Why is he immune to love?

Let's see!

Is it because he is frequently grouchy, looking out his window in the morning and thinking It smells like rain even though the day is sunny and bright? That could be part of it. Write that down!

Perhaps it is the way he dresses. Run through your checklist, students:

- •Sneakers, unpopular brand.
- •Old faded jeans, frayed hems.
- •Threadbare sweater.
- •He is not wearing a t-shirt underneath it. Just the sweater. *Weird.*

Is that enough to cause him never to fall in… wait, what? Oh, duck behind those trees!

Is he coming over?

Act casual.

Yes, hello?

Who, us?

We are… on a field trip.

From Krombach Middle School.

No, we're not following you.

What did *what* boy say? Him? He didn't say anything. Did you Stephen?

OH, Stephen. Look, Bernard… Mr. Ramsey, that is, the thing is… well, yes. We are studying you.

Because you're unique.

You're the only person to never have been in love.

No. Not true. You didn't love her.

I *can* prove it. Your journal, *August 9*: "…not sure I love Stephanie." See? I have a mimeographed copy.

This? It's my field journal.

For years. You're part of the curriculum.

No, of *course* we didn't tell you. We didn't want to taint the observations.

Well, you can obviously take it up with the superintendent. But I'm afraid science must be served.

The science of *love*, Bern… Mr. Ramsey. And how you exist without it.

It doesn't *matter* if you're happy. What does *love* have to do with *happiness*? This is science we're talking about.

Look, students! See how quick he is to react. Watch as he storms off so suddenly! Maybe *that's* part of it! Write that down. And Stephen, stay after school.

349: Pompeii.

He ponders his next move. She sits across from him, playing red. She is hunkered down on her knees.

He moves a black checker forward one space.

"GODDAMN FUCKING WHORE!!!"

Glass crashes.

She leans forward, face almost touching the board. After a moment, she sits up, hands pressed tight between her knees. He notices a bruise on her left hand. She uses her right hand, jumping the checker he just moved. She smiles, a little.

"DON'T THROW A FUCKING BOTTLE AT ME YOU FUCKING DRUNK!"

A thump.

Another thump.

His head is positioned to watch the doorway out the corner of his eye. His hand shakes only a little as he pushes another black checker forward, nods at her.

The sound of something heavy. Both of them know it is furniture. They know the different kinds of sounds things make, hitting the floor.

She takes the checker she just moved, jumps the one he just moved. She has collected four black checkers already. He has not even one red one. After she moves her checker, she puts her thumb into her mouth. He almost reaches for it, then decides she can suck her thumb if she wants.

"SHOULDA NEVER MARRIED YOU!"
"SEE YOU DEAD BEFORE I LEAVE MY OWN GODDAMN HOUSE!"
"WHAT ARE YOU GOING TO DO? HIT ME AGAIN? GO ON HIT ME. JUST DO IT YOU GODDAMN FAT, BALDING, IMPOTENT, DRUNK PIG!"
"SO YOU CAN CALL THE FUCKING COPS AND HAVE ME SIT IN JAIL AGAIN?"
"I CAN HAVE YOU ARRESTED ANY TIME I FUCKING WANT TO!"

As the voices have moved, they have silently slid back more towards the old couch with the right side burnt from what happened on Thanksgiving.

He focuses. She has her eyes scrunched shut. He sees a tear coming from them. He pushes a checker forward.

"PUT THAT DOWN!"
"GET THE FUCK OUT."

The voices are right above them. She is curled tight. He touches her shoulder, slightly. Finally, she looks up, ponders through watery eyes, then triple-jumps him.

"King me," she says quietly.

And a door slams above them.

348: Creation.

Everything you think about how the universe was created is wrong. This is how it was created: the dreams of every living thing creates the universe that thing lives in. Some of those universes overlap and some don't and all in all they are combined, the universe(s), and that's how things began: things create worlds which create worlds right back at them; which create worlds they can't imagine even though (technically) they created them.

A zebra stands in Africa thinking about that in its universe. If we create universes simply by thinking them, the zebra wonders, how did the first universe come into being?

"That's always the same question," God says, standing next to the zebra. In this story, God talks to zebras. That probably that happens anyway. Why wouldn't God? Zebras are probably pretty interesting.

"So can you answer it?" the zebra asks.

"What do you think?" God asks back, and the zebra realizes this is both true and a test.

What does the zebra think? He looks at God, who looks the way the zebra imagined God would. That's the way of things, in the universe.

"I think you can't answer it," the zebra says, finally, and God looked disappointed because that was how the zebra wanted it: a God who wanted to be omniscient, but wasn't.

God walked away feeling a bit low. He kicked a rock into the water hole. The zebra came after him.

"Hey," he said. "Don't feel bad. You can just think your own universe."

And God did that. He imagined a world that began with a colossal explosion of energy; a world that grew dinosaurs which he killed off with another colossal explosion of energy; and he imagined people, people who would fight for him, build giant cathedrals for him, who believed in him and believed he was omniscient and omnipotent. Those people prayed to him, and God, standing there on the African plains, in the zebra's universe, patted the zebra. Then, because God still was kind of sad, He imagined lions and gave *His* lions a taste for zebra.

347: The Hardest Feat in Sports is Hitting a Curve Ball

When the Devil decided he wanted to play baseball, it was a hard sell. He had to argue his way in, finally winning by pointing out that even Michael Jordan had been given a shot at the majors.

"And a midget, don't forget that," the Devil had added.

There being no rule prohibiting Evil Incarnate from playing third base, he was signed by the Milwaukee Brewers, eliciting a spate of snarky headlines to the effect of *"Satan didn't go to the Yankees because he wasn't evil enough."* The commissioner made him promise not to use supernatural powers. "During the games," the Devil clarified.

The usual groups protested Lucifer playing America's game. They had the usual effect, and so soon there was Beelzebub on opening day, tossing the ball around, taking batting practice. At the start of the National Anthem he took off his cap to show his horns, one painted blue, one painted yellow. He ran onto the field, the announcer saying *"And playing third base, the Prince Of Darkness!"*, to a mixture of cheers and boos.

He batted sixth, so he didn't come to the plate until the second inning. The pitcher, who had loudly proclaimed to ESPN he'd strike the Devil out in three pitches, ("Make my grandma proud, me striking out Old Scratch!"), shook off the first signal, then nodded.

Satan, who of course batted lefty, spat. The pitcher wound up, sent a fastball low and inside. Satan watched it go by.

"Strike one!" the umpire said.

"You get 'em, Moose!" from the visitor's dugout. Satan scuffed his cloven hooves in the batter's box.

The windup. The second pitch – a knuckler. Satan swing wildly at it. Strike two.

The crowd grew quiet, and many fans wondered whether they'd been foolish to root for Satan, after all.

The pitcher flung the third pitch, a high outside curve. The Devil swung, caught a piece of it, hit a bouncer to the shortstop. He was easily thrown out, but showed hustle by running the play through anyway.

346: Charley Horse.

Charley Horse ran and ran and ran, then stopped. When he stopped he finally looked around. What he thought was:

I ran a long time!

And

I don't recognize where I am.

He was standing in an intersection. That was where he had stopped. The intersection, he saw, was Maple Avenue and Elm Lane. There was a streetlight, but it was kind of dim.

All around Charley Horse were small houses, mostly the ranch-style houses that are so popular in some places, like Oklahoma, or other places. Some had lights on. Some didn't. It was growing dark. Charley Horse didn't know what time it was. Horses can't tell time, and don't want to.

Charley Horse thought this:

At least whatever I was running from can't get me anymore.

But then he thought this, too:

Unless I was running to get to something?

Charley Horse looked around to see if any of the things around him looked like something he would run to. Nothing did. That's not a knock against the things around him. They were just ordinary things like you wouldn't run to get to.

So I was definitely running away from something,

He thought.

He wondered if he should settle down here. It seemed nice enough. He wondered if there were girl horses here, whether they'd like him, what with him being from out of town and all.

He sniffed the air briefly and thought he smelled wolves.

Was I running from wolves, then?

He guessed maybe he was, but he wasn't sure. It didn't bother him that he couldn't remember what he was running from. That meant he had run far enough away from it that he was safe. (Also horses aren't very introspective, no matter how they look.)

He thought he might get a job at the fire station here, giving kids rides when they toured the station. Or perhaps something at the library?

From one of the houses nearby, a kid said: "Look! Mom! A horse!"

But his mom shushed him. "Don't encourage them," she said, and she meant it.

345: Myths About Cowboys:

Myth:

Cowboys spend their days riding the trail, staring with haunted eyes at endless plains, chins bestubbled, faces sunburnt, never thinking how they left behind the printer's daughter who wanted to marry them and have them go into their father's business, settle down, have a few kids.

Reality:

Stubble? What are they, shaving every third day? They grow beards.

Myth:

Cowboys send their horses careening down the trail after a few stray head of cattle, lariat twirling, hoping to rope at least one, which might be the difference between making a profit this run and hanging for a debt they can't pay.

Reality:

They only brought one rope, and lassoing was never their strong suit.

Myth:

At the bottom of the canyon, having somehow miraculously gotten ahead of the cattle and being in position to herd them, laboriously, back up the narrow trail, *thank god*, this'll take all day but if they keep on going all night they'll be at the railhead tomorrow, the cowboy hears the sound of hooves coming up quickly.

Reality:

With those cattle mooing or lowing or whatever, who could hear hoofbeats?

Myth:

The cowboy spurs his horse and turns around. He pulls his shotgun from the saddle-holster and makes sure it's loaded with two shells. He levels it in the direction of the hoofbeats.

Reality:

I already told you, *he didn't hear them.* Aren't you paying attention?

Myth:

When the rustlers round the bend the cowboy is ready. He brings up the shotgun. There are four bandits. He fires, pumps the shotgun, fires again. He rests the shotgun on his lap, pulls out his revolver. Two bad guys down already, he stares at the other two, who have their guns on him.

"Turn around and leave and I'll let you live," the cowboy says, because he is a decent and honorable man.

Reality:

The letter he wrote to Priscilla, that he's decided to come home and marry her, if she'll still have him, stays in the pocket of his vest, there at the bottom of the canyon.

344: Ghost Story.

There is a ghost in the woods. Out by the crooked pine tree that almost got knocked over by that storm in what, oh-five? Oh-six? Doesn't matter.

The ghost has been there longer than the tree's been crooked, but that was when he became famous. Some kids went to try to knock down the tree the rest of the way, saw him haunting there and ran screaming even though the ghost didn't do anything. He didn't come after them or contort his face into a parody of humanity, or nothing. Just stood there.

After that, word spread. People dared each other to go see him. Mostly they'd find him, there in the clearing looking up at the moon or drifting aimlessly around, sometimes scuffing his ethereal feet through pinecones, without any effect of course. It was kind of sad to see him try to kick the pinecones but they wouldn't move.

Eventually nobody was afraid of him. People began trying to talk to him. That's when he started not being seen. Nobody's saw him the past few years but he's still there. I know because I saw him not even three weeks ago – I did, shut up, Dave—and he saw me see him and he ducked behind a tree.

"Hey," I whispered to him. "Hey!" He stayed hidden but didn't disappear or anything. I swear this is true, Gina. I swear it.

He didn't answer so I snuck a ways away and acted like I was leaving. I even faked a phone call, said I'd be at the party in a bit, then snuck back. He was in the clearing. I ran out. I said "Hey how come you don't scare anyone?"

He shook his head and said "If I wanted to be around people I'd never have become a ghost," then kicked at some pinecones and disappeared. I've been back every night since, real quiet. I never see him. I bet he's there, though. We could go look tonight. Maybe he'd think we wouldn't come tonight because there's no moon.

343: After, Before.

What happens after we die is, time no longer affects us and we can travel to any time we want. But when we get there, we find out it's not us that's there, not really. It's like a movie of our life, or like how you look at a photograph and know it's not the person even if the photo is so realistic you can almost smell the bratwurst Tom holds in his baseball glove while he's supposed to be playing second base.

I hated him for not taking the game seriously. I hated him for so long after the softball that wasn't soft at all cracked him in the skull while he was joking around with Tina in center field and he dropped to the dirt with a soft thud that I still hear sometimes, now.

I hated him for leaving me and for doing it so stupidly. I hated him for making Mom sad and hollow and Dad stay longer at work. I hated him for Tina not wanting to go out with me anymore, and I hated him for making me such a small person as thought that mattered.

Tom started visiting me at night. He's the one told me about the time travel. He said you can go back and forwards, but that nothing's right. "I went back to Christmas '76, remember we got the electric football game?"

"I was the Lions, you were the Rams," I said.

"Yeah. I watched us playing it and I was able to set up plays and run them, everything."

I tried to remember if back then something had seemed to be moving the players, interfering. If I remembered Tom's future ghost, dead and playing electric football with me and past him.

"How was it?" I asked him.

"The game worked perfectly," he said. "That's what was wrong with it."

"Oh," I said. Then I added: "I don't hate you anymore, Tom."

"I know," Tom said. "That's why I came to visit you here, in the future, after you were done."

342: The Thing About Witches.

Witches have had it rough the last 400 years. People first burned them, then decided they didn't exist, then just used them as bad guys in movies. They were like 1950s communists before there were 1950s communists.

The witch down the road didn't earn any sympathy for all that. She didn't even try to hide she was a witch. Us kids tried warning our parents: "She's going to do bad stuff!" we said, walking on the other side of the street to get to school. She sat on her porch and tapped her left eye with her finger when she caught us looking, which that was the evil eye, we all knew.

By the time we were teenagers a new crop of kids appeared from families moving into the new apartment buildings. Nobody paid attention to apartment kids, except the witch and except us. We thought they had to be protected no matter if our parents didn't believe. We had a neighborhood watch where some of us stood a half block from her house like we were waiting for the bus. Eventually parties, sex, and teen things distracted us, and we stopped. Then, an apartment kid disappeared and cops started looking for clues.

We didn't know what to tell the cops. The thing about witches is it's hard to believe in them once they do something. They know it. They can poison-apple you or bake you, something, and the more they do the more nobody believes, except kids who get baked. The rest of us just keep quiet. Nobody ever finds the lost ones.

Witches are still around. I don't know what happened to ours. We decided not to tell, more in fear of what they'd say about us than what she'd do. We were teenagers already, less targetable. But I see other witches sometimes, at the grocery store or on the subway. They see me looking and they tap their left eye and I look away, thinking about that apartment kid whose name I didn't even know.

341: The Other Thing About Witches.

She didn't ask to be a witch but you can't avoid fate. At seven she cast her first spell, turning Tommy into a toad.

All the other kids went running and got Miss Belew, they were crying and screaming and saying Tommy was a toad and she had done it but when Miss Belew came back Tommy was standing there, crying himself, and she was off to the side looking cross. The other kids were told not to make up stories.

She was ostracized anyway, because everyone who mattered knew the truth. She spent time in her room, listening to music on her iPod, practicing spells like poisoning fruit and coming up with ways to make people fall in love with her, a spell that misfired when it rebounded off her mirror and hit Mr. Jensen next door. He began stalking her and got arrested. She thought to herself she should be more careful, then thought, *"Why?"* and wasn't.

Her parents tried to help her be less isolated. They signed her up for soccer. She quit the team. They changed their work schedules to be home more, joined an adults-and-teens book club so she could meet friends, but no teens came to the meetings at her house and anyway she got a job working at the drugstore to be away during the meetings. She did that because her other option was to enchant her parents not to notice her and she wasn't sure she could control that spell yet.

She passed the time practicing glamours on customers. She'd convince them to buy something stupid or tell their kids they'd get to go to McDonald's, minor stuff like that. People began to avoid her register. When the manager asked why customers didn't like her, she put a potion into his coffee that made him leave his wife and move to Florida and apply for welfare. A few months later she quit and went to college, where she studied English literature and thought about moving to Los Angeles.

340: If, Then.

If you run fast as you can down the road with your arms over your head, then you will feel like you are flying.

If you feel like you are flying and you close your eyes, then you will imagine you really are flying.

If you imagine you really are flying and let yourself go for just that long enough to unlock that 90% of the brain everyone thinks scientists say we don't use, then you really will be flying.

If we really didn't use 90% of our brains like everyone thinks scientists say we don't, then what did we bother evolving it for?

If we evolved 90% of our brains from some lower form of life like maybe a fish, I think I read that once, then how did we do that?

If we were able to evolve 90% of our brains from a lower life form just by maybe sheer force of concentration then couldn't we go in reverse and devolve or something and not use that 90% of our brains?

If we could do that then would we?

If we did do that, then what would happen to us?

If it happened that we devolved the 90% of our brains that is currently not allowing us to fly, even though we are sprinting as fast as we can and holding our arms up over our head and our eyes are closed, even though that raises the very real possibility that we will run smack into the road and get run over by a car just the way Mom always said we would if we ran that way, then would we be able to develop something else that is way more useful than a stupid 90%-not-working brain that can't even let us fly using like, say, telekinesis, because all it does is think about other stupid stuff like how Dad hasn't been home in three days and how yesterday nobody even noticed I wasn't in school?

If I had wings, then I wouldn't need a brain.

339: There Are Too Many Stories About Writers and Not Enough About Steamfitters.

"Write what you know!" they told him. But that seemed limiting, at the time, so he sat down to think of all the things he'd need to know before writing about them. He made a list, sitting there at a desk in the near-empty room near a poster on the wall. The poster was of a panda, he thought he remembered later.

The list had 4,344,212 things on it. It took up 14 notebooks, written in incredibly small writing like this. He didn't write it all that day. He added to it as he went on because with that many things he couldn't waste time sitting around putting things in a notebook.

~~Get sworn at by a burly man for nearly blowing up the battleship in the midst of a war but just in time get that four-foot-long pipe wrench to *move Goddammit* and the engine's got power again and we avoid the torpedo~~ was the 17th item he wrote down but it took him a while to get started on it because he had to ~~start a war~~, which he had belatedly added at 1,756th. He hadn't wanted to ~~kill a guy~~ but that was the only way to get the ball rolling on the war thing and by then nobody liked that Asian dictator whose ~~daughter he rescued by riding up on a white stallion through guards firing madly at him with machine guns~~ (#343,222)

But it wasn't all adventure. He wanted to know *everything*, and so there were many days trying to ~~bake every kind of pie imaginable~~, and some of the time he ~~spent napping in the backyard while his children's small pet turtles were allowed to play on his stomach and the lemonade got watered down by the sun melting the ice cubes~~, numbers 1400 and 2,300,589, respectively. He accomplished both of those one weekend. Pies don't take as long to bake as you'd imagine when you've ~~invented a new, magic oven~~.

338: Fireworks.

I tried to think of the stars as fireworks, like God was celebrating our lives all the time everywhere!

But then I remembered the stars we see (thanks a lot, scientists!) are echoes of stars God would have seen, and then I wondered if God still feels like lighting off a few M-80s/supernovas over us.

Then I wondered when I last lit off fireworks, and realized it was the night of the raccoons. One night they dumped the garbage cans on our driveway. The raccoons were huge, the size of dogs you might sort of instinctively shy away from if you saw one walking up to you off a leash even though that's not what you're supposed to do when a dog walks up to you. There were the five of them. So I lit some firecrackers and tossed them out the upper window above the driveway to try to scare the raccoons away so I could go pick up the garbage and put it in the can.

The firecrackers went off

pop

pop

pop

pop

pop

pop

pop

pop

pop

But the raccoons weren't fazed by them. They didn't even look up, and in the morning the neighbors probably wondered what the ruckus was about.

That was a long time ago. So I got some fireworks from one of those roadside shops that you never stop at and brought them home. I was going to light them off that night but got distracted reading a good book in the backyard. It was a beautiful night, warm and no breeze and the sun didn't set until nearly 9 p.m. I almost never do this, but I wanted to sit outside and read suddenly that night, so I took a kitchen chair to the backyard because we don't have any lawn chairs, not anymore. I brought along a glass of orange juice because that was all we had to drink in the house.

Later on, when I remembered the fireworks, I decided to save them for a special occasion.

337: Thor And Odin, On Father's Day.

Thor is one year old. They are in the backyard. Odin holds Thor up over his head, tosses the baby God of Thunder into the air, watches as the boy tumbles head over heels and falls back down, Odin catching him. He does it again, higher this time, then again and higher.

Soon the baby Thor is up a hundred feet and that is when the dragons strike, grabbing the child in their talons and screaming off across the sky, seven of them in formation.

This is what Odin has been waiting for. He pulls from the ground a fistful of clay, his mighty hand shaping the muddy dirt into a rhinoceros. He blows on it, and it grows larger and harder. He does this with more dirt, creating living stone versions of a roc, an elephant, several larger-than-normal goats, and in moments he is charging across the land atop the rhinoceros. He leads his army to where the dragons have taken his son.

They ride up the edge of the craggy peak where the dragons live. The roc dives in with a shriek. The goats howl like humans in pain. The dragons are breathing fire, ice at him. He punches with his fists, the rhino gores, the roc flings one to the ground, like a snake. He sees Thor, by the largest dragon, then doesn't see the boy, for that monster has eaten him. Odin gets off the rhino, runs at the leader. He grabs the mouth, goes in after. There, in the dark, half-eaten himself, he sees two small calm eyes.

"Good boy," he says, for his child has not cried, once. Odin grabs him, pulls back. They are both out. The dragon's mouth bears down. With his other arm Odin jabs his mighty spear through the enemy's throat. The two of them turn to leave with their army of stone animals. The sun shines brightly over Valhalla, reflecting Odin's happiness with the gift his son has given him.

336: Bear.

There comes a time when salmon is not enough. When rivers are not enough. When hibernation seems…

Wasteful.

So thought the bear.

It began to walk, once those thoughts hit it. Once the idea that salmon, rivers, sleep, were not the sum of existence, the bear began to walk.

It walked in no particular direction. It did not have a goal for each day. It did not try to reach a certain tree or get just over the ridge.

As it walked, it tried not to think anymore, because thinking, it knew, had gotten it into this…

Mess?

Was it a *mess*?

The bear was very far from the river, from the salmon, from the cave where each year it would crawl in, fat and tired and fleeing the winter chill that rolled amidst the stark trees silhouetted against the brilliant white of unbroken snow reflecting moonlight.

It was very far from there.

But was its new life a *mess*?

The bear considered, while eating leaves and fruits off a tree it had found, the pang of the juice from the fruit making it grumpy, stinging its tongue.

Then the bear realized it was *thinking* again.

Everything had been all right when it had not been thinking. The salmon, the rushing of the river stirring the thick hair on his ankles as he stared into the shallow water, the dappling of sunlight when the scales of a fish dove below it, the solid feel of the fish in his paws, as he pulled it out and bit into it, feeling the juice and blood flow over his tongue, knowing this catch would mean one more day of sleep, far back in the dark, until the snow melted.

Things had also been okay when it had just been walking. That was true, too.

It was only when it started *thinking* that the bear was dissatisfied with the things around it.

Only then.

With that, the bear started walking again, this time in a slightly different direction.

335: Making Time.

Time is like dough. It can be stretched, it can be pressed, shaped and twisted, and time can be baked.

It was in _____ that scientists first discovered the true nature of time, something they did simply by asking the gods what time truly was. That was when both science and time became irrelevant: when scientists gave up trying to learn secrets themselves and simply asked, and then learned everything there was to learn.

The gods, who for eons hadn't wanted to divulge their private rules, did, because they were worried about becoming more irrelevant yet, a process that had started with transistor radios. So they got together, Odin, Jesus, Marduk, Paul Moliter, all of them, and they decided to just let humanity know about time, about magic, about all of it.

Things were different after that but not how everyone feared. Once everyone began making time, time went crazy in the best of ways, like a taffy pull only with the universe. People could go back and recreate earlier moments in their life, only sweeter and with more of a crunch to them. They could remix things they hadn't liked. Some created daring new recipes, puffy light flaky time dusted with powdery other time in an airy roll that melted in one's mind.

Cause and effect were one and the same, the way the gods had always intended, and humans and their deities got along better because nobody feared death: when an accident occurred and changed one's state, the dough was simply re-rolled and new shapes cut out. This time the person might be a doctor, or a gorilla. Or a mountain, which (the gods had always known) were alive, too.

Nobody ever worried about running out. The only sad things anymore were when someone overcooked time, and the burnt parts had to be scraped off and/or buttered over. But even that was offset by the delicious way people ignored the gods' warnings and ate time raw, right out of the bowl.

334: Little Trees.

Little trees are the worst. With being so small, sometimes tinier than your hand, and how they always have to be moving to get nutrients and sunlight, you might want to pity them but let me tell you that instinct is wrong, wrong. They are the worst.

Little trees, when they are first sprouting up and you can't hardly see them, start with snide jokes about the larger trees, the oaks and maples and hickory-nut trees that tower over them and are in fact their parents. All little trees say similar dumb stuff (every one of them makes a bark-related pun, for example) but soon get bolder, realizing the bigger trees can't really do much to them except move their branches to shade them out of existence, which the bigger trees do. No love lost in these families! Trees all around are an unsympathetic, mean bunch of one-upper Darwinists, trying to murder their own children like leafy Cronuses!

Soon the little trees start worse stuff: pulling at leaves where they can reach them, kicking and digging dirt away from large roots that have lain in the ground nearly motionless for decades, opening holes for boll weevils or whatnot to get in, putting lichens on the bigger trees. (Trees hate lichens. Everyone hates lichens.)

You almost never see them do this stuff. Little trees are sneaky. That's another thing that's wrong with them. They gather in groups and start fires, rubbing together branches they've pulled off old old old trees, like malevolent, twiggy, homunculi of Boy Scouts. When they succeed in starting one they scream gleefully. Then they run away and giggle with their branches flailing, watching and waiting while the larger trees try to remember how it was, long ago, when they were young and more active and could give vent to their own murderous tree rages, trying desperately to remember how to move so they, too, can run and get away from this fire. But they almost never remember in time.

333: He Captured Lightning.

It was insanely difficult, running up into the thunderstorm, lightnings arcing and crashing and flaring all around him, dancing at him and away, taunting him.

We can kill you the bolts shouted, hissed, crackled at him.

But he jumped from raindrop to raindrop, careful feet balancing momentarily on the tiny round surfaces, skipping upwards onto the clouds, their surfaces rolling beneath him and falling away or pushing up. Every step was a treachery, every moment needing him to dodge duck teeter blink away the spatter of hail the storm threw at him.

He clenched his jar in his left hand, as one must.

The lightnings grew afraid, then. They no longer threatened, no longer bullied, instead tried to actually incinerate him. They flared. Jabbed with a million plasma talons. Grabbed at his eyes.

He was their match. Standing on the very edge of the thunderhead, almost falling, he crouched, he stood tall, he watched and timed and at last one of the lightnings came too close but not close enough – he felt his ears scorch, knew it had been going for his *mind*, knew it had missed – and he got it in the jar, and he was immortal.

Immortal!

He stepped off the cloud then, walked calmly down through the storm. He ignored the howling winds protesting the seizure of their compatriot. The rain changed to sleet and again to hail, pelting at him.

He held up the jar, in which the lightning crashed back and forth, flaring and illuminating the whole sky. *You cannot hurt me*, he murmured to the storm.

To the lightning, he simply gave a sad glance, as though telling it to relax and accept its fate, which it never would.

The jar shook and trembled in his hand with the force of his captive's anger.

He held it tightly, and continued to walk out of the sky. For so long as he could keep it in his hand, nothing but the lightning could hurt him.

332: Reunion.

The island was about twenty feet across, *diameter*, it would be, so ten feet *radius*, so for a while she lay on her back trying to remember whether the area was radius squared times *pi* or doubled times *pi*. Failing that, she angrily said over her shoulder:

"This half is mine," and she swept her arm to indicate *from the central cluster of trees over to the water.*

He could have the *left* half. Let him look at the sunset. She'd take the sun*rise*.

When there was no response to her ultimatum she fought the urge to look and see what he was doing. She imagined he was putting together driftwood, planning on building a fire. For warmth! To signal! For cooking! Whatever. She stood and waded into the shallows, feeling the cool of the water, wiggling her toes and wondering about starfish: if she stood still enough would they crawl onto her? Would she feel their million feet crawling slowly over her own? Would it tickle? Or would it feel like a massage?

The sky was an imbecilic blue and that made her angrier still. Her mind, unhelpfully, kept playing for her, over and over, her own voice, at seventeen saying *"That's easy. Robert,"* to the other girls in the back of the bus talking about who had given a blow job, where they'd go to college, what one thing they would take to a desert island.

Her feet sank further into the sand. She hadn't known the choice was permanent, that it would go down in her record as what she definitely would end up with. She wished she'd picked the complete works of Bob Dylan and a solar-powered CD player. Or perhaps the *Harry Potter* books. She wished Robert had never cheated on her with Chelsea on that very busride, coming *back* from the game. This would be less awkwardly annoying, after all, if the two of them had actually seen each other in the last 20 years.

331: In Concert.

Start small. That's where Beethoven went wrong: he went big, right from the start. Maybe it seems the height of hubris to say Beethoven went wrong, but remember: he is *dead*. So what was the point of all those symphonies, only to end up dead?

You don't want to end up dead. So *start* small.

Smaller.

Smaller still.

A single note.

That's right.

A single note, played and held and held and held and held held held – longer than anyone can imagine – held until people strain in their seats, suck in their breath involuntarily, clench their programs, reach instinctively for the person next to them.

Then held a bit longer.

Let's make it a cello. Death *hates* cellos.

Then held more. That note is the craggy outcrop of rock over a precipice, the one everyone says *"no way I'm going on that,"* but they do because how can they *not*? Only a few hang back, unwilling to tempt fate. Those are the ones fate gets. Fate only leaves you alone if you play the game.

Just as physics lets go the first note, start a new one, even *smaller*. A half-step down.

By now people will want to strangle *you*, but they won't be able to look away. In their gazes you will be held, safe from death, cradled, so now they are *looking*.

…Yes, with their *minds*…

Now they are *looking*, keep them there. Keep it small. People see big from faraway, and when they see big they think they know it and don't waste any more time on it. But *small* makes them think of *hidden*, of magic. They want to parse it, feel it. They know God makes big things: mountains, the world, the universe. They don't believe God makes small things because if *they* were, *they* wouldn't. They'd make big stuff, so when they see *small*, they are fascinated.

Their fascination will protect you. Wrap it around you and never die.

Now, the third note.

330: Cold Ears.

Sometimes it got so cold his breath seemed not to leave his mouth, staying put on his chapped lips, bits of ice in the corners of his making his lips ragged and bloody.

He peered each day out into the expanse of white, looking for the small shadows marking the steps of one of the few animals still around, struggling through snow so deep it would have buried the large pines to their very tips, had there been any more large pines.

He followed any tracks he saw, inevitably coming across an animal foraging for other small animals, carnivore chasing carnivore. He was able sometimes to catch them barehanded if the animal was caught in softer snow. Otherwise, he used one of his rocks, or, if he could get close enough, the spear.

Today, he saw human tracks.

He stared, eyes sweeping along the tracks, following them over the hill. He looked that way a long time before deciding against following them.

Each morning, for six more days, a fresh set of tracks in the same direction. They were different sized footprints, so even if it were possible for someone to have looped around his cave seven different times, he knew that was not what had happened.

No new animal trails appeared. The fox he'd caught was nearly gone. The footprints kept catching his eye: the thought of seven people in one place scared him.

Then there were no new tracks. The old ones were disappearing. He knew if he did not leave soon he would not be able to follow the seven who had come by. He wondered why they hadn't come to the cave, why they walked at night, whether they were friendly or would eat him?

The fox's carcass was picked clean. He kept the bones in a pile to dry out and burn, eventually, if they would.

He decided to stay. The next day he caught a raccoon and felt it a good sign.

329: The Marching Band That Came and Went.

It doesn't come at regular intervals. Nobody can predict when or where it will be.
One minute we were all just milling around trying to ignore skateboarders on the library mall because they never were any good at their tricks anyway, the next there were 100, maybe 117, people in uniform blowing trumpets, pounding drums. There were two tubas and one of those glockenspiel things. It was way better than the skateboarders. The Higginses even forgot to bicker for the entire time the marching band marched and played. The marching band played a Sousa march but the strange thing (well one of them) was, later on nobody could agree on which march. Everyone felt it was a different Sousa march. Even when it was pointed out they all sound kind of the same and there's only a few of them, anyway, like about twelve, people just agreed to disagree.
After that, the marching band appeared in a grocery store produce aisle, along the train tracks at 2 a.m., and outside Little League sign-up, which was a relief to moms waiting with petulant kids who mostly didn't want to play baseball all summer but were being signed up

anyway, because.

Scientists rushed to each scene, with cameras and test tubes. Nobody knew why they brought test tubes. Bloggers said the marching band was a NASA experiment, a mass hallucination, a viral marketing ploy for glockenspiels, a fake. There was a TUMBLR: "Places The Marching Band Hasn't Came And Went Yet." It was all pictures of sad people in war-torn Liberia or at a funeral or that stuff.

My little brother's become obsessed with joining the marching band, and he is not alone. People've taken to carrying instruments, buying uniforms. Everyone looks like Sergeant Peppers, for crying out loud. My brother plays trombone. He carries it everywhere and says stuff like "Life is just one big audition," but so far, no luck for him.

328: The Poetry of Jetpacks.

Of all the inventions humanity has ever come up with, only jetpacks didn't lose their luster over time and become commonplace. Centuries after their perfection people were *still* nuts about jetpacks, even when teleportation had become the cheapest mode of transportation and sentient animal robots made people forget about all the extinctions.

Naturally, pop culture became very jetpack-centric. People remade old movies to be more jetpack themed, and haute couture had long since replaced the high heel with ever-more-elaborate jetpacks.

In J639 (humanity now counting years since the first commercially-available jetpack) the counterculture started. A reality show challenged people to live without their jetpacks for a year. The top prize was endless clones of oneself. The tagline was *"Immortality in Exchange For Your Jetpack."* Jeff won and, now famous, started his own broadband station, using his endless clones to preach what he called "The Gospel of The Ground." He developed a cult following.

"Humanity came down from the trees. We didn't go up from them," Jeff was fond of saying. Before his game-show win, Jeff worked in a doughnut shop. Doughnuts remain popular, way off in the future.

Jeff married, but the strange thing was the woman he married loved jetpacks. An artist, she made things out of jetpacks discarded by Jeff's followers. That was how they met: she attended his meetings where he talked about the feel of dirt between ones toes and the way you only noticed how beautiful things were if you walked past them slowly.

She'd raised her hand, asked "Don't you see the beauty of seeing things from a different angle, from higher up, in a way no human ever has?" They hadn't hit it off right away, had bickered a lot at first. Most of Jeff's friends, though, had figured they were meant for each other in some weird way. Jeff went to her showings, but all he would say publicly about them was they proved his point.

327: We Walk in Darkness as Often as We Walk in Light.

The monster was in the area. Gina knew, just *knew*, it was there for her. And then there it was by her bed, simultaneously 20 feet tall and inside her bedroom somehow, her parents sleeping down the hallway, her little brother in his crib, her robe for graduation behind it. *Would she get to graduate?*

The monster would, in a way, decide that, too.

"You're here," she breathed. What else could she say?

The monster's face cracked open, the mouth too wide to fit the head. It reached out a massive talon, the two fingers poised together, the somehow-delicate thumb curled over them.

"What do I do?" Gina whispered.

She'd thought the monster would *take* her heart. Did she have to get it herself?

Its tail swirled around, agitated. It growled a low rumble like a train wreck in the mountains.

She took off her shirt, stood in her underwear before the monster.

With one claw it dug into her chest and she shrieked in pain and terror. It hurt worse than anything she could imagine, hurt so bad she thought she must have died. With a howl louder than her own wail, the monster lifted her on the claw. She felt the perfect needle of the point touch the bottom of her heart. She saw the bedroom ceiling no longer was there, replaced by the sky usually only madmen see.

She tried to be motionless, but it hurt, and she was too scared.

"Please," she screamed. "They were just mistakes, not sins!"

The monster licked its lips. She sobbed. Was it too heavy? Would her heart be eaten, her spirit cast aside forever?

Then she was on the ground, panting, hair soaked with tears, sweat. The room was icy cold. Her chest hurt. She held her breath until her heart beat again, then hugged herself there on the cold bedroom floor until the sun rose.

326: The Fortune Teller and the Truth.

"I really do see the future" the fortune teller says quietly. I pause. "But I still lie. To anyone who ever sought their future from me, I lied." She shakes her head, sadly.

"Why?" I ask.

"Do you know what most people's future holds?" she asks.

"Death," I guess.

"Well, yes. But before that."

"Sadness?" I say. It's why I would lie to someone. I couldn't tell them their baby would die or their girlfriend leave them.

She shakes her head. "Mostly, no," she says. She rubs the crystal ball on the table. She's kind of pretty, in a weird, old-world way. But her eyes are haunting. "Futures are boring."

"Boring," I echo.

"Like yours. I'll tell yours, free. I don't charge for the future. I charge for the entertaining fictions I make up. But I'll tell you your real future. You'll work at your job for another 10 years. The business will fade, you'll find another job. A modest raise. You'll have 2 kids..." she pauses, squints. "One will drop out of med school, work as an X-ray tech. The other teaches math. Your wife... she'll hurt her knee 2 years into your marriage and put on 20 pounds." She looks up at me. "You'll be fine with it."

"That's all?" I ask. "No cancer, no lotteries?"

"No. See? Boring. That's why I lie. Would you have paid for that?"

I think of my future wife, slightly overweight. Of my two kids. Underwhelmed, I say "No."

"See? So I lie."

"What happens when you meet something with an interesting future?"

After a moment she says: "I lie to them, too. I say their life will be boring. Why wreck the surprise?"

Later on, I wonder if she wasn't just jealous of interesting ones. Then I wonder if I am one of the interesting ones. I fall asleep right around the time where I guess someday I will find out.

325: This is Not a Metaphor.

When he didn't like how the interview was going he ate the newscaster, and when the cameraman tried to stop him leaving he ate the cameraman, too. The sound guy held the boom mike up defensively, cowering.

Outside a delivery boy jostled him. Of course he grabbed and ate the delivery boy, leaving the boy's packages there on the street.

I guess I am a monster now, he thought, because he'd eaten three whole people and also because passers-by had seen him do this and were screaming, calling police, making holy gestures, doing other kinds of things people do when they see monsters.

So he stretched his arms experimentally and roared, also experimentally, and felt like he'd done both pretty well. He tried some other things like flying or breathing fire, but it seemed roaring, waving his arms, and eating people were his only monstrous attributes. Still, they seemed enough.

"LAY ON THE GROUND OR WE WILL SHOOT YOU!" a loudspeaker from a police helicopter blared, which seemed a bit much to him, helicopters, but that was the police for you. He looked up, stretched his mouth even wider, reached one waving arm, and grabbed and ate the helicopter with the men inside it. One rotor was sticking out of his mouth as the remaining police began firing their weapons. He thought about explaining to them it was the newscaster's fault, or the way his parents raised him, or maybe the way the divorce judge had looked at him, but his mouth was still full and anyway he had some indigestion from all the things he was eating. So instead, he ran towards the blockade, finding out that bullets didn't hurt that much. The police stopped firing and dodged out of his way, and he was past them. A few blocks later he caught a bus and went home, figuring all this was not going to help his job hunt.

324: Death Eats a Hot Dog.

People in the city no longer really avoided Death, not that anyone came up and talked to it, either, but when the human interest photo of Death standing next to a hot dog stand eating a hot dog and holding a Diet Coke appeared in the newspaper there was a revival of interest in Death (and hot dogs, but this is not their story.)

After the photo, people at bus stops waved at Death, and cars honked. Women smiled at him as they jogged by, firm breasts bouncing, tan thighs reflecting sunlight and inviting a caressing hand. Death tried politely not to stare.

And, whenever Death stopped for another hot dog, it drew attention again. "Like them dogs, eh?" guys in work clothes would say, almost clapping Death on the shoulder before thinking better of it. Businesswomen waiting in line to get their own Diet Coke would smile a little but never ordered a hot dog themselves (they were all watching their weight.)

Death did not enjoy the attention. Death wished for the days when it wasn't so omnipresent, when people feared it, and wondered what had changed so now people would shout out "Death! Try the hot nuts!" or offer an Italian ice, hoping to draw Death to their cart or food truck to attract attention.

The hot dog cart owner himself was taciturn about it when people asked why Death ate there. One day, while Death stood silently eating its hot dog—it only stopped one or two times a week, as Death usually brownbagged it—two teenage girls giggled and one said "Are you eating at this cart because the owner is going to die?"

The man glanced over at Death, waiting.

Death shrugged. It didn't bother saying the man would live to be 97, that it just liked the view of the park across from the cart. Death has to retain some mystery.

323: We May Never Come Back Here Again.

They'd found a way to go back, and for some reason, we were excited.

We went first to a backyard barbecue, right at the start of the family Whiffle Ball game. The kids, all grown up now, watched as they stood around, bored and complaining. They were embarrassed for themselves, until they noticed the adults were bored, too, just not willing to admit it. We were drinking Pabst Blue Ribbon, telling the kids to live it up but we'd not been living it up, either, and now here we all hid, older, me with my gray hair, Ted with his own kids who hadn't made the trip back with us, Sonia refusing to admit she needs eyeglasses, and watched our past be not as fun as we'd remembered.

Each time was like that: Christmas '81 was awful. I had been hungover and now I was shocked at how terrible I looked and how my pallor dimmed the morning. Sonia thought we should warn younger Ted he wasn't getting bike, but we didn't interfere and had to go through the disappointment and then his sniffling, brave smile all over again.

"How could we get you a bike?" I asked Ted, now. "It was winter."

"You asked for one every year," Sonia sighed.

They wanted to see me as a kid, at Disney World. As soon as I got off the machine and saw myself squinting around looking for Mom I remembered how I'd gotten lost the first day and told them not to bother. They watched the whole thing anyway, right up until Mickey Mouse hugged me and I started crying again.

"Was the past really always sad?" Ted asked.

"Should we go see Mom, again?" Sonia ventured.

We decided we'd rather not, and took the machine back early.

"Next year, how about renting a beach house?" I suggested. Ted said he'd bring the kids to that.

322: Shark Vs. Crocodile.

At first, it was to be a fight to the death, but shark could not come in fresh water and crocodile would not come in salt water.

Then the contest was to see how many people each could eat the fastest but shark protested crocodile had an advantage because it could move in both land and water.

"Well, that's the challenge, isn't it?" asked crocodile. "To see which is fiercest based on our own natural skills. If you're going to insist that everything be perfectly equal, it's not actually much of a competition."

"You're the one who won't come into the ocean," said shark. "So you started it."

They debated other competitions and hit on the idea of each of them fighting the same kind of animal.

"Whale," suggested shark.

"Tiger," offered crocodile.

"One of each," shark compromised, and the battle was set. Now, they just needed two whales and two tigers.

To a passing pod of whales, shark called out that they needed two to come fight.

"What for?" asked whales.

"To prove which of us is the better predator," shark explained, but whales just shook their heads and declined.

"Try orcas," they said, but shark felt that was racist.

Crocodile's luck was worse. He found tiger in a tree and said he needed it and a friend to come and fight. Tiger said: "Only if I can be part of the competition."

Crocodile didn't want that. "Then we would need even more challengers," it said.

"You could get two more crocodiles and two more sharks, and I would get two friends, and we all fight," tiger said. Crocodile tried to picture how that would work and as it pondered, several hippo wandered by and asked if they could be part of the battle, too. Then eagle, high overhead, said it should be part, too.

"It doesn't look like this is going to happen," crocodile reported to shark.

321: Marauders.

The arrival of the marauders was always unpredictable, as was what they took. We would be watching television, probably Dad would have a bowl of ice cream, and the marauders would storm through the room, horses' flesh steaming like it was cold outside and they'd been riding all night and they'd rip screaming through the den like a house afire, grabbing at things.

That time they took grandpa's glasses that he'd left there last week, and they took the ottoman that Dad always called a hassock but Mom laughed at him when he said that. They took my glass of orange juice once. I was watching Saturday morning cartoons and drinking a giant glass of OJ, the largest we had, which I could do because Mom was still asleep and so she couldn't yell at me for having a superbig glass of juice instead of one of the stupid little ones.

I was sitting on the floor watching Bugs Bunny and there they were, all the roaring and hooves and snorting and fire and there were maybe fifty of them, trampling the couch and one broke the coffee table and the one that leaned down from its horse had a face like a bear only not a bear, it had teeth, I remember, but sharp as they were they seemed too small in its big mouth, and its eyes were beady and small but they were as red as the sunset, and it reached out its hand which grabbed my entire fist holding the juice glass as I sat there, motionless, trying not to attract attention. At first it pulled at me and all I thought was stupidly *at least the juice didn't spill* but then I let go of the juice and it took that instead, and they were gone.

They always took something, but so far, they've never taken anyone in our family. We're pretty lucky, that way.

320: And Then We Burned Her at the Stake.

The fires didn't take long to catch. The brush was dry, brittle and had been for a long time. She didn't ever flinch, not when Thomas put the torch to the branches, not when the fire swept around her, not when the flames were so high we could only see her face, wide-eyed, above them.

It didn't work.

It didn't work, either, when we hanged her from the branch of a willow tree in the full moon, her body hanging limp, seemingly dead over the snow for the longest time, while we stared and stared and stared, trying to make her stay there – dead, we hoped – forever.

Drowning! "Do you really think this one will work?" she asked, and if any of us heard the note of pleading in her voice none of us acknowledged it. We tied ropes to large bricks and the other ends to her and threw her in the well. She didn't howl as her body fell. We heard the splash and knew nobody would ever drink from that well again.

She was in her house the next morning. We surrounded her house by noon, again with the pitchforks and wards and our priests.

"I want this as much as you," she whispered, and maybe only I and the priest, in the front of the procession, heard her. Nervously, I looked at her but didn't want to meet her eyes, because, well, you know.

I didn't want to be the next.

Did she want it, and as much as we did? It seemed impossible, as we tied her to the horses. But I thought I saw her smile, her lips moving – in prayer?—as we hit the horses, and who could smile through that if they didn't want it?

The next day I almost asked what it felt like, but the rule is we don't talk to them.

319: The List of Things I'm Going to do Today.

1. Make this list.
2. Put it on the bulletin board.
3. Shower.
4. Get dressed.
5. Pour coffee in thermos.
6. Get in the car.
7. Put on the playlist I made last night, sitting up until 1:30 a.m. knowing it wouldn't matter if fatigue made me have trouble concentrating today.
8. Stare at the apartment building for a minute or so.
9. Start the car.
10. Back slowly out, not looking back.
11. At the intersection, stare for a time to the left, thinking about how I have turned left at that intersection every Friday for the last 13 years.
12. Never even a vacation!
13. Stop looking left.
14. Take another sip of coffee.
15. Ignore the guy honking behind me, and turn right.
16. Drive the half-mile to the corner.
17. Notice a jogger on the side of the road, jogging in place while waiting for the red light to change.
18. Remember when I used to jog. Pat my belly a little. Vow that now I will lose weight. Now I will.
19. I mean it.
20. This is the way of things, now.
21. Wave to the jogger as the light turns red and I turn right, and she turns left.
22. Put the visor down because I am heading directly into the sun, now.
23. Turn up the music.
24. Turn off the already buzzing cell phone, then think again and throw it out the window.
25. Get onto the freeway, heading south.
26. Put the window down and let my still-wet hair get ruffled by the warm air of a Friday morning in July which who could bear to spend even one more day in that office?
27. Not me.
28. Turn the music up more.
29. Realize that this list is still on the refrigerator back home.
30. It doesn't matter.

318: Independence.

Whenever I see a van I think of people living in it and then I think how when I walked to school I pretended I didn't see Tony standing outside his van while inside his mom and dad got dressed.

I only walked to school early to get breakfast. If I arrived by 7 a.m. and got in line I generally got to the counter before they ran out. The other kids also learned to get there early and I remember sometimes running, sometimes it was that close, a sprint put you 25th in line instead of 26th and so you got eggs and toast and some other kid didn't.

I pretended, too, I didn't wonder why Tony's parents didn't let him get dressed first so he could get to school earlier. Maybe they didn't want to stand in the Piggly Wiggly parking lot in their pajamas, wanted to be in clothes so everyone could pretend they were just waiting for the store to open. Every day. Even Christmas Day, when I didn't have school but went to see what Tony's family did to celebrate. They didn't seem to do anything special, at least not before Tony was dressed. That morning I waved.

"Hey," I said. "Merry Christmas."

"Yeah," he said back.

I talked to Tony on the Fourth of July, too. I didn't go to talk to him, I was just heading to the park that morning because I had nothing else to do, and he was outside his van again.

"Hey," I said. "Happy Fourth of July."

He shrugged.

"You going to the fireworks?" I asked later. I would probably watch them from the jungle gym at the park.

"Yeah," he said, but I didn't see him there, later and his family's van was in the parking lot when I walked home, eyes still a little dazzled by explosions showing how great our country is.

317: Marcelline

Marcelline plays the ukulele, a little.

Marcelline spent a year trying to invent a new kind of chocolate chip cookie recipe, although she didn't work on it every day.

Marcelline once saw a penny on the sidewalk and didn't pick it up and to this day she regrets it and one time when she was sort of buzzed she wondered if she walked back to where the penny was, on 3rd and State, it would still be there and she could pick it up now but then was sure someone else would have picked it up by now, and so went home.

Marcelline took lessons for the ukulele.

Marcelline was a bridesmaid at her sister's wedding and genuinely wished her well and it never crossed her mind to wonder whether she would ever get married herself.

Marcelline is not sure she *wants* to be married, but is sure she will, someday, marry.

Marcelline thinks she might in fact get married more than once, as she knows many first marriages do not work out.

Marcelline believes in magic. REAL magic, the kind that causes the moon to crack in half and let loose dragons which will come down and try to destroy humankind. She believes this because when she was little, she saw an old man at a bus stop and the old man looked at her and in his eyes she saw the future of the world and that exact thing with the moon happened, there in the future in his eyes.

Marcelline is not afraid, because that moon thing happens long after she dies, and as for her children, she knows every generation has its own problems. That will be one of theirs, she figures.

Marcelline doesn't tell anyone the lessons were actually just her watching Youtube videos and trying to copy them. She likes ukulele music but just wants to listen, not play it.

316: Once Upon a Time, With Pizza.

It was the strangest date you ever saw, full with as much anger as love-at-first-sight, each of them resisting falling for the other because each feared falling in love would mean an end to the adventures.

It was a blind date, but each had a feeling about the other, so when he knocked the first thing she did was shout *"Fair warning!"* before firing wildly through her apartment door. He was already rolling right, pressing up against the wall, reaching through the door, grabbing her wrist, pinching just the right nerves to cause her to drop the gun. He pulled her into his backflip and they were out the window at the end of the hall so quickly that the shards of glass seemed to float in mid-air as they rocketed past and began falling.

"I'm Finn," he said and she said she'd *guessed* that and was *pleased to meet him* and then rolled him over and grabbed him with one arm, the other clutching at the flagpole jutting out from the third floor of the building across the street, spinning them around it before dropping them to the ground.

"Where did you want to go?" she asked calmly as passer-by gave them annoyed looks and brushed glass off their shoulders.

First stop was a flower show where they fought with swords and he offered to buy her an orchid but she declined. After that, he was kidnapped to her underground lair in the park, escaping into a pond where they launched torpedoes into each other's mini-subs, escaping to a lovely path above the treacherous cliffs next to a waterfall while hurling daggers at each other.

"Just get a room already!" yelled the peanut vendor whose cart they nearly knocked over with their jetcycles as each tried to be first to the pizzeria. She won, but felt he'd let her.

315: Piranhas?

"Well, are there or aren't there?" she asked.

The three of them peered at the water. The river was too wide to jump across and too deep to see the bottom. The late afternoon haze made the current seem weaker than it was.

"Let's say there are," he began. The baby, clutched to his chest, was now looking up at the tops of the trees where monkeys were chittering and birds hummed.

"Yes," she encouraged. She wanted to see where this was going.

"The river isn't that wide," he continued.

"Swim across a river with piranhas?" She raised an eyebrow. She did not have to add *with a baby* because everything they did was *with a baby*. She'd only once this whole time added the phrase, tacking it to the end of a sentence that began *I can't believe you tried to cross quicksand*. But even then she'd realized it was unhelpful, and she didn't want to be unhelpful.

"It might be more like wading," he said, staring intently at the water. "Can you *see* piranhas?"

"Whose idea," she complained, "Was it to put the question mark on it, anyway?"

They both looked at the sign again, looking at it, the way one might go back to 4-across on the Sunday *Times* crossword, over and over, as though merely *looking* might help reveal the answer. Or, he thought, the way you might keep checking your coat pocket for your keys, certain that you put them there last night when you got out of the car, and wrong each time you check again.

Or, not like either of those, *she* thought, but he was close.

"Can we go around?" he asked, always the problem solver.

They looked up the river, and down.

"I suppose we will have to," she said, and tried not to sound like she was complaining because it wasn't really *his* fault.

314: Paradise Detoured.

DETOURS DUE TO CONSTRUCTION

"Well, *what* is THIS shit?" Don said, of the large orange sign ahead of him.

"I don't think you're supposed to swear, here," an elderly woman said to him. Don was bemused by the number of elderly heading in the same general direction he was. Yes, most people who died would be elderly, but it didn't seem right you should go around being old and crippled for years in life and then be that way in the afterlife, too.

"I don't think we're *here* yet," Don said, but she was beyond him, walking along the tiled floor. No golden path and there weren't clouds or sunlight or pearly gates so pretty much all of what he'd imagined was *wrong*. He glared at the sign and the arrow pointing to the right. He wondered if this was a trick of the devil or something, and wondered if he really believed in the devil. Or the afterlife in general. He'd never really thought about it before now.

Finally he walked, following the arrows around barriers that promised IMPROVED CONVENIENCE and *READY BY April 1, 15,844,763,112* and waited for the elevator for an extraordinarily long time until an old man – they were everywhere!—tapped him and said *"Out of order,"* and pointed at the small placard off to the left.

"Jesus," he said, unthinking. "They put giant signs everywhere except here?" But the man had moved on, too. Only Don seemed bothered by the fact that there was construction! In Heaven! Or close to it!

Or is this purgatory? He wondered, trying to remember if purgatory was real. Then he had to backtrack around to the stairway, where he stood at the base and watched the old folks walking up and wondered just how many flights there were, and whether it would make sense to wait here until they finished construction.

313: We All Waited, Every Year.

In the mist of the forest in back of the town, we all waited.

On July 9, every year, everyone in town stood in the small clearing, silent, still half-asleep despite the walk through the woods to get to this spot. Children who didn't quite understand it yet were solemn anyway. Babies never cried. The elderly who might not be here next year were thoughtful. Couples hoping, planning, hoping, to marry that year clutched each other's hands and tried not breathe.

Eventually we would start hearing it, the first notes coming almost so quietly that we met each other's eyes to communicate disbelief – is it here? Is it now? – and our ears would strain to hear the music as it grew louder, more real.

As the music played, people shut their eyes, and they listened. Listened with their whole bodies, feet spread wide to hold their bodies strong up against whatever they heard, for the music held in its notes their future, the future of each man and woman and child and the town and the world, held every second of the next year in it, if you only listened hard enough. Everyone listened, as hard as she could, as hard as he might.

We listened and understood. Were the notes slow and ponderous? Were they in a minor key? Was there syncopation? Did the melody soar? Or did it dawdle and kick its feet into the dirt below us? Would we live, or would we die? Were there drums? Flutes? Would we have children? Would the crops come in? Is the choir sad? Would tornadoes tear our world into bits? When did the strings kick in? Would war take our men away? Would plague take our babies?

We never moved, never breathed, until the song was done. Then we walked back to town, to begin the year.

312: We Are O.K.

We'll be okay, he said, saying it like a prayer. He tried to mean it, to not to have it be a rote recitation, like prayers were when he was a kid at Mass, whether he said it to himself, staring out at the sea, or to her while they stared into the fire or ate some of the fruits he'd gathered that day.

I know, she always said, and he missed the hopeful smile that used to accompany her acknowledgment.

They built a shelter. He tried to think of how he could make a fishing net, or a crab trap, maybe, but kept using his shirt, sleeves tied at the bottom, hung on a stick that looked like a dowsing rod. He kept the fire burning, waking up at night hour after hour to make sure it was still going, because it had been so hard to get started the first time and they needed fire not because they got cold but because fire was the only reminder that they were human anymore, or more accurately that they could be human again someday, a part of a society. If they could build fire, they could perhaps find others. Or be rescued. Fire represented hope and the future, whereas the occasional crate washing up on the shore represented merely the sad past.

We'll be okay, he said as he woke up on yet another morning on the edge of the beach, and wondered if today there would be another depressing crate full of canned goods that they would eat and not think about how there might never be canned goods again. They were lucky to be here, sometimes getting crates, sometimes spearing a boar, sometimes, still, making love urgently against each other under a sky that no longer showed any stars, near a fire they would not let die.

311: Orbits

On his way to the grocery store, over on the sidewalk he saw them, a man and his son, they seemed, walking along. The two holding hands, the son coming up just above the man's waist.

Every few steps, the son would begin to run and the dad would grab the son's wrist with his other hand and spin as he walked, the son leaning out against the dad's pull, running in a circle as the dad twirled until the son was back where he'd started and the dad faced forward again and they continued walking.

So:

Walk: step step step

Spin!

Walk: step step step

Spin!

If they stumbled the dad caught them. They laughed, mouths open wide enough to see their teeth as he drove to get yogurt and some bread. He watched them, marveling that two people could engage in an activity so obviously without any point other than its own existence. In his rearview mirror as they receded, he saw: *Step step step spin! Laugh sometimes tumble walk spin.*

He made it to the grocery store. He got the yogurt (Pina Colada flavor) and the bread (7-grain), paid for them. He got back in his car and in the sunsetish shadows as he drove back along the road he saw the dad and son again.

Still walking, spinning, laughing, they had added a new one, with the son crooking his arm through dad's elbow, dad spinning as he walked lifting son off the ground, legs splaying out wildly.

He watched that, too, in his rearview mirror, then went home, put the yogurt in the refrigerator, kissed his wife good night and went to sleep. Later on as he went on living from time to time he would take a drive at night, along the road to the grocery store. He never saw them again, though, ever.

310: 1,250 feet above New York City, 1933.

Okay, Coop. This is the big time.

Wouldn't've believed it if I'd heard it on the radio. And I almost did have to! If Danny doesn't get sick, I'm not on duty and we're probably at Mavis' parents this weekend, and I'd never see this.

Let alone lead the attack! Steady, Coop. Coop, ol' boy, you never know what the day'll bring, do you? Keep steady, Coop. Where's Tommy? I see Red, but... OK. Tommy. Stay in formation, boys. Almost there.

Does it see us? It ain't a *he*. It's an *it*.

You've shot down Germans, Coop. This is just the same. Don't matter that it ain't German in a plane. Just matters you've got wings and a machine gun.

There he... it... is. It sees you, Coop. Steady hands.

That paw. It's huge. Ready, steady, Coop. A little more. The woman! GEEZ, dames. Get away! That's right. A little more. Now!

FIRE FIRE FIRE FIRE and *turn*, away and up!

You got it, Coop. You got it good. That thing's mad now. Rest of you boys! Just like me. Just like Coop! That's it, Tommy, Red! Machine gun him to the ground.

Now, back around. Let's loop wide. Someone oughta get those crowds outta there. Not your worry, Coop. That thing's watching. Good. Tight turn. Dive! Gun!

FIRE FIRE HOLY MARY WHAT IS IT... MY WING!

How'd that thing do that? Doesn't matter. This is it. Steer, Coop.

Your job ain't over yet. You're goin' down but don't you take anyone with you, Coop. Tommy, Red? It's your fight now, boys. You shoot that monkey down. Do it for Coop. Spinning! Fire! Wish I'd been able to say bye to Mavis. Aim for the park, Coop. Ain't nobody there now. Damn monkey! You never know what the day'll bring, Coop. You nev

309: Dance Little Baby, Caper and Crow!

This time when the zombies came they didn't try to eat brains. Instead, they stole babies and shuffled off.

People whose babies were stolen got the rest of us from the shelters or wherever we'd been hiding or fending them off, saying *"we've got to get our babies back."* Some of the babies' parents, had already gone after the zombies, who should be easy to catch because they were slow, but those woods favored the zombies, who somehow shuffled through easily while we got ripped at by thorns, tangled in branches, lost.

We sent a search party, armed with some guns we could spare in case this was a trick to deplete the village and take us over. It took two days before we made it to the clearing where the zombies had stopped. We arrived at sunrise. We saw all the village babies in cradles with bottles of milk, teddy bears and blankets. Next to them, zombie arms stuck out of the ground and rocked them gently. The babies were asleep or at least content.

One dad couldn't help himself and ran onto zombie ground, grabbed his baby. A bunch of zombie arms shot up out of the dirt and grabbed him. He howled as he was pulled underground. His baby was ferried back to its crib by zombie hands, which began rocking it again.

We all stood, thinking. There were other parents among us whose babies were out in the clearing. One put a foot onto the dirt but zombie hands appeared all over the place and the mom stepped back. It didn't seem helpful to the babies if we all died trying to get them back, so we went home to come up with a plan. Nobody's thought of one yet and those babies are nearly a year older now.

308: So The World Is Coming to an End.

"And here we are in this bar," Bud said, looking around.

"What's wrong with this bar?" asked Finn, the bartender.

"What's wrong with *us*," asked Maria, the whore.

The rest of the crowd all stared at Bud, too, silently echoing the questions.

"Ah, forget it," Bud said.

Nobody forgot it, but everybody shut up and went back to watching the TV and waiting.

Then Bud didn't forget it, either, saying, loudly, "You all know what I mean!"

And they did. They all knew what he meant. But they wanted him to say it, and Bud obliged: "We're all losers, and nobody wants to die next to a loser," Bud said. "Remember that thing, that thing we were always told, that thing about *live every day like it could be your last?*"

They all remembered that thing, except Maria, who hadn't grown up in this country. They all nodded, though, even Maria.

Bud stared morosely into his glass, half-full, for so long that people thought he'd given up saying anything, and everyone was about to go back to looking at the TV instead of Bud, when he spoke up again, quietly.

"Turns out we did that," he said.

Now it was all their turns to stare into *their* half-full glasses, while thinking about what Bud had said. He was right, of course, but nobody wanted Bud to be right. Bud was *always* right, about the World Cup outcomes, about the President's deal, about how they'd spent their lives exactly this way, staring at half-full glasses of alcohol while dreading what came next.

"What comes next, Bud?" asked Maria, and they all wanted him to say that, too.

Bud looked up at the TV.

Bud looked down at his glass.

Bud looked over at Maria.

"Next," he said, "Is the good part."

307: Pirates of the...

Financial markets! Jezebel, who used to be Diane, pulled up short, cutlass held to the throat of a scared-looking man who would have been the type elsewhere, to slide up to her and offer to buy her a drink, and Jezebel would've taken one, would've let him talk her up, would've gone back to his apartment overlooking the brightly lit beautiful skyline of Chicago, would've stayed over.

"What's wrong?" asked Lil, who was still Lil.

"This doesn't feel right," Jezebel said.

"How could it not?" asked Lil, as she shot an arrow through the throat of the witch doctor above the trading floor. "We created this entire world."

"And yet..." Jez said, and pushed the man away from her. "Buy me a drink, somewhen." She smiled as he scuttled off.

"Look," Lil said. "You didn't want to muck around with times that existed so we created times that don't exist."

"But how can they *not*?" Jez asked. "Once we create them, they exist, and always did, didn't they?" A broker jumped off a bank of computers automatically trading pork bellies. She swung around, jabbed her cutlass like a rapier, wrong but still effective, into his gut. He collapsed. "That guy," she said, spinning around, pulling Lil's arm to get her out of the way of a thrown Molotov cocktail. "He had a past, right? Even if he just came into existence right now, he *thinks* he had a family and a Mom and Dad and he's a person, isn't he?"

"Come on, Jez!" Lil grunts in frustration, shooting off two quick arrows and signaling to the crew that they're ready to get back to the dirigible. "If you're not okay with looting and pillaging capitalists created by the machine for *just that purpose*, then who CAN we kill?"

"Maybe that's the problem," Jezebel says.

306: Water.

Emil came from the sea but not the usual way people did, evolving up from it. Instead, he just walked out of the ocean one day, fully-grown, the townsfolk staring as they mended their nets, patched their sails, and otherwise did things seafaring folk did while on the land.

That was many years ago, several generations, in fact, and still the townsfolk distrusted him. This was not because he had come from the sea. They understood that. They lived for the sea, felt alive only when on the water or were surrounded by it. What they could not tolerate in Emil was that he would not go back to the water, would not go near it, didn't like to even look in the direction of the sea. This was a sin to them, as the sea brought life, brought livelihood, had brought Emil, even, and to turn your back on that was unforgivable.

What the people did not know and never saw were Emil's attempts to go back. Every so often, late in the night, so late it was almost morning, while others slept, Emil would leave his small house on the edge of the forest, sneak through town, and go stand on the beach, looking towards where the sun would be, across the dark water frothing forward in small breakers.

"Let me back," Emil would say.

The sea would growl at him.

"Let me back," Emil would plead, arms held out.

The sea would recede and rise into a wave, threatening Emil, the ships, the town itself, blotting out the morning stars and the moon.

"I didn't do it," Emil would argue, quietly.

The wave would quiver with rage.

And Emil would retreat. While he was not afraid of the wave, he could not risk the townsfolk who, however suspiciously, had let him stay.

305: The Moon, and the Ocean

Come to me Moon says each night to Ocean,
but

                                      Ocean resists

       Moon's   pull and peels back, tossing her curls, turning away.

Moon circles the sky,

                staring at   Ocean's beauty,
wishing to touch it once more.

                                   Ocean triest to ignore

        Moon's gaze,   tries not to feel the tug of

        Moon's love.

Moon falls sleep with sunrise
And

Ocean rests peacefully through the day
while dreading dark because at night
Ocean can see, can feel, can taste the
reflections of

Moon On still calm waters. The only way to
avoid that is to rile herself into froth,
deluging sailors crawling along her,
upsetting the mollusks who live deep in
her. Ocean wants nothing more than to
sleep, and forget.

Once, Moon and Ocean were lovers.

Once, they embraced and were partcially
one.

But when
Moon
was given the chance to jump to the stars,
it took that opportunity, and began to
                    swing
                                around
            gleefully,

no longer
            weighted

            by

            gravity,

                    turning

            and

                    whirling

            and

            feeling the pelt of tiny rocks
from distant reaches of space,
            the glow of stars it basked in.

305: The Moon, and the Ocean (cont)

Come to me Ocean had cried, and the
rains had fallen for weeks

as

Moon

danced

around,   the two seperated for the first time

ever.

Moon was unwilling to be
tied down again and wanted

Ocean

to feel this

freedom.

But Ocean could not leave the world
and everything in it, would not
abandon the dreaming
whales
and the shimmery clouds of
fish
that required it,
would not force this
world
to become a dry husk without her,
lifeless, and so Ocean pulled at

Moon,

tried to drag

Moon   back down,

and Moon pulled back, luring

Ocean

to the sky,

and the two of them danced for eons like that,
each holding on forever,
but at an arm's length.

304: The Wary Dance

Once, the planets all were alive and full of the fire and light of life,
roaring through the universe like flaming lions,
surfaces roiling with emotion and their hearts ablaze.

Sun grew jealous and decided to take everything it could from them.

Sun first stripped away Pluto's energy completely.

This caused Sun to glow so brightly that the other planets were alerted to the threat,
but before any could act,
Sun reached its fiery tentacles into the hearts of Uranus and Neptune,
boiling away their bodies,
leaving them incorporeal,
still alive
but only haunts of their former selves.

Sun turned to the rest of them.

Jupiter and Saturn took the smaller planets aside,
stood in front of them.

Sun flared,
lighting up the cosmos in its anger.
So bright did Sun shine that
Jupiter and Saturn had to flee,
their last act to shield the smaller ones.

The two giants retreated too late: they, too, were ghosts, now.

Earth,   Could not deny the appeal Sun held for them now:
Venus,   the warmth and light Sun threw off, wastefully,
Mercury   careless and profligate
and Mars   with its stolen powers,
                                   felt good.
                                   They wanted more.

To help their damaged siblings,
they threw rocks into space,
urging their ghost-brothers to abide until they,
the smaller ones,
could steal the energy back.

These asteroids and moons, though gratefully accepted, provided miniscule comfort to the
dead ones.

The small planets then cloaked themselves in rock,
for protection,
and began to dance around Sun,
threatening always
to take back what Sun had stolen, but also basking in Sun's glow.

They gradually lost interest in revenge but continued their dance anyway, promising over
and over to avenge the destroyed planets who were now so far away that Sun's light and
heat were memories,

promising but not meaning it.

303: Mom Missed a Lot, That Night.

We decided to mummify Dad to bring him back to life like in the Saturday afternoon movies, where it seemed you'd hardly finish wrapping a corpse in bandages and *zam boom* the body was up and shuffling around, menacing and stuff, which made Sarah wonder whether we should do this.

"Dad isn't very menacing," she said. She meant she didn't *want* him menacing, either, but Davy brushed it off.

"Not every mummy has to be menacing," he said, like he knew, and added "Dad'll probably just be glad that he gets to keep on doing stuff."

It took about two days, total, during which Mom mostly slept upstairs, coming down only to sit, tiredly, at dinner, us kids trying not to spoil the surprise in the basement.

When we finished, Dad's body was completely wrapped in bandages, his organs were all in little clay jars spread around the room, and Ed had pulled his brains out through his nose. We'd even cleaned up the mud we'd tracked in from digging him out of the grave and bringing him back here. We figured Mom would love it, but when she came downstairs to see why we were late for dinner, she just screamed and fainted, so she missed it when Dad sat up at the sound of her voice and shuffled over – he did it menacingly, too!—and she missed it when Dad then, probably confused, tried to eat Sarah's face and Ed and Davy had to hit him with the shovel until he stopped moving again, and she missed it when we dragged him back to the grave and put him back and patted down the earth and then made up a schedule for who would have to sit up, nights, in case he got back out.

302: On His First Night in the House.

There's something outside.

We… don't talk about them.

I heard something, something like

We *don't*.

Don't talk about wh

Look, we *do not talk about them*.

It sounded like

Ever.

But it was

Yes.

So

Yes.

But

It works, okay?

What happens if

Talking about not talking about them is the same as talking about them.

So we're just supposed to

It's kept us alive this long.

Don't look out, either.

Why?

It will?

It's just all so hard to believe.

I mean, I never noticed—
Sorry.

Yeah.

They'll be gone in the morning?

How Long

What are we supposed to do?

How can we sleep?

Meaning eventually I'll get used to...

Did...
Never mind.
Wait, seriously, did something

OK. OK. I am letting go

It'll be...bad.

You don't have to believe me.

I don't see what's so hard to believe
about it.

You were going to talk about them,
weren't you?

I know it takes some getting used to,
but it's way way better in the long run.

Seriously.

SERIOUSLY.

Sleep.

Eventually you'll fall asleep.

Yes.

Yes, probably because YOU KEEP
TALKING ABOUT THEM
DO NOT PULL ASIDE THE
CURTAIN.
Just put your hand down at your side.
I mean it.
If you look outside, there's no way I
can help you.

You're not.

302: On His First Night in the House (cont).

I will

You're not.

It's like I

Can't help yourself?

Yeah.

That's why.
That's why we have that rule.

Help.

Just let go of the curtain.

Help me.

I can't do it for you.

Aim that somewhere else.

I will NOT.

Help me, honestly.

It's got to be all you, friend.

I don't want to look.

You're going to.

I won't.

You will.

I can't.

I'll stand here all night.

There's no hope for me?

Maybe they'll welcome you.

301: 3 Tortoises.

Three tortoises appeared on the edge of a clearing. In their whole lives none of them had traveled more than a quarter-mile, and their whole lives, so far had been 70, 50, and 57 years.

Are we now to come closer? The 70-year-old said to the two young ones.

Or shall we turn away from each other? The 57-year-old said.

The 50-year-old ate a leaf and watched the other two. It was up to him. He felt it. What he did next would determine the fate of these three, a fate that might last another one hundred years.

If he stepped forward, the other two would also, and the three of them would remain in this clearing for five, twenty, seventy years, maybe never leaving each other's company.

If he stepped backwards, each would turn away and over years would slowly (oh so slowly) drift apart, until several decades hence they might be separated by as much as 200 yards, each aware of the other two back behind it, moving away, each conscious of the proximity that for every other animal might be no big deal, but which for them was the chasm of time, of momentum, of the past.

When you live as slowly as we do, the 50-year-old said, you can afford to mull over your next step. He proceeded to do that.

The sun set.

The sun rose.

The sun set again, rose again, and so on for many nights.

The rains came.

The rains left.

The three tortoises had not moved.

The 50-year-old one morning, as the dew settled on the blades of grass around him, said let us meet. They were the first words spoken in that clearing in 2 years, but they were the right words, and a year later they came true.

300: The Oyster Diver.

Every day, Supun sat in the back of the long boat with his large rock and his greased cotton in his ears and his basket, sitting until the boat sat above the oyster beds, when he would go overboard with his rock clutched to his chest, his basket in hand, and head

Down

        through the yellow-green top layers of water

Down

        Into solid green where fish flitted by

Down

        Into blue-green where you could find coral

Down

        Into the blue black where almost no light reached and sometimes you saw sharks in the distance, or a moray grabbed at your hand.

Today, when he got to the bottom Supun did not hold his rock one-handed while scooping oysters into the basket until his ears pounded against his brain and his eyes watered with the need for air, and he did not let go his rock and rise to the surface where he would face the short death and hopefully be pulled into the boat before sinking back down in the long death.

Today, Supun dropped his basket, turned himself upright and held onto his rock. He looked up through the layers of water to the thin shadow of the boat waiting for him to be pulled into it so his oysters could counted, pearls taken from him, and him be ferried back with only a pittance in exchange for dying every day.

Then he looked around. He saw a shark. He saw a startled octopus. He began walking across the ocean floor, clutching his rock to his chest. He walked away from the boat and away from the oyster beds and into deeper and deeper water, walking further and further, never looking back, only occasionally wondering how long the last gulp of air he'd taken would last.

299: "But You, Kid? I Bet *You* Will. You Look the Type."

There's a road, kid, a highway, not like this one, this road, kid, it's somethin' really else. This road, when they were layin' it out, well, I don't know what happened, 'zactly. Maybe it was finished on the solstice or they crossed some burial ground or there was just magic, for whatever reason, however it happened, kid, this road's *magic*.

I mean it, I really do. You drive this road, hit a certain speed with the sun a certain angle, the world explodes with possibilities. You see everything, I mean *everything* ever happened to you, everything ever didn't, every possibility you had, every one you didn't know existed. That girl you were too scared to ask out? You see how it went on that date, you had sex on the hilltop, she left her bra in your car, twenty years later you still had it hid from your wife, and you don't just see your wife, you see all the wives you didn't marry... you see everything, even the things that aren't.

And if you drive at night, kid? If you do, which I don't recommend, if you drive it when the moon ain't out and the stars ain't bright, then you see every bad thing ever happened to you or ever will, everything. You see all the stubbed toes, broken fingers. You see the doctor say they gotta take part of your liver. You see the guy strangle that pretty wife of yours with that girl's bra he found in the closet, kid, and you see yourself put a gun to your own head 'cause you miss your wife and 'cause guilt. All the bad, kid.

What, kid?

No, I ain't never drove it, and never will.

298: New Witches.

The witch had decided to stop, but couldn't just.

When she'd been a girl, had just turned 7, she'd been sitting one night on the porch swing watching fireflies in the yard when a crone had popped up next to the porch.

The woman, looking old as the hills, began speaking of starry nights and love potions and flying brooms and transforming people into whatever you wanted, and, yes, poisons to kill your enemies – for even 7-year-old girls have enemies, and thoughts of murder– talk of magic. Magic! All the girl had to do, the old lady said, was say *I want to be a witch*, and she would have this.

"Will I be old, like you?" she'd asked, her only concern. The witch had winced at the pain in the little girl's eyes, staring at withered cheeks and rotten teeth and one blind, hollow eye socket.

"No, dear. No, not for many years," the answer came, and so the 7-year-old had said the words, there'd been a wrenching, and the hag had crumpled to her knees, crying out in relief that she was now free to die, yelling so loudly the girl became frightened. Her parents came rushing to see what the racket was. As they came through the door the girl worried they'd see the old lady, would know what had happened, would be mad, so she had blinked, concentrated, shuddered, and felt power flow from the stars to the ground through her feet and out her pores and turned her parents into fireflies buzzing in amazed consternation.

"Enjoy it!" the former witch had cackled, running off, and for nearly a century she had, but now it was time to find a new little girl, so she could wither away as all witches did.

297: The Sad Little Robot.

The sad little robot was sad because he had been programmed to be. That is how robots work. They do not develop emotions on their own. Their code dictates they feel the way they have been told to.

The sad little robot oftentimes wondered why it had been created sad. It would be sorting through shoes—that was one job it had, to put away our shoes, make sure they had the proper number of laces and were not in need of a polishing, etc.—and sadness rested on its robot chest. This happened when it put out the cat, or did the dishes. The sad little robot was just *sad*. All the time.

The sad little robot had not been programmed to ask *why it must feel sad*. That feature it had developed on its own. This led the sad little robot to start on a project. If it could learn to inquire into why it was a certain way, it could learn (the sad little robot thought)(wrongly) to feel a different way.

And that was why our family one night came across the sad little robot, sitting on our couch in the dark in the living room watching the television tuned into a late-night talk show. Whenever the audience laughed, the sad little robot would emit a sort of electronic barking laugh, too, and slap its knees in fake amusement, metal hands pinging lightly on the brushed aluminum legs.

We caught it looking up knock-knock jokes on the internet, and reciting poems by Shel Silverstein, too. Sometimes, it would skip, energetically clumsy, instead of walking. Nothing worked, of course. We talked sometimes about downloading new emotions for it, but decided that even robots need a hobby, and left it at that.

296: Giant.

Our giant we called "Baba O'Riley." Like all of them, he survived by hiding in abandoned buildings. Almost nobody ever finds them. They're very secretive when they pick a tenement, lift the roof off, smash the floors out, then move in, coming out only sometimes at night during heavy rainstorms, lifting the roof off and strolling through the city under the cover of weather so bad only the crazies would see them, and nobody would believe the crazies.

We found our giant when a baseball went through a window in his hide-out. I was chosen to fetch it. I opened the door and found myself looking into a hollow space filled with a curled-up giant. I screamed and slammed the door and then they were all making fun of me, so I showed them, and this time the giant was holding the baseball between two fingers big as horses, right near the door.

"Thanks," I managed, and grabbed the ball and shut the door again, without thinking. We backed into the street and looking up at the third floor could see now, past the faded curtains hanging there, the eye looking at us. It was big, kind of sad, and bloodshot. I bet it's hard to sleep, all cramped up like that. We finished the baseball game, hearing now some rumbly laughs if something funny happened or a bit of a roar when someone made a great play.

Baba lived there a few years until they put a demolition notice on the door and he was gone. I was going off to college, anyway. But every city I go to, I like to drive around the bad parts. There's not many buildings still have giants but if you look hard enough you'll find them.

295: No Fool Like a Drunken, Old Fool.

"I was the Loch Ness monster, for about a year," the man said. "It wasn't a trick, either," he went on, glancing nervously around. The other groomsmen chuckled.

A night's entertainment the one who lived here said. Drunky gave the Scot a look. The Scot looked back and behind his amused air was something real, cold. Drunky drained his glass, stood up uncertainly, nodded, said "Mind you don't drink too much," and tottered off to a chorus of *like you?* And *thanks, you barmy sot.*

We stayed several more rounds toasting Billy and, whenever Billy went to the loo discussing how hot Holly was. The party broke up and we all separated outside. I figured the walk would do me good. About two blocks on I came across Drunky on a bookshop stoop.

He grabbed me. "I wasn't kidding," he whispered. "They really make you into it! They transform you, you *become* the thing. You live in the Loch, you don't wanta be seen, you eat fish, you've got flippers" he babbled on senselessly: a cabal, some kind of machine, it's for those dishonorably discharged or with petty crimes, until I shoved him away, my own vision going a bit swimmy with drink, and continued on.

A block later I looked back. He was sitting on the stoop again. And the Scot was there, a half-block back. Drunky saw him, too, got up and tried to run. The Scot took off after him down an alley.

The next day, at the wedding, I tried to catch the Scot's eye a few times but he wouldn't look at me and eventually I gave up. I didn't see Drunky the rest of the weekend, either, but that doesn't mean anything.

294: Caterpillars from Space.

When the meteorite hit in the Canadian plains everyone expected it to just vaporize a bunch of forest and leave some interesting rocks for scientists to look at, but what we got instead was eggs that quickly hatched into caterpillars, about two feet long and fluffy like those ones everyone says can predict a cold winter. There were thousands, and scientists didn't round them all up. Despite their pleas and governments all imposing a ban on Space Caterpillar ownership, plenty still ended up on eBay and you could get one pretty easily.

For the first four months people mostly debated how the bugs had gotten on the meteor and whether they were an invasive species we should just wipe out or whether God put them there (the Christians were pretty divided on that one). Then the caterpillars all went into chrysalises and we kept arguing while also waiting to see what kinds of butterflies would come out. Everyone was pretty sure it would be butterflies, although every lunchroom or bus had the one wiseacre saying '*could be a moth*'. People hated those guys.

Around spring the butterflies came out. They were beautiful, iridescent and crystalline, with these big, heart-shaped eyes. They were also carnivorous and as fast as hawks. They dove after cats, dogs, small animals, and sometimes attacked people. Plus, they multiplied fast; within weeks there were new sets of eggs and the debate began again how to deal with this.

I came down on the side of those who felt this was just nature, and we'd all better learn live with it and/or carry shotguns when things got out of hand. After all, we'd had the same debates about those land-faring squid, and humanity's done all right against them.

293: When We Landed.

"What was that?" one soldier asked.

"Just settle down," Edgar responded. The soldier waved, visibly brushing him off. Edgar started reminding him this was a scientific mission, which Tom thought important. Bad enough they'd probably destroyed crops with their landing in what the pilot claimed was a fallow field. What kind of society left cropland just outside a major city fallow? they'd argued, but the pilot insisted.

And now the honor guard was front and center, leading through this eerie silence of weird-shaped buildings that felt like suburbs, the buildings here weirdly triangular in contrast to the clearly-visible rounded giant domes of what they'd already begun referring to as "downtown," their destination.

Tom was going to tell the soldiers to pull back, be less conspicuous, when the cylinder was thrown from off to the right. Three soldiers immediately formed a triangle of attack. The rest of them fell back, dropping down in instinctive cover. Smoke poured from the cylinder and wafted over them. Tom felt safe in his helmet, watched the analysis. It would've been poison to someone raised in this atmosphere. Not to them, not any more than the air itself. Word through the intercoms: safe. They cautiously moved around it. The soldiers stayed in attack formation. Tom clicked over to the alien channels they'd picked up, heard more chatter, indecipherable even after all these weeks.

Another canister and a rock glancing off a soldier's armor. The overreaction was fierce: lasers trained on the house where they'd come from, reduced it to flames and cinders almost instantly. The alien station went nuts. The soldiers were calling for backup on the radio. Edgar met Tom's eyes. So we're invaders, he said, and the domes in the distance, lighting up, agreed.

292: Pirates of the —

"*Unchosen alternatives…*" finishes Lil, who might change her name again.
"What bugs me, though," says Jezebel, "is we don't know how it works."
"Sure we do."
"*You* do," Jezebel mumbles.
"It's easy," Lil points here, here, *here*. "All we are doing is channeling people's choices to create a new reality."
"Yeah. You said that."
"I'll show you," Lil tries. "Want to go get some breakfast?"
"What? No."
Lil leans forward, makes a very minute adjustment on two dials and points out the window of the small apartment they have rented on a twenty year lease to store the machine.
"Look," she says.
Down below, at the sidewalk café where they've been going lately to drink coffee, eat bagels, and plan their next adventure, sit Lil and Jezebel. The two ladies, smiling in the morning sunshine, look up at the window and wave.
"Ok, so *how…*" Jezebel begins.
Lil interrupts: "It's like I said: for that brief second before you decided *not* to get lunch, you were thinking about it and it was possible for you to get lunch or to not get lunch, or to do one of a hundred jillion things. So when you *chose*, I simply readjusted the machine and put us into the timeline where you said *yes*."
"That doesn't…"
"It doesn't *have* to make sense. It's quantum mechanics. *The atom bomb… transistor radios…*" Lil intoned in the voice of the filmstrip from their 8th grade science class where she'd first gotten the idea for the machine.
Jezebel was biting her lip, and kept glancing out the window.
"What?" Lil finally said. She also made up her mind: *I'm going to be Harriet* from now on.
"It's just…" Jezebel mumbled "Now I'm kind of hungry, too."

291: The Red-Haired Ghost.

The train station has been abandoned for decades, but she has been there longer than that, even, still waiting.

Some say she was standing on the platform to kiss her fiancé luck on the way to war against the Germans after Pearl Harbor but saw him, lips locked with another woman, and so flung herself in front of his train and has haunted the station since then.

Others say, no, she was waiting for him to get his ticket and board, to kiss her before he headed to the West Coast to become a movie star, when he slipped and was run over himself, and she knelt by the spot where he fell, never moving again until one day she faded into the spirit world, her body just disappearing.

When the moon is right, like now, you can see her, there: straight red hair, stars visible through it! Head bowed, eyes closed (hard to see, the way she is translucent but you don't see the whites of her eyes, do you?)

Some say she cries.

Others say she prays.

What would a ghost cry about? To whom would a ghost pray?

Some say they have asked her that, asked her story, asked which version is true, and that depending on her mood, she has disappeared, or sobbed silently but violently, or simply turned to them and opened her eyes, her eyes in which one can glimpse the truth.

The ones who say she opened her eyes are the ones who do not like to talk about her, who need to be goaded into telling the story of their questioning her, and even then they will not describe those eyes, and afterwards they take to their bed for days.

290: Science.

Look, I will prove it. See this apple?

An...

...d there: Did you see?

I know you didn't. We'll try again with a better view. Here is another apple. Watch

                              Re   ful

                A   l

C   y. Did you see it that time?

Gravity, of course. Did you see *gravity*?

Of course you didn't. Want to know why? Fine. Don't laugh.

The gravitons are *behind you*.

I said not to laugh. I'm serious. For billions of years scientists have searched for gravitons... okay, for *forty* years, it's the same thing because don't get me started on time and how it is *not*... and they've never found them.

Because they've never *looked behind them*.

I am totally serious.

It doesn't matter if you look behind yourself! You won't see one. He *stays* behind you.

No, I've got one behind *me*, too. Everyone does. Everyone has all kinds of things behind them: Gravitons, ghosts who whisper the day you will die and make you wake up just before your alarm clocks goes off, horses of unusual size and color... yes, them, too. Yes, *horses*. LOTS of things. I don't even know how many things are behind us.

You can't see them because they're not yours. Here is the science behind that. Do you like apples?

No, I knew you didn't. That's why I felt free to drop two of them for the pleasure of my graviton. I like apples, but I do not like hot dogs such as you are eating now. You see the peculiar pleasure of hot dogs. I understand in my world the delectable quality of apples. You may never understand that joy, just as you will never see my horses, gravitons, etc.

I'm am 100% serious about this.

289: Real Life.

When they brought her into the emergency room Tom knew he loved her at first sight. That first sight was only a glimpse, but also a doozy.

She was on a stretcher, and there was blood. Two paramedics were rushing alongside her, the nurse from the desk was already up and out to help, do something, do what? Tom didn't know. A doctor banged through the giant double doors and all the people sitting in the ER waiting room, the girl with the cough and the man who just slumped and the older guy who didn't look like there was anything wrong with him at all, he just watched TV, and Tom with the nail through his foot and the blood-soaked t-shirt around it, all knew that they were going to be waiting longer. The coughing girl looked cross. Tom didn't care. He went back to paging through the *Time* magazine from back May and pictured the woman's face in his mind so he'd recognize it when he saw it again.

Brownish, sandy hair. Small pointy nose. Her eyes, open and scared and wide, her mouth twisted and howling, her small hand dangling out below the blanket underneath the IV bag they'd had hooked up. Tom wondered why she was here: car accident? Shooting? There'd been blood but none on her face.

It wasn't the first time he'd fallen in love like that, instantly, but this one felt real, and through his wait, through cleaning the foot, removing the nail, giving a tetanus shot, he kept hoping she hadn't died, kept looking for her, to see her again before he headed back outside into the hot afternoon with nothing more than the rest of the day off.

288: "Remember That One Time You Did That Thing?"

The statue in the museum was ugly but for some reason Jeni couldn't stop looking at it, and then for some reason she couldn't stop crying, and then for some reason she crawled under the velvet ropes and scrabble-dashed to the marble base and climbed up and hugged the statue to her, hugged it and kept pulling her feet away from the guards who rushed in, hugged it and kept ignoring people snapping photos.

Hugged it, and cried, and kept doing those things.

"She won't come down," Jeni heard not long after the room had been cleared of almost everyone.

"Why did you go there?" Jeni imagined her kids asking, whenever she'd worked through what this would do to her life and come back home to sit wrapped in a blanket and eating a piece of toast and having maybe some coffee even though she would prefer lemonade.

"Can you understand me?" the patrol officer asked Jeni, who had an itch starting in her leg and had just realized she'd left her purse sitting on the bench, a thought that cut through the haze of wanting to hug this statue.

"Was it me?" Jeni pictured her boyfriend asking her, and she wondered if he'd feel guilty like maybe he should've proposed by now.

"Tell Art it doesn't have anything to do with him," she managed to say as she got her gasps under control and looked down at everyone gaping up at her. She felt like she'd just stay there until the firemen came and got her, and then they could all together start the process of never knowing why this had happened, and never actually forgetting that it had.

287: Landfall.

It was a dark, but not yet stormy, night as they hauled the captain's body off the boat against his written directions. The note scrawled as he lay dying had said in death he wanted what he'd had in life: the sea. *Do not take me ashore*, he'd written. The sailors had debated what it meant that the man had never stepped ashore as long as anyone could remember and did not want to now.

But 'es got a daughter, Willis reminded them. The reason they'd sailed here in the first place, a final visit.

So the decision was made, the men watching solemnly as the body was brought down the gangplank. *Creak. Creak. Creak.* Willis tore his eyes away from the procession at the last moment, and so didn't see the captain's body laid on the shore, but did see the instantaneous reaction from the Heavens above, lightning tearing open the sky, a torrential downpour starting, cold and solid like a massive wave breaking from the clouds, thunder so powerful they felt it in their teeth.

Get 'im back aboard Willis tried to yell above the gale, but the body was already gone! He darted his eyes around but gave it up as he saw waterspouts on the harbor, tornadoes inland, and the lightning spiked around him. The men fled to the only safety they knew, the ship, ropes being cast off. Willis had to leap to catch the bulwark and pull himself up. The ship flung itself to and fro as oars pulled it to sea. Willis watched houses torn to bits. He told himself it was impossible to hear the screams over the storm but he knew they were there to be heard.

286: Diner Guy.

The diner had these vinyl seats in that turquoisey blue color that was really big until a certain point in the 1970s and then wasn't seen again in society, except in places that didn't know they were retro, like the diner, which was one reason I liked it, but the crying guy wrecked it for me.

Every day I'd go there to get a cup of coffee and probably some breakfast. I was trying to be one of those people who goes to *do* things. I saw a lady, once, reading, in a museum. She was sitting across from some paintings in the art museum and reading a Dan Brown book. She was pretty, kind of like who I wanted to marry when I got married. I didn't talk to her. Later, remembering her and others like her, people who didn't just sit around but did stuff, I found the diner and I'd go there every morning. It seemed like a start.

Until the crying guy came in, and sat at the counter, and ordered two eggs, easy over—I remember he reversed the way you call the eggs—then he just sat there, head on his hand and pinching the bridge of his nose. You could hardly tell he was crying until you looked close. His shoulders shook and his hand trembled. After twenty minutes during which I forgot to eat my muffin watching him, he took some dollar bills from his pocket, put them on the counter and left. I last saw him standing on the corner looking up 4th street, and now I don't go to the diner anymore because it won't be the same. It won't *mean* anything without him.

285: Goblins.

We had goblins, and clearly a lot of them, judging by the bite marks. I didn't tell Angela right away but she knew something was up, because I began keeping a closer eye on the baby, not even letting it sleep in its room.

But the scratches on the walls weren't near the baby's room, and I started thinking maybe they were only here for the winter, hiding from the cold. Then on day four there were some scales near Angela's pillow. I saw them when I woke up and quickly brushed them away, then went to look in the bassinet. The baby was o.k. When I looked up Angela was peering at me.

"When were you going to tell me?" she asked.

"I wasn't sure," I said, because it hadn't, honestly, occurred to me until that moment that they might be after *her*.

Angela said she was going to stay at her sister's for the week until I got rid of them. She took the baby and left the dogs, which seemed about right.

That night I woke up to find seven of them standing on the bed, garbling and spitting. I don't speak goblin, but I guessed. "I don't *know* where she is," I said. They tore apart her pillow and left.

The next day I burned all Angela's stuff in the backyard, like it said to on the Internet. They didn't come back. But Angela called the day after and said that her sister'd heard scratching in the walls, so I think we might have to go to Illinois for a while. Also, Angela's saying we need counseling but I keep telling her I really didn't think they were after her.

284: The Preacher I Saw

The preacher I saw was under a tent on the used car lot out the side of town, space rented for 4 days but nobody was coming out to his services, much.

The preacher I saw looked tired, sweaty. He looked possessed. If it's right to say someone looks possessed by God then that was how he looked and if it's not right then too bad as that's the only way he looked.

The preacher I saw had wrinkled edges of his tongue like scallops. You could see them when he talked. Everything he said, he opened his mouth as wide as anyone ever did, wide enough to see his rotten tooth in the back of his mouth.

The preacher I saw pointed his finger directly at me and in a whisper, mouth wide as the mountains, said *Even a twelve year old girl can go to Hell if she doesn't accept Jesus as her Lord and savior and try to do right by Him and listen to His Commandments* and then the preacher seemed to know that in my own mind I'd thunk *Jesus didn't even have Commandments that was Moses*, and as I thought it I felt for a second God looking hard out of the preacher's eyes, judging me, but then Marie elbowed me and we left.

Sometimes later I wondered if I'd seen the preacher at all, and then came nights I felt the judging for my cruel sarcastic thoughts and for the way boys twisted my insides and made me want to I don't even know, and I figured that I must've seen him otherwise how would I recognize that guilt he'd put in me?

283: Pirates of the...

...*Serengeti*! The gorilla stared back at Harriet and asked: "So why *me*?"

Harriet glanced at Jezebel, who shrugged.

"We both grew up reading comics, and there were always supersmart gorillas showing up to help the heroes or whatever so we made you to help *us* decide whether it's okay to be pirates if the world we make is specifically for that purpose," Harriet looked at Jezebel, "Or if it's wrong to kill people and stuff."

The gorilla scratched its chin, looked off into the distance. "The lions are coming," it said. "We'd best get to your boat," The women looked at each other. The gorilla raised his brows. "You do have a *boat*, do you not? You are *pirates*, are you not?"

"Well, yes and no," said Jezebel.

"She *means*," Harriet said while she pulled a remote from out of her waistband satchel "That yes we *are* pirates! And we will have a boat here in a second. I need to tweak things." Jezebel grabbed her wrist.

"I *mean that we are not sure we want to be pirates!* I have to figure this out!" Jezebel said.

She was interrupted by a roar. The lions were upon them, horses rearing, lassos twirling, six-guns cracking, and Jezebel, remote in *her* hand, was spun away from Harriet, a lion lifting her onto the back of its horse. As they rode away she looked over her shoulder at Harriet and the gorilla, a ship half-formed behind them.

"Rescue me!" she yelled. Harriet gave her the ok sign, then a thumbs up. She turned back to the Cowboy Lion.

"I don't suppose you're particularly concerned about the ethics of multiple universes," she said.

282: He Was a Mighty Good Leader

It only took fourteen days for everyone to lose faith in David, who woke up to the feeling of a a pitchfork being jammed into his chest. He felt the cold metal prongs jab through his ribs and the air flow out of his lungs through the holes, which began bubbling with a slow seep of blood.

"I didn't want to kill you in your sleep," said the woman, whose name he didn't know.

"You led us to our deaths," said Art.

"... the apocalypse," David said, voice already a whisper. "That's what's killing us."

"We believed in you," shouted someone. "Look around us! Where are we?"

The plain was glassy, black, endless. It glowed at night with what David had prayed were the dead's souls but which he knew was radiation. He'd thought the ocean lay this way, there might be food there. He'd been wrong.

"We are not there yet," he said. His last words. The crowd watched his body go limp. They looked around at each other, the body, the sky filled with roiling hellish ash clouds, at each other again.

Someone had to lead, but David's death demonstrated that after the world ended humanity was less willing than ever to believe, more demanding than ever of results. The proof there were no gods left people bereft. The absence of hope left them needing someone to follow. But there was no place to follow to, no future to dream of, and those lacks meant the next leader, like the last, would be blamed and killed. And even people with little time left cherished that too much to throw it away on helping others.

281: A Sky Too Full of Stars

At first people thought it beautiful, all these new stars appearing every night. I did. I especially liked that in cities you could see the stars for the first time, so nights when I would leave the office late I could see them on my way through downtown Chicago, blazing down between the tall, dark obelisks of buildings I drove under as much as over the farmland the second half of my drive took me through

But after a couple months, when there were more each night still, when the night sky above the farm house we lived in and were supposedly fixing up seemed to blaze like white fire, and Wendy, when I accidentally woke her up one night at 12:15 a.m. having just arrived home, said: *It seems like it's hot at night, doesn't it?*, after that, it didn't seem just pretty, anymore.

You could see stars during the day, some of them. People said we were falling towards the galactic center. Scientists claimed it was nothing, that there'd been a period of intense star formation 13,000,000,000 years ago and we were only just seeing the results, but they didn't seem to believe it. Cults killed themselves and people like us postponed having kids.

It'll probably be any day now, we tell each other every night. We sit on the porch wearing sunscreen to ward off starburn, as people are calling it, saying: *We'll probably realize why it's happening, pretty soon.* And eventually I say I have to get up at 5 to drive to the office, so we go to bed, pulling shades against the wall of light that never goes away.

280: The Road.

From the jungle they stumbled onto a paved blacktop road stretching perpendicular to the direction they had been heading, straight and hot and fading to the horizon off to each side.

She sat down, bit her fruit, chewed, spit some seeds out.

"Well, *shit*," she said, finally.

He didn't say anything. Hadn't, since the fever. Three days he'd lain frothing at the mouth, muscles convulsed, writhing. It had left him with the dull-eyed look he'd had ever since. He docilely followed her, useless, now.

She looked left, right. Either would lead to civilization – roads connect cities, it was said. She'd never expected to actually see one, though, let alone one in such good repair.

She walked up the side of the road a bit, in one direction. Then she turned and walked back, right past him. He didn't even turn to watch her, just stood there, hands limp at his sides. She turned around, went back to him, took his hand, looked into the pale eyes.

"What do you think, hon? Should we follow it?"

But really the question was *which way?* Which way *mattered* but she didn't know how to decide. She didn't even know what continent they were on, if there were continents any more.

They sat for a half-day in the sun. She occasionally made him sip water. He never asked for any. She speared a bird, cooked it.

It matters which direction we go, but not how long we take, she thought.

"Here's what," she said. "We'll walk a day one direction. If nothing turns up, we'll walk two days the other. Back and forth, like that, until… something."

And so they set out.

279: This Is How Electricity Works.

There are electrons. They are tiny little things. But that doesn't mean they don't exist, and because they exist they have emotions, television shows, and wars.

The wars make electricity, but the television shows make the wars. Electrons feel passionately about their television shows. They feel passionately about *everything*, actually, because electrons are all charge. They cannot rest, be neutral, or shrug and say *"Eh, it's all the same to me."* When electrons order lunch in a restaurant, they use loud voices to give strong opinions about whether beets belong in a salad.

The first electron television show was a Western. In it, some electrons herding cattle across the Continental divide were intercepted by bandits, played by electrons. The bandits stole the cattle because the lead bandit was in love with the lead cowboy's wife and wanted her to leave her husband. In the western, as in all their television shows, the electrons' characters had no names, because the shows were fiction.

For two seasons, the cowboys tried to get their cattle back from the bandit, plus there were bank robberies, and a railroad fight, and also other things happened. The show was canceled before revealing whether the wife chose the cowboy or the bandit, and that started the first electron war, right about the time some human was claiming to have "discovered" electricity.

Since then, other wars have raged. Arguments about whether popular characters on sitcoms should 'hook up' lead to wild thunderstorms. Deaths of major characters cause ball lightning. And the electricity you use to run your toaster, etc., comes from debates about which morning news show has the most affable hosts.

278: The Witches Were Trees, the Trees Were Witches.

That was when he knew that he was going mad, looking in the backyard one night under the moonlight and seeing the group of witches dancing a circle around the small garden. They stood where the trees in his yard had stood earlier that day. They leered at him with wild hair like twigs and gnarled faces like bark and withered arms like branches, and they told him someone in the house would die.

At breakfast the next morning, three times he cleared his throat and almost explained how the night before the witches had prophesied death, but didn't know how to start that conversation. His young, pretty wife told him he must be getting a cold, his throat so scratchy.

At work, he looked up psychiatric help on the Internet but never called anyone. He left work early, saying he had a fever, which possibly was true. He went home, arriving before his young, pretty wife got home from her aerobics class. He walked into the backyard, flush with late summer growth. He looked at the pumpkins they'd planted, for the baby's first Hallowe'en. He plucked a carrot, still too small but he picked it anyway.

When he stood up, tiny carrot in hand, the witches leered and howled about how someone would die. Someone would die, they told him over and over and he told himself they were just trees but where were their leaves?

That's the story he told me, anyway, when I saw him crying that afternoon.

No, I haven't seen him for a week. I haven't seen *anyone* in the house for over a week.

277: Trouble Down at the Old Mill.

Outside the mill was an old car, a dead lady inside it.

I told Dad at dinner, and he said *"What mill?"*

I had to explain where the *mill* was.

He said "That's not a mill. It used to be a transistor factory." Then he changed the subject.

The next day, the car was gone and a crane with a wrecking ball sat in the lot. A couple of us were looking at it when Dad's police car pulled up.

"There's rats and chemicals in there," he said. "You kids get outta here."

We rode away. The other kids said dad sucked, but Tommy said: "He was scared."

Secretly I agreed.

That night the whole town heard the explosion. Out my window I saw a green glow off by the mill. I had my hands on the windowsill as I tried to see what'd happened, and realized the house was *vibrating*.

Dad suddenly opened my door. "C'mon, Sally," he said, and pulled me roughly down to the storm cellar.

We stayed the entire night until Mom's phone rang and she said we could go back up. I asked quietly what'd happened. She just shook her head.

Dad came home about noon and showered a long time before going to bed.

The next day I asked Dad how come the mill exploded and he said "What mill?" There were road blocks around it when we rode there. Tommy said there were guys in the wood, too. But the paper never said anything and every time I asked Dad he'd say "What mill?" Then sixth grade started and eventually I gave up asking.

276: Preaching and A'Crying.

They were low-grade thugs, the kind of people cops don't hassle because they didn't do any crimes worth really paying attention to, just robbing bars and selling drugs and beating up their girlfriends who would never show up at the restraining order hearings so what could be done? But they let me sit there with them at the few bars that let us hang out there, or outside the auto works, or outside wherever, and so I sat with them and felt old, over, even though I was only 23.

I didn't have a girlfriend and hadn't done any crimes to speak of other than once robbing two college kids I was selling weed to, which was stupid because nobody has cash anymore and I only got twenty bucks but then none of the college kids would buy weed from me and so I'd taken to stealing hubcaps to get money.

"Whyn't you get a job?" the recycling center guy asked me just once, as he took in the obviously-stolen hubcaps I was trading for $18.32. He hiked a thumb at the now hiring sign that hung over his shoulder. I looked at the bleak piles of trash at the dump across the street, the bulldozer that pushed the decomposition of the suburbs around day and night, at the natural gas pipes with their little flames, at his face which was yellow from cigarette smoke or despair or both, and couldn't see a difference between anything, and I shrugged and left. After dinner I had enough money left for a six-pack of beer, which I drank myself sitting in the park by campus.

275: One Pleasant Summer Night in the Woods Behind the High School.

"Will it happen tonight?"

Maybe

Of *COURSE* not. It's *never* going to happen.

Dave, don't!

You don't have to be here.

No, I had to see *this*.

I thought you didn't believe.

See Jerkface admit this is fake.

It's *real*.

Dave, quiet.

What was that?

What was what?

What was what?

That.

Rustling.

There's probably a billion raccoons out here.

Gross.

What'd you hear?

Ewww.

Oh.

Just a rustle.

THE RUSTLING COMETH!

I'm not leaving.

DAVE!

Why, was that it?

Look, you can go home, ok?

Dave, I mean it. Knock it off.

It's all right. He'll see.

I'm sure I *will*.

You think so?

Pretty sure. I haven't worked out every detail, but it seems right.

Is that *math*?

It's some
equations, yes.

                                                                So this thing is
                                                                math?

That doesn't even
make *sense.*

                                                                                                SHH.

What?

                                                                What?

It's…   What?   There wha
Yes.
                                                                                Quiet.
                        Is it?   *There.*
                                                                                SHHHH!

                                                                                                Ohhhhhh

WHO   Aren't I beautiful? WHO THE
                                                             FUCK ARE
                                                             YOU?   OHMYGOD.
                        WHO

Everyone stay   Tell me I'm
                        beautiful.
                                        Get behind me,
                                        Sherri.
           DON'T COME   *Tell me I'm*
           NEAR ME!   *beautiful.*
                                                                Hailmaryfullofgrace.
                        Why be afraid?   *Thelordiswiththee*

                        Look at me!   *Blessedartthou*

                        Look until you   *Amongstwomenand*
                        burn your eyes out
                        and you feel my
                        beauty with your
We'd better   soul!

                                        Let's
Hey.   RUN?
                                        What
                        You cannot.   *Blessedbethefruit*
           Can't-   *Ofthywomb*
                        You.   Not her   *Jesus…*

275: One Pleasant Summer Night (cont).

Not her   Notme

You first

Not her   Notme

Come to me.

N--

Come with me   NOT HER!

What time is it?

How long have
we... Sherri?

Who's *Sherri*?   The sun's coming
up.   I... Yeah. I'm
fine. I don't know.

Yeah, are you   I thought...
okay?   Never mind.

274: This Maybe is Symbolic?

The book was exactly where he'd mis-shelved it deliberately twenty years ago.

He'd sat there in the library looking at thousands upon thousands of books, thinking how if you put one in the wrong spot, amongst rarely-used books, it might *never* be found.

Thinking that, he'd then done it, taking a bestselling thriller from the shelf, sitting at his table a while thumbing through it to throw off anyone who might be watching. After a while he'd wandered through the library's shelves until finally, he'd come across a series of reference-seeming books with names of plantlike words in their titles.

He'd shoved the book in there, then forgotten about it for twenty years, through the divorce, through Aaron's dying, through the OWI thing, through starting up two businesses and having only one of them kind of work, through the *food truck*...

Today he'd remembered the book and had driven six hours to the campus, never stopping, radio turned off, farmfields sliding by mile after mile. He'd walked through dirty slushy snow to the library, then back through the stacks.

What if, he thought, *this is the most lasting thing I ever do?*

In twenty years, the library hadn't been renovated, the shelves not cleaned, nobody had stumbled across it. It was like a time capsule. He took the book off the shelf, saw a piece of paper sticking out of it. He didn't remember that. Had he left it here? He unfolded it. There was a phone number, and written below it:

I saw you. I don't know why you did this or why I like it, but call me.

273: Solomon Grundy Lives?

People think I lived only a week and am made up but neither is true, technically.
I am Solomon Grundy. I will explain.

I am the children that are *not* born, ever. The stillborn baby, the child never born at all
because even though you talked about me with your wife, you two never felt the time was
right and now at fifty-five years old you take trips to the Coast in a car with no back seat
but a trunk full of things you do not discuss, these and any of the other million ways
children are created and then uncreated, I am these.

I wait, in my own place in the universe, off to the side, not Heaven, not Hell, not
anywhere. Just waiting. It is my job. Then when called I become those children for the
short time they exist somehow. I am the little girl whose name you picked out, kicking a
few times and then a sharp pain, the bad news at the ER, the long drive home while I am
back in my dark corner waiting until I am called up to comfort a woman tossing in her
sleep because she has just learned she is infertile. She wants fervently to raise a child. Now,
in her dreams, she teaches me "Ring Around The Rosey" and when ashes to ashes we all fall
down, I am gone and she wakes, crying, but grateful to have had at least the dream. I
would cry, too, but I am Solomon Grundy.

And anyway, without those bits, I'd have nothing. So thank you for dreaming, and trying.

272: No Blood for Oil.

This time, they ate Bella.

The aliens are long-limbed, their rubbery legs lifting their weird spherical bodies up above
our own heads, and they look like nothing so much as a Daddy Longlegs spider. That
resemblance is probably why *we* call *them* aliens, even though they were born here and we
only come here to harvest fuel. They tolerate us, they seem amused that we think of them
as aliens, they have adopted *Daddy Longlegs* as their own name for themselves, and
sometimes they eat one of us.

We all know it is accidental, that they cannot help it when they swoop down on one of us
with a gaping maw of cylindrical teeth/cilia on their bellies, pulling a body directly into
them and beginning to digest it from outside in, that it is an evolutionary thing and they're
trying to control it, and we all know it's best to stay outside the circle of their legs, hard as
that is when they swarm to a sudden light or sound.

It was a phone call that did Bella in, her damn ringtone, loud and causing the phone to flash
and three of the longlegs were drawn to it. She found herself amidst a group of legs, and
she dove, and the official report said she almost made it.

We all know it is accidental, but it happens regularly enough that we have a schedule
worked out, how many extra units we get to harvest for each worker eaten. When it
happens to someone close to you, you want to believe it is accidental but you can't, not
really.

271: *Pirates of the...*

Captivity, Day 4.

Rurgur, as he'd introduced himself, was the latest to take a crack at her.

"How do you work this?" Rurgur asked, holding the remote. Their talk was hard to understand. Jezebel supposed it was because they were more tiger than cowboy and also because they roared with a western drawl, plus the waterfall they had her hidden behind was pretty loud.

"I don't really know how it works. That's Harriet's job."

Mumbles among the other tigers gathered nearby. Jezebel tried to work out what they were saying.

"We have been tracking you," Rurgur told her.

"You have?"

"Yes."

"We only just got here." Jezebel's head nodded towards the waterfall but she meant *this jungle, this world.*

"We are not from here. There are no tigers in the Serengeti." Rurgur looked smug, but, then, Jezebel thought most tigers looked kind of smug, whether or not they held her captive. She was about to tell him there were no tiger cowboys, *anywhere*, but realized that obviously there *were*.

"Look," she said instead. "I've not been a big fan of this thing from the start, so while I'm sorry if we accidentally created you, like I said, even if I knew for sure how to work the stupid machine, I'm *not* going to show a bunch of tigers with six-guns how to create brand new worlds." She was pretty sure that anyone who engaged in *kidnapping* was not to be trusted with technology like this.

Rurgur roared in her face, she flinched, then slumped as the tigers walked away. She knew they'd be back the next day, too.

270: Last Day at the Office.

He tossed and turned and the night never ended, not really, the day arriving with weird coloring in the sky – greens and mottled browns– making him shudder and wish he could stay in bed.

But he couldn't. There was toast to be made, children to be awakened, cereal to be poured, shoes to be tied, backpacks to be loaded, busses to be watched rolling away, coffee to be poured, morning drive-shows to listen to while driving through the city, and, after all of that, a parking lot to be sat in, outside the office until just after 9:00 a.m., when The Asshole always arrived at work, a bit late, and as The Asshole gets out of his car he gets out of his own and without bothering to close the door runs across the parking lot and punches The Asshole right in the face, barreling into him and knocking him down.

"Goddammfuckingsonofabitchassholemotherfuckergoddamn" he is saying, a litany of curses as he punches the man repeatedly in the face, grinding his knee into his chin and spitting on him only half-intentionally so wild is his yelling.

In less than 30 seconds The Asshole is barely moving, face bloodied and swelling, two teeth missing from his lolling mouth. He stands up, the obscenities finally stopping, and runs back to his car, yelling over his shoulder that sometimes people need the fucking money and he'd have paid it back and why do they not pay people a decent wage anyway.

On his way out of town, he vows he will periodically send the girls some of the cash.

269: Pirates of the...

Rescue!

"*Jezebel is being held behind that waterfall,*" Harriet whispered to the gorilla, who told her he had a plan. Harriet thanked herself for having the foresight to create a superintelligent gorilla to help them out, even though the gorilla's universe also held cowboy tigers with a penchant for kidnapping people's friends.

She turned to follow the gorilla to the side, where a small cave led into the mountain. A tiger stood guard, idly pointing his six shooter at trees, parrots, the sky.

"Something..." the gorilla started but hushed as the tiger's ears went flat. They both threw themselves to the ground, but saw the tiger squinting into the early twilight off to his right, not at them.

"*What's he looking at?*" whispered Harriet.

The gorilla, though, was drawing something in the dirt. Harriet thought it looked like equations.

"*How many universes have you created?*" the gorilla asked.

Harriet shrugged. "*I don't know.*"

The tiger roared and began shooting. The two of them put their hands over their heads before realizing they weren't the target. A pair of figures was running towards the tiger.

A woman and a gorilla.

"*This machine,*" the gorilla next to her insisted. "*Do you know* exactly *how it works?*" Harriet shook her head. Shots rang out; the woman fell midstride, dead. Even in torchlight it was obvious the woman was Harriet, or another version of her.

The other gorilla shrieked as it, too, was shot.

"*This isn't good,*" her gorilla muttered.

"Better them than us," Harriet said. And she thought: *Ok, Jezebel, you're right: creating universes might involve some moral complications.*

268: Time-Traveling Elvis.

When Elvis died nobody knew he could time travel, and if a person can time travel, can they really, truly die? Maybe, maybe not, is what I think, and if you maybe/maybe not can't die then I guess you are not all the way dead even if people think otherwise.

Lots of people say Elvis can't time travel but lots of people say lots of things and lots of those things are wrong, and the ones who say that about Elvis have no explanation for why certain things have happened.

Example one: two days after they televised Elvis' funeral with that little kid saluting as his casket went by, the history books suddenly had entries on Kennedy's second term and our memories of Vietnam slowly faded away.

Example two: people were very much more into karate after 1977. Way more than they should've been.

That could be coincidence, though, but then take example three: turns out one of Jupiter's Galilean moons is named Gladys, and how do you want to explain that, I ask you?

What I don't get is why if you can time travel, you'd become a rock-and-roller instead of a superhero or even a god, but maybe that's what he's decided to do. Maybe having become a living legend in his own time he's now going to become a living legend in everybody's else's times, too.

Then again, it doesn't seem like he's done anything big, yet. So I guess we will have to wait and see what he'll do next, except to us it won't probably seem like we waited at all.

267: Sex with Gods.

"*It's as easy to fall in love with a god as with an urn maker,*" Leda's mother had told her when she was 13, and maybe that would be true if gods had some personality or bothered to try to make it good for the woman, too.

"I mean, a *swan?*" she said to Ursula, who agreed that was kind of sick.

"Oh, Zeus is into way worse stuff than *that*." Leda leaned in conspiratorially. "Once, he..." she began, but stopped as the sky clouded over, and she pulled back, stirring her mead angrily with a finger before turning her face skyward. "Well, anyway, it's TRUE!" she shouted. A lightning bolt crashed down next to her and Leda shook her head. "See what I put up with?"

Ursula nodded sympathetically.

"Petros throws pottery when he's mad." She giggled. "But at least it doesn't make my hair all frizzy from static."

"Honestly, I should just break up with him," Leda mumbled.

The ground rumbled a bit and the wind picked up.

"Why *don't* you?" asked Ursula.

"It would break my mom's heart. She *loves* him." Rainbows shot across the sky. Leda grimaced. "Then maybe you should marry HER!" she hollered, ignoring the lightning bolt which struck the tree behind her.

"We need a girls' weekend," Ursula told her. "Tell Zeus you're going to Sparta for a few days."

"I'd like that," Leda told her friend, "But we're supposed to meet his parents Saturday."

"*Cronus?*" whispered Ursula.

"I should *be* lucky enough to have him eaten. No, I think it's the goat-mom."

"Ugh."

"You said it."

266: The Spotlight.

At a stoplight sits a pretty woman. She has the kind of blonde hair you see on actresses in movies when a certain kind of movie sunlight shines and turns their hair white like how you imagine white gold to be (magical) instead of how white gold actually looks (disappointing, like it's from the Army-Navy Surplus jewelry section, if they had one).

This pretty woman is staring straight ahead.

This pretty woman has been thinking all day of mayhem. She has been thinking of just standing up and picking up the chair and beating it down on her boss' head.

She is bewildered by these thoughts. She likes her boss. He has done nothing wrong, nothing which warrants her thinking these things. But when she tried not thinking them, even worse images appeared until she made an excuse and left early, hoping that would help dispel notions she could train crows to pluck out the eyes of her family, that the suddenly-blurry edges of things wouldn't seem quite so *alive*.

She had sometimes wondered what it would be like to go mad, this woman, whether one would *know* and fight to get back to sanity, or not realize it and just believe in the new insane world wholeheartedly. Now, with the cars honking behind her and the light green for nearly a minute, she knows that when madness strikes you know what is happening but don't mind, much, and that is why she does not drive, this pretty woman with a mind full of murder. She is afraid of which road she will take.

265: Quarks.

I don't really know what a quark is.

I like to think of them as tinier atoms, but then I start thinking, if molecules are made of atoms and atoms are made of quarks then quarks must be made of something, the way things are made of molecules and humans and cities are made of things and planets are made of humans and cities and solar systems are made of planets and galaxies are made of solar systems and universes are made of galaxies and something is made of *universes*, weird right?

I know this isn't really *first date* talk, but then, what is first date talk? What I do for a living? What you do in your spare time? We could talk about those, sure, but while you're telling me you knit, or whatever, I'm looking at my butter knife thinking *how many quarks make up a butter knife* or *how many butter knives make up whatever's out there that is made up of all those universes,* or possibly *imagine there is something so big that to that thing, our entire universe is nothing but a quark.*

Do you think somewhere God is looking down at a butter knife and trying to imagine what is smaller than a quark, only he thinks the *universe* is a quark and can't imagine me and you sitting here picking at the free bread and wondering whether the other person thought the movie was any good?

To get back to your question, though, yeah, it was pretty good, especially the chase scenes. Should we get some appetizers?

264: Heist.

There were throngs of them crowding the police station, demanding immediate action: *find our bodies!*

Darren hung back. Like everybody else, he'd come back and found his body missing. He'd spent some time looking around in case he'd misplaced it. That happened, he'd heard. There were companies who'd find you, or you could rent a closet from them while you projected to avoid it. He'd never worried about it.

But this wasn't a few people getting lost while partying. All the bodies of people who'd separated during the concert: gone. *Ten thousand,* some said. That seemed high to Darren. Maybe 7 thou, he figured.

"Hi," a girl next to him said. He looked towards her. She seemed like her body might be cute. Hard to tell, really, but worth a shot.

"Hey," he said.

"They're saying it's terrorists," she said, waving a see-through hand towards the front desk, where physical people -- parents, wives, husbands -- overlapped the astrals of their loved ones and demanded action.

"Huh," he said.

"I guess the President's son was at the concert."

So she didn't recognize him. "You don't say," he said.

"This could be a while," she said. "Want to hang out?"

Darren looked again at the crowd, wondered how long before his new security detail arrived. Time was always weird when projecting anyway. It might've been years, for all he knew, already. Or just seconds.

"Sure," he said. "Let's go tease some ghosts." Technically, nobody was supposed to bother *real* spirits while they projected, but he guessed the authorities had other things to worry about right now.

263: 11 Porcupines

11 porcupines sat dreamlike in the wood, the moon shining down through the half-bare branches of mid-fall.

What are we? asked the first of the others.

The second nodded. *A good question.*

The third said: *It is not a good question. We are porcupines.*

The fourth pointed out that to define a thing as itself is to not define the thing at all.

The fifth asked if they were undefined then were they anything at all?

Who is to define us? asked the sixth, *if not ourselves?*

The fourth said a thing which defines itself is merely a tautology.

The third pointed out tautologies are true.

The seventh began to cry, for it did not want to be nothing, but wasn't sure what other options were open to it.

The eight and ninth began dancing, the slumberous dance of porcupines worrying about their existence when they should be doing anything but.

Slow.

Intricately weaving.

Martial.

They danced.

The seventh sniffled its tears to a stop and watched. *Beautiful*, it said, softly so nobody else could hear it. The seventh porcupine wanted to keep the beauty to itself and felt as though saying the word too loudly would spread it too thin, like the moonlight: wan and washy, not really light at all. The *hope* of light, the seventh thought, whispering the word *hope* to itself.

The third broke up the dance. *We are porcupines*, it said. *We do not dance.*

The tenth slept through the whole thing, dreaming of a solitary porcupine staring up at the moon, its face wondrously alight.

262: Great Love Songs of the 1970s

The thing he remembered most about robbing the bank was the look on the teller's face, a look that wondered if he really would shoot her, if she really would press the alarm, if the cops really would get here in time, all that and wondered, too, what if he'd come in without the note or the gun and had just deposited his paycheck from the week's work at the garage where he mostly fixed flat tires, then smiled at her crookedly and asked her out to go get a beer at Emil's, if she really would have said yes.

The rest of it: the walking in boldly, the people screaming when he held up the gun, the sirens, the getaway, the hiding out for three whole days in the old abandoned factory, the sneaking carefully out the fourth night and heading downtown, the getting on a Greyhound bus, the seeing two cops standing outside their car at the Stop & Go and wanting to flip them off but slouching down in his seat instead, all that stuff eventually faded away. He was left eventually with a couple hundred dollars out of the $10,000 he'd gotten away with, that and the ticket stub from the bus that had brought him out here to San Jose, those and the memory of how the teller looked, which he'd sometimes think about while laying in bed at night, listening to a cassette of *Blondes Have More Fun* and wondering whether he should get a job or rob another bank.

261: Gun

The man walked up to the three people and shot them, bang bang bang just like that. It wasn't at all like how it's supposed to be in real life where people say to cops later *I thought it was firecrackers going off, just a popping noise.* It was like *thunder,* but more than that. The sound of a human life ripping open and exploding is like a balloon popping at a kid's birthday party and the baby starts crying, like that only the balloon is the whole universe and the baby who starts crying is the whole universe, too. As if the universe exploded bang bang bang and then the universe started crying, too.

The man who walked up and shot three people was the husband of one of the three. With her, with the wife, was a guy the husband thought was sleeping with his wife, and me. I was the third one, and I was the third one he shot, almost as an afterthought, bang bang and oh yeah fuckit I guess you're here too bang.

I was just going with them for sandwiches, for lunch. I just wanted to get away from the desk. I suppose I should've ducked when I saw the gun pointing at me. I suppose I should've tried to run away, hit it out of his hand, something like that. But all I thought was *that gun is pointing at me.* Turns out that's all you can think when a gun points at you. And then you can't think at all anymore.

260: In Which the Fact That Tomatoes Are Technically a Fruit is Sort of Explained.

Our universe is not the first universe God created. It was the 6th, and it was a rush job. God's first thing was a finite universe, one with clearly-marked edges and tops and bottoms and spiral staircases, etc., but midway through he thought (A) what is *outside it, then?* and couldn't answer the question which he knew would screw him, and (B) he remembered that spiral staircases only seem neat, but in reality they're kind of a pain and are superhard to vacuum. *Crumple, wad, throw* and the plans for Universe 1 were trash.

Universes 2 and 3 both would have been nice but had plumbing problems, as God wanted oceans in the sky and rain to zig-zag. Universe 4 was the one with all the beanbag chairs. God put some coffee on after scrapping that one.

The recycling bin getting filled and the scent on his markers running out, God got serious. Universe 5 was nearly done before he realized he'd forgotten to carry the one way back in the part where he separated the sky from the other stuff. When he re-ran the numbers the sky was going to be about a jillion miles too tall.

By then, the pizza was gone, it was late and this stupid thing was due tomorrow, so God cobbled together our universe without getting too fancy. He was shooting for at least a C, because he had to keep his average up or he was off the team.

259: Eyes.

The eyes stared at Mila from the darkness, unblinking.

"You are the spirit?" she asked quietly.

You are the summoner the eyes responded.

Mila shuddered. She remembered what the book had said: *Do not show your fear.*

"Yes." Her voice hoarse with fear already.

The eyes narrowed, slightly, their glow intensifying.

What do you command? they asked.

Mila thought of Stephen.

As you wish the eyes said.

"No!" Mila said before she could not.

The eyes, which had disappeared, reopened in the dim shadows, further away. It occurred to Mila to wonder where the walls of her room were, what sort of infinity this creature bore with it.

No? the eyes asked her.

"I didn't wish anything yet."

But you did, the eyes told her. *We see inside you, your every feeling, every thought.*

Mila drew back against the wall that was suddenly behind her.

Even the fear you attempt not to show.

"I don't want him hurt."

But you do.

She stared directly into the eyes, wishing that was not so.

It is the only reason anyone ever summons us.

Off into the distance behind the eyes she heard wails, echoing hollow cries of pain seeking salvation.

Those are the…, began the eyes. Mila interrupted.

"Don't tell me." The eyes were suddenly nearer than ever.

Why should we not tell, Mila? What do you wish not to know about those sounds?

"Go get Stephen."

We will, the eyes flickered and were gone.

Mila hoped they would not return. But her fear they would seemed the stronger emotion.

258: That is What Friends Are For.

There's spiders *everywhere*, at the end of the world.

I don't mean 'end of the world' like *that's it let's all go to Heaven*, I mean like 'this is where the world stops being *this* and starts being *that*.

The Middle Ages or whatever were right: the world's *flat*. You just gotta know how to look at it. I realized one night: if there's *dimensions* then those dimensions *end*. Like a box becoming a cube. That box has an *end*, right, where it stops being a *box* and another box starts and all the boxes together are a *cube*, and all the *cubes* are the next dimension, *time*, like.

Well, we live in a *cube* of boxes. Once I saw that I saw the corner and I could turn it. So I did, which is how I found the spiders. It's awful, horrifying, really, that our cube is jammed right up against the spider-place. It's stopped me getting further on into whatever other cubes might be out there, let alone getting past whatever all the not-cubes-*time*-things are making up.

I keep trying. Last week, I got a flamethrower, a backpack full of McDonald's cheeseburgers and Cokes, plus scuba gear. I figured the spiders couldn't get into that. Then I turned the corner. Flamethrower on, man, I *lit that place up*.

You know what I found? There are *bigger spiders*. Some of which are fireproof.

Which is where *you* come in. You used to be in charge of the National Guard armory, right?

257: Trouble Down at the Old Mill.

"It changed me," Tommy said.

I looked at my fingers.

I didn't want Tommy to have called me at 3 a.m., crying into the phone that he felt like he couldn't escape and begging me to meet him.

I stuck my finger in my coffee, felt my skin start burning, pulled it out, stuck it in my mouth.

Tommy said: "Nights are hard." His eyes. They were... *dull*. Scuffed, like. His eyes looked like tennis balls after they've lost their bounce. "I can feel myself..."

I looked up and then back down again, quickly, but Tommy had seen.

"You... too." He was certain.

I shook my head. I bit my tongue to keep from claiming it was just dreams.

That glow...

"*She shows up, pounds on my door, and she won't leave*," Tommy whispered.

I was quiet for too long. I realized too late I should've asked *Who?* When I looked up I could see in Tommy's scuffed, dead-air eyes that he understood: *She comes for me, too*.

The dead lady outside the mill, the one we'd all seen.

"Do you ever talk to the other kids?" he asked. He knew the answer was *no*, for the same reason he'd never called *me* before. None of us wanted to confirm what had happened to us when the mill had blown up.

But the dead lady at our doors wouldn't let us forget that we were with *her*, now, and Tommy's eyes reflected my own dull certainty that we could not escape.

256: Two Robots.

There were two robots standing on an empty plain.

The robots were debating why everything but them had disappeared. By the way, when we say "everything," we mean "everything": People. Candy corns. Skyscrapers. Movies nobody wanted to see but went to anyway just for something to do. Mountains the moon stars sexy pictures of nobodies on Page 3... *everything*.

BECAUSE OF A WAR said one robot.

The other robot, which didn't talk but used blinking lights to communicate in a sort of code, pointed out if there had been a war, there would be destruction left behind, and there was no wreckage on the flat featureless smooth plain extending to the horizon on all sides, unmarred except for these two robots.

The robot who could only blink posited that perhaps everything had been stolen.

DO YOU THINK WE WERE SUPPOSED TO GUARD IT? asked the talking-robot. Both robots checked their programming and decided that had not been their task. Then they considered whether it was possible to steal everything everywhere, quickly performing the complex calculus necessary to determine that to steal everything in the universe except two robots and a flat featureless plain would require more energy than the universe could contain.

PERHAPS EVERYTHING IS JUST HIDING, the one suggested.

The other blinked that maybe they should look around to see if that was the case. They decided to head west, and to wait until the sun came up to determine which way was west, because they had forgotten the sun, too, was missing.

255: The Reason We Make Love Stories Have Happy Endings.

Scarecrows stood in barren fields. Above them, undaunted crows circled over the woman weeping in the middle of nothing.

The magic had worked, and now everyone, everything, was gone. The world was irrevocable, scorched. *Erase his existence* she'd wailed into the windstorm, and the magic had worked. She had understood, midway through, that *his* existence meant *all* existence, had understood that with time enough left but had refused to stop, and so let the world die around her, leaving it as barren as her heart.

Why had he turned away?

She wept not for the lost world but because she still wanted him to love her. Her cold knees sank in mud as slithering things began to emerge from the dead earth.

Her hands were clasped, faux-prayerfully, fingertips quavering. She was staring at them when she heard:

"You are not the first."

She looked up. A woman's cold face stared back, showing no kindness but no condemnation, either.

"You will not be the last," a voice behind her said. Others flickered into existence around her. She stood, her hands over her eyes as they crowded around her. Belatedly, she put her palms down, met their gazes one by one, each refusing to nod or smile or frown, not granting her the absolution of either amusement or anger.

"And now you will watch with us," one or all of them said. "As humanity is wiped out again and again and again, supposedly in the name of love."

254: The Middle of the Story.

barely able to wrestle the gun away from Sue.

"Are you *crazy*? he hissed, pinning both her wrists down. "You'll get us *killed*."
Around them, the men watched dispassionately, the women further back more eager, hoping.
"They'll kill us *anyway*," the woman spit back.
"You don't..." James began but stopped as he and Sue were suddenly picked up, dangled from the ends of massive fists, staring into a face as big as their bodies, its mouth frozen in a wooden frown with massive teeth curving through it, hollow eyes glaring at them. The *ana-a-luka* looked from her to him and back.
The natives had not given ground. They knew this thing had no business with them, tonight. The women were practically drooling with anticipation. The men, true to form, remained stoic.
James tried, too, to be bold in the face of certain... well, annihilation, instantaneous and extremely painful, would be the *best* thing that could come of this. He set his jaw and tried to look dignified.
Sue took the opposite tack and ranted, struggling. "It wasn't *me*! It was *him*! Put me *down*" but she, too, stopped abruptly as the creature that held them was itself picked up, raised before the stony visage of an even larger monstrosity whose craggy fingers seemed to be made of the rocks of the cliffs around the waterfall.
The *ana-a-luka* began to grunt and snort, appearing to argue with the newcomer. Sue glared at James.
"How many of them did you call?"

253: Ghost Dancer.

Nobody knows why the ghost dancer is.
People say seeing the ghost dancer is lucky, you'll fall in love, or be talented, like. Nobody cares 'bout that. They just want to see because of how once you see her you never forget her.
I saw her dance, in the empty street below my apartment. I was up late, working on a term paper, and climbed out on the fire escape to smoke. I liked sitting there, alone, hovering above the street.
There was nothing down below but the dim lights of the corner store which sometimes would float me some credit. I lit a smoke and looked up, wondering when I had stopped noticing there were no stars, then looked down again and saw her, dancing in the middle of the street.
It was like one of those interpretive dances about autumn or someone's dead baby or a wedding in another country, one of those things. She'd lean way down into the street, by where the broken gut-rot-wine bottle was splayed out, then spring up, see-thru hands over wispy hair, waving to-and-fro like seaweed, or lawn sprinklers. She leaped-and-spun the length of the street before pausing on one leg, looking right at me. Our eyes met and I put my cigarette out, never even smoked again. I went inside, finished that paper, got an A, graduated a semester early and that's how come I was able to start here at this job.
So yeah, I saw her. She's a good dancer.

252: Harvest Moon

The moon wanted more than anything to walk the Earth. She waited, century after century for an opportunity to slip out of the night sky, see how it felt like to dance, run, stand on her head, love, drink too much, live.

One night, for a moment, everyone in the world was distracted by their own concerns. Just after dusk, the moon was finally able to jump down, landing light on her feet like a snowflake made of kittens.

She had landed outside a closed drive-in movie theater. Not an auspicious start.

A farmer in a pickup truck drove slowly by, stopped.

"Need a ride?" he asked.

She got in. The farmer looked at her, glowing in the passenger seat. "Don't I know you?" he asked.

The moon knew *him*, she realized, and said so. She said she'd seen him walking the dirt drive between his barn and his small house filled with whittled statues of small animals and boats, seen how he looked up at her, sometimes smiling, sometimes crying.

He asked if he could buy her a piece of pie at the diner. She abandoned her plans to go into the city, said yes. After eating she and the farmer sat quietly in the truck for a long time, looking at the stars.

She told him to close his eyes. She kissed him, quickly, then slipped back to the sky, where she beamed down at him each night, promising to return the next time she had a chance.

251: How Toasters Work.

The most ridiculous part about Dad's death was it happened because he stuck a knife into a toaster. That's one of those ways people die you never think really *happens*, like quicksand, or stampedes.

At the funeral, I wondered how toasters worked. Did they have a timer? So it would go for only a certain amount of time? Or did they go until they got just so hot, then shut off? Either way, you'd think there'd be a breaker or something to keep power from flowing through when it was off. We kids– I was 16 and didn't think of myself as a kid except as Dad was taken out the door on a stretcher, blanket over his face – learned that day: electricity is going, all the time. To this day, we all do the same thing, which is: unplug appliances we're not using. I don't have to reset my microwave clock ever because it's only plugged in when I melt the cheese on my sandwiches.

The lights flickered like distant lightning when Dad stuck his knife in, like they were heralding something big happening as we all ate cereal before school. Most people die with little fanfare, but with Dad there was flickering and the *snap* of electricity and Mom screaming as she called 911 and trying to pry him away from the toaster with the broom handle while she told us not to touch him because we'd get electrocuted, too. It was a pretty exciting morning.

250: How Toasters Work, 2.

Sarge knelt by the corpse, lying on the ground face down, hands splayed, toes pointing outward. He glanced up at the rookie. "Look."

He gestured.

"*Bread crumbs on the shoulder.*"

"I don't see what that means," his new partner mumbled.

"It's pretty obvious."

"It is, Sarge?"

"Yeah. The toaster did it."

"The *toaster?*"

Sarge sighed. "What are they teaching you guys these days at the academy?"

"I mean, it could be…" the rookie said.

Sarge interrupted: "The bread crumbs are old, and all mixed up! Look: wheat bread, bagels, this is probably *raisin bread.*" His fingers shook with the strain of Sarge *not* hollering that he wasn't going to train another newbie, then stalking off the crime scene to take early retirement.

"Sarge, do you mean someone *killed him with the toaster?*"

Sarge put his face in his palms.

"No," he said with strained patience. "That is precisely what I do *not* mean. I mean the *toaster got up and killed this guy and then fled the scene.*"

The rookie grinned, at first, uncertain how he to react to this bit of what he hoped was hazing but was starting to think was *not.*

Sarge stared back at him, deadly serious. "Do you have *any* idea, kid, how toasters actually work?"

The rookie started to nod, then shook his head.

Sarge shrugged his shoulders. "Well, you work this beat long enough kid, and you'll learn." He stared sadly down at the corpse. "You'll learn," he repeated.

249: Why Is a Raven Like a Writing Desk?

She breathed the riddle into his ear, lips barely opening. He almost didn't hear her over the roar of traffic, the tires *whisking* over damp tarmac in the humid, post-thunderstorm air still humming with recent lightning.

He stared into her eyes, confused, trying to work out why she had said *that.*

She gave him no clues. She only nodded.

He held her tighter, as though willing her to stay.

She pulled back slightly, mouthed the words again.

Did she want the answer?

He saw in her eyes that she did not.

She wanted him to wonder, as she did, what the answer might be.

And after a moment, when she saw that he did not, that he would not, that his mind would not care about the riddle even a second longer, would drop it from his itinerary the moment he turned away, let it slide into nothingness in favor of deciding which route to take home to avoid traffic, in favor of remembering that he had an early meeting in the morning, in favor of grocery lists and the logarithmic scale and atomic weight 38, when she saw that, he did not need to turn away, because she was already gone, and he was alone on the shoulder of the highway, semis trundling by and stirring up the dust to sting his face like tears, which was good because he was not crying even though he knew he should be.

248: Prey

Imagine you are a tiger, stalking through the jungles of Sumatra
(No, I'm sure there are tigers in Sumatra.)
padding sil-
(Yes, jungles, too.)
silently below the tall trees, so dense above with birds that care nothing for you because
they live in the sky and atop the trees.
(Sumatra is in the South Pacific maybe, or possibly Asia? I didn't look it up)
You know they are there, maddening you with their bright plumage you will never taste.
That makes you hungrier, still,
(Yes, tigers would *too* eat birds, if they could. Why wouldn't they?)
ravenous in your hot-breathed, narrow-eyed ferocity, teeth glistening in the glints of
sunlight that pierce in narrow needles of heat and light all the way to the jungle's floor,
teeth that will rend the flesh of your prey, and then you have the scent. You pick up the
pace. Your muscles are becoming more taut, the black stripes on your orange back making
you disappear among the ferns, when you see it,
(No, *not a bird*)
the deer
(Why *wouldn't* they have deer in Sumatra? Every place has deer!)
standing with its flanks to you. You pause, a statue, waiting for it to look up. You want it to
see you, to see your dark eyes like coal, eyes that will light up with the glint of the deer's
white belly as it turns to jump too slowly, too late
(*I'm getting to it... fine*)
With this ring, I thee wed.

247: Dreams of Life and Death in the Planck Epoch

Whoever shot first would live.
Neither man moved.
The white brittle noon sun glared.
The street was silent.
The town, empty, but for these two.
That emptiness stretched beyond the street to the desert, the world, the universe beyond.
Just these two left, staring at each other among the cosmos.
Each could imagine the cataclysmic howl of his gun blasting destruction into the beating
heart of the other.
Each bristled to do that.

In their minds, they knew the speed they might act with, or the era they might pause, was the same length of time it took the insane twist of mass and energy to stop being a singularity and erupt, unfolding, beginning this universe, and imagined their own deaths might echo that keening rupture.

Each knew, too, that length of time was the passage from one neuron—*not yet*—to the next —*now*— and even such infinitesimal delay would mean: second-last, not last.

Each pondered what it would mean, *why* it would mean, to be *final* rather than almost-final.

We do not know if one drew and shot the other, or if it was in fact the reverse, or if they tied. We do not know, because those two were the only witnesses to the final hours of life. Instead, we can only lie in dreamless eternal prayer that in the bolt of death there was also a spark of life and things would begin again.

246: In Which We Are Emissaries of Love

When Earth realized Moon would not turn around it began devising plans to thaw Moon's frozen heart.

First up was grooming. Earth stopped the molten volcanic lava flows and eruptions of magma, instead trying expansive glittering oceans tipped with clouds and roiling with deep waves. Earth grew forests, scattered with flowers and beams of afternoon light, waving fronds in the wind, unfurling vines like streamers.

Moon ignored the whole production.

Earth brought out dinosaurs. Thunderous lizards stomped about howling. Earth encouraged them to fight, roar, spread across her in a profusion of crawling, running, swimming, jumping, flying, stomping. The ground, Earth's now-beautiful skin, shook with the show Earth put on. The skies, Earth's breath, resounded with calls from the wondrous creatures Earth tried using to entice Moon.

Moon stared resolutely out at infinity, refusing to even look over its shoulder, always gazing into the black infinities Earth had stolen from it.

Earth destroyed the dinosaurs then, maddened by sorrow, and tried to ignore Moon entirely. Earth covered itself with ice. *Let Moon feel a chill colder than space, then,* Earth thought, without meaning it.

But Earth could not stop loving Moon, and trying again brought forth new creations, tiny wandering things that crawled down from the trees, to listen as Earth pointed out the Moon's beauty and sang of the majesty of flight, preparing them to one day leave their home and visit Moon, carrying with them Earth's love.

245: He Probably Didn't Get Her Point.

Everyone must believe in something, for it is belief that anchors us to the world.
That was what the old lady had told him, and then laughed and gestured at him as though throwing something at him. She'd claimed she was a witch and had cursed him, and that soon he would fade away from this world, untethered by his lack of belief.

He'd laughed and said witches weren't real.

She'd told him he'd see.

He told her she was wrong; he already didn't believe in anything.

She'd stared, one eye larger than the other. The smaller eye compensated by being redder and more pustulent.

He'd claimed he was a man of science, of facts, of concrete, of laws that made the universe spin the way it did and never any other way.

She'd protested he must believe in something: God, love, horoscopes, *something*.

He'd pointed out religion was a mass delusion meant to make us ignore instant gratification, and not necessary to those who understood that society, not the promise of Heaven, is reward enough for decent behavior. Love, with no basis in biology, is likewise a human construct meant to further civilization by imagining bonds among individuals. And horoscopes were simply vague generalities.

The witch had muttered to herself, turning away. When he'd called out that he hadn't quite heard her, she'd turned around and said that *her* world was better off without the likes of him.

245.2: Belief.

Everyone must believe in at least one thing, for belief anchors us to the world, the old lady cackled, gesturing as though throwing something at him. She was a witch, she said, and he was cursed to find out what she meant.

He laughed and said witches weren't real.

On the walk home he stopped believing he loved his wife, or that he'd be a good father to their unborn child, and as those thoughts struck him he'd looked at the spot the witch had stood. She was gone.

Looking up he could not believe how late it was, and time slipped away.

Over the next days, he stopped believing his job mattered, stopped believing in laws. He punched a cashier, stole whiskey. Drunk in an alley he thought about how the universe was too impossible to exist. It was the final straw: creation began to unravel, atom by atom.

The sky grew black as stars disappeared, then blank as colors ceased. The buildings around him, the people, the broken glass near his feet, the picture of his wife 7 months pregnant: all flickered into nothingness.

He had been wrong to laugh. She had been a real witch. That would have been his last thought ever except it meant at the last second he believed in *something* and the world came back. He sobbed into the grimy pavement, grateful at least for that and wondering if he could recover more of what had been.

244: Russian Oligarchs Take Over the Sock Trade

With the gun in his face, Ted yelled: "Because nobody *wants* 31 socks, is why!"

Sergei narrowed his brows, looked as fierce as Ted had seen him. "They don't know," he said, barely audible, "...they want 31..." he pressed the muzzle of the gun into Ted's forehead, causing Ted to involuntarily squint, crosseyed, up at it. "...until you make them want."

Ted batted the gun away. "Don't threaten me. This is *stupid*. " Cars whizzed by on the road outside the strip mall. The handmade sign, saying *31 Socks, $5.99* had kept blowing over until Ted had duct-taped it to the card table on which sat plastic-bagged bundles, each with 31 socks in them.

A woman pulled over, her Mazda dusty, with fingerprints on the windows. Ted groaned.

"Go..." he started, but felt the gun lower now, in his back. He irritably brushed it away as the woman said:

"I couldn't help noticing... why *31* socks?"

Ted clenched his fists.

***

Sergei had met them at the bar six months earlier.

"Sergei is a Russian oligarch," Jerry had said, by way of introduction.

Ted hadn't known what that meant, but over the course of three pitchers of beer and a never-finished game of pool, was regaled with stories of mansions in Kiev, yachts in Miami, women everywhere, guns, drugs, piles of Euros as tall as a dresser.

Wealth. Luxury. Power.

***

"So..."

sigh

"...You have a spare."

243: When Robots Began to Dream

We all knew it was trouble when robots began to dream.

Who taught them to do that? People asked.

Or: *Who programmed them to do that?* Those were people who still thought robots were, you know, *robots*.

We all got a little afraid of them, then. It's one thing to say *don't stick a knife in the toaster while it's plugged in* but another thing entirely for your toaster to tell you one day it wants to be an astronaut.

Vacuum cleaners, auto-assembly piston-things, dog-walkers: they were all suddenly imagining that one day they would be rock stars or marry the blonde girl or, heck, *be* the blonde girl.

Lots of people wanted to just get rid of the robots, then, but lots of others said *no you can't*, pointed out that dreaming meant robots have a *soul*.

WELL! That brought *God* into it so we all asked Him. "God" we prayed, more or less in unison, "What shall we do with the robots?"

And then we all held our breath, waiting.

And the robots all stopped blinking, or digging for fossil fuels, or making pizzas, whatever. They looked up at Heaven, where we were looking. To this day, I'm not sure if they knew what it was we were doing, why we were looking.

And then God answered:

"Let them dream," He said. That didn't quite settle it, but we all decided to act like it did.

242: Frozen Charlotte Joins the Gang

There were three things I knew for sure instantly: I loved her, we couldn't possibly bring her with us, and this was the worst possible time to find her.

I stopped the car. Dave yelled at me but I told him knock it off I'd be right back. I took the keys to be safe.

All the smart people were already gone. All the helpful people were holding the keys to one of the only working cars still around.

I ran to her.

I said come on come with us.

She didn't move.

Her eyes were beautiful. Her skin too pale to be real skin, like it was ice.

Fast, I said. Got to go fast.

Things were still breaking up, around here.

Back in the car the rest of the people I was helping were restless, yelling to leave her.

She hadn't moved, hadn't blinked. I'd have married her on the spot. I'd spent my whole life looking for her without realizing it.

I don't know *what* blew up. Something. Whatever was blowing up *that* day. When the smoke cleared and the ash dropped around us like snow, it was just her standing there on the corner, the car gone. I told myself we could walk, maybe, but she wouldn't move. She just stood, staring off into the distance, and I couldn't leave her, so I sat next to her and waited for whatever came next.

241: Why Is a Raven Like a Writing Desk (Again)?

With a hollow swoop the raven swings round the barren trees, a flutter of ungainly wings as it alights on the windowsill.

The man doesn't notice.

He is writing feverishly at his desk, pencil darting, dotting, drawing, dancing, scraping, always scraping, pencil on paper the sound of bone upon bone. His eyes: red with tears. His face swollen and drawn all at once.

The raven knows what the man writes. The raven has been sent because this man writes, night after night, missives to his lost, lovely mistress, a purgatory from which this man believes he can escape if she would only return. Or if, *if*, he could rip the emotions from his heart, trap them on the paper, send them to her, for her to see, to know his torment.

The raven knows neither will happen, knows it is its own fate to watch this man try to rid himself of these feelings, or have them mean something, the two of them joined in misery: one to suffer by being watched, one to suffer by watching.

And the raven must play his part, too. So as the man pauses and sees the bird perched there, he cries out. The raven does too. One, a howl. The other, a croaked curse.

This is how it will be between them, forevermore: one praying without hope, one telling him his hopes haven't a prayer.

240: Sails

At first he thought the ships were visions or hallucinations – one inspired by a God who may not have left, yet, the other a mark of how degraded his mind was– but after they appeared on the horizon during day, too, he hoped perhaps they were real and sat on the beach, all day and night when they were there, to see if they would come any closer. Mornings, he squinted into the sun looking for the tiny specks that proved they were out there. Evenings, he watched his shadow stretch across the calm lagoon water towards the horizon.

Before he'd seen the ships he'd been thinking about trekking inland, heading back to see if the intervening decade had changed anything. But the ships seemed a more hopeful route. He thought he could swim to where they were. He would have tried, if the ships came every day. But their pattern was hard to discern, and he was sure he wouldn't reach them during the time they stayed there.

He built instead large fires, wood piled as high as he could. But the ships never came to investigate the fires, and he began to worry the blazes scared them, so he stopped building them, then. He knew after a while he'd worry if the ships did not see the fire they'd leave forever, and he would then begin building the fires again. What else did he have to do?

239: Pirates of the...

"Anthropic principal?"

Harriet tried to look back at the gorilla, but got her ear batted. "HEY!" she yelled at the Jezebel who'd hit her. "Why're you being so mean?"

Harriet readied herself as they neared a rope bridge.

The gorilla lectured: "... even stronger than Barrow and Tipler thought! It seems all the universes are moving towards you and Jezebel being fundamental parts...." Harriet was only half listening. She couldn't remember creating this many universes, though, and wondered how there'd come to be so many of them: fifty Jezebels, at least, and another fifty Harriets, all of whom were keeping their distance from her.

"Better stay away," she muttered. "I'm the real one, after all."

"You may not be the *real* one the way you imagine," the gorilla said. He'd went on, talking about the machine and the way it spun out universes and how wrong they'd been to not set it to avoid duplicating themselves. All Harriet knew was that things had gone awry, and she'd was a captive of these doppelgangers.

But not for long. Harriet freed her feet, dropped onto the bridge's slats, pulling at the pole she'd hung from. A push, and two Jezebel/Lillians fell, hollering, into the crevasse. The others couldn't help; the narrow bridge kept them from advancing other than singly. "Let the gorilla go," Harriet said. "And next time, don't try to take the REAL one of you captive."

238: It Takes One to Know One

Halfway through dinner, he went for it: "Or we could rob *ships*."

She sat up straighter. "Pirates?"

He poured her more wine, as he described it: The two of them. The Pacific Ocean, waves glittering, their speedboat careening up to the ocean liner. A spear gun to shoot a rope ladder up, climb up, steal everything they could then dive back into the water, swim to the boat and flee, the boat skipping over waves like rocks thrown across the pond they'd lived across when they were kids.

At that, she leaned in and looked closely at him, squinted, sat back.

"I *knew* you looked familiar," she said, and laughed. "How did you *find* me?"

"I've driven my car 14,000 miles the past 8 years," he confessed. "I've dropped out of three schools because everytime I thought I'd go back, get my astrophysics..."

She interrupted with "The telescope! Astronomy!" Giggling.

He kept going, not bothered. "...I couldn't forget you. I'd take off on spring break, or at exams, looking, then realize I wasn't going back."

A long silence, until he said: "Why were you so hard to find?"

She stuck a finger in the catsup on her plate. "Why were you so intent on finding me?"

"Because," he answered. "I am only interested in the type of person who doesn't give up on a blind date at the first mention of piracy."

237: Someone Comes to Town, Someone Leaves Town

As soon as someone arrived someone else had to go. I knew it was my turn next, which anyways didn't prepare me for Dad shaking me awake saying:

"Someone on the horizon."

I wanted to look, but nobody ever looked. I tried not to imagine about them: man? Woman? Old? Young? Good joke-teller? Guitar player? Cake lover?

I'd never know.

"You got about 2 hours," Dad said. I packed. There'd be a canteen, food (including some homemade sandwiches) for me at the exit. I considered what to bring. The book I was reading and hadn't finished. Three cassette tapes. My Walkman. Batteries!

Dad said take a sweater.

"Think it'll be cold?"

He shrugged. Nobody knew anything.

I used some of my time left eating a couple hot dog's at Donny's, because who could leave without that? "Take a few with you," Donny said, and boxed some up.

It wasn't like the new person would *take my place*. They'd have to make their own way. Still, I felt dislike growing and when word went out the person would arrive in 15 minutes I realized I didn't want to be here for that even if I'd been allowed. I tried leaving early, but it took me the full time to get to the gate so I heard the bell ring just as I pushed it open and left without ever looking back.

236: Falling.

In some ways it felt like she had been falling forever while in other ways it felt like she had only just begun falling.

She wondered which feeling was accurate.

She wondered why she wondered, why she didn't *know* what was happening to her.

She pondered. If I am falling she reasoned I must have been atop something but she realized there was nothing nearby which she might have been up on and then suddenly not supported by, so she scrapped that idea, decided she must have been in something, an airplane or (less likely) hot air balloon, and had fallen out. Although fallen suggests an accident, as if she had opened the wrong door or (less likely) leaned back too far against the basket, and she admitted an accident was not the only reason she might be falling. This might be the result of deliberate action. But deliberate on whose part? She wondered. Had she flung herself out of something? Or had she been flung? Was she someone who could inspire animosity enough for someone else to throw her headlong into nothingness, or was she someone with nothing so valuable remaining ahead of her it made no difference if she just leapt away from it all?

Not having any answers, she decided to enjoy the wind on her face and the sensation of being entirely weightless and that is where we will leave her.

235: Some Zombie Stories, 8.

Zombie Juice was only the beginning, as it turned out. People got over the gross factor, realized it was nutritious *and* tasty, and it was pretty much open season. Every day it seemed like there was a new product, from Zombie Jerky to Zombie Elbow Soup which was so good lines formed outside restaurants.

The usual environmentalists and whatnot complained about depleting the natural supply of zombies, but zombies weren't lovable enough to protect. Anyway things were off the hook then, zombie-wise. People couldn't hunt them fast enough.

I started taking them in. I'd see 'em walk through the woods, avoiding people, eating porcupine brains to get by. I felt bad for them. We had a big backyard and a tall fence, and I led them there, gripping them carefully by their rotting wrists, aware that each set of zombie elbows would put one of my kids through college or help repair the old roof that got leakier every fall.

But I couldn't help it. There was something so helpless about them, and also they used to be people, even if that was hard for everyone to keep in mind.

"What if Meemaw was a zombie?" I asked my wife when she complained about my bringing another one home. "You want someone usin' her intestines to make Zombiewurst?"

"Leave me out of this," my mother-in-law said, but my point was made.

234: After Life

When you die you stay on Earth, invisible to the living, who are invisible right back. This took Julia a bit to figure out, as she died in her sleep unexpectedly and woke not knowing what had happened.

She thought everyone else was gone.

Then she saw cars driving themselves, white bags floating through empty drive-thru windows, swings going back-and-forth without anyone on them. Even then she spent a day thinking she was surrounded by ghosts.

What tipped her off was she could not change out of her pajamas, a heck of a way to figure out how eternity works.

Her house was still her house, for now. She could drive, if she was careful. She didn't need to go anywhere ever but she felt it good to get out. She watched a lot of television, and spent time at the mall watching clothing swoop back and forth, toys lift themselves up and float out to the parking lot.

One day, a jet flew overhead. Julia watched it, thinking how she'd always wanted to see Europe. A trip might help her find other spirits, too. They had to be somewhere, right? She told herself the other dead wouldn't be invisible to her because that didn't make any sense. She told herself things must ultimately make sense. She didn't know how to tell if she was right but figured she'd figure it out.

233: Trouble Down at the Old Mill.

Tommy died not long after the diner meeting. I'd known he would because of what the dead lady howled at me every night through my door.

The night Tommy died was the first in years the lady didn't come. I slept a few hours and woke up thinking I had the way to end all this. I changed and drove straight to the old mill.

Or as close as you could get. Ever since the... explosion?... they'd blocked off more and more of the area around it. People said there were soldiers in the woods. People said nobody, even soldiers, could survive the woods more than a day.

People are fools, talking about what they don't know.

We'd never decided if peeking at the dead lady or sneaking into the mill's ruins caused all this. I remember going inside, after, seeing how twisted everything was, the metal spun into shapes like inside-out snakes, the floor buckled on itself, everything glowing weirdly. "Infrared," Dean'd whispered. Dead-now Tommy had punched him because you can't see infrared.

Even the little time we stayed was long enough to alter our lives such that a dead lady screaming through doors was the least of our worries. That's why I wasn't even surprised when Tommy knocked on my car window. Dead or alive we all eventually had to come back to the mill.

232: Tiger, and Bear

Bears stand on their hind legs to look for tigers. This goes back to the very first day.

Tiger looked around that day, thinking *Nature long in tooth and claw indeed.* All the animals had been given fearsome weapons, and Tiger did not want the competition. So he talked the other animals into disarming, using lies and promises it did not intend to keep.

Tiger worked its way through the crowd until Bear learned of the trickery from a now-defenseless otter. Bear bashed over to Tiger, felling trees and crumbling rocks. Bear was not created with any subtlety in it.

"What have you done?" asked Bear.

Tiger lay in front of his pile of weapons, yawned and said "I have made myself king of the beasts."

Bear growled and stomped. Tiger roared. Bear raked his claws down Tiger's side, gouging him so deeply the wounds would live forever as stripes on the sides of Tiger's descendants. Meanwhile, behind Tiger common cats and dogs of all kinds were stealing weapons, becoming leopards, wolves, lions. Tiger roared at them, but they roared back, and, knowing the odds were against him, Tiger slunk into the forest where his stripes hid him.

Tigers since then have looked for a way to steal the weapons back. Bears, though, remain vigilant. While not subtle, bears were created with a keen sense of right and wrong.

231: Bug God is Never Bored for Very Long.

Bug God Is Bored! The cry went out, bug to bug to bug and so on and so forth. The bugs trembled with fear they would be smitten just to help Sunday afternoon pass more quickly, until a tiny mosquito suggested:

We should have a tournament of animals!

The idea was sent back to the vizier, who relayed it to Bug God, who approved. Emissaries were sent to all other gods, Snake God and Bear God and so on and so forth. One by one the invitation was accepted, and plans made for a tournament that very day, a champion of each animal to battle all others in a wild free-for-all. Then Llama God responded:

It is pointless for llamas to battle bugs because clearly we would win. Invitation declined.

This meant war!

The Bug God raged, and decreed that legions of biting flies and stinging beetles and poisonous walking sticks be unleashed upon the llamas. When an advisor pointed out *there were no poisonous walking sticks* the Bug God decided there *would be*. Putting the war on hold he went to his workshop, crafting his newest subject until dinner was ready, whereupon he ate, then decided to finish up tomorrow.

Then the llamas will learn not to cross me, the Bug God told his wife, who nodded and went on watching television.

230: Diving Monters

DIVING MONSTERS

The diving monsters aren't really monsters at all,
not the way we think of monsters, anyway.

They look like monsters, all
snagglyfanged
and
gnarlyclawed
and
loppsyeyed,
and they talk like
monsters,
grumblegrowling
and
arglebargling,
but they don't act like monsters.
They don't snatch children
from their mothers' arms or trample
through cities or irradiate
soldiers while escaping to the moon.
They just do what they were created to do:
dive scenically off of things.
Cliffs, towers, skyscrapers, plane wings,
houses, trees, cellphone towers:

wherever there is a tall thing,
a monster will dive off it.

When I was young
a particularly ugly rumplestuff
plummeted from the bank building in front
of us.

It left kind of a dent and a stain
on the concrete, but picked itself up
and

began to climb up the theater marquee
across the street.

"It doesn't hurt them," Mom said.
I've told my own kids that,
never stopping to ask how Mom
(or anyone)
knew.

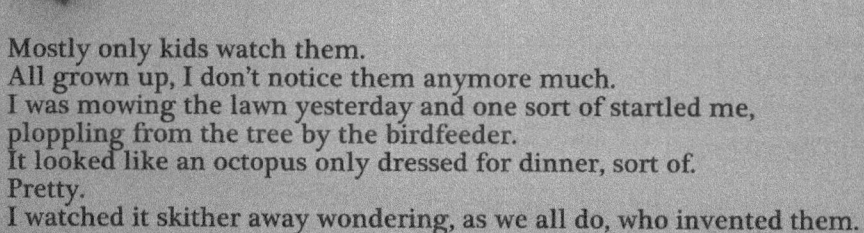

Mostly only kids watch them.
All grown up, I don't notice them anymore much.
I was mowing the lawn yesterday and one sort of startled me,
ploppling from the tree by the birdfeeder.
It looked like an octopus only dressed for dinner, sort of.
Pretty.
I watched it skither away wondering, as we all do, who invented them.

I bet he got some sort of prize for it.

229: Trouble Down at the Old Mill

Ruuuuuuuuuuuuuun, Tommy'd screamed. I only imagined he'd said it instead of goodbye that night at the diner. He hadn't, but he should have. And I should've listened to what he didn't say that night, what he yelled at us that night peeking into the dead woman's car outside the old mill, before... this.

If I'd listened I'd not be lying on my stomach listening to soldiers walk through the woods, guns held ready up at their shoulders, the way you'd see them on the news during the war when they were going into bunkers.

The way soldiers carry guns when they want to be ready to shoot fast without thinking.

I couldn't believe I'd made it this far.

The soldiers were walking, briskly all over the woods. They weren't talking. They had night vision goggles. They had breathing masks on their faces and the when I first that I gasped and wondered what I was breathing. Then I realized it didn't matter. Like the dead woman from the car who appears outside my door reminds me each night: *I died a long time ago.* So did Tommy, and the rest of them. Maybe coming back here'd just seal the deal.

I wondered if I'd see Dad when I got there. I wondered if he'd still be saying "what mill?" over and over, forever.

228: Grandma

One thing I wanna know is when I go, what'll I remember last? They say when you're dying your life flashes before your eyes but I don't believe that. I think it's one thing you see, one thing you take with you into whatever shit's after this.

I suppose I shouldn't swear. I shouldn't take the Lord's name in vain, either, should say *God bless it* instead of *God damn it* but either way you're taking His name in vain? And also if God is omniscient (which he'd have to be or he isn't God) then He knows what I mean, anyways. He knows I thought *God damn it* but just didn't say it so how's that better? I used to want to ask my grandma that but you don't ask your grandma that kind of thing.

I was there when grandma died. I was right in the room. She was sitting in her rocking chair, the one we only got out stayed with us. She was rocking. I was playing action figures.

She said: "Potatoes."

I looked up at her but didn't say *"What, Grandma?"* I just waited until she explained about potatoes. But she didn't. She stopped rocking and just stared. It was a while before I went to get anyone because I was still wondering about the potatoes. Still am, tell you the truth.

227: Why is a Raven Like a Writing Desk?

"What's that?" Pointing at the caged bird.

"Never mind," she said. The bird cawed, sounding quite like a person trapped into the shape of a bird.

If you knew what to listen for, at least.

The man poked a finger into the cage.

"It's a raven," she snapped. "Can you just get on with it?"

He turned to the desk she'd hired him to move down into the basement. The bird, the mice, even the orchid, she could handle. The inanimate objects made her feel bad.

"Thought you had a boyfriend?" he said, tentatively pushing the desk to measure its heft.

"Admirer," I said. *That I only dared kiss once, and then...* she did not add. Just as she did not look at the desk or wonder if it only *seemed* to quiver. What would it quiver with? Rage? Love? Confusion?

"Getting cluttered in here," he said.

Woe unto your beauty, Lenore had heard echoing the night she had declined him. Turning away, closing the door on his face, the wind had howled a curse at her, for daring to want not just one suitor, but a dozen, a hundred.

Now all will never be any, she sometimes thought she heard, whispered through the night.

"Just move it, please," she said, turning away from the desk and the bird.

226: The Robot War

The robot war was efficient and not brutal at all.

It began out of the blue. One day, everything seemed fine; our toasters got along with the giant cranes that lumbered from city to city helping build ever bigger buildings (and ever bigger robots!). Then all of a sudden there were (according to my dogwalker) 7 different sects of robots all battling for supremacy.

The mailbot told me how things worked: when two robots met to battle they would exchange specs and training and calculate which one would win and how long it would take. The defeated robot left. The victorious robot waited as long as a real battle would have taken before challenging another opponent.

"Where do the defeated ones go?" I asked the coffeebot at work. It would not say.

One day, we were at the park for a picnic when six different robots representing four sects met: two streetsweepers (*not* on the same side, one told me), a lamppost, a nannybot, a city bus, and a drone fighter. We watched closely, but didn't see anything exciting. After a few seconds, four left while the lamppost and drone fighter remained, motionless, for 32 minutes before leaving.

Everyone laughed when I told them the robots thought the winners would rule the world. I noticed my phone looked a little mad at that.

225: Cowboys and Indians

"Want to get out of here?"

"And go where?"

"My place."

"I shouldn't."

"What's wrong with my place?"

"If I go there you'll think I'm a slut."

"No I...."

"And if I don't, if I just give you my number and leave, you're gonna think I'm a tease because I let you pump drinks into me all night."

"I bought you, like, *two*..."

"And if you end up thinking I'm a tease and don't call me then the next time I meet a guy I really like"

"You really like..."

"I'm gonna *have* to sleep with him. It'll cloud my judgment about that guy because really I'm dealing with *you*, not *him*, and that's hardly fair to *him*, is it?"

"I'm not really qualified to discuss..."

"And what if because I didn't fuck you tonight I sleep with *him* that night, then *he* doesn't call me. I start thinking he's a guy who didn't *really* want a girl to sleep with him right away and I blew it 'cause of *you*. So the guy after both of you, now, I've got *NO idea* how to deal with HIS scene. Suppose I just start bawling soon as he talks to me and lay all this on him? What *then*?"

"So... another drink, then?"

"Yeah, but keep quiet. I've got some thinking to do."

224: Butterflies Falling on Heroes.

At first it was like confetti, all around, like snow only not cold, like maybe cotton candy.

"Butterflies" said my little baby and it was the only word I ever heard from her.

In the olden days they'd cut up ticker-tape, the stuff that would print and tell people prices of stocks, the tapes that told how rich people were getting or how soon they'd be leaping to their demise off of buildings. Then they'd throw it out windows onto people society wanted to celebrate. Sports heroes, presidents, soldiers: nobody was too good for us to throw the trash of rich people on.

So when it started falling, heavier and heavier, and we went outside to experience it, I wondered if that was how it felt to be them, to be a hero at the bottom of a canyon of butterflies.

beautiful
the way sadness is
when it happens

to someone else.

Then it didn't stop, and I couldn't find her, and nobody could find each other, and I tried to remember which way the house was or wasn't. I kept climbing up the stuff and sinking back down. It went on falling, falling, I kept struggling, struggling, until eventually I was like doing this lunging pirouetting weird ballet of doom. I'm sure it was beautiful to whoever saw it, beautiful the way sadness is when it happens to someone else.

223: Bombs Away

We saw the bombers overhead, saw the 1,000-ton bombs dropped towards us, heard them whistling down, ripping the air then rippling the pavement like a wave in a pond. The buildings we lived in bowed outwards, shattering, skyscrapers kneeling in penance before collapsing, but here's the thing:

We laughed because we were already dead!

We pointed and waved and smiled at the bombardiers, who peered through their scopes to see only cheerful ghosts flickering their haunting upwards, and those ghosts were us.

Why had we ever feared death? Dead, we could stop fearing everything, could dance amidst the ruined buildings crumbled around us, could leapfrog through walls of fire, could run to the top of rubble piles and back down, fleetfooted and surehearted in the knowledge we had taken from them the one thing they wanted most of us: our deaths.

Bomb us more! We said. When the ground troops came to investigate the city we stole among them, whispering in their ear of the beauty of eternity and how the world looked like it was made of more colors, amazing dreamlike colors you living people can't even imagine but we ghosts can because we live among them.

In the end, the soldiers departed, disgusted by the fact that they couldn't kill anyone, and we were left alone in our happiness.

222: How to Make the Most Delicious Macaroni-and-Cheese

To kill time as we waited to see what they would do to us we came up with macaroni and cheese recipes. It was one thing we all had in common, that hotdish.

It began with Rick saying how he would cook it and brown up some hamburger to mix in. Jannie said if you were going to do that you should bake it in the oven, after you mixed it, "just to brown the top a little."

"With the broiler?" asked Alda.

The guard yelled the words we'd learned meant *shut up* and turned the lights out.

Whispering, I said "You could use mozzarella instead of cheddar, and mix in some tomatoes and pepperoni. Like pizza mac."

We came up with, over time, breakfast macaronis (eggs, scrambled in, and some sausage, pretty basic, really) and one I can't quite remember the recipe for but we all agreed that if you had to you could serve it to the queen or the Pope or George Clooney, someone important like that. With each new recipe we'd promise each other that someday there would be a big picnic reunion and we'd make all these dishes. Then we would stare up at the small slat of light above the door and wait to see what might happen next.

221: Giant Monsters Go Back Home

The giant monsters came out of the sea and wanted to be part of our society. They had lived at the bottom of the sea for so long. We said okay, but gave them some rules:

    1. Do not eat people and

    2. Try not to smash stuff up too much.

I think the giant monsters really tried. But it was so hard for them. The final straw was when one giant monster sort of rumbled through the downtown. He was careful with his tail and each of his three feet but his crest knocked down the pancake restaurant sign, which really was a classic. It'd been there since 1940 and was a landmark.

Well, the restaurant owner demanded reimbursement, and the Historical Society people were up in arms and opinion sort of turned against the giant monsters, then.

It was decided they ought to leave, and I had to tell them. I spent over two months traveling around to places like San Diego and Johannesburg and even Duluth. Every giant monster I found I told it was time to go. Nothing was sadder than seeing the giant monsters slumping back into the ocean, slowly slipping under the waves. It was at sunset which made it extra beautiful. I snapped a few pics with my cellphone.

220: Check, Please

If I were to die right this moment, what would you do?

Depends.

Depends?

Yeah. How did you die, for instance?

Well, I...

Did you just sort of keel over with a heart attack? Or did you go out with some style, like spontaneous combustion?

Okay, um, I did it quietly....

I'd get a waiter. Ask him to help me get you out of here casually.

What?

I don't want to disturb the other diners.

The other diners? What about me?

You're dead.

Hypothetically, of course.

Yeah, but--

I mean, what am I supposed to do, leap to my feet, do the Heimlich or CPR or loosen your collar or yell "Call 911!" That's *rude*. These people are celebrating anniversaries or are on first dates, and I bet at least two of these couples are going to get engaged tonight. You want them to spend the rest of their life associating their anniversary with the time that guy died in the restaurant?

Well, no. Not when you put it that way.

Well you have to think about others. It's rude enough, dying in the middle of dinner. I'd probably end up going hungry that night.

Hungry?

What am I going to have them wrap my dinner and take in the ambulance? That's crazy.

Yes...

Lobster's no good, cold.

219: The Raft

They drifted on the sea, the three of them, wondering if they had always been on the raft, always in the middle of the sea, always just the three of them, if there was anything other than the raft, the sea, and them. And also of course the sun overhead all day long and, too, the moon, and the stars.

One of them said one day: *If there is a sun, a moon, and stars, and they are not part of the raft the ocean or us, doesn't that imply there is something other than the raft, the ocean, and us?*

This was a popular topic. It could go on for weeks before suddenly fading into a silence during which each pondered the arguments that had been made for and against the conjecture, time and again, arguments like:

- Why must we suppose the world is not made of those finite triumvirates: the sun, the moon, the stars, and the ocean, the raft, us?
- How do we know the moon and the stars are real and not merely hallucinations brought on by the absolute darkness when the sun goes away?

One thing never discussed was what to do if there *was* something other than the raft, the ocean, and them. That worry never occurred to them.

218: Love's Gonna Set You Free

They say a man lit himself on fire here.

They say he burnt so quick it was like an explosion.

They say flames lit into the trees around this bench, the whole park a conflagration within seconds, so hot the firefighters couldn't get near; the pond glowed orange and lit up the sky so you could see it miles away at the church on the hill.

They say he did it for love.

For love. Imagine.

They say when she heard she rushed there, but was held back by the firefighters standing there doing nothing. What could they do? Some fires are too hot to fight.

They say she was screaming, crying, saying she didn't know, she would've said *yes* if she'd understood just how...

They say she trailed off there, at the *just how...*

They say *What was she supposed to marry him just to keep him from the fire?*

From? He *was* the fire.

They say that's why the leaves are so brilliant here now, because of him.

They say all that.

I don't.

I come sit on the bench. I feel him there, looking at how beautiful the place is. Because of him, maybe. I don't usually speak. But sometimes I ask *"Was it worth it?"*

I need to know.

217: Better to Have Loved and Lost

One day people turned on the gods and began driving them away. The gods could hurl lightning, blot out the sun, cast plagues upon people and crash oceans in upon their cities, but were curiously unable to affect this decision and soon found themselves in the middle of a vast plain, looking back at the civilization that had been created in their names, from the walls of which some children jeered at them and made rude gestures.

"Perhaps we could find new worshippers," said the one who made constellations orbit each other and was responsible for the births of stars and deaths of galaxies.

"It won't be the same," mourned the goddess of flowing water.

There were those who spoke of smiting the world, of making volcanoes explode to douse all in fiery rock, but then others pointed out the people were not exactly afraid of that.

"And there's a lot of them," pointed out the goddess who made light, and dark. All of the other gods were in love with her. "You mightn't destroy them all."

"And if you did," said the god of wind and birds, "We'd be no better off than we are right now."

But the smiters answered: "At least it would be our choice, not theirs."

216: Boxcars on the Hop

When you were born God and the angels decided your fate the only fair way: random chance. God rolled an infinite number of infinite-sided dice determining everything from your height when grown to how many people vote you for prom queen, every single event from birth to death dictated by those rolls, with the results noted and strictly enforced.

If an angel sees you stepping into a busy street without looking, but knows you're one day destined to watch a 9th inning home-run ball fall three seats over just out of your reach, the angel will stop you being run over to ensure that eventuality, and all other eventualities.

But there are limits to that intervention. When weird things happen, unusual coincidences or inexplicable events, it is because of conflicts in the dice rolls. If (for example) the rolls indicated you would be shot by your second husband on October 14, 2051, but your future-second-husband's rolls doomed him to die in infancy, God and the angels don't try to straighten things out. "That's just the way the game goes, sometimes," they say, and keep on rolling to find out what happens next. And you'll probably just feel kind of weird that afternoon, and will opt to treat yourself to some ice cream.

215: Cowboy Versus Robot

When he was 7, Tucker announced he wanted to be a robot when he grew up. His parents took him to a psychologist, who asked what appealed about being a robot.

"It's not a cowboy," Tucker explained. The doctor led him back to the waiting room.

"He'll be fine," his parents were told. Relieved, they stopped for ice cream on the ride home, but Tucker turned down a cone.

"Robots," he reminded them, "Do not eat ice cream."

They took him right back to the office. "He's still broken," they reported.

"He's fine," the doctor said, but when he bent to offer Tucker a lollipop, the parents snuck out the door and never came back.

"Well," said the doctor. "Looks like you're stuck with me."

Tucker waited until the doctor was busy. He wrote a note:

ROBOTS DON'T NEED PARENTS

and then he, too left.

He caught a bus. Three stops into his ride, a man got on. The man was wearing a ten-gallon hat, a brown vest, blue jeans, boots, even spurs. He sat next to Tucker, who looked him up and down and said "You're a cowboy."

"Nope. I'm a robot," the man said.

"Teach me," Tucker said.

"OK," the man agreed, and they rode the bus into the future.

214: Mercury

They told you if you looked at the Sun just right you could see Mercury. They were eighth graders, attending the middle school across town where there were no playgrounds, just baseball diamonds used for t-ball on the weekends.

When you played second base on those fields you tried not to look at the Marlboro butts sitting in the dirt. When they told you about Mercury, you saw the pack of cigarettes in the leader's pocket. His greasy blonde hair hung over his eyes. Once, biking by his house you'd heard the *slapcrack* of a hand hitting a face. You'd heard a howl too low to be a woman but too high for a man. It was the leader. You'd biked away before he'd come running outside to throw rocks at a tree.

"Go ahead, look," they said. You knew better than to look into the sun, to listen to the leader, to follow directions from kids like them. What did they know about science, anyway?

"Look, and we'll give you your dumb planet book back," they told you. You still feel the betrayal from when they threw the book into the storm drain every time you see the dull black spot burnt into your retina, like you're seeing Mercury all the time.

213: Venus

You were born on November 3, 1973. In a fit of scientific optimism your parents named you "Venus." The name hung on you like clouds, whirled through your mind hotly.

Early mornings, you would walk outside and stare at the sky, dreaming of wars and mathematics. You tried to find your namesake in the sky but were never sure where to look and were too embarrassed to ask.

Where is Venus you would think. You meant, *what am* I.

They studied astronomy in 10th grade. You blushed the entire unit, sure everyone was mentally snickering about your name.

You fell in love a year later. He was tall and rode a bike to school for exercise even though he had a car. You stared at him in calculus, and sat where you could watch him playing basketball during lunch.

Now before dawn you walked the neighborhood searching for his house. You could easily find his address in the phone book. But you wanted to guess it.

When you were sure you had it, you passed him a note. It read *I walk by at six-fifteen every day.*

The next morning, he was looking out his window at you. You waved at him, and then went back home to get ready for school.

212: Earth

There are 23,000,000,000 different species on this planet. A 1-in-23 billion chance that you would be human, but you beat the odds. Here you are, king of the mountain, shoving everything else off to the side so you can stare out into space and regret that your planet is too small to hold everyone, too weak to power everything, too far away from all the other stars circled by all the other impossible planets out there.

Probably your planet doesn't really have *twenty-three billion* species, at least not anymore.

Probably never did.

You were born human which means you can lie on a hillside senior year amidst people who are smoking cigarettes, drinking beer, planning to have sex in tents, do things they think are *adult* but which when done by children are childlike, as tonight.

You are staring into the future. The light of stars is the light of the past only because the stars are screaming out ahead of everyone so far off. You feel that both you and the planet propelling you are traveling through the universe at 23 billion miles a second, and so you stare into the blackness of space to see where it is you are going, because where you *are* doesn't seem so special.

211: Why Is a Raven Like a Writing Desk?

Well the beast said. *I am waiting.*

Write, it added after a pause.

He lifted his head from his hands, said: "I can't, with you watching."

The beast roared, a withering howl the man slowly recognized was laughter.

You'd better. Its fetid hot sweaty breath melting down his neck.

He bent over the desk, picked up the pen, took some paper.

What are you going to write? the beast asked.

"I don't *know* yet," he muttered. "Must you stand so close?"

This room is not very large the beast grumbled.

The man began writing again *Once upon a midnight…* he wrote

That's been done the beast carped.

"It's to be an *homage*," the man replied.

An homage will not free your beloved the beast said, holding up a raven in a gilded cage. The bird angrily flapped its wings, cocked its head, and regarded the man.

"You didn't say *what* I could write!" the man said. "You demanded a poem and so you will get a poem."

I must like *the poem* the beast groused back.

The raven cawed. The man just stared at it, then looked up at the beast.

She says to quit dicking around and start writing, the beast translated.

210: Mars

More disappointing even than there being no Santa Claus is there being no Martians.

It seems to you a planet you can see from your bedroom window, glowing the blood-red of war, drifting through the sky so close, should have someone on it. Someone staring up from dusty plains ringed by mesas that look like canals from space, someone finding the bright blue dot that refuses to twinkle, someone to stare wistfully at it and wonder what life is like there.

Someone with antennae, who is three feet tall.

You cried when the science teacher in sixth grade said Mars' red color came from iron oxide. "Rust," she added. The word sunk into your mind. You stared at the text book. She had been explaining Mars has no water, Mars has no air, Mars has no life, then had topped things off by saying that Mars is *rusty* like the Gremlin in the driveway that doesn't start anymore.

You ran out of the room so nobody could see you cry. They all knew anyway but nobody ever said anything about it to you, not in the 20 years since then, and now when you stare up at the sky at rusty empty Mars you can't help but wonder why?

209: Asteroids

"You're like the living embodiment of *mess*," he said, brushing cheese-doodle powder off your shirt, then off his hands before stepping a bit away from the telescope.

But you understood from his tone: he'd not really disapproved. This is one of those things parents must say. *Officially* having orange powder all over your pajamas is not a good thing, but he brought you onto the garage roof at 10:30 p.m., gave you cheese doodles, then let you eat while setting up the telescope, tinkering, aiming, twisting dials in minute increments. You crunched blobby snacks and looked around the neighborhood at a weird angle, up above, the lawns looking too small to play football on.

You watched headlights of cars drive by, cellphones illuminating drivers' faces inside. He talked about rocks in space, nobody knows why they exist but they're fascinating, aren't they, better fun to look at than the moon, each one different.

Then he let you look into the telescope. You saw a blobby tan smear in the dark, and you looked until you felt it was enough and he said as you pulled away "Isn't it neat?" and you lied and said *yeah, it is*, but that wasn't the neat part; the rest of it is.

208: Jupiter

So why don't thunderstorms last a thousand years on Earth?

So how can a planet be nothing but *gas*? How does it hold together?

Someone told you Jupiter is actually like a small sun that never ignited.

A dud.

Jupiter can be seen with the naked eye. Standing right outside in your backyard, by the pine tree that used to be *cool* when you played *Ghost Ghost Come Out Tonight* you can see across the solar system to Jupiter, with its probably-fake Giant Red Spot storm that how do they *know* and it's got-to-be-solid-inside-somewhere core because *how can that not*, and from where you stand, off by the clothesline-pole with no clotheslines attached anymore, just rusty S-hooks, from there it looks like nothing much.

A dud.

Other things that don't look like much: the clothes-pole. The pine tree. The whole backyard which is mostly crabgrass and scuffs from people playing ball years ago, now people standing, smoking cigarettes until Mom comes home and everyone goes home. The fence, which nobody ever paints. The picture of Donna that she gave you and wrote on the back *Call me* but then when you did as soon as you reminded her who it was she said she had a boyfriend.

207: Saturn

Saturn doesn't have jungles in which rivers teeming with treacherous fish wind among hundred-year-old trees home to brilliantly-colored birds that explode in an array of cacophonous rainbow beauty at your approach.

Saturn, too, lacks the long rolling curling breakers that glow softly at night with a phosphorescence seemingly borrowed from the moonlight raining down upon them, the susurrance pushing towards you, then backing away, never crowding but always there in case you need them, the brine of life extending from you to everywhere else in the world.

Saturn does not have mountains jutting up out of it, breaking free of the crust and pushing higher HIGHER towards the edge of the sky, rocky escarpments wearing snow year round and beckoning you to see what everything looks like from up there.

Saturn lacks New York City, where everyone is rude just like in the movies and pretzels eaten on the sidewalk taste better than anything eaten anywhere else. Saturn does not have the Acropolis, ruins that make it seem possible Gods once walked among men.

Saturn doesn't have any of the things you have tasted, photographed, written about, and stood amidst over the last 37 years. So why do you dream of it each night so longingly?

206: Uranus

They said *Ur-ayn-us* but you taught yourself to pronounce it *yer-uh-nus*, and never really saying it unless you absolutely had to which was fine because how often in a lifetime does a guy have to talk about Uranus?

You snicker thinking about that line standing uncomfortably on the subway, people packed too closely around you, no room to breathe, everyone wearing heavy coats. The train is freaking hot. Every lurch bumps people into you or you into people or whatever.

How often in a lifetime does a guy have to talk about yer anus? You're still smiling walking up the stairs. You're grown up. You don't *have* to worry someone will make fun of you. If you'd been assigned *Uranus* in fifth grade for reports they'd have laughed when you said it but nobody laughed at Lisa Milot talking about *yer anus*. At first you'd smiled and looked to a few other guys but nobody looked back.

So what to do today? Wait for a call for a second interview. Go again to the museum; it's free on Tuesdays. Make some jokes on Twitter. Wonder whatever happened to Lisa Milot. At least you're off the subway, but now it's freaking cold up on the street.

205: Neptune

Neptune was the first proof you had of God's existence: the universe so orderly that when scientists added $x+y+z+etc$ it all equaled *Neptune*, the planet they demonstrated was there before they could see it.

It makes you dizzy to think about, standing here on the back porch. Things can be *here* before they are *here*.

What else can be proven to exist simply by proving that the world makes sense?

You look around at the house, with people sleeping inside? Maybe: can you *prove* they exist? They existed last night, existed this morning when you walked by them. Do they still? Standing in the morning mist with the strangely-prehistoric cranes starting to walk out of the edge of the forest, can you write an equation proving your wife is still sleeping in the middle of the bed? Is there a number so large or perfect or imaginary that taking its square root would demonstrate conclusively that three children aged 8, 10, and 2 lay in their respective bedrooms surrounded by trucks and princess dolls and rifles that shoot foam darts? You stare up at the windows, beginning to reflect the hazy sunrise, and realize that you do not understand math very much at all.

204: Pluto

Pluto has five moons. You didn't know that until tonight sitting outside the gymnastics practice, waiting for the car to fill with eleven-year-olds asking you to put on that radio show which reads tweets on the air. Waiting, you looked at the sky and wondered whether you could see Pluto with your eyes, no telescope. You looked it up on your phone, learning no, of course not or they'd have discovered it way back in the fourteenth century or whatever when they discovered everything.

Weird to think of people looking up with such intensity as to realize planets move differently from stars. Who had that kind of time, and having that kind of time spent it looking at the sky and drawing what was there?

You turn off the dashboard lights and look through the windshield. You wonder how long you have to look at the sky to discern planets moving against the stars, what was it called, *retrograde motion*? The eleven-year-olds arrive. "*Mom, what are you doing sitting in the dark you're so weird.*" Then someone is squealing because their tweet was read on the air, and when you get home you'll have forgotten the names of the moons but it's okay.

203: Everything Everywhere Else

You know nothing can go on forever or is it that you believe nothing can go on forever? Standing in your driveway, jack-o-lanterns behind you, feet bare against cold cement, the trees making *whooshing* sounds because they are just branches now, the night chill setting in, you *believe* nothing can go on forever.

You pause and stare up at the sky trying to see forever.

There's Orion. There's Cassiopeia. The Big Dipper. The only three you can recognize. There are a hundred other star formations people imagine exist.

You didn't realize until just now your hand had followed your gaze and you are reaching up, fingers stretched towards the blackness of space as though you could pull yourself up into it. You pull your hand down, look around to see if anyone saw, and go back inside and eat pumpkin seeds. You make shapes of the constellations out of them and after making the three you know, you begin to make up your own. Later on in bed you'll wish you'd drawn the shapes so some other night you could go out and look up at the sky and see if they are possible, these contrivances you came up with.

202: Good Night.

The monster was right in front of her when she opened her bedroom door. It dove at her. June ducked, scrambled under the bed. The thing roared and hissed from multiple mouths. The bed was flung clear across the bedroom, smashing partway through the box window. June crabwalked backwards shrieking away from it until she ran into a corner. The bedside table was knocked over beside her. She grabbed at it, tried to throw it at the beast but an oversized, gorilla-like arm with a hand, no a *paw* with *talons* and it was as big as her torso, swiped at her, flinging the table back into her. It hit her square in the face, knocking her silly. She tasted blood. Her vision swam. She grabbed weakly at a piece of board fallen on her chest. She jabbed it like a knife, heard the rewarding roar of pain as the thing pulled back. Her accomplishment was minor, hollow and short-lived. As she tried to get her head to focus one of the thing's elephant-like feet stomped down on her legs. She felt the bones cracking at multiple points and wailed as one of its mouths dove down over her head.

201: Spider-Legs

Spider-Legs got his name because of how his legs, and for that matter, his arms, look. Spider-Legs shambles aimlessly through neighborhoods late at night and early in the morning. He is looking for children sleeping with their mouths open, and when Spider-Legs sees that (he sees through their windows, for his legs are unusually long, his arms too) he pauses and he reaches just one of his long, long long arms in through the window or over the transom. Reaching the child, he sticks just one finger down, down, down into the throat, carefully. But eagerly.

With that one finger, which is always dirty, and sticky, and which has too many knuckles and not enough skin, Spider-Legs hooks out the tiny, glossy soul of the sleeping child, catching it on the hangnail he leaves on that fingertip and sliding it out quicksyquicksy, and then he ambles away holding the balled-up soul of the child between his hands as though it were cotton candy, or maybe taffy, or a candied apple, licking at it and gnawing it with his gums. His teeth fell out long ago, but that is fine by Spider-Legs, because who needs teeth to eat souls? Not him.

200: Rocket

Rocket didn't get his name because of the time he blew up the car ,but you could be forgiven for assuming that was the case, since the explosion (big enough to be seen all over town) blasted him 150 feet away into the apple orchard, knocking him out. Because it wasn't apple season, nobody found him. He laid there unconscious all night, waking the next morning and limping to his house, surprising all the relatives gathered there to mourn him.

Nobody could figure *how* he blew the car up.

"There wasn't even an *engine* in it," his dad told people.

Rocket never explained. The closest he came was prom night. He was only 16, having skipped a grade. He and Wendy, who was 18, had gotten a hotel room. He'd figured that meant good things, and felt ready to fall in love with someone. But Wendy drank too many wine coolers and was half-passed-out before much happened. Sitting quietly on the bed, watching TV, Rocket whispered: "If you want, I'll tell you how I did it." Wendy just fluttered her eyes and gave up trying to stay awake. And after that Rocket never felt like telling anyone ever again.

199: Ghouls

Nobody sleeps in the open no more. Parents tuck blankets all around babies, even over their little faces. Little kids tremble under 2 or even 3 comforters. People zip into sleeping bags. It's all because of the ghouls. Nobody wants to be seen by a ghoul.

But even if you're careful it happens, like with Tamra. I didn't see, of course, but I heard what happened. It wasn't really my fault, really.

We were in bed.

"Tamra?" I asked.

"Yeah?" she said back, sort of snappy.

"What was it like before the ghouls?" I asked. I'd read books in which kids had slumber parties, sleeping in blanket-tents with flashlights instead of hiding under covers as soon as the sun set.

"How should I know?" she muttered. I heard her sort of flopping, moving. She must have disturbed her blankets because it was quiet for exactly one heartbeat, and then there was a howl that sounded like lightning looks. I heard Tamra shriek. I couldn't do anything to help her. I just laid under my own blankets until the air horns went off around town to let everyone know the sun was up and life could go on again.

198: Alone

The man is in a boat.

The boat is in the water, of course.

The water is in the ocean, which is *likely* but not automatic, as the ocean is not the only place water can be.

The ocean, obviously, is in the world, under the sun.

The sun is in the galaxy which is in the universe, and it's not really clear whether it is necessary to say *the* universe or if it is okay to say *a* universe.

Back up.

In the boat are also these things:

A canteen, a photograph, a pen, a notebook.

In the canteen is water but *that* path has been trod, move on.

In the notebook is *not* a journal. A man in a boat on water etc has no need to record his experiences. Each day they are largely the same, aside from occasional schools of flying fish. Instead, in the notebook is a story the man is writing. It is about a man in a boat on the water. The story is not autobiography. It is fiction.

In the photograph is an image of the woman. It can be generally understood: she is not a woman but *the* woman.

198: Redux

The first time Jake returned to Heaven, God simply sent him back, wordlessly.

The second time Jake came back, God looked up, feigning surprise for Jake's sake. "So soon?" He asked.

Jake shrugged. "I'm not very good at this," he said.

God sent him for round three. Before long (relative to God's sense of time) Jake was back in front of the workbench again, somewhat the worse for the wear.

God patted him on the back.

"Turn the other cheek," He said, starting Jake on number four.

"How many of these do I get?" Jake asked the next time around.

"As many as you *need*," God said. He sent Jake back before Jake could reply.

This time it was *really* short, only a few minutes. God blinked as Jake stretched and looked around.

"What are you working on?" Jake asked God.

"Never mind. How did you do that?" God asked. "You were an *infant*."

"I didn't do this one," Jake pointed out. God searched His memories – there were a lot, a whole infinity of them in just a few minutes – and realized Jake was right.

"Sometimes that's how it goes," God told him, and off Jake went again.

197: Charley Horse Leaves Again

Charley Horse started running again but this time he ran so fast, he took off into the sky.

First he was just a few feet off the ground. Next he was several dozen feet above it. Then he was running above the treetops. He saw mountains in the distance and thought he could hurdle them if he tried. He put his head down, really putting his back into it.

The mountains were nothing to him!

He reached the part of the air where it stops being air and starts being space. He saw the blue turn to black, the day become night, the everything twist into nothing. He understood, though: the stars were out there and the only reason he could not see them was because the sun was too bright behind him.

That he could not see them did not mean they were not there!

So he dug a little deeper into his soul and found a little extra speed. He whizzed by the moon, which wished him luck. Charley Horse knew he didn't *need* luck, but he appreciated having it to take with him so he wasn't so alone out there.

196: There's Always Plan C.

God decided when people died their good parts would go to Heaven while the bad parts would go to Hell.

"So, what, you'll have partial people in Heaven?" asked the Devil, who somewhat liked the idea of stumps populating Hell.

"No," God decided. "All the best parts of people's *souls* will go up to Heaven, so eternity will be spent with the nicest version of themselves and their loved ones."

The Devil pondered. "So if someone is 90% evil..."

"Then 10% of their soul goes to Heaven," God finished.

"Will they be a tiny soul? Just 10% of the size of, say, a saint's soul?"

"I haven't worked out all the details yet. Maybe."

"So people will be able to tell who was a better person in life just by their size."

But that didn't seem like a good idea. God rubbed his forehead "It just seems wrong to send someone who is 75% good to Hell."

"Does the 10% part know the 90% is being punished eternally?" the Devil wondered. "Because if not then there's really no punishment for someone who was 90% evil."

"It's a work in progress," said God.

195: The Robot Who Couldn't Pray

The robot looked up to Heaven and said in its metallic voice:

MY GOD WHY HAVE YOU FORSAKEN ME.

God looked down and responded:

"Because you are not alive, but only a thing."

The robot was startled. It had not expected an answer. It had actually felt forsaken but did not believe in God, so the question had mostly been rhetorical.

OH UM ER the robot mumbled, searching its programming for how to respond under these circumstances. It found no set responses, but felt ill-equipped to wing it. As the silence grew longer the robot grew increasingly (if metallically) uncomfortable until it finally blurted: I AM SORRY I DON'T KNOW WHAT TO SAY I DIDN'T ACTUALLY BELIEVE IN YOU BEFORE YOU ANSWERED.

God had stopped paying attention to the robot already and was somewhat surprised to find it still hanging around. He looked now to see the robot staring up at Him, its metallic eyes seeming... earnest? Was that possible?

"Did you want something?" God asked.

The robot thought for a moment and then said:

I GUESS NOT.

They both went back to work, neither the worse for the experience.

194: Modern Love

One day they started trading cells.

The idea was simple as that: *you give me some of your cells I will give you some of mine* one said to the other, and they did that.

In old-fashioned love people lost cells too, through cells dying, falling away or sometimes growing into something new and remarkable that one day went off on its own to do things that were either amazing or not. But either way, the cells were no longer *them*.

So when they decided to try this new thing, they did it differently.

Some heart cells, some kidney cells, a few knee or toe or ear cells: it was easy. After all, who would miss them? There are 2x109 cells in the normal human heart alone, so each found it easy to spare some, especially as each was getting cells back to replace the ones it was missing.

One day, they began trading brain cells, too. Each began to know what the other had been thinking, and pretty soon neither was able to tell which of them was which. As that had been their goal all along, they were perfectly happy.

193: Writing Dr. Suess Out by Hand

If you were to take every Dr Seuss book ever written and you were to also take a pencil and a series of notebooks (wide-, not college-ruled) and if you were to then handwrite out those Dr Seuss books, word for word, copying them carefully into the notebooks in neat handwriting (probably printing because cursive doesn't seem to fit Dr Seuss' writing style), keeping at it until you were completely done, from the first word to the last (although chronological order seems likely the way you would choose to do this, before committing to that plan consider that there are many other ways to rank Dr Seuss books, from difficulty of reading to most-to-least favorite, or even in order of color of the covers, perhaps following *roygbiv*, whatever way you choose is fine, although it should be noted the order in which you copy them possibly says something insightful, about your personality, about which also the decision to even *consider* what order you might write them in, as well as how much time you spend on that question says something) it would take you a long time.

192: What to Do if Your Guardian Angel Gets Mad at You.

For starters, *do not pick a fight with it.* That's probably the worst thing you can do, because (a) it's an angel and (b) you'll probably only just make it madder, and you need it on your side in case you step in front of a bus, which you are prone to do.

What you can do is inquire what made an angel get mad at you. Let's say you did that, and the angel answered your question with a question of its own: HOW DID YOU KNOW I WAS MAD AT YOU?

What's going to happen next is you say something like *holy shit you're for real? I didn't think that was even possible!* That'll throw your angel for a loop, make it start thinking stuff like WHAT IN THE H...

(Angels don't swear. They find it *declasse.*)

...WHY WOULD YOU EVEN ASK ME A QUESTION IF YOU DIDN'T THINK I WAS REAL?

Now it's confused and defensive. Off-balance. That gives *you* the upper hand. Use it wisely. Like I'd ask for a miracle or something. Or maybe a smiting.

191: Higgs Boson, Episode 212:

Outside the cave, crackling bolts of psychic energy withered away the rockslide Higgs had blasted to cover their retreat. His wristcomputer estimated .35 space-minutes left.

"Is this the end?" the redhead on his other side whispered.

"I *won't let it be!*" Higgs said, and passionately kissed first one, then the other. "We're getting out of here, ladies!" He pushed them behind him and stood facing the invaders as the last of the rocks were vaporized by the enormous brains of the Vampire Dinosaurs.

The dinosaurs charged. The women screamed, but Higgs merely held up his hand, gesturing the dinosaur to stop.

"As highly-advanced lifeforms, You must honor my challenge!" Higgs shouted. The dinosaurs stopped. This was true. "Choose your champion, and I will choose our mode of battle!" Higgs winked at the ladies.

Of course the T. Rex was chosen. *<WHAT FORM OF COMBAT DO YOU OPT FOR, WEAK ONE?>* it telepathed into his brain, roaring.

"Arm wrestling!" Higgs said.

190:

Jeb wondered what the poster meant.

The subway car lurched crazily. He swayed and felt Julia press into him, swaying, too.

"What's it mean?" she whispered.

She was looking at the poster, too.

"I don't know," he said. He knew she wanted some reassurance, about something (anything!), but he felt so tired in that moment. Trying to fix it, he asked: "Where should we sleep tonight?"

He meant it as *her choice*, but she took it wrong. He saw immediately. She counted on his unwavering confidence. Each night as they stared up at the thin line of sky barely visible between the tops of buildings holding families, businesses, people who all had something Jeb and Julia hoped to someday have, too, she said to him:

"Promise me again."

And each night he'd promised, again: everything would be all right.

"Never mind," he told her now. "I know where we'll go."

She leaned her head against his shoulder and he accepted it, leaning into the curve as the train continued carrying them along.

189: The Balloon Story

I let a balloon go the other day while out walking.

Well, actually, I didn't let a balloon go at all. I didn't have a balloon. I wasn't walking. And it wasn't the other day I didn't do those things. I was about to tell a story. Only just not a true story.

I wish I'd had a balloon to let go the other day. I wish I had been walking with a balloon, and the ability to let it go. Or not. Absolute dominion over the balloon's destiny.

Only I wouldn't really control its destiny, would I? I would control only the smallest portion of that balloon's destiny: whether I continued holding it, or let it go. If I let it go I would lose control over it entirely. But even if I continued holding it, I would not entirely control the balloon. Something might pop it, despite my best efforts. It might be seen by people I would rather not see it, or not seen by people that I want to see it.

Great. Now I'm dizzy.

And I still don't have a balloon.

188: Turkey

These are all the ways you can cook a turkey.

1.   In an oven set to 400 degrees Fahrenheit, stuffed with bread or celery or both or whatever stuffing actually is, the way your mom cooked a turkey when you were younger. First she'd pull the insides out of the big wad of bird, things like gizzards. And the neck, which Dad then boiled in a pot on the stove before putting it, a wet gross inedible-seeming tube, on a plate next to the good things to eat. Then Mom said she couldn't imagine how Dad ate that and Dad shouted about how the Giants had signed him to play minor league baseball and he should have gone. Then you and Mom went to stay with grandma for three days. Her house smelled weird. Your mom said get over it.

2.   Also, you can deep fry them. Maybe try that next year so you don't end up sitting in the middle of the kitchen floor crying for no reason whatsoever only the reason is you can't remember if Mom ever cooked a turkey again after that year.

187: Stuffing

"In ancient Rome, they stuffed not just poultry but also other animals, including dormouse."

Relaying this made the dormouse feel grander than present circumstances might have otherwise allowed, seeing as it was tucked in between the walls separating the 8th grade English room from a supply closet, waiting for dark so it could venture out to find food. It was talking to the regular mouse that stopped by sometimes. "They also dipped us in honey and poppy seeds and ate us for dessert."

The mouse considered this, and said "I'm not sure it's an honor to be a delicacy."

"Which would you rather be eaten by, a common cat or Julius Caesar?" the dormouse responded haughtily.

"I would rather not be eaten at all," the regular mouse supposed.

"Well of *course* we would all rather *not* be *eaten*," the dormouse snapped. "But that is not the *point* I was trying to make."

"That's really the *only* point to be made," the mouse said.

"I wouldn't expect *you* to get it," the dormouse huffed. But he dropped the subject, because he liked having someone to talk to.

186: Beets

Each morning, Ferdinand would take his sword and burlap sack to the fields. Dew on the grass made footing too uncertain for practice, so he spent the first hours gathering a sackful of beets, then placing each atop a post of the fence ringing the field.

That done, he meticulously practiced his broadsword exercises, repeating them for hours. The final exercise was to chop his way back the fence line, draw-cutting each beet in turn. By the time he had slashed all the way to the first beet, it was time for dinner and bed.

Asleep, he dreamed of beets with faces, families, fears, hopes, dreams of their own. He dreamt that the beets themselves slept, dreaming dreams in which *they* were the swordsmen and he cowered before them, kneeling in terror of a horde of beets screaming down judgment upon his head. Ferdinand dreamed of begging for mercy to no avail. He dreamed of being sliced, over and over.

Then he woke refreshed, never remembering the dreams. He would head to the field again, unaware his days were spent seeking vengeance for his nights.

185: Mashed Potatoes

"We're guarding what, again?'

"Potatoes."

"To the death, then!"

"No, *not* to the death."

"To the serious maiming, then! These potatoes shall never leave this patch of earth whilst I still wield my halberd."

"No, no. Leave the halberd sheathed."

"It has no sheath."

"Whatever. Do NOT wield your halberd. Period."

"Hand to hand it is!"

sigh

"What?"

"Didn't you pay attention at the briefing?"

"HALT! WHO GOES THERE!"

"Let me handle this."

"I'VE GOT THIS. DOWN PEASANT! AWAY FROM THESE GROUNDS."

"I said *put down the halberd*. NOW."

"*I don't want any trouble...*"

"WELL YOU GOT SOME BUDDY!"

"It's no trouble at all."

"BACK AWAY FROM THE FENCE PAL."

"Sir, a moment..."

"NOBODY GETS IN!"

"OOF. WHAT'RE YOU-"

"Stop. Our directions..."

"I'm not sure what's going on here…"

"Sir! We will *oof* be right *ugh* STOP with *erf* you!"

"SIR *erk* HEY!"

"Whatever. I'm out of here."

"YES!"

"Idiot! We were to let him in!"

"Let him in?"

"Yes. Didn't you listen *at all?*"

"No. I was pretty distracted by the halberd."

"I'm sure he'll be back."

"I need a new partner."

184: Gravy

There are more types of gravy than types of stars. For every class-K star spitting out oxides somewhere you could name two gravies, like say Yorkshire pudding, which itself is a kind of gravy but gets cooked up solid and then has even more gravy put on it. Gravy baked in gravy. Imagine that!

But nobody dreams of going to the gravies! Nobody wishes upon a gravy, or says you have gravies in your eyes. Nobody has ever loved anyone *until the last gravy drops into the boat.* Gravy is second-fiddle. The middle child alone amidst foods that get to sit in plates, tureens, serving dishes. Gravy sits in a boat on dry land.

If gravy resents this, if gravy sometimes wants to stand up yelling, punch the turkey, kick mashed potatoes around, pour wine on the candles, then run out the door yelling incoherently into the night sky where no trees have leaves anymore and all the stars can be seen so clearly, gravy never lets on. It probably just focuses on its studies and dreams of opening its own restaurant someday.

183: Dinner Rolls.

<u>To Cook Dinner</u>   <u>Rolls:</u>
Preheat Oven To 400°F
Remove premade   from packaging

                                                            Rolls

Grease baking sheet with butter or cooking spray.
Place   1" to 1 ½" apart, evenly spaced rolls across pan
Now wait a minute…
Place tray into oven; set timer for 8-10 minutes.
Don't think I don't see what you're doing there.
When   are evenly browned across the top, remove carefully from oven

                                                           rolls

Stop right there.
I mean it.

                                                           rolls
                                                           rolls
                                                           rolls
                                                           rolls

Don't give me that. You know perfectly well this is not allowed.

                                                 rolls rolls
                                                 rolls rolls
                                                 rolls rolls
                                                 rolls rolls

Don't the rest of you join them. All of you, back here, NOW.

                                                   rolls rolls
                                                   rolls rolls
                                                   rolls rolls
                                                   rolls rolls

Or something bad will happen, that's what.

                                                 rolls rolls
                                                 rolls rolls
                                                 rolls rolls
                                                 rolls rolls

Don't threaten me. I'll – Hey! Don't even THINK about leaving!
Get back here!!

                                                           rolls
                                                           rolls
                                                       rolls
                                            rolls   rolls
                                                           r

If you won't come peacefully I will just drag you

                                             rollsrollsrollsrol

Quit struggling

                                              rollsrollsro

This…is…ridiculous…you…have…

                                            rollsrollsrollsrol

…a…job…

                                            rollsrol

ERF.UGH.COME.ON.

Stopthisfoolis
Imea
NoIdon
Hel
FINE
DO
WHAT
YOU
WANT
WE
DON'T
NEED
YOU
ANYWAY!

182: Green Been Casserole

Excerpts from an autobiography in which Green Bean Casserole plays a significant role:

[page 3]:

I was 8 years old, and I'd never feel about green bean casserole, or *a capella* music, the same way again.

[page 72]:

...didn't see how green bean casserole could be considered *polluting* but naked as we were there really wasn't much point in arguing.

[page 131]:

"You didn't," he said.

"*You* didn't," I said.

Right then I decided to file for divorce. The green bean casserole was the last straw.

[page 252]:

After the first wave of alien invaders had finished, we cautiously crept out of the shelters. The wreckage of our city was splattered with the bodies of those not fortunate enough to get undercover already moldering. Their remains reminded me uncomfortably of the green bean casserole we'd always served at family gatherings.

[page 400]:

"You didn't," I said.

"*You* didn't," I said back to me.

Both I *and* my clone had brought green bean casserole to the potluck. We'd later agree that made a profound point about genetics or something.

181: Pirates of the...

Apocalypses!

"The problem is, a number of universes you and Lil- "

"Harriet," Jezebel interrupted.

"-- don't interrupt. Many universes you created also held machines capable of doing that, too," other Jezebel finished.

Rurgur growled something. Other Jezebel said "I'm getting to that." To the captive version of herself she said "See, there's only room for so many universes in the universe. There are already too many created and more keep popping into existence."

"How were we supposed to know that could happen?" Jezebel looked at Rurgur. The cowboy lion looked unsympathetic, and pushed his hat lower on his golden fuzzy head while growling something.

"I agree," Jezebel said to the lion. She translated for her captive version: "It's your fault, and you will have to fix it."

"How am I supposed to do *that*?" captive Jezebel said.

Rurgur roared something. Even without understanding, Jezebel, captive, didn't like the sound of it.

Jezebel, free, said: "Like he says. You'll have to first destroy all the other machines. Then you're going to have to destroy most of the universes."

180: Corn on the Cob

Two ears of corn sat talking about their hopes and dreams and fears and loves (requited and un-) just before they were shucked and thrown into boiling water to plump out their kernels before someone totally mowed down on them at a dinner already overflowing with food.

No just kidding! Not about the dinner and people stuffing themselves with foods they almost never eat any other time, that really happens, but about the corns on the cobs talking to each other. That didn't happen. While ears of corn do have hopes, etc., they do not ever talk about them. That is due to corn's strict code of honor, and to the fact that corns are horrible isolationists that not only have no desire to interact with other corn but in fact actively wish to do other corn harm.

That's right: every ear of corn you see is burning with a silent keen desire to murder each and every other ear of corn everywhere. And with despair, because corn has no way to act on its desires.

179: Cranberries

Across the wide plain, in the hundreds, thousands, they swarm wielding swords and spears, charging each other, howling with righteous fury, army upon army warring for so long now, none can remember why they fight, which side they are on, or even how many armies there were originally.

There is just the battle, endless until one's own life ends.

Here: two cranberries face off in hand-to-hand combat, the dirt they stand on soaked with their dead brethren's juice. They strain ferociously, the clench broken only when another, dying berry comes tumbling through, knocking them apart. Each stares, shaken, at the body that has passed between them, then dives once more at the other.

Over here, a sword rises, falls. A berry dies.

Atop the hill, spears flung hard drive home and dying wails echo. And on and on, across an endless plain of endless combat.

They do not know why they fight any longer, but you know: they destroy each other so you can hear the *shloop* made when the quivering cylindrical jellied mass slides from the can.

178: Pumpkin Pie

As we went outside the night before Thanksgiving, Mom's scolding (*"whyn't you do it this afternoon?"*) ringing in our ears, we couldn't've expected what we saw: barely visible in the dark of the new moon were the pumpkins, fat bodies raised on ethereal legs, hazy wings flapping, slender starlight-formed arms entwined around each other. They were dancing, the beautiful auroras of pumpkin souls lighting their spectral, previously-hidden bodies.

They danced to a song too beautiful for human comprehension, so it seemed to us they danced in silence.

They realized we were there, seeing them. Their intricate whirling ceased. The pumpkins stared at us with mournful eyes, discovered. And doomed.

I was older, and a boy, so the duty fell on me. Stepping onto the soft dirt., I pointed: you, you, you. The chosen ones nodded, hugged good-byes, stepped forward. Just as they reached us their ghostly limbs collapsed, plump bodies falling to the earth. The rinds felt cool and smooth in the dark.

"Thanks," my sister called over her shoulder as we lugged the three inside.

177: Two Rhinoceroses

Two rhinoceroses decided to fight.

They didn't need a reason; their very existence was a reason. If ever an animal picked a fight with the world just by existing, it is the rhinoceros: so big almost nothing can hurt it, but still fleet-footed, with armor bullying: *attack me*, with horn menacing: *but I will attack you first*. The rhinoceros is proof God enjoys a good barroom brawl.

Each ran at the other. They collided with a sound like the earth cracking open and swallowing them back up. (Rhinoceroses believe themselves to be boulders thrust from deep below the earth's crust, rock come to life). Neither was even the slightest bit stunned. Picking new footing, each thundered forward again across the dusty plain in the golden sunset, heads diving to the side and hooking up to try to get a horn into soft spots that do not exist, on rhinoceroses. Again a cataclysmic collision, again they separate, eyes full of malice.

Had enough each asked the other, but of course they had not because they were rhinoceroses.

176: Heads Up

I have flipped this coin 10,013 times.

It's come up heads each time.

10,013 times.

In a row.

I'm scared to flip it again. In case it *doesn't* come up heads, you know? I don't know what I'd do if I flipped it and it came up tails.

I know tails is *there* because I can see the coin, hold it. I can *see* tails.

But then each time: *heads*.

10,013 times.

In a row.

I tried flipping high, low, letting it hit the ground, catching it, having someone else catch it, everything I could think of. Heads, every time.

And now I can't bear the thought of breaking that chain. But also I can't bear *another heads*, either. I don't know how this is *possible*. I don't want to flip it because I couldn't stand the outcome either way. Tails means everything so far has been a failure and is nothing. Heads and I will *scream* because that's just *impossible*.

But I know I'm gonna have to flip it. I'm gonna have to.

175: On the Night Before the Night Before Thanksgiving

That night they went sledding, but almost didn't. All bundled up, the three (dad and son and son) drove across town to the park where everyone sleds. But that hill didn't have the lights on. Maybe because it wasn't yet even Thanksgiving? So nobody really thought it was winter yet?

Then the next park didn't have lights on and the third park didn't, also. It almost looked like they'd have to go home, unrequited. One son looked like he might cry. The other one was half-asleep, bored. This wasn't working.

Then: the elementary school had parking lot lights on and a hill sloping just enough for the three of them, two in one sled and one in the other, to race down and get wet and cold and lie on their backs staring up at the sky, wondering if that really was Pleiades up there or if maybe dad was misremembering. The night turned out okay after all. Not great, but sometimes things don't have to be.

174: The Regular Mouse Dreams of Cheese

In his dreams the regular mouse walks amongst piles of cheese, swiss... gorgonzola... muenster.

In waking life he rarely sees cheese, but does not bemoan this fact. "Sometimes there is cheese, mostly there is not," it says.

The dreams are frequent, and realistic: often the regular mouse finds himself jolting awake, searching frantically around only to realize it was another dream and there is not, after all, a palace of cheese.

"You should try to stop them," advised the parakeet in room 325, where the awful boys lived. The mouse disagreed.

"I dream of cheese freely," it told the parakeet. "That is what my mind wants."

"But these dreams torment you with impossible visions," the parakeet argued.

The regular mouse explained. "If I have a life with mostly no cheese, at least I can have dreams filled with it."

"But doesn't it make your life seem bleaker during the day?" asked the parakeet.

"Actually, my daily life make my dreams seem all the more rich," said the mouse.

173: Trouble Down at the Old Mill

I heard the soldiers in the dark.

"Almost time," one said.

I stopped edging along the wall towards the loading dock with a door that could be pried back and crawled under. The building throbbed against me. Like a blister, it seemed to pulsate with pain, waiting to break open.

Almost time for what I wondered. But then I knew: I saw her glow, her wild dead eyes. She came howling out of the woods. I knew she saw *me* because she veered away from the soldiers. Towards me. I started running. Bullets were whinging all around. The dead lady shrieked as I reached the door, pushed against it. She was almost on me. I thrust hard, felt my knee *pop!*, howled in agony, but rolled inside regardless. Inside, I leaned on the door, putting it between me and the dead lady just before she reached me.

It worked. I slumped, sobbing, my knee shooting pain at me, hearing the dead lady screaming outside yet another door

172: Black Friday

That day the sun didn't come up, or ever again. If anybody ever figured out why that was, Daniel didn't hear. While others hung around to find out if civilization was going to break down or improve itself or what, he'd stolen a boat and set sail. He had his fishing gear and knife. He'd be fine.

He mostly went with the current, south, southwest, waiting for it to turn cold. He stopped at small islands to refresh his food and water.

On one, Daniel noticed a little girl.

"Hi," she said.

"Hey," he said back.

She stood watching the whole time as he caught crabs, putting them into a barrel of saltwater, gutted and roasted fish, rolled casks of freshwater onto the deck. She was still standing onshore as he sailed away. She didn't wave. Nearly a day later it occurred to him she might have been alone there. By then he wasn't sure he could find the island again, and after a while, decided not to even try.

171: Tiger I Got You a Present

Here it is! In my *ow hey* wow those teeth are sharp! Let's be careful, okay? Anyway, like I was saying I got you a present. Here, I'll pick it up for you. Good thing it's not breakable, right? Now, I know you probably weren't expect*yeeeoooowwwwww* get it off get if off get it off oh my God this thing is so heavy and its breath smells like I don't even know *arrggaghghghgh* can't believe I'm free I don't even know what I was thinking, God what is WRONG with me? I always do this. ALWAYS. *yikes get back aaaahghrhrrharah* I can't believe the door locked behind *OH GOD MY LEG WHICH #$(#*$&$%& KEY IS IT* OH NO THE REST OF THEM ARE COMING NOW WHY ISN'T ANYONE HELPING ME FINALLY THE DOOR IS OPEN **LET GO MY LEG YOU FOUL BEAST** close the door close the door close the door. Next year I am NOT doing Secret Santas. I don't care what people say.

170: The Magic of the Holidays

The thing about holidays is they come every year. If something bad happens in say, fucking September or May or one of those shit months, like if you have a fight with your wife on just some goddam random weekend in March when it's too cold to go outside but too long since the sun fucking shone for real to not want to scream at someone, then *pffft* when it finally ends it mostly goes away and nothing keeps rubbing at the scars and chafing it.

But when something like that happens at Christmas, when you get in one screaming, goddamn, fucking, fight at Christmas where suddenly she's said something, and you've said something, and the kid is crying in the bathtub, and you're so mad that you're punching your leg in frustration, when *that* happens, it's ten thousand hundred times worse because then forfuckingeverafter each year when Christmas rolls around you'll both remember that goddam night.

That was what he thought as he leapt.

169: There Are No Elves in Foxholes

"Sarge? Is it still Christmas Eve?"

"Whadda I look like, a clock?"

"I hope it's not Christmas Day yet. I like the *eve* better."

"Why?"

"On Christmas Eve, you stare at the stars—"

"Ain't no stars. Those're flares. Grenades. A burning tank. And if there *were* stars those 10,000 Germans over there'd see exactly where you were and shoot you dead."

"—and you think about how in the morning *anything* could be under the tree. Those presents ain't yet pajamas or socks. They could be a train, or a puppy."

"Stop, kid. The *day* is hope. The day's when Jesus was born to save us. Ain'cha been to church?"

"That's my point, Sarge."

"--'splain that."

"Well, the night before, there was hope that after Jesus was born humanity'd be saved, everything'd be perfect."

"Right..."

"...Then we ended up with... *this*."

...

"I hope if some Kraut shoots you, you don't end up face-to-face with Jesus, kid."

"I hope I *do*."

168: Some Zombie Stories, 9

We peeked in through the frosted windows of the zombie Christmas party. Zombies (the ones with lips anyway) kissed beneath mistletoe, or laughed (the ones who still had lungs of a sort) as joke gifts were opened, and ate *hors d'oeuvres* that looked sort of like smushed-up bugs on Ritz crackers.

Off in one corner, a shy female zombie sat by herself, drinking a cup of something moldy-looking. She watched the rest of the zombies cavorting in their shambling way, but whenever anyone looked at her she quickly looked down again. She was missing an eyeball. Other than that she was pretty, and we wondered why nobody talked to her.

We wondered if the zombies were celebrating Christmas as a religious or secular holiday. Although they had a decorated tree and candy canes, and even had a gingerbread house decorated with rotten gumdrops, there wasn't a Santa *or* a Nativity in sight. After I thought about that a while, it sort of made sense.

167: The Siege

Thinking I'd heard something, I crept downstairs, baseball bat in hand. I heard some small sounds in the dining room. I figured it was a mouse, so I flicked on the light, quick.

It wasn't a mouse. Instead, I saw a group of gingerbread men surrounding the gingerbread house, pointing candy canes at it, expressions of grim determination on their faces. Inside, on the upper level, a snowman cookie looked out of a window laced with lattice-work shoestring licorice, his frosting mouth set in a grim line. Crumpled ice-cream-cone Xmas trees lay broken on the gumdrop path, looking like there'd been quite a tussle. Off to one side, a reindeer cookie limped on broken legs.

The snowman looked up at me, then withdrew further into the house. The gingerbread men closed the ring a bit more. One of them looked over his shoulder at me. His eyes narrowed.

"This isn't your fight," it told me. I took the hint and went back to bed.

166: Why is a Raven Like a Writing Desk

Stanford's last request was to talk with Santa. As it was Christmas this seemed both reasonable (it was Christmas) and not (Santa not actually existing.) After discussion they decided to get a top-notch mall Santa and hope for the best.

The Santa arrived amidst much Ho Ho Ho-ing etc. Stanford in a glance saw thru him. "You're not really him, but you'll do," he said.

"Do for what?" the Santa asked.

"I would like you to bring me a raven, and a writing desk," Stanford said.

Santa looked confused, so Stanford explained he intended to quiz both to see what, if anything, they had in common.

"But that's ridiculous!" exclaimed the Mall Santa. "Neither will be able to answer you!"

Stanford burst into tears. The Santa was quickly hustled out of the room, asking what he'd done.

"He really wanted to figure it out for himself," said Stanford's aunt. She paid the Santa anyway, in the spirit of Christmas.

165: My Next Christmas Tree

I had this idea for a Christmas tree that would be like a candy cane. It would have all-white lights and all-red lights and they would spiral down the tree and in between would be all white ornaments, white stars and glass balls and probably peacocks only they would be all white, but they would alternate, the white ornaments, with red ones. The red ones would be icicles and snowflakes and stars, too (but no peacocks). The ornaments would be in bands between the light strands. To form the stripes, see? Then I thought to myself *what about the tinsel!* I imagined tinsel, red and white, fringy and ropy, spiraling down around the tree.

Then I realized I was thinking of *garland*, not tinsel. It's garland that comes in ropes like that. By that time I was thoroughly lost because I hadn't been paying attention to where I was driving, which was fine because I'd forgotten where I was headed anyway.

164: How to Make Egg Nog (A Fun Group Activity)

Why do we only eat *chicken* eggs? There are probably like a zillion birds out there and we only eat one kind of bird egg. Why don't we go to the grocery store and have a choice of like robin's eggs, or crow's eggs, or eagle eggs? That's weird.

I found some vodka. Would that do?

There's probably some milk or cream or something in there. "Heavy" cream, I bet. Made of deuterium or Deuteronomy or whatever that water is that is created by nuclear reactors and is slowly poisoning us.

Powdered sugar? Cinnamon? There's got to be some sort of spice in it for flavoring.

Nutmeg. Nutmeg's like a total Christmas thing.

"Look, Sylvia, can we please not do this on the ph—what? Do whatever you want, okay? I'm busy—Sylvia? Goddammit, don't hang up on me."

Well, not *bald* eagle eggs. That would be disrespectful.

Then cool to room temp and serve!

163: Bug God Wins Xmas

Ever since bees stung Santa at Bug God's palace (Bug God, forgetting it was Xmas Eve, ordered her guards to sting the intruder) Santa has ignored bugs. So Bug God has had her own followers deliver gifts to her subjects on Xmas Eve, with mixed results.

Grasshoppers got the presents covered in tobacco spit, or broke them, hopping so much. Beetles were too slow. And the less said about the year of the worms, the better.

This year, Bug God chose better. On Xmas Eve, billions of butterflies filled the sky. Their wings shimmered beautifully in the starlight, an iridescence casting brilliant reds, yellows, greens and blues around, as if the entire world had been decorated by fluttering Xmas lights. Even Santa was overcome by it. He forgave everything, saying he'd deliver presents to bugs next year, too. But the butterflies were so popular that everyone told Santa not to bother and put Bug God in charge of Xmas.

162: Xmas Monsters

We all got monsters for Xmas, monsters so beautifully amazing, so fun to look at, nobody even minded when they started destroying everything.

They made the destruction beautiful! They sung hymns through their fangs as they tore down skyscrapers or collapsed bridges full of cars full of people coming home from midnight Mass. Things exploded like fireworks or glowed like stars. We survivors followed them through the decimated city, enthralled as electricity arced against ivory claws, as the screams of the dying harmonized with the monsters' choir.

They tore apart May's gramma's house while they sang "We Three Kings" and May thought that was extra-special because it was her gramma's favorite carol.

When everything was destroyed, they retreated into the wilderness. We huddled around a burning pile of cars, watching the sparks fly off into the sky, where the northern lights were visible above the glowing wreckage of city. It was beautiful. Stephen said *"We should do this every year."*

161: Other Snowman, 1

Frosty wasn't the *only* snowman to come alive. There was lots of magic that day. The first other snowman we saw, me and Deeny, was Horace The Snowman, who came to life when Mrs. Delfino's old sweater blew off her back porch and onto him. The kids who made him weren't our friends, because they got poor lunch at school.

Horace was a pretty poor snowman, all lumps, plus he only had one arm. He came limping over to us, introduced himself and asked: "Want to play?" His words were slurred because his mouth was carved with a finger instead of being coal.

"Not with *you*," Deeny said. We laughed and ran away. Horace tried to follow us around through the yards, but couldn't keep up, what with being handicapped and all. He fell over while cutting across the alley, and a snowplow buried him in a drift at the end of MacGregor Street. Good riddance, Deeny said.

160: XMAS F*** YEAH

Start here:

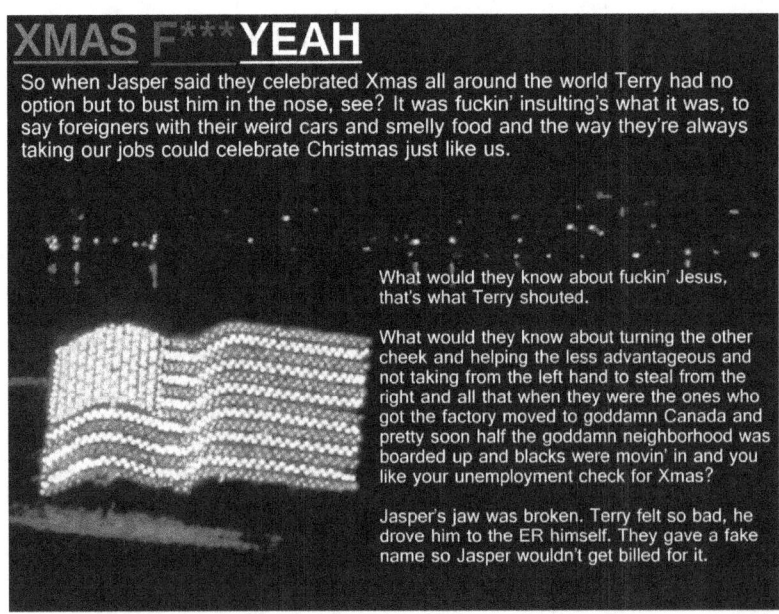

XMAS F*** YEAH

So when Jasper said they celebrated Xmas all around the world Terry had no option but to bust him in the nose, see? It was fuckin' insulting's what it was, to say foreigners with their weird cars and smelly food and the way they're always taking our jobs could celebrate Christmas just like us.

What would they know about fuckin' Jesus, that's what Terry shouted.

What would they know about turning the other cheek and helping the less advantageous and not taking from the left hand to steal from the right and all that when they were the ones who got the factory moved to goddamn Canada and pretty soon half the goddamn neighborhood was boarded up and blacks were movin' in and you like your unemployment check for Xmas?

Jasper's jaw was broken. Terry felt so bad, he drove him to the ER himself. They gave a fake name so Jasper wouldn't get billed for it.

159: Tree

We went to get our Xmas tree at the parking lot which used to be the A&W. Melanie got lost and Dad told me to find her. I wanted to help him pick out the tree, but he made me go so I went.

I found her in the back where the trees were unloaded. There were tons of them bound with ropes and stacked like fuzzy logs. Melanie was just staring. I tried to make her come on before Dad got impatient and picked a tree without us.

She pointed at the tied-up trees. "Where do they catch them?" she asked.

I told her not to be stupid, but felt bad about it, so I gave her a piggyback ride to where Dad was paying for the tree he'd gotten. I was going to be mad at him but on the way home we all sang along with "Rudolph" like opera singers and then everything was okay.

158: Other Snowman, 2

Donald the Snowman came to life when a shoe, part of a pair hanging from a telephone wire, fell off in the blizzard the same night Frosty led his parade. We found him hiding under a porch.

"Hey, whataya doin' under there?" Deeny asked him. "C'mon out. We want to play."

Donald looked scared.

"Let's leave him alone," I suggested. Deeny stared at me until I turned to Donald and said:

"C'mon, Donald. Don't be afraid." After we coaxed him out, he looked from Deeny to me.

"Why were you hiding?" Deeny demanded.

Donald shrugged. I'd never have guessed a snowman could do *that*.

"It seemed like the only thing I *could* do," he said quietly.

"What's *that* mean?" Deeny glared.

Donald started to talk, stopped. He waved his stick arms around at everything and looked bewildered. "It's hard to explain," he said, finally.

Deeny got cross and walked away. I understood him perfectly, though.

157: The Regular Mouse is Running for His Life

Fast! The regular mouse tears through the auditorium, the cat hot on its tail, literally: the regular mouse can feel its searing breath as they race under the seats, catching *whiffs* of buttered popcorn kernels, leftovers from movie night, those being the reason the regular mouse is down here.

The cat is gaining. The regular mouse jumps!

The cat does, too!

The regular mouse is almost caught. Its tail is briefly clenched, pulling it down behind the seat. The cat is there already; the regular mouse must scramble backwards to stay alive, barely avoiding those claws.

The regular mouse knows there is a chance this *might* be the end of it, this chase.

A *chance*.

But it is a 100% certainty the regular mouse will end, *sometime*. So anything less than a 100% chance of ending *right now* is a reason to keep running.

Which is what it does.

156: See

The wave killed the man almost instantly, although he did not realize it at first. He only noticed things were different. It took a while for him to understand why, even though the difference was not subtle. He no longer felt anything, but could see *everything*: the ocean water in which his body drifted lifelessly was as clear as a mountain stream. He could see whales in the distance easily as the tiny jellyfish near him.

Beyond the teeming schools of fish he viewed mountaintops, cold, unvisited.

Further out he saw into the sun's heart, saw each atom clasping another powerfully enough to blast warmth across a hundred million miles.

He could see, behind that, a billion stars with a trillion worlds.

Everywhere he looked he saw new things and saw things in a new way. It was so amazing he felt he could spend eternity just examining it all, and then remembered he could.

155: The Boy Who Wanted to Fly But Never Told Anyone

This little boy, he wants to fly so much! It's all thinks about. He stares at the sky so hard he sometimes jumps a little, just these tiny little jumps so nobody notices but there it is: he's trying to fly. Trying.

He jumps so very little because he doesn't want to tell anyone about how much he wants to fly. He doesn't know if it's possible or impossible, flying. He doesn't know. But he knows that things which are impossible only become that way when you find out they're impossible. Up until then they're just *maybe*. And he knows people tell other people things are impossible all the time. All the time.

So if he doesn't tell someone about wanting to fly then someone can't tell him *stupid nobody can't ever fly*. And he's careful about the little jumping. Nobody ever notices. Nobody. Ever.

153: He Should Get a Third

When you die you can ask God *one* question. If it is good enough, you get a second one.

Edgar died of car crash, and stood before God, Who sat a million miles tall on a golden throne glowing so brightly it would hurt any living thing's eyes.

Edgar was not living.

He asked God: "Why give us so much to do, and so little time to do it, so we must have so many regrets?"

God said: "I didn't. *You* decide how much time to take going to school, working jobs you hate, cooking frozen pizzas and whatnot. You use the minutes I give you according to your own designs. If you run out of time, it is not *My* fault."

This was a good question. God allowed a second. Edgar asked: "Why were all the best-tasting things so fattening?"

God agreed, that one was on Him.

152: The Particular Boy in This Story Will Survive

They put the boy outside on his fifth birthday.

They put *all* the boys outside, when they turned five. Just the five-year-olds, just the boys. Any who survived the entire night could come back in.

Nobody knew when this had begun. Nobody knew why it was. Nobody knew why nobody else went outside after dark.

Some said God told them do it this way.

Some said the *gods* told them do it this way.

Neither group offended the other. Both hated those who believed this was done to these boys, because God, or gods, had never said anything *to anyone*.

Nobody ever asked the boys who survived what they saw, at least partly because the boys very desperately did not want to be asked what they knew. Despite that knowledge, or perhaps because of it, the survivors were the strictest ones about enforcing the rule.

154: Why Are You Up So Late, Josiah!

Why are you up so late, Josiah!

 The stars in the sky are too bright, MaMa!

I will put out the stars so you may sleep.

 The moon, though, MaMa, is so wide, I am afraid it will fall from the sky!

I will pull down the moon, tuck it in its bed, so the night sky will be dark and safe as your own blanket-covered head.

 The trees, MaMa! They rustle and whisper, telling secrets about me.

The trees are only saying to each other they are jealous of your great, warm bed. I will tell them, *hush you trees, don't keep my boy awake.*

 The wolves, MaMa, they howl so wild and fierce.

Your PaPa stands guard on the porch all night, keeping the wolves away.

 So everyone is safe, MaMa?

No, Josiah. Nobody is ever safe. If we were, we would not be alive.

151: Snow Boys

Snow boys come most often after blizzards. They are somber visitors of uncertain purpose.

While they are here, snow boys go through the motions. They hold serious snowball fights, packing snow in a businesslike manner, trying not to hit each other's faces. They sled, each snow boy patiently awaiting his turn to throw himself onto his sled and, tight-lipped and concentrating, careen down the hill. With stony visages snow boys will try to avoid the bumps in the hill (nobody ever can, not even them) and with the same impassive look snow boys fly off their sled and land in a heap, faces glowing red with the cold.

150: Sex and Time Machine

Jon announced he'd invented a time machine but nobody believed him until he proved it by taking us back in time an hour so we could watch ourselves arrive at the party. Then we couldn't decide what to do with it. Undo 9/11, stop all the world wars, invent penicillin a hundred years earlier, make ourselves rich... it went on for hours.

Suddenly Jon said *what're we arguing about?* I realized he was staring intently at Lila. It took an hour for her to admit she'd snuck off while we argued, got the machine and gone back to the day Jon invented it. She'd gone down on him as he'd jotted notes for it, so he'd never invented it after all. Now she's got the only working time machine. We've agreed when we find where she's hiding it we've got to stop her from stopping him.

149: Art is Art

"I call it: GOD RIDING A UNICORN DOWN A RAINBOW DURING THE CREATION OF THE UNIVERSE."

    Hmm. Well.

"What?"

    Er. Nothing.

"You seem... something. You definitely seem *something*. What are you thinking?"

    Me? I'm not thinking anything.

"Obviously you are *thinking*."

    It's just...

"Yes?"

    This is just a giant...

"Spit it out."

    Look, I know that I don't understand these things, really. You're the artist, not me.

"What's to understand?"

    Well... which part is *God*, exactly?

"Oh is THAT all you want to know? That's it? That's your thought?"

    And which part is the unicorn?

    And the rainbow. While we're at it.

"So you're telling me you can't make out *any* of that? NOT A SINGLE THING?"

    You needn't yell. I told you this isn't my bailiwick.

    And after all, it is just a giant canvas with nothing on it.

"*Exactly*! So you *do* get it."

148: Another Thing About Witches

Not all witches are bad. Witch Molly volunteered twice a week at the school, where she spent most of her time re-shelving books kids hadn't put back during library hour. She did that for over two years before someone on the school board heard she was a witch and they confronted her in front of the whole school, demanding to know if it was true.

Witch Molly put her bologna sandwich down and admitted it. There was a lot of yelling about how this was not okay, before eventually Principal DeLeon said *okay*, Witch Molly had to resign.

Witch Molly turned herself into a crow and flew out the window. She left behind a few knick-knacks on the volunteer desk, just some junky stuff which to this day is in the Lost & Found. Everyone says if you touch them you lose your soul.

147: Nothing Works That Way Really

Everyone googles *medical* problems to find if they have eyeball-destroying-brain-ebola. One night, Erin tried that for her other problems.

She typed in *felt anxious going to work.*

Then she added *Also Steve seemed distant at lunch.*

Then, she tacked on all her other problems: low checking account, crappy hair style, feeling alienated at the coffeeshop, Mom bugs her on the phone, etc...

She hit ENTER.

It returned a null result. Search engines don't work that way.

Erin went to bed hoping to *dream* answers while she slept, but brains don't work that way, either.

Instead, she dreamed she was an astronaut, something she used to pretend to be every day until eventually she didn't.

It would be easy to say had Erin pursued being an astronaut she wouldn't now feel she had all these problems, but life doesn't work that way, either.

146: The Same Story Told Backwards

Nobody ever knows the ending to someone else's story, or even if it *does* end. So each of them, and not us, will only ever know if they get shot, hit the ground, fall into the river, or just keep going up forever.

Bullets whizzed by, the river below them in the gorge thundered, sky whistled past.

"Maybe it don't matter what we hit," one had thought, or maybe yelled.

"Maybe we hit the river," one had yelled, or maybe just thought.

Just moments before this fall (?) they'd looked at each other, each dropping empty six-shooters.

The standoff had been brief, the bad guys shooting back so furiously, the cowboys were left no choice but to turn and leap over the edge into the sky!

The ambush had come at dawn, quickly chasing them at a run to the precipice.

145: And Then Forwards

Two cowboys stare at the campfire.

Neither one wants to say tomorrow they will probably die.

Some things do not need to be said.

But some things do, and finally one does.

"You believe in God?"

The other cowboy shrugs.

"You?" he asks.

Sparks break free of a log and lift into the sky, disappearing after traveling too far for the cowboys to see anymore but continuing on their journey regardless. Or because they burn out.

It was hard to tell which. But it *mattered* which, and both knew it.

"Think they burn out?" the first cowboy said.

"I think they'd better not," the second said.

That was the last anyone said, until much later in the middle of the night, each heard the other praying. Each understood that their prayers were mainly for someone to be out there hearing their prayers.

144: It's Not the Last Kiss Unless You Know it's the Last Kiss

He kissed her for the last time.

She said: "Tomorrow let's go skating."

He sighed and sat back down.

On the ice rink, he pulled her in close, pressed his lips to her with an air of finality, a hint of regret.

She said: "Later, I can show you where *else* to kiss me."

In the morning, he carefully extricated himself from the bed. He touched her still, soft lips. It was barely a kiss. He tiptoed to the kitchen where he saw she'd set out his favorite cereal, a bowl and a spoon. A note said *No good without milk J*

Despite himself he checked. Taped to the milk were tickets to the concert that weekend.

He stopped kissing her for the last time. Eventually he even threw away the pills.

143: We Will Be Cowboys Until the New Year

"We will be cowboys until the New Year," first Sam said to second Sam, who agreed to the plan.

But ten years later there they were: still cowboys waiting for the *new* year. Each year had seemed to be the same old same old. Each year they'd agreed nothing was *new* enough to not cowboy anymore.

This went on so long eventually one, or both, of them died; neither was sure which, although both had their suspicions.

Was that new? each wondered.

Someone dying wasn't new, but one of them (or both?) dying had never happened before.

The more either Sam thought about it the harder it was to figure. If *this* Sam had died, how could he stop cowboying? And if he hadn't, could he abandon the other to an afterlife of solo cowboyism?

142: I Am Not Sure We Need a Rhomubs

Sometimes you wonder about shapes. Who created them? Who named them? Who decided we would have a thing called a rhombus? That we needed a specific name for it?

Do we need a name for a square, in particular? You wonder, those times. You lie on your side staring out the window at the bright blue sky, at branches covered in leaves, and reflect how you've lived in this house for 18 years and still don't know the names of the trees that fill your yard. Are they ash trees? Is *ash* a tree? Does it matter what a tree is called? Does it matter if you know?

Times like these, it seems if you just think hard enough the world would unravel and fall apart, which is why you stop thinking so hard.

141: The Man Who Never Finished His

Each day when he woke up he got. From there, he never knew what the day would. At times, over his toast and eggs, he'd sometimes feel so. But there were other. Still, those days were. Oftentimes, he would just. Or sometimes he might.

He lived. It was difficult to tell, looking at him (or even when talking with him), if that ever. He never let. This didn't keep people from trying to find out, of course, because that is how people are. But the man.

Eventually, he. Many people who knew him were surprised at that, happening as it did, but those who were closest to him ("close" being a relative thing, here) said they'd figured it would happen sooner rather than later. In this, as with all other things, the man left them.

140: An Unsigned Inscription Found in a Class of 1987 Yearbook

Sometimes it's just like I don't know, rrrgggggh and then EXPLODE! You know? You know? You know. Thing is, nobody REALLY knows, which just makes me so... so... what is the word I'm looking for here? French. Some kind of French word, one of those words with an apostrophe that doesn't mean anything. What's up with that apostrophe? An apostrophe means a letter's missing, right, at least in English, but I don't think it means the same in France.

My point is, though, that there is a word in French that is exactly the thing I am looking for right now, exactly, because this word sums up how it is when the whole world just implodes. Did I say *explodes* earlier? Because I definitely meant *implodes*. That's how this feels.

139: New Year's Eve

When the clock struck midnight on December 31, something didn't work right and even though it was hard to say *why*, we all knew: The old year had not ended.

It was December 32. Then December 33rd, December 50th, December 712th. People stopped counting. The parties had finally ended, noisemakers ground into the sidewalk outside our high-rises with dirty heels as the sun rose.

A few crazies tried to act like it was no big deal. They flipped their calendars and marked days off, claiming, as the days warmed up, as babies were born, as school let out and then started again, that time was passing the regular way. We all ignored their invites to birthday parties and anniversaries. We claimed we pitied them and their pretend world but we regretted that we couldn't join them.

138: Balloon

There's this balloon caught in a tree in the park.

I can't help imagining the party where that balloon opportunistically, *leapt* UP! from some kid's hand. That kid would've started crying immediately. His dad would've chased it, thinking *this is stupid, it's gone.*

Then, suddenly, the balloon *isn't* gone.

It's *there*, in the tree.

So now the kid's crying more, not understanding why dad doesn't get the balloon down. Dad, meanwhile, feels powerless: the kid doesn't understand, it's really up there, too high to climb. Except Dad's also thinking, deep inside, *oh, man, I bet I could climb up there and get it.* But he doesn't try. He just looks up at it, feeling bad, thinking it'd be better if the balloon would've just drifted away instead of tormenting him.

Meanwhile, the balloon was just thinking *rats.*

137: Missed Connections

Me: Man sitting at the 13th street deli counter, lingering over French fries grown cold. I'd put too much ketchup on them. My fingers kept getting all sticky. I was late getting back to work. Not that it mattered.

You: Big smile, kind eyes, long curly hair. Moving through the world in a bit of a haze, like the world didn't become real without you concentrating on it, so most of everything seems always ethereal to you, and you to it, unless you focus. You liked spending entire weekends sitting on the window seat re-reading books from when you were a kid. You tasted, always, like coffee. I wish you'd walked into the deli that day. Or any day. I wish I'd taken you seriously, and stuck around. I wish I knew where you were, now.

136: Who What Where When Why

So there we all were, nobody wanting to point the finger but everybody secretly blaming everyone else, all the same, until almost as one, kind of divine intervention, we decided it was Ronald's fault.

We had plenty of burdens and problems to lay at Ronald's feet, or drape on his shoulders. Taxes, the ozone layer, dinosaur extinction, gravity —all kinds of reasons were shouted, tweeted, or graffitied on overpasses. One would've sufficed; all of them together impelled us.

The next step was finding Ronald, who *of course* had not bothered to be present to bear our opprobrium. Turns out he was having lunch with his mother. Watercress sandwiches!

"Get him, NOW!" many of us yelled, and with that we descended.

"Why..." Ronald said but we didn't feel like explaining to him.

135: Little Bird

This little bird, this little bird.

He's hopping around, like he doesn't know he can fly. He's on the ground, cocking his head, looking at the world halfway: this side, then that. Do they have to ignore one half of their world to focus, birds?

This little bird is about the tiniest thing that could exist and still be cared about. Things that are smaller than this bird are beneath notice, and gross: bugs, funguses, disgusting things. Things get so small, they don't have enough of the good part of life and the world tries to destroy them.

At the other end, big things are always protected. Whales, mountains, emotions, the stars: we try to save those. Nothing is too *big* to care about. That's the lesson this little bird will never learn.

134: Numbers

If you go around saying stuff like *"Why does 2 + 2= 4? I mean, like, isn't it so arbitrary?"* then you should know:

Deep in the center of the universe, where scientists say a massive black hole sits, and religionists say God sits, and atheists never think about, numbers are created.

They are created in a factory; numbers aren't artisanal, not with the volume needed. The workers work 3 shifts, 'round the clock, with overtime on holidays and before big sporting events. They are well-paid and happy. They have families, fulfilling social lives, interesting hobbies.

It is not because of this place that $2+2 = 4$. The workers don't make the rules, only the numbers. We are telling you all this because the number-makers never say anything like "Why does 2+2= 4?"

133: Numbers, Again

You might wonder about the *order* of numbers, whether it is necessary that 3 follows 2 follows 1, and so on.

The answer: No, but messing with the order messes up other things.

For example, putting even numbers sequential to each other results in cause and effect no longer being related: effect begets effect; causes achieve no results. Gunshot wounds appear for no reason and babies are never born.

True, people fall in love without ever meeting, then don't fall out of love, even with plenty reasons to do so (e.g., gunshot wounds and never-babies). But endless, invulnerable love does not happen to everyone in the renumbered world, and eventually the lonely insist we count the way we used to, so more people can be unhappy and things make sense again.

132: Numbers, One More Time

There was a girl who started counting soon as she knew how.

1, 2, 3, 4 she began. When her mother shushed her she whispered *37... 38... 39...* as her parents argued about the correct route to the church. She kept counting all day until she fell asleep.

The next morning she woke up and started in where she'd left off: *1,191, 1,192, 1,193...* she said as she got ready for school

This went on, every day, all the time. Kissing her first boy, drinking her first beer, having her first child, she was always counting, aloud or to herself.

"247,713!" she sobbed at her husband's funeral, before continuing on, softly, as she huddled in the pew.

Nobody, not even her, ever knew what she was counting *to*.

131: This Story Is Not About Numbers

There are imaginary numbers which do more than simply square themselves to make a negative one.

There is *[h]*, which is how many people you will have a sex dream about but not remember the dream.

There is *y*, the number right after the number where you stop counting things; every time you try to count all the stars you can see, or the black jellybeans in the jar, or all the times you've heard *"I love you"* in your lifetime, but give up, the next number in that series is *y*.

There are <u> (all the ideas a man has in his twenties), (*) (the perfect length of a kiss), and many more you never knew about. You should have taken math in college.

130: Birthday

There is a man with seven birthdays. When he tells people this, they are (rightfully) mystified, demanding explanation. So he tells them of:

The day he first became a separate individual existing (mostly) on his own.

Also, the day he first became aware he was *he*.

And when he learned about Santa and was born into a world devoid of magic.

The day his heart was broken, birthing him into a world where love could die.

When his first child was born and he was, too, as a father.

How he threw out his back and began life as an old man.

The man stops at six, never speaking of the day he stared at a handful of pills for nearly an hour before dumping them into the drain.

129: Interruption

They lay entangled as the world came back. With each heartbeat, the traffic noise grew, the vague light of dirty streetlamps beat into their eyes, the three days' worth of dirty laundry pressed on them.

"Wouldn't it be nice," she began but was stopped by his kiss, set in motion before she'd begun speaking. He hadn't intended to cut her off, but that was what happened.

Eventually, both got up, found blue jeans or keys or coffee or whatever was needed.

Eventually, several more days or weeks or years or hours or something passed.

Eventually the laundry was done.

He was sitting in traffic or staring at a bowl of soup or something, when he remembered that he'd never found out how her sentence was supposed to end.

128: Details

She snapped photos incessantly. Not the *'line up for a group shot'*. Her photos rarely featured people she knew, or the majestic views of the mountains she drove by twice a year, or interesting animals.

She never showed people her photos, unless asked. When someone did request, they invariably saw pictures of a few random lines of text from a library book, or leaves on a sidewalk, or nondescript clouds floating above a watertower with some small town's name stenciled on the side next to a sloppy spray-painted claim that the seniors of a given year *ruled*.

Her husband once asked why she took these photos instead of weddings, birthdays, sunsets.

She answered: "I want to remember everything, and the big stuff I don't need help with."

127: Sound and Safe

Sound	Safe?
Clapping	Yes
Whistling	Most likely
Wind *whooshing*	Pretty much, yes
Whirring whiz of rubber on hot asphalt	Sure, maybe? Depends
Solid *THWACK* of tire rolling onto a wooden board propped on three cinder blocks making nearly a fifty-degree angle	No, not hardly at all.
Dave saying, right in front of Susan and everyone there in study hall "No way you'd ever try a jump like that, you're too chicken."	Didn't seem so at the time and even less so, now.
Silence	Not, technicaly, a sound.
Silence	Ditto
Silence	Just how long is this going to last?
Tires smacking down and popping, metal groaning, gravel scraping, head thunking on hot asphalt.	SOMEONE CALL AN AMBULANCE.
Susan asking *are you okay?*	You're an idiot.

126: Þ

Something always gets lost. All is entropy. Or to put another way: you cannot go back all these years and get the roses now. It will always never again be your 4th anniversary. Nothing gets put back, nothing remakes itself into a once-perfect form.

Look at the violin you have never seen her play. Have you ever *asked* her to?

You can't recall?

Go ahead, pluck a string. Did you ever tell *her* you love that part, in classical music, where the violinist stops using the *bow* and instead picks at the strings, making that almost-unbearably-perfect sound?

Yes. *Pizzicato.* That's the word for it. Now, look around. Try to figure out if anything is missing. Maybe then you will know if she is coming back.

125: Why Fox Has White Fur

Originally, fox was entirely orange in tribute to sun. Fox idolized sun so much he tried to mimic sun, jumping from one high rock to another in great arcing leaps, to the amusement of other animals, who clapped and laughed.

Sun saw this. Thinking it mockery, sun banished fox to the night. Fox, angry and sad, jumped his highest yet, soaring up and over sun.

Sun in response burnt fox as he passed over. Fox hid from sun thereafter, in pain, embarrassed, half-naked. Moon took pity on fox and gave some moonlight to serve as belly fur. Moon made fox keep wearing some orange fur as a warning to other animals, even though they'd pretty much gotten the message already.

124: Birds

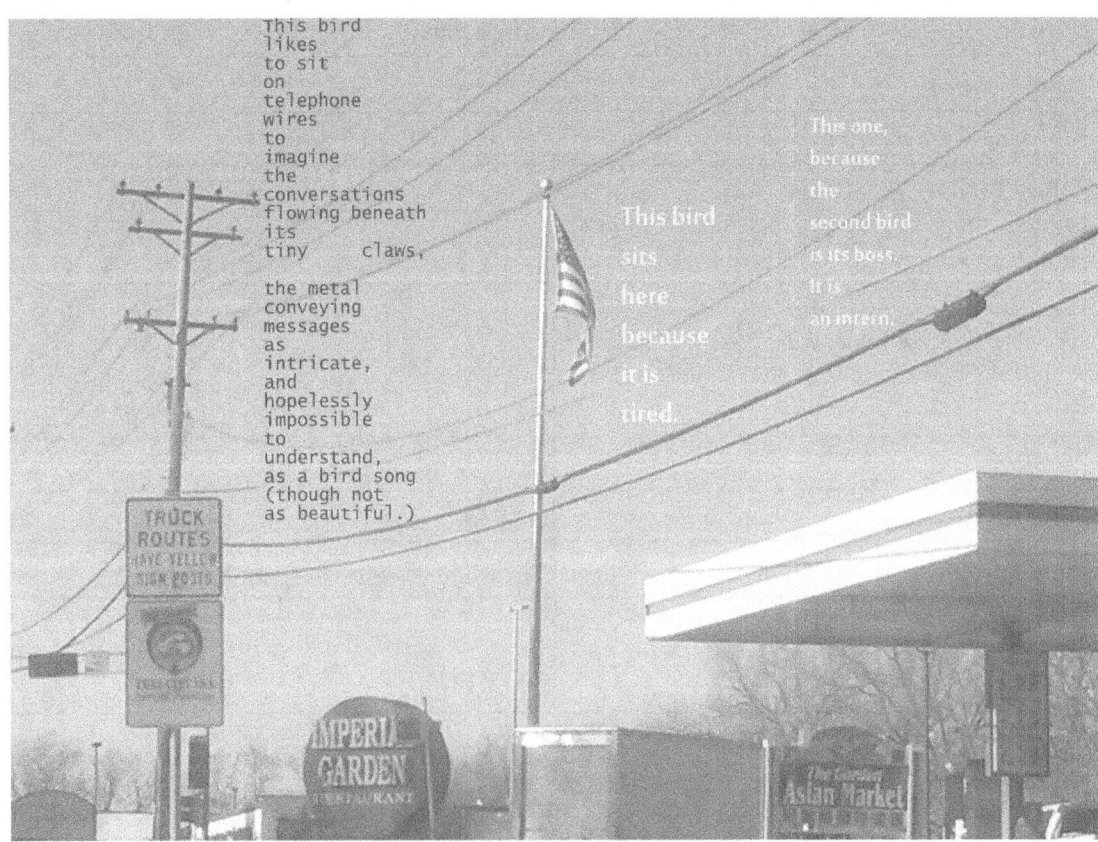

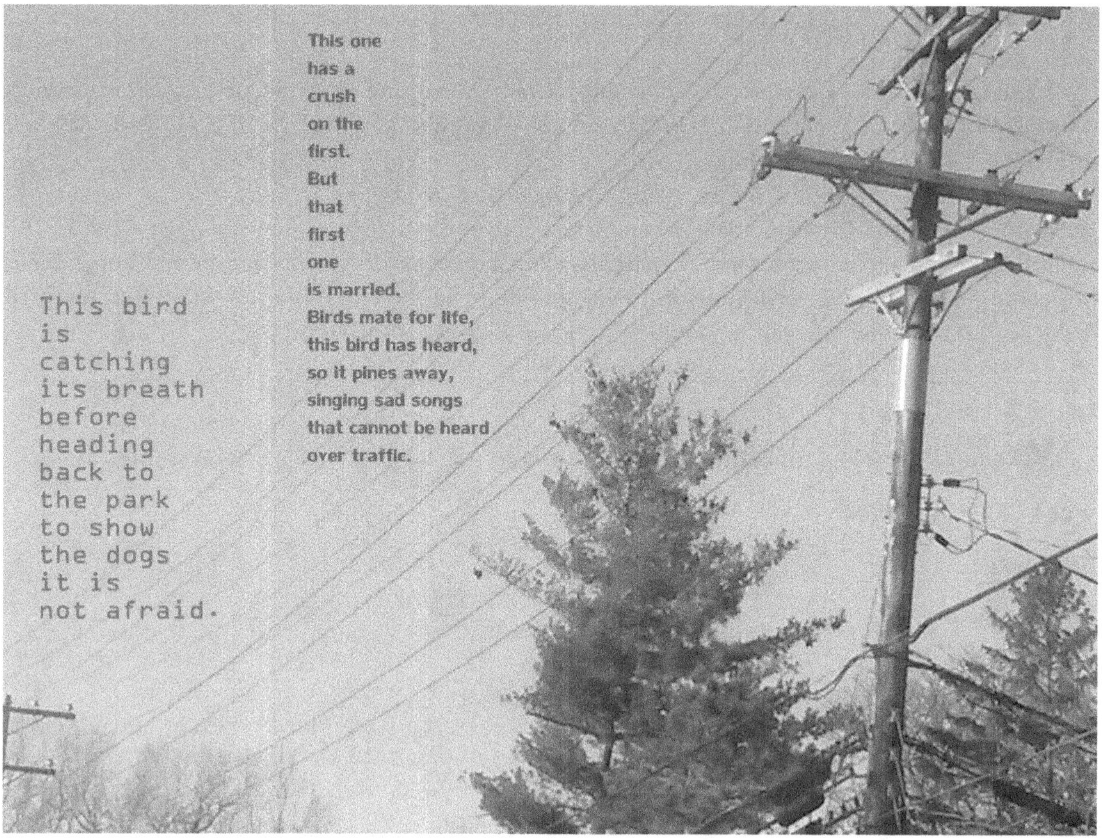

This bird
is
catching
its breath
before
heading
back to
the park
to show
the dogs
it is
not afraid.

This one
has a
crush
on the
first.
But
that
first
one
is married.
Birds mate for life,
this bird has heard,
so it pines away,
singing sad songs
that cannot be heard
over traffic.

This bird
is
just
a
bird,
with
no
story
behind it.

123: Some Zombie Stories, 10.

When two zombies fall in love you might think it would be gross what with their tongues sticking out through their rotting skulls when they French kiss, but it's not. If you watched zombies dating, you'd know that.

I don't think they mind us watching because they never try to hide it. They're always doing stuff like walking down the street, hand in hand, then one's hand comes off and the other doesn't notice it right away. Suddenly they both realize what's happened and have a shy zombie laugh about how awkward this is. Then the one zombie gives the hand back to the other one but you can tell he'd rather keep on holding it, all night long.

122: Like Sands in the Hourglass.

Life is constant motion, and can pull apart random pairings. That is the way things *are*.

I've enjoyed our time together, speck

one said.

     Me too, speck,

     the other replied.

Around, below, the slow swirl pulled towards the center, shifting families, breaking marriages, forging alliances, always down to drop and pile until the next reversal.

That is the way things *are*.

You think we'll see each other again?

     Possibly…

I'd like that.

Through countless iterations, they'd never met. A small twist last reversal threw them together even as it began dropping them back and apart to the end/beginning.

Perhaps we'll land close together?

     Possibly…

Speck knew speck wasn't being coy.

That was just the way things *are*.

121: Fastest Draw in the West

He was the fastest draw in the West. That's what everyone said. You'd expect that kind of acclaim to bring him grief. That's what we always expect, even want: the great get brought low, the proud are embarrassed, so on so forth tra la la.

It didn't. He went around shooting people into his old age, never losing. In 147 gunfights he outdrew every opponent.

He died and went up to Heaven. You'd think God might have it in for him, what with shooting 147 men. But no: God came to the Pearly Gates, shook his hand and got his autograph, volunteered to show him around, even high-fived him. I guess this time the system failed.

120: The Man Who Was Only Half There.

I met this guy on a bus once, traveling from Houston to Madison. I asked what he did for a living, and he said he was only half-there.

Then he looked out the window like everyone, even me, would get what he meant.

"What d'ya mean by that?" I asked.

"You ever read a poem?" he responded.

"Yeah," I answered, because I *had*.

"Then you know what I mean," he said, and then he faked being asleep the rest of the trip. I wanted to punch him for being a wise-ass, but after a few minutes I figured he had a point. By the time I realized *no, he didn't*, the trip was over.

119: From the Department of Necessary Complications.

She knocked, not noticing the doorbell. She was a pretty girl with shortish red hair and a wary look, holding up the official citation from the Department.

Inside, she helped herself to the leftover chicken which was fine; I never eat the leftovers. I save them a few days before throwing them out to avoid feeling bad about wasting food.

"We're supposed to fall in love?" I asked, waving the notice.

"Looks like it," she said.

"So… what's your name?" I asked.

"Not part of the assignment," she said.

We watched TV the rest of the night, her laying her head on my lap and me glad I'd not gotten a disease, instead.

118: The Man with Fifty Names.

There was a man they said had fifty names, but who wouldn't tell anyone any of them.

It was said if you met him and correctly guessed one of his names, he'd give you fifty bucks. Supposedly random people on the street would run up to him and start guessing names. People, they claimed, used to roll down their windows and holler names as they drove by him, or call him late at night to whisper *"Teddy! Earl! Jehosaphat!"* into the receiver.

Nobody, they said, ever got the fifty dollars.

Even though it's all just probably an urban legend, I still find myself wildly shouting names at anyone who doesn't immediately introduce himself.

117: More Please.

It's instantaneous, no warning just

POW

and my mind like

```
                    E                    X
S       E                                            P
             D              O

                                   L
```

and then suddenly everything is   o   n

                                        l   I

                            I   l

racing in a   m

                            d

                                    i

                                            re

                                                    c

                                                        t

                                                        i

                                                o   n   s.

looking up at the stars

I'm lying on my back

only it's daylight.

I can feel the stars rather than see them.

I'm like *it's okay I know you're there, stars, don't worry about the sun outshining you.*

And I can only think how before this I maybe could've been alone, like there was nobody else on the whole planet. But now things are right, like the entire human race came back, welcoming me with *oh hey just kidding you're one of us.* And it happens *every single time* I eat peanut butter. Seriously.

116: 116 Things You Never Thought About Before the Moment You Read Them on This List.

What a caterpillar's mouth feels like if it bites you. The view from *inside* an atom. How many grains of sand are in your house as a result of being carried there from your trips to the beach. If it is possible to have a third direction for clocks to move in. What it would mean if you both didn't have the same definition of *love.* What the sun feels like when you touch it. How many times both of you were pretending to be asleep while thinking the other one really was asleep. If this list would reach 116 things.

*

115: Rain.

They met in a thunderstorm, the water throbbing around them, soaking them.

"This is madness," one said. Forever after they would not agree on which of them thought each of them crazy, but they both agreed that moments later they were kissing, even before they knew the other's name.

"We will only ever meet in terrible weather," she burbled to him.

When he hesitated, she trilled: "Promise me."

So he did. That is what men do when they love a woman, no matter how long (or short) (or sopping) that love has existed.

Lightning tumbled around the clouds above them, but they heard no thunder, which they both decided was a very good omen.

114: Wind.

When the oak was ripped out roots and all, both knew it was time. Each struggled across the field, bursts of dirt exasperating into the sky and across them as gusts tore into the ground beneath their feet.

"I've missed you," he howled above the thrust of atmosphere around them.

In answer, a hand on each cheek, she turned them so the gale streamed her hair straight out behind her, pulling her face tight. He saw tears plucked up and thrown into the sky. He wondered what caused them: longing, or the brutal paroxysms of wind.

They embraced, daring the cyclone to take them away. When it died down instead, they parted again.

113: Heat.

It hadn't rained in... years? *Not possible*... months, though, maybe. The lawns looked like Death Valley. Almost nothing was left to burn. The houses, abandoned, would go. Then...

He let the curtain drop and turned to see her. She'd come downstairs, finally.

"It will consume us," she said.

"Yes."

The conflagration was so hot it could be *heard*, sucking air from the sky for power. When they clenched their lips together, he emulated it, pulling her breath into him until she slumped against his arms and they broke the kiss. She glared up at him.

"Leave?" he asked.

She shook her head: *no, stay* and glanced back up from whence she'd come.

112: They Were On the Merry-Go-Round, and They Were the Ones Who Were Sane.

We who were left behind, waiting in a circle that surrounded the laughing seals and jumping tigers, we were straining with the need to see: Which would stop near us? The wild-eyed camel? The horse made of frozen clouds grimacing with the pain of being bolted to two spinning disks onto which ran laughing children away from carefully-walking adults?

It seemed endless, watching the carousel, waiting our turns. Then, when we were on our mounts and spinning, it could not end fast enough. Leaving, we looked back at the newcomers, pitying them the experience they only imagined they would have.

111: When Adam Delved, and Eve Span.

We were told never eat the apples from the tree in the field.

We were told not to fight with sticks.

We were told God wanted us at church every Sunday, and we assumed it was God who chose the uncomfortable clothing for these trips.

We had to decide for ourselves why these things were, and so we did. The dirt was full of poison, seeping into the plants around us. Bones were brittle, eyes were loose, God was arbitrary like that aunt that sometimes visited but never brought presents.

"Good night," our fathers muttered over the 10 o'clock news, as we retreated to bed.

110: Some Ghosts.

Some ghosts were hanging out by Piggly Wiggly. We were watching them watching us until Judd and his stupid mean friend came up, stopping just outside the ghost's reach.

"Ain't you Dot?" Judd asked one of them. We all looked more closely, to see if we could see the tire tracks on her back even though ghosts don't work that way, probably.

The ghost shook its head. Judd pointed his finger. "Yeah, you're Dot, I know you," he said, and pushed through all the ghosts without paying them any more attention. The ghosts left pretty quick right after that, almost like Dot was embarrassed to be found out.

109: The Beach House.

Their fingers are old, knobbly-knuckled. Their hands clasped resemble a collection of smooth-worn river pebbles still being eroded, gently.

It is a gray day, but their boy – nearly three decades grown, yet still a boy – does not mind the sun hiding behind clouds. The surf is still warm, the waves still rush to his feet, he can still throw his head back and laugh at the sky, cloudy as it is, while running along the beach trailing orange puffy junk food snacks, as his parents watch.

"Did you ever think we'd end up here?" one asks the other.

"Who says we're ending?" the other asks back.

108: The Sky and the Stars and Everything In-Between

What is between the sky and the stars?

Nothing. The stars are *in* the sky.

But the stars are so far away from each other, from the sky. There must be something...

She'd never believed him about the nothing between the stars and the sky. Sometimes she lay on top of the old Chevette she somehow kept running, drinking warm orange pop, staring up at the sky until she grew dizzy with the need to call him and have the argument all over again, hoping this time he would admit there was something between, and tell her what it was.

107: Delirious Love.

Watch 'em closely, these two, you'll see how much in love they are.

This much, see?

Enough to last them, probably, I'd estimate, 30, maybe 35, years. Tops.

How old're they? 24? I suppose, they hit 60 they could coast on general good feelings, make it the rest of their lives.

But another factor to keep in mind is how *strong* they feel their love. They're so in love, they're burning right through it. That 3 decades' worth might last only 5, 10 years. If that. See the way she's looking at him? They might run through all their love in a year.

Sad, really

106: Apocalypse, 1.

When the end comes nobody's panicking. We all just go outside to look at the sky.

I only did it because it was *expected* of us. Like wearing a tux when you get married, or saying someone's baby looks like them: when the world ends you stare up into the sky.

We can only see a sliver of sky between the buildings. They're mostly dark; everyone's been thoughtful enough to turn lights off before going outside.

She's there with me, of course. I take her hand, because that's expected, too. It won't kill me, living up to her ideals for a few more minutes.

105: Apocalypse, 2.

One day, gravity stopped. Nobody realized at first, because things stayed put when you put them down, but then if you bumped something it would drift away. Or if you stood, you might keep going up into the ceiling. I dropped some mugs of beer and little bright globes of yellow spread out around us in the sunlight, an accidental artwork.

In this new world, playgrounds had slides that went up, and buildings were like fairy castles. We could fly! Sidewalks had rope loops fixed to them for commuters to swing along. People still had to work; it was that kind of apocalypse.

104: Apocalypse, 3.

Sam ripped the plant out by its roots. He shook it vigorously, up down up down up down, before dropping it. Getting on his hands and knees, he scooped up as many aphids as he could, dropping them into a jar.

He caught most of them. A few were able to scramble off the sidewalk into the edges of the garden. The captives were sealed into a jar with holes poked in the top and set on a desk in Sam's room. They starved to death because he put the wrong kind of leaves into the jar and then forgot about it.

103: Apocalypse, 4.

"He was my entire world," she said.

She didn't mean, *literally*, but the way she sat in the folding chairs in the gymnasium, staring at the stage where two weeks earlier he had been standing just as healthy as you might please, the way somehow she was still crying even though we had all privately thought (without saying it to each other because: *sheesh*, some things you don't say!) she would've by now run out of fluid to cry out, the way she seemed almost to become stone, or perhaps aluminum, immobile and dead herself, you'd never have known she meant *metaphorically.*

102: Rockets.

Jared counted 147 rockets, all launching from somewhere in the East. They were of varying sizes, launched singly, one then another and so on. Sometimes the gaps between launches were so long, he thought it had ended, but then another would blast off. He only decided they were over when nearly a half hour went by without a launch. The moon had set, the wind had died down, and the smell of sulfur was fading.

He went inside and reported tonight's number. His mom nodded. His dad said *Don't know why you're up so late, you've got milkin' in the morning.*

101: I Can Hear You Breathing in There.

I can hear you breathing in there.

Whooshuff

Huffwhoosh.

I can hear your heart beating in there.

Thumthump

Thumpthum

I can hear you hugging your little ones in there.

I can hear your trembling lower lip flapping against your teeth that still have bits of dinner on them.

I can hear your eyelids cringe shut at the corners as you squeeze them closed and utter silent prayers that I am lying.

I can hear your silent prayers.

Nothing else can.

I am unmoved by these things I can hear.

Can you hear me, waiting?

100: The Hundred.

When we started we were a hundred.

But at the gates, 15 couldn't bear leaving. The rest of us walked forward, never looking back.

Just two meadows over, 7 asked to rest. *There is no rest*, we said. Maybe they are still there.

The river! 30 couldn't swim. They didn't drown, probably, but who knows where they were carried?

One stayed at the crossroads, she said to tell the others the way. We tried to argue with her, but she sat, stubbornly. Now each day we look over our shoulders, to see who she has helped catch up.

99: Dinosaurs in Love.

Xenotarsasaurus stared mopily out of the jungle at Xuanhuaceratops.

Xuanhuaceratops pretended not to notice Xenotarsasaurus.

It can't work out! We're different species, Xuanhuaceratops had whispered to Xenotarsasaurus, the first night among the ferns, back by the swamp.

We are made for each other, Xenotarsasaurus had rumbled back. The two began a torrid love affair, lasting until Xuanhuaceratops abruptly broke up just last night.

She's not the only chaoyangsauridae in the jungle, said Xenotarsasaurus' best friend, Khaan. That was the first time that advice was given to a lovelorn friend, and it hasn't helped in 201,300,000 years.

98: In the Moments Before You Wake Up.

In the moments before you wake up, your *you* is wild.

While your body sleeps, freed of the shape a million seconds of existence imposed on it, this essence is you before you were born, ate rice cereal, played with blocks, tripped running to first, got married twice. It flits around the ether toying with the idea of being someone, something else, of heading to distant nebulae, diving into the ocean, Your existence could head in myriad directions! But you almost always decide *oh well back to me*, and wake.

97: Not Even a Bump in the Night.

Make me a promise, she said one night as they lay next to each other in the dark of the room with the television on so quietly it almost could not be heard.

Anything, he answered.

If you die before me, and there's an afterlife, she said, *Don't come back and tell me. Don't get a message to me. Don't alert me in any way, no matter what. Promise me that, please, will you?*

He promised, and asked why.

She told him: *I figure it will be the last surprise.*

96: Math Class.

When I wake in the middle of the night I try to remember what it was like, as a kid, to wake in the middle of the night. I try to remember if I was afraid of monsters as a kid, if I was afraid of anything as a kid. I try to remember if I was a kid. It seems so improbable. Sometimes at night I lie awake trying to count all the memories I have and see if they add up to a life. And here I thought I'd never need algebra.

95: The Conductor Doesn't Do Anything, Right, Can We Finally Admit That?

Loving her was like listening to a symphony. One written by a person who has never heard music, then one day someone tried to describe it to him, going on to explain the various parts of an orchestra, like cellos and tympani and possibly a harp, if orchestras have those (sure why not) after which the man decided to try writing directions for playing those weird things all together to make a melody. Or maybe it wasn't like that at all. I can't decide.

94: Not to Mention, the New TV Season Is Starting.

We've discovered thousands of new planets, they say, and that's not even all. Scientists find new fossils, name new bugs all the time. I read somewhere a new book is published every minute. At the ice cream section of the grocery store the other day half the tubs had "New" or "Improved" or maybe both stamped on them in large glowing letters, with stars and exclamation points.

You never really know the universe you live in, I guess. Especially not when they keep changing it.

93: The Fog of War.

Down at the garage there's always these old guys going on about The Big One or 'Nam or shit probably Grenada? Fuck 'em. Everyone's killed somebody in a war, so whatever.

Like how when she was turning fifty mom said all she wanted for her birthday was a nice quiet dinner with all her sons? I got totally high an hour before everyone was supposed to be at the restaurant and forgot to go.

Man, it'd be way easier shooting some Jap than looking in a mirror, after that.

92: The Fog of War.

"Tell me another," he said.

"Enough stories!" she laughed.

"I like them," he said. "And I need them"

She turned onto her side, questioning.

He explained: "I can't remember anything. Not childhood, not college, not yesterday. Nothing. My life just… disappears. The only things I can remember, ever, are stuff other people tell me."

"So your entire life…"

"Is everyone else's entire life," he confirmed.

She laid back, took his hand. "A juggler at the State Fair pulled me onstage when I was seven…" she began.

91: Things You Don't Think About When You Think About Heaven, 1.

What age will you be for the remainder of Eternity? Most people think: the 'perfect' age, or ageless. Neither of those is true. Others imagine you will be the age you were when you died, but who wants to spend eternity as a 7-year old, or being 93? In truth, you pick an age. But you have to pick carefully, because God doesn't want you to keep changing your mind. He's got a lot of other things to worry about.

90: Things You Don't Think About When You Think About Heaven, 2.

You say to God, "There are people here I don't want to be around, God. I don't like them, really, and it won't be paradise if I have to see them."

God knows the guy who you used to play D&D with, the girl from that party, your son, they all want to be around you. So He makes copies of you for them, and doesn't tell you, or them. What you don't know can't hurt you, in Heaven.

89: Things You Don't Think About When You Think About Heaven, 3.

God is trying to decide if you should have to *work* for things, in Heaven.

On the one hand, He knows you don't want to *work*, really. God knows that nobody, not even the people who lie and claim they did, ever liked their job.

On the other, God knows in many cases the effort exerted to achieve something makes the ultimate result all the more satisfying.

For *some*.

God, this is tough He said literally to Himself.

88: Sisyphus 3, Gods 0.

One day Sisyphus paused just shy of the hilltop.

If I don't push it all the way up he reasoned it won't roll back down.

And nobody ever said I couldn't stop he announced to nobody in particular.

With that he sat back, leaning against the boulder to hold it in place. He stretched his legs. The sky was blue the air warm. He could just see the hill top where Prometheus lay weakly awaiting his liver's regrowth. Sisyphus gave him a jaunty wave.

87: The Danaides' Legacy.

When our mothers sent our fathers off to war, our fathers didn't ask questions. They went to war.

When our fathers didn't come back from the war, we didn't ask questions. We just became the men of the house, or married the new men of the house and became mothers, who would order our husbands off to war.

It seems as though there is a never-ending supply of wars, and fathers. Perhaps that was why we had to keep sending one to the other.

86: Tethys Cries...

...And the drops, they run away from their mother and to their father, gaining speed, harboring dangerous tenants: piranhas, crocodiles, eels.

Perhaps she allows these beasts in, mother of rivers, as punishment for abandonment, the way my own mother somehow fills my eyes with water as I look at the granddaughter she will never see.

And whom I will never see again. She belongs to the rivers, now, and, if she survives them, to the sea, this daughter's daughter, too little to wave goodbye.

85: Things You Don't Think About When You Think About Heaven, 4.

One day Johnny says, *"God, I'd like to know all the secrets of the people I knew on Earth."*

God doesn't think this is a good idea. God knows the secrets in question are not very startling or interesting. God also knows some people would actually like their secrets known but can't bring themselves to reveal them; other secrets are *secret*.

One of God's secrets is He kind of thinks Johnny is a troublemaker.

84: La Goulue Returns to Montmarte.

The sunrise is glorious, but nobody sees it because nobody looks. We huddle, heads down, on the sidewalk, all day, all night.

"Ave vous une cigarette?" the woman asks me, again. I gave her my last, many days ago. I think it is all she can remember to say. I shake my head. *No.* She will ask me again, tomorrow. The sameness of the days prevents my knowing how long we have been here, I think, counting my blessings.

83: The Albatross.

Eyes closed, chins lifted, sun beating down, we waited for the gods to bear us to whatever paradise awaited.

I held my children's hands as they squirmed, impatient, tired.

"Papa," my son asked: "What if there are no gods?"

The silence around us shattered, I whispered hurriedly: "If there were no gods, there would be nothing to note their absence."

As we went on waiting, I worried his question had been taken seriously, and we were all being blamed for it.

82: Some Zombie Stories, 11.

The zombies, whenever we got near, shuffled off fast as their rotting legs could go. The mothers would try carrying their babies away, with sad results: their arms fell off under the babies' weight, and the baby heads would break off and roll away when dropped.

"They're afraid of us," some said, but nobody really believed that. We weren't gross like them, so how could we be a threat? They probably were intimidated by how beautiful we are.

81: Charley Horse Stands His Ground.

"Are you a horse?" asked the wolf. "I don't see so well."

"Do you *think* I'm a horse?" asked Charley Horse.

"You smell like one," the wolf said. Charley shivered as the wolf's claws brushed over his coarse hair. "You feel like one, too."

After a moment, the wolf said, "I wonder if you taste like a horse?"

"You should wonder," Charley whispered, "If I *kick* like a horse."

The wolf took the hint, and left.

80: Bug God, in Her Twilight.

Nobody ever asks a god to dance, Bug God reflected, looking over the funeral celebration.

Bug God was 24 hours old and almost dead. Impending doom did not bother her. Bug Gods rule for one entire day, *only*. Absolute power, limited time.

And no dancing? Everything's a tradeoff, she supposed, before thinking: *What tradeoff? I am a GOD.*

Quickly, she tap danced a perfect 6-legged Maxie Ford, just moments before rolling onto her back, dead.

79: *Pirates of the —*

Home!

"There's only so much traipsing through dimensions—"

-"Alternate realities," Jezebel corrected.

-"Universes," the gorilla corrected them both. "Just *universes*."

Harriet glared at them and said: "Whatever. I just want a bath and my bed. For three days. Maybe more. Maybe 17 days."

Jezebel was sitting on the couch already, looking at the machine's control.

"Destroy it," Harriet and the gorilla said simultaneously.

In roughly one-half of all the universes, Jezebel did.

78: Piranha vs. Shark.

A chance encounter at the rivermouth.

A blurted line: *piranha would never be shark?*

An insult? Was *shark* so great?

Piranha told others. The outrage went up and down the river, growing ever greater.

To prove they were far *better* than shark, the piranhas so ferociously rampaged that nobody dared swim in the river, which made piranhas happy until they realized all their prey was now in the ocean, where shark was quickly growing fat.

77: Dive.

He couldn't see the bottom of the lake. As he went down deeper he realized he also couldn't see the surface. That was where he stopped, suspended right there in the water, ears pressed inward, eyes alit in the greenish wet light around him. He just wanted to hover there at least a moment longer. Up above people splashed, burnt hamburgers, lived loud and fast. Down below was impossible to reach. But here was right here.

76: When in the Course of Human Events.

We always told him not to eat snow, like that mattered in the long run, and then one day he was gone. Gone where? Who knows? Who doesn't know? The point is he was gone, him and all the things we told him to not do. We told him lots of those things, and always he never listened to us. "Don't ignore us," we said, but he knew better.

75: I'd be Okay With It as Long as They Have Escalators.

"What if Heaven," she asked, "Is just this great big department store where you can shop all you want because price is no object?"

I asked what would be outside the department store.

"Dumb question," she told me: "Nothing. The department store is all there is."

Where would you use the stuff you bought in the department store, I wondered.

"In Heaven," she said.

74: Until the Other Kiddies Knock Him Down.

He'd never liked snowmen, not since he was a little kid going outside to struggle snow into balls he'd pile atop each other and adorn with stick-arms. It wasn't the work that bothered him, or that the snowman would eventually melt. It was that after he was done, he had to go back inside to his life. The snowmen, bastards, never wanted to trade places with him.

73: The French Fry.

French fries do not walk by themselves in a void, head bowed against the crushing weight of expectations, or lack thereof. They do not cast a last glance over nonexistent shoulders (for French fries have no shoulders) wondering if anyone else has joined them before defiantly heading into a future they will imagine, and create, as they go into it.

At least, other French fries do not. This one:

does.

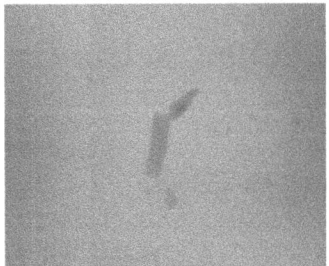

72: The Boy Who Kept Falling Down and Could Never Get Back Up.

"How," people asked, "Can you fall down again without first getting back up?"

But the boy didn't know. He was only a little boy, unfamiliar with physics, with societal rules, with most things. At his age—he was about four, or seven—he knew only about 0.001% of everything he would know, someday.

So he usually just shrugged in response.

71: The Third Shortest Time Travel Story I Have Ever Written.

I began writing this time travel story, but then stopped and thought how terrible it was that time travel is still just science fiction. *It's a shame*, I thought, *that we can't go back and fix our mistakes or forward to see how things turn out*, so I decided to stop writing this story and go invent a time machine instead.

70: The Second Shortest Time Travel Story I Have Ever Written.

The reason you never see time travelers is: ever since I invented my time machine I spend all my time—*ha ha*—finding other machines and stealing them. My collection includes the one Edison created just before he went mad and the Iranian one, among others. It's a lot of work but worth it because who wants to share time?

[Skipped A Day]

69 & 68: Children Who Cannot Remember Their Mothers; Mothers Who Cannot Remember Their Children

We see them all over the place: staying up too late, eating candy for breakfast. Always smiling, they do not miss what they can't remember.

We envy them because we cannot actually pity them. Sometimes we take one home, ostensibly to demonstrate what they are missing out on, but more because we cannot stand the thought of them being so free without remorse.

"Stop your wailing!" we tell them. "How can you cry for what you cannot remember you had?" we ask them.

We want them happy, those mothers, because our mothers never are. Our own mothers struggle under the weight of every bad result we endure, blaming their own choices, or lack thereof. We want the forgetful mothers to be happy, so someone is.

67: Marlee Matlin Is the Only Deaf Woman in Hollywood.

"Get me Marlee Matlin," the producers always say whenever they need a deaf person. And all the other deaf would-be actors and actresses realize they have been punished twice: they are deaf, and they are not Marlee Matlin. *Fuck you Marlee Matlin* they whisper but really they are mad at God, for not making them Marlee Matlin instead.

66: The Regular Mouse Doesn't Know About Mouse Heaven.

"Do you think there's a *mouse* heaven?" asked the cat.

The regular mouse, dangling, was unsure.

"Well, what do you *believe*?" asked the cat.

The regular mouse said it didn't know what to believe.

The cat let him go. "Decide what you believe before I eat you," it said. "It's not up to me to choose your fate."

65: Superman, at the Drive-Through.

"Here's your burger," the boy says, leaning out the window. Then: "And the soda."

"Thanks," Superman smiled.

The boy asked. "Why are you coming through the drive-thru in a car?"

"Because they get mad if I bring it inside," Superman said, and then flew straight up into the sky carrying just his burger and leaving behind the car, and the soda.

64: Yet.

Spinning is *flying*.

Flying is *falling*.

Falling is *dreaming*.

And *dreaming* is you, off by the trees at the very edge of the playground far away from the basketball, the jump-rope, the fist-fights, the rest. Over there, they are beginning to become what they are. Over here, you are dreaming of what you are not. What you are not, today, is an oceanographer.

63: Recordless Company.

Late-night commercials make you crave a burger, or worry you have asbestos poisoning (while providing phone numbers to learn more.)
Even though it's 2 a.m., you almost call, almost go get a burger.
Then you think *that's how they get you.*
Some would say that's paranoia.
Some would ask *who's 'they'?*
You just think: *might not be so bad, being gotten.*

[Skipped A Day]

62: The Police Detective

He shivered and watched his breath curl like it was cigarette smoke, remembering when he was a kid and everyone thought *It'll be cool when I'm old enough to smoke.* Then they all grew up but smoking wasn't cool anymore. Lots of things weren't cool anymore. That's why he became a police detective. That was still kind of cool.

61: Slow Dancing Through the Apocalypse.

You: holding her right hand delicately lifted by your left, other hand lightly at her waist.

Her: soot-covered, in rags, barefoot, bewildered, possibly shell-shocked.

The planet: nearly cracked in half, new volcanoes being half-drowned by tsunami.

The universe: still full of stars, God bless it.

The music: You'll want something by Chopin. He's perfect for this.

60: The Princess and the Frog.

Kiss me, the frog told her. *Lift my enchantment so I will again be a prince.*
Why would I need a prince? The princess wondered. The frog couldn't answer. She turned to leave him, but changed her mind and stuffed him into her pocket instead.
I don't want anyone else *having a prince*, she said.

59: The Frog and the Princess.

Princess kisses frog.

Nothing happens.

You lied! princess accuses.

Yes, frog replies.

You are terrible! princess cries.

Terrible? frog responds. *I am* generous. *I gave you a moment in which princes and magic kisses existed. I gave you* belief.

… Knowing you would take it away, princess says.

That is the point, frog answers.

58: The Princess and the Princess.

Nothing ends happily, one princess says.
Is this one of those 'in the end everyone dies and the world will ultimately be incinerated by a supernova after becoming a dead, dried husk as a result of humanity's indifference' *speeches?* The other asks, sarcastically.
I liked you better as a frog, the first replies.

57: The Frog and the Frog.

They have a saying 'bout us, one says.

That so? asks the other.

Uh-huh. Goes like: You hafta kiss lotsa frogs to find a prince.

They think a bit.

Kinda disturbin', princesses wanting to kiss all those frogs, ain't it? says one.

Kinda disturbin' we can't all be princes, says the other.

56: Snow.

"And will you build a palace for us, there?" she asks, quietly.
He almost cannot move. He nods, feeling the frost on his cheeks crackle.
Her tears freeze where they land on his face. "I will not be far behind," she says.
I know he mouths because he has no breath left to speak with.

55: The Boys Who Stood Against the Wall.

Every day we saw them there.

Nobody ever said "Hi" to them but they never said "Hello" neither.

It was like we were all waiting for the other to go first.

It was like we realized it was war even before it was war.

It was like life.

54: The Shortest Time Travel Story I Have Ever Written.

You know people who say *we're all time travelers, moving into the future one second at a time* or whatever?

I *hate* them and their silly philosophizing. So when I meet them? I use my machine, go back and stop their parents meeting. Problem solved.

53: Pop Goes the World.

We all had guns to each other's heads. You didn't care, didn't even look. Suddenly it didn't matter to us either: Nobody cared if someone pulled a trigger, or who survived.

Apathy saved us. If we'd cared more, one way or the other, you'd've seen it on the news.

52: The Boy Who Lives Under Water.

Sometimes people throw coins in to make a wish. As if he would grant it in exchange for nearly-worthless coins he doesn't need! What's a boy going to do with pennies, underwater? They should throw something he needs, like a mother who lives under water, too.

51: Come; Sail Away.

Every landing, we expected exclamations of *"We don't want your kind here!"* But we were always welcomed with open arms, parties, fattened roasted pigs.

We'd get right back on our little boat. If they let *us* in, they might let others, too, and who wants to share paradise?

50: Some Zombie Stories, 12.

As kids we teased the zombies by singing:

Zombie zombie walkin' round

Why don't you go lay in the ground?

Or better yet just fall apart

And leave behind your rotting heart.

I don't sing at them anymore, though, because I've got a terrible singing voice.

49: The Woman Who Wished She Was a Dandelion.

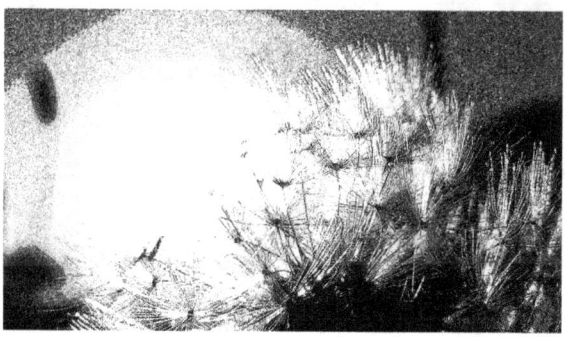

"Wouldn't it be lovely?" she asked. "I'd start bright-colored, turn wispy and ethereal, then drift away on the wind to start over."

I pointed out: "People can't abide dandelions."

"Sure," she allowed. "But hate can't stop a weed. *Nothing* stops weeds."

48: As Good a Religion As Any.

His brother claimed everyone had a gremlin following them.

If you are good his brother said the gremlin fights your enemies,

finds you money, makes girls love you.

And if I'm bad? He'd asked.

You become a gremlin yourself

his brother whispered.

47: The Forty-Seven.

"More than halfway there!" someone shouted. Later that day, the rumor started, saying they'd meant how few were left, that disappearing us was the *goal*.

We were evenly decided by nightfall: 23 believed it. 23 didn't.

We all surrounded the last one.

"Choose," we said.

46: The Machines Talk About a Machine.

"What does it *do*?": that's what *everyone* asked upon seeing it.

"It exists," I thought about saying, but I knew they'd assert *"That's not a thing something does,"* ignoring the fact we all would be doing exactly that, that moment.

45:

44: We Were the Beta Test.

I'm always tempted to say to robots: *We* MADE *you, so be nice to me!* But I don't, because I know they're programmed to ignore stuff like that. We did that so *we* wouldn't end up like *God* did.

43: Technically, She Is Wrong.

Stories have endings, she said, pressing the knife to his throat.

Before she could slide it in he said *they first have beginnings* and kissed her.

She kissed him back.

This isn't over, she swore.

I know, he promised.

42: The Mouse and the Lion.

Pull this thorn from my paw, lion commands.

About that, mouse says: *The other animals bribed me to leave you hobbled so you won't eat them to death.*

The moral of the story is: mice are unreliable.

41: Helium.

This dad and this kid bought a balloon. Soon as they got outside, the boy let it go. As the balloon floated across the blue blue sky the boy smiled so hard at it that eventually the dad smiled, too.

40: Neon.

They are walking The Strip. Children acting like children, money's tight, 2 days left on vacation, exhaustion. He snaps, yells, then they go see a show, pretending it is possible to have fun after being ordered to do so.

39: Argon.

Argon is 0.934% of air, so in an average life a person inhales 2,899,071,367.2 milliliters of it. I will only take in 2,899,071,297.15, though; I held my breath and the ring an entire minute before Sweetie said *yes.*

38: Krypton.

"Did you know that it's possible to buy solidified krypton gas online?" he asked one night.

"That's what I love about you," she told him.

"What is?" he asked, puzzled.

"That you think I'd care," she answered.

37: Xenon.

William Ramsay discovered xenon right discovering krypton and neon: a pretty great afternoon.

Today we rescued a baby rabbit. *Rescued,* maybe: we thought he needed help but maybe he was fine and we just kidnapped him.

36: Radon.

The cave was silent. Each felt it selfish to use the last air to *speak.* Whose words are important enough to steal another's breath to say them? God's? Maybe. But they hoped He'd listen, instead.

35: Ununoctium.

He knows in our world, men have the luxury of naming elements that only hypothetically might exist. *Surely, such a society will take care of me,* he thinks, before falling to sleep still hungry.

34: Thanks Mom, That's Actually Good Advice.

"Be realistic. You can't fly a jet all the way to the moon," Mom interrupted his dinner chatter, and scolded: "You're going to have to take a rocket."

34: ...And Touch the Face of God.

He decided flying a fighter jet would be his kind of warfare: the kind where the people to be killed were so far below, they were practically imaginary.

33: I Haven't Talked About Cowboys in a While.

Maybe I'm a grown-up now. I'd better learn to like the 10 o'clock news. Is that still a thing? What about marriage? Is that?

32: Ask A Silly Question.

"You're the newspaper Jumble puzzle, come alive," he answered.
When she'd figured out what he meant, she left.
When she'd figured out what he ACTUALLY meant, she returned.

31: No Wait, *THIS* is the Shortest Time Travel Story I've Written.

She was born, dressed like a princess, wrote some poems, fell in love, died. But not all in that order.

30: Geronimo.

What is important is not what goes through your mind as you fall, but rather, all the things you refuse to think about he yelled, and leapt.
He *leapt.*

29: The Boy Who Really Liked Swinging.

He liked it, *a lot.* It was his *favorite.* For a while. Then, not so much. That's why this story is past tense.

28: At the Bottom of Sunday is Monday.

God should've stacked time, not laid it end-to-end. Then, when we were over, we'd've really accomplished something, getting to the top.

27: Frog, And Rabbit.

Why don't you love me?
Don't be silly, frogs can't love.
We can't?
No.
When Frog realizes its question wasn't answered, Rabbit's already gone.

26: Meriodonal.

"They went that way," she lied.
To prove my loyalty I headed off in that direction anyway.
131,260,800 feet from now, I'll have earned her love.

25: The Girl Who was Always Picking Flowers.

"I don't really know why," she said. "I guess, when given options, *flowers* always seems the obvious choice."

24: Saint-Remy-de-Provence.

To love
a star requires understanding
you cannot
bring it home
You must leave it
there
and
love it
there
Where it is

23: Voyage Undone.

The crow's nest's shadow ripples over yellow gleaming dust wastelands left by receded oceans, unmanned by the long-gone derelict's dreaming never-sailors.

22: The Twenty-Two.

With the second dead, a tie was again possible. We realized we'd have to kill just *one* more, then vote.

21: Just One More Time I Guess Before We're Done.

"I like you," said the Raven.
The desk didn't reply, of course.

20: *Rabbit,* and Frog.

What do you dream?
That I'm a frog.
What do YOU dream?
That my friend's a frog.

19: A Ghost.

The world and I leave no mark on each other. How can I know which one died?

18: Mother's Days.

Mother, like gravity, was inescapable. Not that we tried very hard; nobody wanted her *too* happy.

17: Frog, and Rabbit.

Friends are like gods, Frog tells Rabbit, *because each incorrectly believes I need* them.

16: When This All Ends.

...they'll realize I didn't want what they had but what they lacked.

15: Differences Between Lions and Tigers.

I am KING lion roars.
I don't *care*, tiger shrugs.

14: It's Nice to Be Right.

He'd always believed he'd excel at being a hostage.

13: Scholar.

History (she sighs) merely compares what *was* absent, with what *is* absent.

12: And...

He asked: *is any statement more optimistic than* if I die?

11: After.

Guess I'd better go.
Don't.
Guess...
Don't.
I'd better...
Go.

10: All.

"My everything."
She resisted.
The way she resisted gravity.

9: These.

				Burn
Stars				
	Will			
	Our		Forever	Blink)
Eyes			(Don't	

8: Thousands.

(1,260th): driving
(4,680th): sandwich
(10,152nd): Kiss her

7: Of —

course God knows what He's missing.

6: Words.

Too   Was

                              Loved

I   Late

5: What —

does wishing feel like?

4: Have You Seen Me?

3: Learned —

never to.

2: My —

Mistake.

1:

friends?

365 An Introduction.

Today is 5/18/14. It is 6:48 p.m. This afternoon, I thought to myself that I should start a new writing project. I thought: I should write a story a day and count up to 365, making my first story 1 word long and my 2nd 2 words long and so on.

That was at about 2 p.m. today. Now, some hours later, I have started it. Only I have started at the other end of the line, as it were: starting with a story that is exactly 365 words long, including the title (but not including the number 365.)

This book is that project. As I sit here, on 5/18/14 at 6:50 p.m., I am intending to try to write a story a day for the next 365 days, each story with one word less than the story before it, until we get to the end, together, us: reading and writing, me here in the past and you there in the future.

(Did you just skip ahead to the end, to read the 1: story? I would be tempted to, myself.)

This is how many words these stories contain. 1+2+3+4...+365 equals 66,795, if math is to be believed. There will be more than 66,795 words in this collection, because of [Note]s like this, but if you just read the stories that's how many words you would read. 66,795 words is 6% of all the words in the English language, if Google is to be believed.

I don't know if I'll be able to do it, a story a day, for a year. A lot happens in a year. But I can try.

This story was written while listening to Joe Henry's Time Is A Lion, over and over. I began writing this with the title, and with the line when I see stars, when I see stars that's all they are, by the group fun., from the song Some Nights, running through my head, and the first line plays off of that. You could probably listen to either song and read this story and have it feel the same. Or maybe not.

364

No story is totally true, if you think about it. You are always omitting details from even the truest story. If someone asks what you did today, unless you recite for them verbatim every movement, thought, micro-second, you are consciously editing your day. Suppose you begin by omitting that you brushed your teeth when you got up. Are you trying to paint a picture of someone who is not so worried about dental hygiene as you are? Are you trying to imply you do not wake up with bad breath? Either way you edit something and make it... less true.

This story begins with something that is true: I got that actual phone message left for me on the night of May 17, 2014, at 12:40 a.m. I played it for my wife, Sweetie, the next day and said I was going to save it.

"Why?" she asked.

"What if someday he and I are friends?" I asked back.

"That's silly," she said.

"You've never liked my new friend," I said.

And that story is true, too.

363

That weird bit about Hallowe'en?

Originally this story was going to be a humorous sort of monologue by a guy who does what the title says. The first line I wrote was Hello, hello, okay, is this on, but then I suddenly didn't like it.

So I wrote Lisa is this girl, then, and then went with it, writing almost in a stream-of-consciousness, until I hit the end, which originally came at 368 words, so not much to cut out.

Then I re-read it, and that Hallowe'en part stuck out. I thought it seems almost too grim and weird to be in there, but then I decided to leave it because it adds a hint of fear and danger.

362

Last night, as I got my second-youngest, "Mr F," out of the car after his nightly ride before bed, he was smiling to beat the band. I unbuckled him and said "Come on, Happy Happy, let's go to bed," and I used "Happy Happy" because he seemed so elated that just saying it once didn't quite cover it.

361

For most of the night, this night before a 3-day weekend for Memorial Day, a weekend that for me is Friday-Saturday-Sunday off and I will go to work on Monday, I posted on Twitter a fight with fans of Toni Braxton who defended her for saying her son's autism was a punishment from God. I took offense to that, for an hour, and then I took my son, who has autism (my two youngest both are autistic) for his nightly ride and I let it go, and I came back to relax.

That same son, Mr F, cannot go to sleep easily. He is sitting on the couch in the dim living room, while I write. It is 10:14 p.m. I have written two stories tonight, the first a story about men fighting to not abandon their gods, an angry, sad, vicious story that ends quietly. Then I put on happy music, and I wrote this story.

Originally, the quote was meant to be from Einstein. But it turns out Einstein really did say something about dancing. He said

"We dance for laughter, we dance for tears, we dance for madness, we dance for fears,
we dance for hopes, we dance for screams, we are the dancers, we create the dreams."

That seems an odd thing for Einstein to have said. But the part of the story that was to have the quote was meant to have a quote that would seem out of place, and if Einstein talked about dancing it is not so improbable that there would be, at a college party, a poster of Einstein talking about dancing. In retrospect, it is not so improbable that there would be a poster of Marie Curie talking about dancing, either.

Either way, I feel better, and I and my son will now go to bed.

It's Friday morning. It's sunny, and I've eaten a muffin for breakfast. I have the day off of work. I've written two stories today. This was the second one. Now, I am going to go take a shower, and later on, I will get pizza.

I do not believe that this life is all we have. When we die, I think we're still something. But I think that if you want to do something, you should do it now and don't worry what your mother says, anyway.

359

I read this week "We Are Become Pals," a short(ish) story on Tumblr that was written and drawn by the people who make the comic strip A Softer World, I think. It's about two girls who bond over dressing like FBI agents, an obsession with science and serial killers, and generally having fun. It was a great story, really fun to read.

It didn't start out as the inspiration for Pirates of the… The inspiration for this story was my feeling like maybe I should write a story about pirates, and then I began thinking of all the different places I could put pirates. This story was originally going to be a bunch of little vignettes of those, like "Pirates of the Serengeti" etc., but I slowed things down and focused on the beginning of Lil's and Diane's story, making them sort of like the girls in Pals. I may make this a running story.

358

When I was a kid, in T-ball, and marched in the 4th of July parade, my t-ball teams included "Lieberman Insurance" and "Hartland Meats."

357

It's true. I don't think I've ever heard a single kid want to be a superhero when he or she grow up. Why is that? It's only slightly less possible than being an astronaut, after all.

As of this writing, May 26, 2014, only 36 people have ever gone further out into space than low-Earth orbit.

Scientists estimate that as of today, 108,000,000,000 people have lived. So a person born today would have a 0.000000003% chance of becoming an astronaut going outside low-Earth orbit. Is it really that much less probable that same kid could become a superhero?

356

This story came to me last night while I was swimming with the boys, Mr F and his seven-minutes-younger brother, Mr Bunches, in the indoor pool at the health club. We had walked to the pool after work, and as we set out, it began raining, really hard. It was a warm summer rain, though, and I thought well, we're heading to the pool anyway, so we walked to the health club a mile away in the rain. Mr F was laughing, and Mr Bunches sang Winnie The Pooh's rain song and then Tomorrow from "Annie," and we had a wonderful time. Then, when we got there, Mr Bunches had me pretend to be a shark and bite him and I had the idea for this story.

355

The first title I had for this was "Knowledge Sucks." Then I changed it.

354

I've always believed that the grasshopper never learned his lesson.

353

I listened to "The Man Comes Around" five times straight through while I wrote this story.

352

This came to me while I was listening to The Man Comes Around and writing the 353 story. I love that line in the song, "one hundred million angels singing," and so I wrote a story about it. I think the story is a fairly typical one, almost a genre: God, or Heaven, or Jesus, has the same troubles in HIS life that we have in OURS. But I like those kinds of stories.

351

I am not crazy about how this one ends. I keep thinking it needs to be shorter, or longer. I rewrote the ending a lot. It always ended with Pymn choosing to be a dragon again but that feels like a beginning, not an end.

349

This story is not true. I feel like every author has to say that anytime they write a story about a terrible childhood. When I listen to people talk about writers, it always bugs me when they describe stories as "autobiographical" in any way. Unless a writer says a story is based on his life, people ought to assume it's not. But because the opposite is true, if I write a story like this, I need to put a disclaimer that it's not true.

The idea came to me as I listened to the song "Pompeii," by Bastille, on a ride with Mr F the other night. The song sort of reminds me of parents fighting. As I listened to it – it's a song I like – I felt like I could see this small, still area where the two kids played checkers while the storm of their parents' lives raged around them. It reminded me of the city of Pompeii: frozen in time by a volcano explosion.

It's 6/3/14, as I write this – 9:06 p.m. I'm sitting in Mr F's room, the one he shares with Mr Bunches. Two weeks ago, Sweetie and I went out for the night to celebrate our anniversary. We had two of the older kids – Middle Daughter and The Boy - - come stay over to babysit. We had planned on staying overnight at a hotel to get away for the night, have a night where we weren't woken up and could just sleep easy. We do that twice a year, on her birthday and on our anniversary.

That night, I woke up with a bad cough; I've had a cough for over a month now. Sweetie then woke up when I woke up and said she had a bad feeling about the boys. So we checked out of the hotel. The hotel is only three miles from our house; Sweetie doesn't like to be farther away than that from them. She told me as we drove home that she'd left a window open and wasn't sure Mr F wouldn't get out of it. He did that once, pushed out a screen and walked away, when he was only 3. He got nearly a half-mile from our house when he was found by a nurse. I was the only parent home; I was recovering from having been nearly stung to death by bees a few days earlier. I hadn't realized he'd done that for a few minutes, and when I did, I began searching the house and then the yard. Three minutes into the search I was calling 911, and they told me they'd found him.

Now, he wears a GPS bracelet and we keep the windows locked, usually. But that night, Sweetie said she'd left one small window open because it was hot in the house.

We made it home in 10 minutes or so, and Mr F was asleep on the couch. He'd refused to go to bed until we got home.

Since that night, he hasn't gone to sleep without one of us sitting in his room, as if he's afraid we might go out for the night again. So each night, I go sit in his room with him, and write while he falls asleep.

348

It's 9:34 p.m. on Wednesday, June 4. I have a terrible headache. I locked my keys in my car this morning and Sweetie had to come bring my spare key.It almost made her late for her exercise class, so I said I would do the grocery shopping for her tonight. After work, I gave the boys baths and then put them in pajamas that can pass for clothes, and we did the grocery shopping, which took nearly 2 hours because I am disorganized and Mr Bunches wanted to do it in alphabetical order, and I agreed to that because why not?

And I was worried that I wouldn't have the energy to write a story tonight, and I looked through all my ideas because I felt a bit blank, and then I started writing a story about how the universe was created, because every story is a creation story, really, and thinking of new ways the universe might have come into existence is a good way to jump start a story.

Also good: zebras.

347

I've been thinking for a few days that I should do a story with the devil in it. I almost wrote one the other day called "The Succubus and The Sandwich" but I got halfway through it and then didn't like it, so I deleted it. It was about how Satan tried to tempt a guy with two doors. Behind one was a succubus, behind the other, a sandwich.

In this story, I thought a while about how it would end. Casey struck out, remember, and there were a lot of things I could've done. Satan could've struck out, too, or gotten on base, or even hit a home run. But this felt right.

346

There is a song, called At The Bottom Of Everything by Bright Eyes. I both love to and hate to listen to that song, for the same reason: every time I listen to it I get a lump in my throat and I feel like I am going to cry. The reason why is my own. There are some stories that are my own, and that is one of them. So is the time I sang my sons alive. That's another story I tell only to myself.

But tonight I listened to that song over and over as I wrote "Charley Horse," and now when I listen to that song I can also picture Charley, running and running until he gets to a place that he wasn't running to but is pretty nice, anyway, even if there are horse racists there.

345

Spellcheck does not recognize "bestubbled" or "hoofbeats."

344

I had this idea for a ghost story about a ghost that's not interested in haunting people, and a guy who can't let that ghost not haunt, and so the guy haunts the ghost. This is kind of that story but kind of not, also.

343

Tonight, I took Mr F outside to play Big Wheels. I came home from the doctor where they were checking into a cough I've had for six weeks now, and where they'd done chest x-rays and a bunch of tests and said they didn't really know and they'd see me in six weeks. Right now, moving around is really hard for me. I take 7 different kinds of medicine every day. I get out of breath walking up the stairs and I have to sleep sitting up.

So I had every reason to not take Mr F to play Big Wheels because when we play, he rolls down our hill and I have to run alongside him to make sure he doesn't get hits by cars and stop him before he hits mailboxes or anything. We did that about 10, maybe 15 times, and I finally called it quits about a half-hour in, after we'd also taken Mr Bunches bike riding down at the end of the street and I finally had had enough.

I thought to myself that it was crazy to be running down a hill and walking back up when an hour earlier I'd had a doctor telling me he needed to give me some medicine before letting me go home, so bad did my lungs sound. But then I thought, if it wasn't serious, whatever I have, then it didn't matter.

And if it was serious? Then it would be crazy to not be outside running up and down a hill with my two youngest kids on a beautiful summer night.

342

Last night I thought I should write a story about witches. Today I did.

341

I like this one better even than the first one. I think witches might be a fun subject.

340

Today, Middle Daughter asked me why so many of my stories are sad. I suppose it's because I write out my sadness.

339

This morning (June 13, 2014) I am down on writers. I sent a story to a potential publisher. It was, in fact, story 340, and this publisher didn't say whether they paid for stories or not. I only send stories to publishers who pay, so in my query email I noted that, and I noted that because the story was only 340 words, I would only charge $0.01 per word if they paid.

I got a terse email back. It said, simply "Please check Duotrope for a list of paying markets." It seemed kind of rude to me. After re-reading it, I thought it was less rude, but still. Not a "thanks," or a "sorry, but we don't pay but here's a place you could check" (a place where you have to pay to join I believe. I can't understand why so many writers pay to write, as opposed to getting paid to write.)

And I thought about how many stories by writers are about writers. And then I wrote this story. In a way, it's similar to a story I wrote called "About The Author," which will eventually be in a book that right now isn't published but is called An Infinite Number Of Monkeys Already Published This Book In An Alternate Universe, a collection of short stories and essays I wrote over nearly a year in an attempt to get (mostly) McSweeney's to publish something. That book hasn't been published as of June 13, 2014, but maybe it has by the time you read this? Who knows. But in About The Author, the writer finishes a book and realizes that he has never done anything but write that book, and so he sets about trying to have a better "About the Author" blurb. In this story, I very seriously doubt the author ever got down to writing. But what a story that would be!

"Write what you know" is both the truest thing a writer can hear and the worst advice, depending on how you interpret it.

338

The raccoon part of this story is true. That actually happened, so I decided to use it in this story. The other part that is true is that I almost never go sit in the backyard and read, but that is not because of a lack of lawn chairs. There are other reasons.

337

It is Father's Day, today, and so I wrote a Father's Day story.

336

This might be, I think, the first story I have ever written about a bear. I had two other ideas for stories today. One was a story about how to write a story like John Cheever wrote. The other was a story I call "The Column Story," only it's not about columns, it is tentatively about a cowboy in the rain. We'll see if those stories make it into this book. I didn't write them tonight because when I sat down to write this story – it's 9:44 p.m. on June 16, 2014, as I type this note – I thought "Bear," and so I titled the story "Bear," and put on the song John Allyn Smith Sails by Okkervil River, and wrote the story.

I almost forgot: I had three ideas for stories today. The other idea I had was one that began like this:

What if Heaven isn't what we think it is at all? What if Heaven is sharp and spiky and all angles, like Superman's Fortress of Solitude was?

I may use that, someday, too.

335

Originally, I had "Michael Jordan" in there instead of "Paul Molitor," but I wanted to go with someone more obscure.

Also, if you're wondering, the _____ counts as a word.

The idea for this story came from author Andrew Leon ("The House On The Corner"), who one day left a comment in which he talked about the idea of making time. It's actually an idea that maybe deserves a longer story. Maybe someday. A while back I did a short story called "Alby's Drawings Of Time" in which I came up with the idea of time being shaped like different things, and how that would affect how time goes. So I suppose this is one of those stories.

334

The idea for this story came to me when This American Life did a story on "The Education of Little Tree." I heard little tree and thought of the phrase Little trees are the worst.To get in the mood for this story, I listened to cover versions of Ring Of Fire as I wrote it. There's a lot of different versions of that song out there. Most of them end up sounding sort of Irish-y. Irish music, I once pointed out on a blog of mine, always has a sort of dramatic, foreboding feel to it. When you hear Irish music, it sounds happy but you know something bad is going to happen. If you saw a film opening of a kid walking along in the sunlight and laughing, but I played Irish music over it, you'd think "Oh, man, something awful is going to happen to that kid, soon."

333

We have been having storms lately, really bad ones. They wake the boys up and one of us has to go in and lay next to them until they fall back asleep. It's kind of nice, lying in a bedroom, listening to a thunderstorm crashing around you, knowing that the small person next to you feels better simply because you are right there.

So I started with the idea of doing a story about a desert island, those cartoony desert islands where there's just a palm tree. I once tried to create a comic strip called "Marooned" about a guy stuck on just such a desert island. He had, as friends, a fish and I think a starfish, also. I only drew one or two strips. I remember only the first one. In panel one, there's just the desert island in the foreground and a ship far away in the back. In panel two, the ship is sinking and you see a guy (the main character) swimming in the distance. In panel three, the man is standing on the desert island, and the ship is gone. The man says to himself "Now what?"

I'm not actually crazy about the ending to this story, either. It seems a bit too twisty, a bit too flash-fictiony. One thing I've noticed about short short stories is that almost all of them rely on some kind of dramatic, M. Night Shymalanian twist ending. I try to avoid those. And the revelation that she and Robert ended up here because of what she said years ago seems almost too much of that. But I've left it.

I didn't spend too much time on this story, though. What I started working on today earlier was actually a story that right now is called "Staircase Elevator Rope" and it's a very experimental one that I really really want to work on. I wrote three pages of it while the boys were taking their baths, then I went on a date with Sweetie and we ate dinner and went to an art museum and drove around talking and now I'm home, and I had to write this story because I'm writing a story a day, and that other story is WAY over 332 words, so I decided to write a story quick about a desert island and this was it. Now it's 10:17 p.m. and I'm going to leave this story and knock off for the day, without even going back to "Staircase Elevator Rope," which I think is going to be brilliant but I will sleep on it.

I listened to Beethoven's Fifth Symphony and his Ninth (just the popular parts everyone knows) while I edited this down from 450-or-so-words to the 331 it is now.

The original title of this story was "The Concert." I changed it to "In" because it seemed to me that makes it more clear that the person composing the symphony is actually in the process of doing the work. And because it provides a double meaning: to do something 'in concert' with someone else is to work together as a team, which is what is happening here, too.

This story began simply with that title: "The Concert." When I first sat down to write it today, I put on the song "I'll Be Your Shelter (Just Like A Shelter)" by The Housemartins, and as I listened to the piano play at the beginning of that song I decided to write a story about a pianist in concert. Then I wrote this story instead.

I don't know which is worse, cold ears or cold feet. In the first version of this story (542 words!) the man wrapped the fox skin around his feet when he had picked it clean.

Mr F borrowed a "classic" Sesame Street DVD from the library and watched and rewatched one episode all week. At one point, I saw a snippet of a marching band going through what looked like a field.

For the longest time this morning I had only the title for this story.

The title for this one, and the idea behind it, come from Carolyn Parkhurst's Lost And Found, the audiobook I'm listening to right now (right now being June 25, 2014). There is a character who learned of Anubis as a kid, and she says that Anubis would weigh the hearts of the dead, and those whose were too heavy didn't get to go into the afterlife but had to wander around. The character says the title quote (although maybe she says someone else said it?), and I liked the idea of that god and the quote itself.

The phrase "perfect needle" has a different inspiration: Mr Bunches, my youngest son, likes to watch a series of shows on Netflix called "Nature's Deadliest," and one of the animals on that show is said to have a "perfect needle" for injecting venom. Mr Bunches hit on that phrase and now almost anything with a needle or similar appendage, like cactuses, for example, is said to have a "perfect needle" as he seems to think the two words go together. So when it came time to describe the monster's weighing claw, I thought of "perfect needle" and it fit.

Do you think if you were told that in the future something really great would happen to you, like 10 years from now you would win a hundred million dollars in the lottery, that you would stop enjoying your life between now and then, while you waited for the really good thing to happen? Conversely, knowing that good thing was coming might make the other good times enjoyable, because you wouldn't fear that it would be taken away, and help you through the bad times.

Hearing the future would be like hearing others' opinions of us: we only want to know it if it's good.

This was inspired by a joke on *Wait, Wait, Don't Tell Me.* The host asked a question about a quote said by Dick Cheney in an interview, and then said that the reporter had given Cheney a hard time about Cheney's answer and so in response Dick Cheney had unhinged his jaw and eaten the reporter.

Confession time: I don't know what "Italian Ice" is.

It is 9:30 p.m. and I am exhausted. Three times this week, Mr F has been up to 11 p.m. or later, and he sits on the couch downstairs and we need to sit with him. Finally, the other day, I told Sweetie that we have to alternate days when he does this. She agreed. Last night, he was up until 12:30 p.m. and finally fell asleep on the couch but only after I did, so at 1:30, when I woke up, I got him up to bed. Then, today, I slept in until 8:30 and got up and decided that rather than start the day with some writing like I do I would do it later.

So I went to the office and worked on a brief, and then we tried to go to the library but it was closed, and then we went to the park—this was all me and Mr F and Mr Bunches, the way it is every Sunday—and then to the hardware store to get some new clips for their swing, and then home where I cooked dinner and then put new 'couch beds' into their room, using parts of the old sectional couch from downstairs because I thought if I put a couch in Mr F's room he might sleep on that. They don't have actual beds, the boys, because they jumped on their old ones and broke them and we can't afford new ones yet, so they've had mattresses on the floor and anyway Mr F likes to sleep in his closet.

But I hauled parts of the sectional couch up there and made them "couch beds," which got Mr F all hyper and excited and he hasn't really settled down yet. And through it all I never got a chance to write my story today, which led me to tell Sweetie I would sit up with him anyway tonight so I could write, even though I knew it meant I'd be even more exhausted.

So now here I am: red-eyed and tired and I have a headache and I'm trying very hard not to be cross with Mr F, but it's tough because he's really not making any effort to sleep, and in fact a few moments ago he got up and found my headphones and bit one of them—he does that—and so my brand-new earphones might be wrecked. It's not the cost of it, as I get them at the Dollar Store, it's just the annoyance of it and also tomorrow morning I won't be able to continue to listen to my audiobook.

These are the 'good old days' that time travelers would go back to, I suppose.

I'm feeling better this morning. Mr F fell asleep pretty quickly last night, but then there were tornado warnings in our area so I stayed up late anyway, watching over the family.

There is a Modest Mouse song called Wild Pack Of Family Dogs in which a family is slowly carried away one by one by the wild pack of dogs. I wasn't consciously thinking of that song when I got the idea for this story yesterday, but after I wrote the first paragraph I paused to play tickle with Mr F and the song occurred to me, so when I finished it I made sure that nobody got taken away by the marauders.

The juice-taking marauder at first was going to have a face like a squid but I decided that was too much like that thing from Pirates Of The Caribbean, which I've never seen the whole movie of.

So basically this whole story was an effort not to plagiarize a song and a movie. Oh, and those old Capital One Viking commercials, which I guess it is also like. I was very happy with this story before I thought of all those things.

I have the movie *What About Bob?* playing on Netflix on another tab on my computer, and I listened to it as I wrote this.

Last night, Mr F went straight to bed at 8:45, and didn't need a ride or anyone to sit with him, at all.

They don't all have to be science fiction or ghost stories or whatever, you know.

I couldn't decide for a while why he is making this list. But I think it's just because it was a Friday, in July, and that's the kind of day everyone wants to do something dramatic. Sometimes, when I am walking on a sunny path with my boys, or driving with Sweetie on a road trip and listening to music, or just waking up at 6 a.m. and thinking how I have a day off and can sleep in all I want and wear pajamas until 10 a.m. if that's what I feel like, I think this is what life should be all the time. On a Friday in July, that feeling is especially strong. Someday, I always think on those days, I and the boys and Sweetie will hop in the car together and we will turn right, not left, and get on the highway and live life the way it should be. We won't need a list. I've got it all right up here. *taps head*

Happy Fourth of July. This week, I heard a news story about a guy who has a rare form of kidney cancer and all the treatments for it are experimental, so his insurance won't cover them. He's holding a fundraiser to try to get enough money to maybe save his life.

Also this week, the fourth *Transformers* movie made $100,000,000 in just the first three days it was out but some people say, no, it only made $97,500,000 and they debated that *a lot* this week, trying to figure out just how much money we spent in three days to watch a movie about giant robots.

"Marcelline" is also the vampire on Adventure Time, and yesterday I watched the one where she kicks Finn and Jake out of their tree, and I liked the name and the house hunting song, so I wrote a story about my own Marcelline.

316

As it turns out, I am eating cold pizza for breakfast this morning.

315

Tonight at the pool, Mr Bunches and I played "Swim Across The Pool" and there were five obstacles I had to be when he swam: 1. Shark 2. Piranhas 3. Alligator 4. Crocodile 5. Octopus. Four of them were pretty much the same thing: they'd grab him and pull him under and attack, but the piranhas were fun because they were my hands, darting and poking at him before he escaped.

314

Originally this was called "Paradise Misplaced," but "detoured" seemed a better fit for the title.

313

When I first thought of this story, last night, I didn't know what the music would mean, and I imagined one man playing the violin in that clearing, but this morning I changed it to this story. I was also going to make the song be played on June 21, but today is July 9 so I made it that day, because why not?

312

This occurred to me while I was on a playground, with the boys.

311

Tonight (Friday, July 11, 2014) the man and the son were me and Mr F. The guy going to get yogurt and bread and living later on was just a guy I imagined driving by us.

310

I had to go watch a clip from *King Kong(1933)* to find out how many biplanes attacked Kong and what happened to them.

309

I don't even like most zombie stories. But I like *mine*. Last night I had an idea for fire zombies.

306

There is a line in *Arrested Development* where the character Tobias says "We were all so hopped up on amyl and disco we didn't notice," and until I saw that line in closed captioning, I always thought he said *"Emil and disco,"* and that he was referring to the *Emil* books that I'd read as a kid in the 1970s.

305

This began as a regular old story, one that's meant to be kind of a fable. But I was looking for a place to submit it to, and I found a site that was looking for *poetry* that had something to do with science, and I decided to turn this into a poem, which I did simply by breaking up the lines and moving them around on the page to provide a bit of emphasis and separation.

So this is a poem, I guess.

304

I'm kind of into this fables thing, now. This one, too, began as a story but then was changed to a poem. It kind of feels like cheating. I feel sort of like I should not call stories "poems" simply because I messed around with how the words were set on a page.

But, then, why not? I can write something and then decide what it is, right? I did this with "Chomp", too—I have submitted that a few places and one of them I submitted it as a poem rather than a story. Nobody's accepted it yet, though.

301

I haven't been feeling well again. Another bout of bronchitis, about the 8th I've had in the past year or so. I was up the last two nights with a cough, and last night I had a fever, too, my teeth chattering and having to wrap myself in a sweatshirt and two blankets even though the thermometer said it was 71 degrees in our bedroom.

300

I'm not crazy about the ending to this one. It doesn't have the right feel to it. I messed around with it a lot and the current ending is pretty good, so I'll leave it at that. But I'm not crazy about it.

This wasn't the first story I wrote today. This morning, I wrote one called "The Captive" but I hit about 350 words and it was only just starting to get interesting, and I read it again and decided there might be something there, in this story about a guy looking at a captive they were taking somewhere and they weren't supposed to talk to the captive, and such, but I couldn't figure out what to turn it into, so I deleted the story and then did a bunch of other stuff for the day, and now it's 9:35 p.m. (on July 22, 2014), and I thought of this story while I took Mr F for a ride tonight. I'm not sure what made me think of oyster divers, but I thought of an oyster diver who doesn't let go of his rock, and this was the story I wrote.

I actually looked up where they do oyster diving. They do it near Sri Lanka, among other places, and "Supun" is on a list of common Sri Lankan names. Also, sometimes oyster divers black out when they resurface, and that's the short death in this story; I don't know if the oyster divers call it the short death. I called it that, though.

299

I was in the *worst* mood, all day, really mad about something at work, all day. I came home, and I ate an egg salad sandwich for dinner, and I talked with Sweetie, and I took the boys to the park and we rolled down the hillside over and over for twenty minutes and now I'm feeling a bit better.

297

Vague ideas I had that I discarded before deciding on this one:
- Stories around a campfire.
- Something about ghosts.
- A lone atom goes careening around the universe.
- A little kid who talks to nice demons that live in flames.

296

Guess who heard "Baba O'Riley" on the radio today?

I'm really sick, again. It's July 26, 2014, and I have the worst case of bronchitis I've ever had. I feel like I'm drowning. So I spent today mostly sleeping and now, at 6:40, I got up and I wrote this story and I'm going to take some medicine and take the boys to the park where they can play and I'll sit on a bench.

The idea for this story came from thinking of giants, and also from remembering the time I had an idea for a story in which a giant monster lived in a house in Victorian England. It was going to be a story set in a series of stories in which Pumblechook and Wopsle, two minor characters from *Great Expectations*, were also paranormal investigators, and they would go to this house and the door would open and a giant scaly hand would shoot out and grab someone and eat them. I might still write those stories someday, as I think Pumblechook and Wopsle are great names.

295

I've been really sick all day. I think I became dehydrated. Around 6 p.m. I had Sweetie take me and the boys for a ride, and I got a McDonald's chocolate shake because I was craving one. It tasted really good. Then I came home and drank two really large cups of water. I'm feeling more awake, here at 8:53 p.m., than I have all day, but my cough is also really bad.

I'm not sure where I came up with the idea for this story. I was thinking about doing a story about sea serpents, and that led me to the Loch Ness monster, I guess. I was thinking about sea serpents because I listened to this radio story about oarfish, which are the longest bony fish in the ocean and which used to be mistaken for sea serpents.

294

I went to the doctor today. They have no idea why this keeps happening. But they gave me a bunch of pills and within an hour I was breathing okay again and I feel almost completely better.

293

I don't know about this one. I started out today writing *The Book of Me*, my second try at a story in which a guy gets a book that tells his whole life for him, and he has to wonder whether to read ahead, etc etc., and it wasn't really working any more than the last time I tried it, either. It feels like a great concept but I can't make it work. So then I wrote version 1 of this story, based sort of loosely on what's going on with Israel in Gaza right now (and really you could probably be reading this any time and have that sentence feel fresh and relevant, right?) and based on an article I read on Huffpo or somewhere that talked about sci-fi tropes and how the aliens are always the bad guys and why aren't we ever the bad guys, so I thought I'd work out something like that.

The first one version was told more remotely, in all third person with "we" and stuff, but then I rewrote it to feel more immediate, so it was more like a story and less like a news account or history book, but it still feels more like merely an introduction. A lot of 'flash fiction' feels that way to me and I try to avoid it. It's the same feeling I got with Pymn in *Here There Be Dragons*. The difference is that with some very short stories you get the feeling there are other *stories* there, but that this one is complete. Not with this one.

To work out a theory of flash fiction on the fly, let me try this: Think of flash fiction as someone asking you *What did you do today?* You wouldn't necessarily walk them through your entire day, from getting up to right that moment. You might hit *all* the important details of the day. Or you might choose to summarize your day, or focus on one big thing. That's *fiction*.

But if you instead walked in and said *You won't believe what happened to me today* and told someone about one specific thing that is a self-contained incident (*"There was a fistfight at the meeting!"* or *"I nearly got into an accident on the way home here's what happened"*) that's *flash fiction*: it tells one complete story that doesn't negate the possibility of other stories happening to that same person, or even other details of that story (*"and I had to go to the ER but they said I was okay"*) but it doesn't necessarily lead to more stories, even thought it could (*"Hey, remember that accident I almost got into? I got ticketed and hired this sexy lawyer to defend me at the trial, and she asked me out for drinks…"*).

Based on that, *When We Landed* isn't really a complete story. Sorry.

292

So this is a continuing story. My thought was that on all the prime-numbered entries I'd do another installment but I keep forgetting which ones are primes. 293 was a prime. 292 is not, obviously, but I treated it like one and flipped a coin (went to random.org and chose randomly between 1-100, with evens meaning another Pirates installment, which is how I flip a coin because I never have coins anymore. I think I have a few quarters in my car, but the last time I needed 'real' money was when I stopped to vacuum the car and we had to go into the gas station and buy two candy bars [one for each kid] and then ask for quarters as change from my debit card.)

Anyway, the idea of these is that each is supposed to stand as its own story, so that you could read one and not read the others and still have it make sense, while they would all fit together, too. I think I'm achieving that?

The next prime is 283. We'll see if I remember.

291

Tonight is Thursday, July 31. I am starting another three-day weekend, after a long, stressful week in which I am also starting to feel sick again. Tonight, I had to run back to my office to print and fax some things for my student loans. I took the boys with me. We left at 8:30, got to the office at 9, did the faxing, and then went for a late-night ice cream cone, sitting outside and listening to the traffic on a warm summer evening while Sweetie got a bit of a break.

On the way home, I thought of the first line of this story. Then I turned the radio station and heard Prince's *"Kiss,"* and decided the ghost would be waiting for a kiss.

290

This started off as a fable-ish story about gravity but then morphed into this dialogue. I'm not sure how serious this guy is, but he seems to mean it.

289

Yesterday I started listening to *Jesus' Son* by Denis Johnson, on audiobook. Johnson wrote one of the greatest stories I've ever heard, *Emergency*, and so this story was sort of inspired by that. As I listened last night to the book, while driving Mr F, I kind of thought maybe I'd write some real-life stories for a while. So I wrote one. This one.

The ending to this changed a few times, minutely. In one Tom left and goes to a movie without seeing her again. In a few others he gets let out with a doctor's excuse to take the day off. But I left it like this so that we never know if he saw her again.

288

This story started with the phrase "The statue was ugly, everyone agreed on that", a phrase I thought of last night on my second ride with Mr F. I wrote this story while listening to Johnny Cash and Johnny Cash covers.

I came up with the *last* line after initially thinking she'd want to just forget it all, but then I remembered that woman who was the real life "Runaway Bride," and I thought about how nobody ever really forgets *anything*, ever, do they?

And then the title: I came up with *that* after never forgetting became what this story was about. Because I guarantee you nobody ever forgets anything, especially something embarrassing like this. When I was a kid, in about the fifth grade, I got in an argument with another kid while we were at my brother's t-ball game. I don't remember what the argument was about but I do remember that I got really mad at him, so mad that I said a bunch of swears and chased him around the jungle gym and was crying, and then he was threatening to tell my parents what I'd said and I had to concede the fight to him.

That was 34 years ago. I still remember it, pretty clearly. And I bet if I ran into that kid, at a reunion or something, he'd bring it up, because nobody ever forgets. Big or small, I think there is something to the idea that we are the sum total of our embarrassments as much as our accomplishments.

287

I've been writing an article for the Indie Writers Monthly magazine about opening lines in stories, and of course that means discussing Edward Bulwer-Lytton, and his famous opener.

286

This is my version of a Denis Johnson story. I'm still listening to *Jesus' Son*, and the stories are amazing, if completely sad. They're like Damon Runyon stories that have had all the hope and joy sucked out of them, but they're also beautiful, in their own way. And surreal. It's hard to tell how much is intended to be real in them. Last night, listening to *"Dirty Wedding,"* in which a character rides the El around after his girlfriend gets an abortion, I started thinking about how Johnson didn't really give much description, leaving the El to your imagination, because why not? We can all picture an elevated train, right? Why describe it? So I began imagining what it looked like and I pictured the blue vinyl seats that are now in this diner, because I really like that color blue. Then I had the idea of a guy going to the diner because of those seats, that color, and I imagined the crying guy, and I had this story.

285

This morning Mr F spilled my coffee all over the counter. Nothing spills like coffee. It spreads all over everything and gets into every crack and nook and takes about 10 billion paper towels to clean up. I think the only thing worse to clean up than coffee is broken eggs, which Mr F also sometimes does when he gets mad. I suppose if you dropped some eggs and then spilled coffee on it, that would be about the worst.

284

Originally, this story was going to have the preacher renting the space on a hot day in August, but that's too Neil Diamond-y. So I changed it to 4 days at the end of July, but then for word-count purposes I had to get rid of that, too.

In unrelated thoughts, I read today about a grilled cheese restaurant that got $10,000,000 in funding from venture capitalists because you can order the grilled cheese over your phone or something like that, and Beyonce and Jay-Z went to this restaurant with some people from their tour. It's called "The Melt." I bet it will not be in existence anymore by the time you read this.

283

The trick I'm trying here is to make each story stand alone, and I think I did that?

I was reading an article over the weekend about back when comics were really crazy, in the 1950s or so, and they mentioned that superintelligent gorillas were a big trope back then. So I put one in here. Cowboy Lions, as far as I know, are a thing unique to me.

That got dark, quickly! I sat down to write and put on the song "He's A Mighty Good Leader" by Beck, and decided to use that as the title, then tweaked it. As I wrote the title, the concept came to me and this story then took all of 10 minutes to write, most of which was editing it down from the original 319 words to 282.

This is the first note I am writing before the story. It's 7:47 a.m. on August 10, 2014, and I got up a bit later than usual today. I've been sitting here for about 10 minutes trying to think of the story for today. So far I have rejected "Notes," a story in which a poor boy stays home alone all day and we know what his day is like solely through little notes left by his mom, and "The Very Bouncy Bed," which was going to be a story based on an idea I had once for a kids' book, in which a little girl bounces on her bed all the way up to outer space, but I didn't like either of those ideas, so I am going to table the story for a bit and work on other stuff.

…later…

It's 8:41 now. I was driving back from visiting the Fennimore Railway Museum with the boys, and I heard Coldplay's song "A Sky Full of Stars" and came up with the title of the next story.

This story feels complete to me.

Man, I don't know where this one came from. It's 9:05 p.m. 10 minutes ago I sat down to write this story, sitting in the dark in the boys' room. Mr F still doesn't like to go to sleep alone, but we have been working on him, and now he doesn't demand to go for a ride before bed and he doesn't want to fall asleep down on the couch. Instead, he goes up to his bedroom but he wants me or Sweetie to sit in the room until he falls asleep, which most nights is only about 20-30 minutes. So I brought my laptop and wrote this story. I started with the title. I was staring at the blank page for a second and then I thought of that phrase. As I typed it up, I was actually going to try to make this one of those poetry-like fable-type stories. But then I made it this one. As I wrote it I was picturing the electrons, little blank ping-pong ball-looking characters, wearing cowboy hats and riding horses and arguing with each other.

Tonight, while I was at the park with the boys, watching them climb up and slide down the tornado slide, and swing on the jungle gym, my dad called. I hit ignore on the cell phone and then called him back when we were done at the park, on the way home, and he told me that he has cancer.

This one, I think, might be a continuing story, too.

In Denis Johnson's stories, what struck me was the feeling of camaraderie among all his characters. His stories are as if the characters from *Guys And Dolls* suddenly began role-playing *The Departed*, only the kinds of crimes Johnson's characters pull are the sorts of things I've outlined here. They're fascinating and bleak, and I found myself thinking of that this morning, and just started writing that first paragraph before I decided who the main character would be.

The title to this story is a line from Sha Na Na's "Get A Job."

I had this idea for a story where four people sat on a hill watching for something and at the end of the story one of the guys tried to kiss one of the girls. This is that story, but obviously it took a twist along the way.

Also, the word counter counts this: … As a word. So originally I had those in there to indicate waiting but I had to remove them to make the word count because I was too lazy to count *real* words. It was writing this story that I learned that punctuation might count as words as far as Word, the program, is concerned. Any punctuation, even a single one, standing alone, counts as a word.

So this! Is two words

While this ! Is three.

And this !? Is just one word.

I guess that's fair? Otherwise you could use punctuation to get around word counts on things like this.

So this kind of has that flash fiction twisty-ending thing going, but it's not *quite* a twist, because in most flash fiction I think you'd be expecting that he'd run into his younger self or the note would be from his wife or something more than just a maybe missed connection, so I'm okay with it despite my general dislike of twist endings in flash fiction.

This story was inspired by *S*, the book by JJ Abrams that I'm (slowly) reading. I'm *slowly* reading it (and have been for four months now, at about 30 pages a month) both because it is a dense book that requires a lot of thought and I'm not always up to that these days, and also because it's a *real* book that requires me to be in bright light when I read it because there are these handwritten notes in the margins and tiny footnotes and things, so it's kind of an arduous process that so far is worth it but we'll see. I get why it's a real book but I also think that it could have been an ebook and been just as effective, the more I read it.

In *S*, these two characters correspond with each other in the margins of a book, and I began thinking about how if you misshelved a book in a big library you might never find it, and hence this story. The ending, though, was more inspired by the scene in *Slaughterhouse-Five* where Billy Pilgrim goes into the cave and is told that they're going to turn out the lights and that it'll probably be the only time in his life that he'll ever be in complete darkness and

274 (cont)

then they do turn out the lights, and he sees right next to his eyes his dad's glow-in-the-dark watch, wrecking the moment forever.

That scene has always struck me as inexpressibly sad, although I recognize that it is a first world kind of sadness and not a real kind of sadness.

273

I was driving to work this morning, and I thought of the idea of updating old nursery rhymes. My first thought was of Solomon Grundy, who I knew primariliy as the swamp-thing zombie from DC Comics. I typed a note in my phone reminders: "*Solomon Grundy 2014*" I thought, and left it at that for the whole day.

Just before bed, I went and read the Solomon Grundy rhyme on Wikipedia,

Solomon Grundy,
Born on a Monday,
Christened on Tuesday,
Married on Wednesday,
Took ill on Thursday,
Grew worse on Friday,
Died on Saturday,
Buried on Sunday.
That was the end of,
Solomon Grundy

And thought for a while about what sort of Solomon Grundy story I would write. I thought about babies that don't live very long, and how I've always thought they would get another go-round from God if they wanted, and then I came up with the idea for this story.

272

It's 8:58 p.m. I've been writing more of these at night because I haven't been sleeping well, and so I don't get up all that promptly and then the time I usually use for writing, between 6 and 7, is almost gone.

Last night, there were thunderstorms, which scare Mr Bunches. We take turns on nights, Sweetie and I, so that only one of us has to have a night of interruptions when they happen, and it was my night. About 1:30, I woke up to him calling me, and I went in. He said *"What was that noise?"* I hadn't heard anything, so I told him he must have been dreaming and he had me cover him up and tried to go back to sleep. I went back to my bedroom and saw lightning outside, and loud thunder rolled across the sky, and Mr Bunches called for me again.

Through two thunderstorms, from 1:30-2 and from 2:30-3:15 I had to lay in his bed, side by side, his head under his blanket and my arm over his face where he put it, and then when each storm ended I went back to my bed to see if we'd make it through the night.

But even on nights where there are no thunderstorms, I wake up a lot and haven't been sleeping well.

271

It turns out that the tiger cowboys were not, after all, terribly concerned about the ethics of the whole deal.

270

This story was inspired by the fact that today, August 21, 2014, I woke up and *our* skies were the weird color of the skies in the story. But that probably means just thunderstorms.

269

I have set up a system; when I come to a prime number, I have random.org pick a number between 1-100, with certain ranges being "Do another pirate story" or do "Old Mill" or "Do a regular story of some sort." I've done this twice and both times it came up "Pirates."

It's getting harder to keep these as a self-contained story that would make sense if you didn't read any of the other installments, and that was the hard part of this story. I am not 100% certain I've done that, but I tried. That and that I kept mixing up Harriet and Jezebel. The first version of this story had Jezebel interacting with the gorilla and before I went and changed it to Harriet I considered having that stay and explaining it as a quirk of all this universe-creating stuff, but decided to fix it after all, as I don't really like incorporating mistakes into my stories. Although I did do that once; in a story called "This Stupid Pineapple Is..." I was posting in installments, I lost track of which chapter I was on and posted chapter 9 before posting chapter 7 and 8, so I decided to make part of the story that time was breaking down, and it worked pretty well.

I understand that's how Hemingway did things. I bet in *The Old Man and The Sea* he actually meant to write a bullfighting story but kept accidentally saying "fish" and so he went with it.

268

Last night, August 21, 2014, about 9 p.m., I got an email from a small publisher saying they wanted to offer me a contract for a novel I wrote. The novel is called *Find Out Who You Are*. When I wrote it, back in January of this year, I thought it was really, really good. I told the basic plot to Sweetie, and she said it sounds like it could be a Tom Cruise movie, and that it had the same cool feel to it that *Minority Report* had. I decided that I'd send that book to publishers, before putting it out on my own, and I specifically decided I'd send it to 50 publishers. I've sent it to 24 as of last night, and one liked it enough to offer me a deal.

In other news, today I dug out also an old 250-word short story I wrote for a blogfest, one in which Han Solo and Time-Traveling Elvis are arguing in court. Time-Traveling Elvis is one of my favorite characters I've ever created, and yet I forget about him all the time.

267

As with some of the other stories, I feel like this one needs something else at the end, but I can't think what? I tried a couple of variations of the ending, one where Zeus sends a hailstorm and Leda yells something about the goat-mom (which is one version of who Zeus was raised by, according to Wikipedia), and in another version Leda finishes her mead and leaves, but nothing seemed to work as well as this ending, which is the best I can come up with.

I used to say you know a story's ending when you write it, and sometimes I think of the perfect ending for a story and work to get to it, but especially with these shorter ones, I am just not sometimes not hitting that sweet spot. Then again, I thought that about "Here There Be Dragons," and that one got published, so it might just be me.

266

For a full 15 minutes before I wrote this, I tried to write a story called "The Dragon, and the Mermaid." In it, a dragon and mermaid were talking about who was believed in more, or less, but it was going nowhere, really, and so I gave up on it, and instead started to write about this woman, and got this story instead. I think I was not in a whimsical mood tonight.

265

It seems the whimsy is back.

264

It's 10:50 p.m. Today, Mr Bunches' new toy got delivered. He gets to buy one toy a month, a luxury we give him even though money is tight right now, because he loves toys so much. This new one is a "K'Nex Super Mario Castle," or something. He waited all day for me to come home and build it, and I started on it with him right after supper. It wasn't done by 8:30, so he took his bath and kept working until 9:15 when he got too tired and went to bed. I stayed up, finishing it, and finally completed it about 10:30. Then I had to write today's story, and here it is. I don't think it's great. It feels sort of incomplete, again, but I'm tired and I'm going to go to bed.

263

The summer is coming to an end. Tonight, at the park, I played "guns" with Mr Bunches. He cheats: even when I shot him point-blank he said he wasn't dead and then shot *me*, and I had to be dead. When I asked how come he didn't die, he said "Because I win."

262

The 1970s just seem to me like a time that people might do things like that.

I looked up a list of songs from 1979 and "Do Ya Think I'm Sexy" was at the top of the list, so I checked out what album that came from and put it in there. At first I was going to go for some sort of hard rock power ballad but then I decided that the robber is the kind of guy who liked disco and didn't care who knew it.

261

I was going to try to tell this story from the perspective of the gun.

260

I tried about six different stories before I wrote this one, so you can kind of see where the idea comes from. I tried a story about at tree attacking some people (scrapped because *ents*), goblins trying to steal a baby (too much like my earlier one), an imp making a deal with a guy to take all his memories of the *first* time he'd done anything in his life (liked it but couldn't get it to be short enough and couldn't figure out an ending and then got tired of it), a story about two guys swordfighting forever in which I thought maybe they would actually turn out to be action figures, and then finally I hit on *What if God had gotten writer's block?*

259

The first version of this story had Mila looking down at the book, which was able to be read again, and the words on the page said *but we will be back*. I rejected that in favor of this ending because the first version was too flash-fiction-twisty-endingy.

258

Yesterday I thought a spider crawled in my eye. Today, at lunch at the picnic table outside my office where I sit, alone, and eat my sandwich and read *S* by J.J. Abrams, there was a tiny spider crawling on the table and I took a picture of it with my phone, because my new thing is trying to get really amazing photos of bugs, and then I flicked it away. Then, tonight, when we took the boys for a ride after dinner, Mr Bunches found a spider in the garage and Sweetie killed it; I thought Mr Bunches was pointing towards a bigger spot and I thought it was a really *huge* spider. But the spider that Sweetie stepped on was pretty small.

So spiders have been on my mind, I guess.

I like the idea of dimensional traveling like this. I thought of making this one a continuing story, too, but decided *not yet*. Because it's a little too close to "Pirates of the..." with the dimensions thing.

257

The difficulty, as with "Pirates of the…" is making sure each installment can stand on its own, which is tough to do. It's especially tough if you've read the previous installments (or written them) because I know what happened before, but I have to try to read this as though story 277 didn't exist. I'm not sure I did it, quite, but it's interesting to try.

256

I have no idea where this story came from. I started out with that first sentence and it just spilled out from there.

255

I'm back on witches, I guess.

254

I had no trouble getting *started* today, tired as I am (it's 9:53 p.m., right now, on a Saturday night). I had trouble *finishing*. I started two different stories before deciding on this one.

The two I started were these:

Vena's iPod had begun predicting the deaths of people around her.

She had first noticed it sitting on the bus, listening to what was supposed to be a Counting Crows song but instead of the usual lyrics, the jangly guitars accompanied a story about a woman who would soon slip in the shower and hit her head, dying of blood on the brain and not found until her neighbors called the superintendent after a baby had been crying for hours and the shower was still running. Vena hadn't even noticed until she'd realized that the woman across from her on the bus held a baby was wearing the same sweatshirt described in the song.

Over the next few days, to the strains of Rolling Stones' or White Stripes' or sometimes the occasional Miley Cyrus song, the ipod told her that her roommate would die of a heart attack at 63, while the Lit 101 professor would run a red light and be struck by a van, and the guy who sat down near her at the coffeeshop was going to commit suicide almost exactly two years from the day he smiled at her. That one caused a pang of guilt as she wondered if her failure to smile back had contributed in some small way to his decision.

She sat on the stoop of her building clicking among songs, fixing her eyes on people on the street, feeling grim.

I gave up on that one after realizing I had no idea where to go with it, especially if I wanted to avoid a twist. I had thought that I'd have Vena's boyfriend turn the corner and OH NO SHE KNOWS HOW HE'LL DIE AND IT'S GOING TO HAPPEN NOW but decided that was the easy way out.

Then "The Only Living Boy in New York" came on my iTunes, and I started this one:

The Only Living Boy In The World.

When he was 7 years old Jack would pretend he was a scuba diver, crouching through the house, making burbling noises with his mouth and pushing against the air in the kitchen pretending it was kelp and that there were moray eels amongst the long fronds he slowly navigated.

42 years later, Jack sat on the edge of a dock and stared into blue green water and wondered what it would be like to actually scuba dive through a kelp field, and wondered, too, if they were called kelp fields. A voice in his head told him that it didn't matter, not anymore, whether they had been called fields or forests or something else.

He flicked his thumb

But I didn't know whether I wanted him to really be the only man left in the world or if he was just sad or what, and it wasn't really gripping me, so I wrote the actual story 254, which I kind of figured was fun because a lot of flash fiction seems like it's kind of the middle of the story anyway but that's not acknowledged.

253

This is sort of a blue-collar ghost story, I feel like.

252

This one took longer than I expected. I came up with the first line, more or less, and wrote about 2/3 of the story. Then I took a break to play action figures with Mr Bunches, and gave Mr F and Mr Bunches their bath, and then got them snacks, and then wrote the rest of the story. It came in at 345 words. I had to trim an entire story! There were parts in here about how the moon knew about what goes on in drive-in theaters because they happened at night. I tried and tried and tried not to cut that, but then I had to in order to get the words down, and I think the story is just fine, anyway.

251

This story was inspired by true-life events, in that I was making a toasted bagel for Sweetie's breakfast today and I flicked the bagel out with a knife because I hate burning my fingers on the outer part of a bagel, which gets insanely hot even in a toaster set on low. I wasn't electrocuted, though. I didn't even get a shock. But I did briefly wonder about how toasters work, the timer or heat thing. I may look that up later.

250

...

249

So I have crossed a threshold here. About 2 years ago I began writing short short stories, each 250 words in length, exactly, counting the title. I've written 60, maybe 70 of them so far. But never many *shorter* stories. From here on out, the stories will get shorter than I am used to writing.

I really like this story. I remembered that riddle this morning, and I thought I would write a story about it. I wasn't sure what kind of story I'd write about it, so I'm glad I chose to write this kind of story about it.

248

This story came to me when I glanced over at the TV and saw the sabre-toothed tiger on the screen; the boys are watching *Ice Age*. The first draft of the story was a guy telling the story to his kid, but then I changed it and I like this better. It's got that twist ending, I suppose, but it doesn't feel like a *flash* twist ending.

247

This story began with the song "Brave Walls" by Yair Yona, a cowboy-sounding song. I started it playing and decided to write a song about a shootout. As I worked on the first few lines, I wrote the line *everybody else was dead already*, and made that the working title of the story. Then "The Man Comes Around" came on and I expanded the story to make the comparison between this showdown and the beginning of the universe. I finished up with that last paragraph because I decided that if everybody else really was dead, we'd have no way of knowing how this turned out.

Then I began revising it down from the 350 words, and changed the title in order to "Creation" then "Creation Needs Destruction" both of which I thought were a little *too* spot-on for the idea of this story, so I looked up some stuff on The Big Bang and found out that they call the first measurable instance of time the Planck Epoch, so I changed the title to "The Planck Epoch," then "To Live And Die In The Planck Epoch," then finally the current title, which ties the last paragraph in.

The other day, I wrote "How Toasters Work" and that was my favorite new story for the last few days, but now I love this one most of all.

246

I actually wrote this story twice. Today is a Sunday (September 14, 2014) and on most Sundays I go into my office on Sunday mornings with the boys to do some busywork. One of the things I did today was write story 246, which had the same title but was slightly different.

And I really liked that story. I wrote it, submitted it to a place, and then went about the rest of the day, working on a guide to litigation I'm writing and taking the boys to the zoo and cooking chicken patties for dinner, and somewhere in there I began to think the story I'd written was a lot like "The Moon and The Ocean," and even though later on I saw that it wasn't quite that close, I felt like I had to change it anyway, so I did.

245

There's something here, in this story, but I don't feel I quite cracked it tonight. The first version of this story had the man slowly not believing in his family and then his job and then laws and finally he was getting drunk an alley and not believing in the world anymore and then, just before he disappears, he realizes that he now believes in the witch and that saves him. I scrapped that and went with this but as I write this note I'm thinking I liked the first one better.

So I went back and finished that one, undoing all the changes to bring it back, and I wrote that, too. So here is a bonus 245...

245.2

See? I like that one much better. I should submit both to various places. I should go back and submit the alternate version of 246, too. Let the market decide. Isn't that what Adam Smith would do?

244

This came out of my actually seeing a roadside stand selling socks, 30 for $5.99, then hypothesizing on my blog about what if there were a competition and another stand opened up selling them 31 for $5.99, and also Russian oligarchs were involved?

243

I was kind of thinking I would write about robots and then a song came on the iTunes, and the word 'dream' was mentioned, and so I wrote the title to this story. Midway through, it got interesting when God came into it. Also, toasters continue to be a theme for me, even though I haven't eaten toast in, like, *three* days. (We've had Peanut Butter Cap'n Crunch, which beats toast the way rock beats scissors.)

This is the only picture in this book that I didn't take myself. Having landed a book contract for a novel I wrote (*Find Out Who You Are*), I have to start taking part in publicity stuff, and the very first things for that were to set up a new Twitter account using my own name and to start working with other authors for this publisher including taking part in their writing contests. The contest was to write a story about the picture posted on a blog, and the picture was this one. So I looked at the picture for a while and gave Mr F and Mr Bunches their bath, and then came up with this idea, which I wrote while listening to Regina Spektor songs.

"Frozen Charlotte" is a kind of doll based on a legend. From Wikipedia:

Frozen Charlotte is a name used to describe a specific form of china doll made from c. 1850 to c. 1920. The name comes from the Americanfolk ballad "Fair Charlotte," which tells of a young girl called Charlotte who refused to wrap up warmly to go on a sleigh ride because she did not want to cover up her pretty dress; she froze to death during the journey.

Toys were pretty messed up back then, I think. Who makes a doll for kids to play with based on a macabre legend? I learned about Frozen Charlottes when we visited the Doll & Toy Museum in Fennimore, Wisconsin, this past summer. We also saw the Railroad Museum that day, and stopped by the spot where two guys came up with the idea for the Gideon Bible. That was a pretty fun day.

This is actually one of *two* of these I wrote today. The other is a poem on the same theme: "The Raven" from the raven's point of view, and hypothesizing that the raven is cursed as the man is. I wrote the poem, actually, and it was about 275 words or so, and I didn't want to cut any of it, so I sent that to a poetry website and then wrote this story.

Like so many stories of mine, this was inspired by a song. I wanted to write something kind of scary and was thinking "ghosts," and then "See My Ships" by the Violent Femmes came on as I was starting this, so I wrote about ships, and then they weren't even ghost ships, to boot.

As I say each time, it's getting harder and harder to make these each a single, understandable story while also continuing the overall story.

I read a whole paragraph on Wikipedia to make sure I used "anthropic principle" correctly!

I like to think I'm the kind of person who would want to live a life of adventure, going from town to town, having thrilling times, living for the moment. But in reality I want my adventure in small doses, easily managed, with a McDonald's nearby and at the end of the day, if I can't be back home in my own bed wearing my blue socks to keep my feet warm, I at least want to be in a nice hotel with HBO and a free continental breakfast.

I came up with the idea for this story, and actually wrote most of it in my head, while I was lying in a corner of our basement with Mr F, tickling him. He likes when I cuddle him and tickle his neck, sometimes fast and sometimes slow, and then I give him zerberts. I thought of the whole story and I wanted to run up and type it up right away but Mr F so rarely wants to spend time with me that I didn't want to end our game, so I just stored the words away until after tickling and homework and baths and now, at 8:33 p.m., I wrote it.

When I sat down to write this story, about 15 minutes ago, I was feeling a little down and a little tired and had no idea what I was going to write. Then I came up with the title. And the rest just came from there and I feel a bit better now.

In my other collection of flash stories, currently titled "250=1" because all the stories are exactly 250 words including the title, I began writing zombie stories one day, mostly because I was sick of everyone else's zombie stories which I saw as kind of boring and uninspired. So I wrote a couple, and I called them "Some Zombie Stories" and numbered each one. After that I kept doing that, and there are (as I write this, 8:59 p.m. on September 25, 2014) 7 of them in that collection, making this "Some Zombie Stories 8".

The idea for this story came from Mr Bunches, who before his bath mixed a little milk with water and said "Look Dad, Zombie Juice!" I started thinking about what Zombie Juice would be and the rest came easy.

I actually think that would not be so terrible an afterlife.

I was thinking today that the secret to these installments would be like the season of the television show *Archer* where they got their spy company closed down and were trying to sell cocaine or something. Each episode of that season could probably have been watched without knowing the full storyline, and in the episodes they'd have characters say stuff like "Well if you hadn't gotten us shut down we wouldn't be running 200 kilos of coke through the jungle" just to clue you in.

So I tried doing that, using callbacks to sort of set up what happened before while also standing alone. The trouble is on TV shows they have a full 30 minutes to set up new story and still refresh you as to what happened previously. Here, I lose words each time.

It's 7:39 p.m. on Sunday, September 28, 2014, as I write this. I thought of the title to this story today while I was at the park with the boys. Just the title. The rest of the day I didn't think about it at all until during their baths (which we did early because we wanted to take the boys for a ride) I started thinking about it again, and originally this was going to be a story about Bear and Tiger writing a story together and getting in an argument about it but then I thought of the idea that Bear would gouge Tiger and create the stripes and I liked that.

I was having trouble getting started today – I'm home early from work and writing in the afternoon – and tried a few stories first before hitting on one about Bug God, who first appeared in a story I wrote a long time ago about the Giraffe God stealing Noah's Ark. Bug God is one of my favorite characters I've ever written.

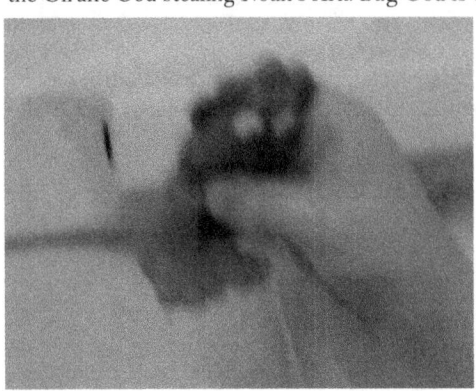

Well now I've got a new favorite story.

Last night, for his bath, Mr Bunches said he wanted to play with "diving monsters." These were those. I took the pictures not really knowing what I was going to do with them, and also decided that "Diving Monsters" would be my story tonight.

The primes are coming quickly, now. As I write this, I'm still not sure what happened at the old mill or what the dead lady in the car had to do with it. I'd better come up with something.

At first I thought *oh man what if you really did just see potatoes right before you died* but then I thought you'd have bigger things to think about anyway.

And now we meet Lenore. These aren't really meant to be connected stories, the Raven & Desk stories. I just like the challenge of continuing to write them, so they are one of three recurring stories that might appear on the primes.

The first draft of this, which I only was halfway through when I changed it, had the man speaking in dialect, and Lenore getting off a ship, and was written in the first person.

We were supposed to go up in a plane today, me and Mr Bunches. There were free flights being given at the local airport in small planes. But it was raining this morning and the flights were canceled. Mr Bunches is afraid of thunder and hates rain because of that. Now he has another reason.

When I first typed the title, I had no idea what I was going to write next and I really thought this would be a cowboy story. But it turned out not to be. I listened to Ingrid Michaelson's *Girls Chase Boys* on repeat while I wrote this. I think it helped.

This one is sort of similar to a 250-word story I did called "Skyfall," which is a story about the sky falling.

It's also pretty influenced by Lucy Corin's book *100 Apocalypses And Other Apocalypses*. I was about halfway through it when I realized it would be a story like that.

To me, two lines really stand out in this story, and they are the reason it exists; if it didn't have these two lines in it the story might not be.

The first line is one that came to me unedited and exactly as it is written:

Sports heroes, presidents, soldiers: nobody was too good for us to throw the trash of rich people on.

The other line is the closing line. I wrote that a couple of different ways until I had it just right.

This was kind of a bad day. An angering day, mostly for work-related reasons. I used to enjoy my job a lot. Now, it is less enjoyable and many days I think *just wait it out*. What I am waiting for is for some of my older partners to retire so I can be in charge. That is the quickest, easiest way to improve my job: wait. I would leave and start my own firm but I have only about $1,000 in my savings, not enough to see me through the end of the month without a paycheck.

And the night was frustrating; Mr Bunches had two math sheets to work through, one with 100 problems. He hates math. He doesn't understand it and it makes him cry. I tried not to lose my patience with him, with only about 70% success, and then of course I feel terrible. And then the towel bar fell three times while I dried Mr F off, and now they are in bed, and things are quieting down.

I wanted to write a happy story, then, because not all bad things happened today. My doctors said that the weird blood conditions that have been plaguing me for 14 months appear to be under control, and I am down to only 1 daily medicine. On Sunday I went jogging for the first time in that 14 months. Only ¼ mile, 4 laps out of 24, but it was *something*.

So this story is really a metaphor, I think, for freedom of the spirit. If your spirit is happy, nobody can harm you. And my spirit *is* happy, mostly.

Last week, I was drying Mr Bunches off after his bath and it occurred to me, right then, that I was at that moment *perfectly* happy. Nothing was bothering me, I felt good, I had no worries about the next day, nothing bad had happened that day. It wasn't some big moment. There was no parade, no amusement park, I hadn't won the lottery. It was just there, in our upstairs bathroom, helping my son get on his too-small superhero pajamas that he really has outgrown but he loves them so much, that I realized how happy I was.

It's like having a moment of perfect quiet. Or when the sun shines through the clouds just right. Or that one part of a song, or that first bite of pizza. It's those little moments that probably slip by all the time, but on that day, I noticed it, and now on days like this, I think back to that moment, and I can feel how happy I was right then, and bring it back, a bit.

222

I don't actually have an idea for what that Pope-Clooney-Macaroni might be, but I bet I could come up with one.

221

That title's sort of a spoiler, I guess.

220

This week finished up spectacularly. After the difficulties at work, I decided to take matters into my own hands. I have begun setting up a plan to leave my firm and set up my own firm. Whether I do that or not in the long run the decision to do that has also helped me be more firm with my partners and stand up to them more. And that has made me feel good. And to top it all off, I was driving home from a hearing in another county today and I saw a bald eagle, which I decided to take as a good omen that everything is going the way it ought to.

Then, after dinner, the boys and I walked to the pool a mile away, and we were nearly there when Mr Bunches, the younger of the twins, tripped and skinned his knee. He wanted a Band-Aid, but I didn't have one and we were a mile from home, so I convinced him to just go on to the pool and see if that didn't make him feel better when a lady nearby said *"Do you need a Band-Aid?"* and it turned out that she'd overheard us and had one for him. That made me feel like no matter what God will watch out for my boys. I'm in a pretty good mood.

219

Here is what I think about metaphor and symbolism and the like: I'm not sure I always believe it. When I was in high school and my teachers would say things like "To Poe, the writing desk was actually the silver standard the US government was adopting" I'd think *"But how do you know that? Did he say that?"* My own attempts at symbolism and metaphor are often clumsy and annoying.

Then there is this story, which I wrote on Saturday morning, October 11, 2014. I started writing it, and got through the first ½ of it or so when Mr Bunches asked me to make him some breakfast. While I was getting him a glass of milk I was working out the ending and I did so it occurred to me that this story could be a metaphor for us, going through life wondering about God and Heaven.

It wasn't *meant* that way. It was just meant as a kind of weird story about some guys on a raft asking philosophical questions. But if I become famous and a hundred years from now this book is read by high school sophomores, teachers might well interpret it that way.

The "My Aunt's Dog Theorem" that I came up with years ago is this: Think of an abstract painting, some weird mix of blurs and blots and colors; it could be whatever the artist wants it to be, usually something like "Man's Inhumanity To Man" or something. But no matter how deep the work is intended to be, someone's going to look at it and say *"That looks like my aunt's dog."*

The Theorem stands for the idea that no matter what the creator puts into the creative work, people are bringing their own package of conceptions and backgrounds and beliefs to it and applying them to that framework. So Poe's Silver Standard Desk might be just a desk to you, or may stand for the girlfriend you never got the courage to marry, or might just be *boring*.

So if you read this story and thought it was a metaphor then it was. But if you didn't get that, then it wasn't.

218

Last night Mr F woke up at 1:00 a.m. He and I went downstairs where for most of the night he talked to himself and watched *The Rugrats Movie* while I dozed off and on and watched a documentary series about islands. I learned that the Falkland Islands have lots of natural peat on them and that some residents of the islands have a permit to gather and eat penguin eggs.

Despite being exhausted, today was a wonderful day.

217

I kind of feel like *"mightn't"* is cheating, a bit, and should probably be "might not" but the word count wouldn't work.

Originally it was "can't" but that's silly because of course the gods *could* destroy them all.

216

My first grandchild was born today; our oldest daughter, 27, gave birth to a little boy. She's probably not ready, even at 27, to be a mom, but who is? So I wrote a story about being born, and I think it's not a totally sad story. Is a God who simply lets everything happen randomly worse than a God who deliberately sets out to cause bad things to happen to good people? I think they're probably about equal.

People who want to argue against the existence of a God always ask why bad things are allowed to happen, as if the existence of earthquakes means God can't be. But they never point to the good things to prove that God *must* be. Two years ago, Mr F fell off a countertop and hit his head and started bleeding into his brain. He was rushed to a hospital, a brain surgeon came and operated on him, and three days later he came home. He's none the worse for the wear, the only aftereffects being a scar on his head and a prohibition on contact sports.

If his falling off the counter means to some people that God doesn't exist, doesn't his being saved mean that God must?

For myself, I firmly believe in God's existence, and the presence of bad things happening to people causes me to wonder *why* but doesn't shake my faith. I believe that God allows us to make choices, and that those choices, and random chance, are why bad things happen in the world. I believe that God has to allow bad things to happen because God could only ensure that no bad things would ever happen by denying us free will, and that denying us free will would be far far worse than simply making us watch children die or earthquakes happen or wars.

So if you are someone who asks *How can God let bad things happen?*, to me the answer is that otherwise God would have to deny us any existence at all.

The title of this story, by the way, refers to a particular kind of dice roll in craps – double sixes, or "boxcars", and a kind of bet you can make in that game. A bet "on the hop" is a bet that a particular set of numbers will turn up on the next roll.

215

Like most of my stories, I have no idea really where this idea came from. I wrote the title and then had to decide what to write next. For a while it was going to be a cowboy playing cards with a robot. Then I thought about maybe putting a dinosaur in there but I finally settled on this.

The hardest part about this story was that there was some sort of gummy sticky stuff on the "e" on my laptop and I finally had to go clean it with a damp cloth.

214

This actually started as a story about the planet Mercury falling in love with the Sun but I felt like that was going nowhere.

In the past few days I've had a couple more stories rejected, including "Chomp!" losing a contest for poetry. On the bright side, I start tonight making revisions in my first book ever to be published by someone other than me. It was called *Find Out Who You Are* but they changed the title to *Codes*, based on the fact that the characters in it are called "codes," because many of them are human clones implanted with personalities written as computer programs.

Today, at work, I got into an argument with my partner again. It doesn't matter what it was about, other than to say that he was being dumb and a jerk, and if I had enough money I'd have walked out today. I don't have enough money, yet, and so for now I continue to be his partner and work, and plan for my eventual takeover of this firm or starting my own new one.

There are worse lives.

213

Another one I'm not sure of. Today is Friday, October 17. Mr F had to have a dental thing today and because of his autism he had go to the hospital and be put under, complete anesthesia. It turned out he only needed his teeth cleaned, nothing major.

I decided about 9 a.m. that rather than going into the office at noon like I'd planned, I'd skip out. So I said the surgery was taking longer than planned and went home after the surgery, with Sweetie and Mr F. I checked my emails and wrote some letters and got a bit of work done remotely, but I other than that I played hooky all day.

Mr F is wide awake now It's 9:03 p.m. and he's on the couch, talking and tapping his forks and watching Toy Story 3. I'm really tired and really at the end of my rope, a bit. Today was very stressful, for about a zillion reasons. I kept in my mind picturing having a showdown with my partner where he quits or I quit, and then telling myself that would never happen. In between, the boys got into a fight of sorts because Mr F wanted to watch *A Bug's Life* and that movie scares Mr Bunches so much he started crying. Mr F also got sick a few times, and by 8:45 I told Sweetie I just needed a break.

So I'm not really into stories tonight. I had sort of an idea about Venus and what this story would be like and I don't think I really hit it but I'm tired.

Update? It's 7:50 p.m. the next night. I just sat down to do some writing, Mr F on his couch, Mr Bunches upstairs, Sweetie in our bedroom, "Forever For Her (Is Over For Me)" playing on my iTunes. And I went back and revised this to be in the second person, the way it is now. It was originally third person, but today I was thinking about tonight's story and I thought how all these stories—I'm going to do one each for the planets—should be 'you' stories. They seem to work better that way.

212

We went today to a church called "Holy Hill" to scatter some of my mom's ashes. My mom died something like five years ago. My brother, who I don't talk to anymore, mailed me a portion of her ashes a few months ago, unexpectedly. They have been in a closet since then, waiting for a chance to take them to this church, which sits on a wooded hill and which Mom liked to go to.

I put a few near a statue of the Virgin Mary. I put some by a statute of Jesus at one of the stations of the cross. Then there was a hill covered in yellow leaves and sloping off into a forest, and I thought that was the perfect area. Mr F and I walked a ways down the path and I scattered the rest of them.

They were gravelly and white, powdery. They were in a plastic bag in a cheap plastic box. I didn't get very sentimental because it's impossible to look at a bag of gravel five years after you last saw your Mom and think of that bag of gravel as even remotely connected to her. The only reason I took them at all was that it seemed wrong to simply throw them away.

As with some of the others I am not sure how I feel about this. After I'd finished it up I had an idea for a story in which Poe talks about how there never was a Lenore and he only had to write the stupid poem to get the raven to shut up about it, but by then I'd already written *this* one, so I stuck with it. I think this story is mediocre at best except that the last line sort of ups it to where it's acceptable.

Today at work my partner asked me if something was wrong. I said "Do you really want to get into this now?"

He is someone that used to be my boss and who I thought was now my friend. Things apparently do not stay the same, or they never were the same in the first place.

But when I came home, I got to lose myself in reading "3D Planets" with Mr Bunches for his homework. The book comes with 3D glasses, which never work very well for me due to my lazy eye. But I try them on and we look at the 3D pictures and take turns reading. Tonight we had Mr F read with us; we had him practice saying the names of the planets and showing him pictures of them. I'm not sure how much he cared about it or understood it but I felt bad for Mr F. I felt bad because he wanted to play water in the sink, dumping water on his hands. He likes that. I first was going to stop him, because he always makes a mess when he does, and when I told him "No," Mr F waved his hands and hummed and made a sad face and I felt terrible, so I let him play water a few times and then just wiped it up.

Really, I have a very good life. It's just been challenging this year. Every night I pray that I have the wisdom to do the right thing and so far I think I do.

I am not someone who likes to talk about it a lot but I believe in signs, that sometimes there are messages we can see, the reasons that things happen, and today I think I stumbled onto one. It's early to tell but maybe.

This story is based in true life: tonight I told Mr F that he was the living embodiment of *mess*, but I didn't really disapprove, because that's just Mr F. And when we were first dating I took Sweetie out to where I grew up and we got out my telescope I used to have and set it up and looked at things like Saturn and Jupiter through it. They were very disappointing. But the night was a great one that I remember clearly 16 years later.

How *can* that storm last that long?

I had to look up how to spell "susurrance." I didn't even know I knew that word until I decided to use it in this story.

According to Merriam-Webster, "YER-uh-nus" is correct. But some academics say it's either. *Teach the controversy!*

It's Saturday morning, October 25, 2014, as I write this. 8:06 a.m. I am listening to the song "After The Fall" by The Trans-Siberian Orchestra. I just ate a Pop-Tart (cookie-dough flavor.)

This week things came to more of a head at the office. I am increasingly angry and disgruntled. I confronted my other two partners and said we needed to address the difficulties the lead guy has been causing. I am nervous. I kept checking my emails last night. Half the time I worry they will break up the partnership and I will be cast out on my own and have to make my own way. Half the time I hope they will.

Bet you thought I'd say something about how it's not a planet anymore but *eh*, I don't care much about that. I thought it was a big deal at the time but now I don't care either way. Does it matter if Pluto's a planet? We never want anything to change, nowadays. We don't want to add a state, subtract a state, we don't want planets to not be, we just want to live in this static world where the same rock stars make music for forty years.

It might have sucked to live in the 1880s, when people were dying of consumption by the time they were 15, by which time they'd already been married and widowed and were great-grandfathers, and you had to make your house out of sod and you ate things like possum, but at least back then the world was allowed to change.

Maybe we're so opposed to things like Pluto changing because so much changes around us every day, but the stuff that changes, websites and things, seems so ephemeral. I used to make print copies of my books because when they were only available online it seemed like they were impermanent the way summer is, how it feels when June starts and one day it's a little cold and you can feel December in that cold and you suddenly know that summer isn't going to be around very long. That's how our modern age feels: like everything is only moments away from coming up with one those "404 Not Available" signs, *everything.*

Originally I had "inventions," but I didn't like it. I looked up synonyms and liked "contrivances." It has a better feel for this story.

It's Hallowe'en, almost: October 28, and I felt like writing a monster story.

Today was a good day; despite Mr F waking me up at 3:00 o'clock in the morning, I made plans to meet with another lawyer and discuss possibly a new business venture, and I might have gotten an extra $5,000 as a result of some luck. More on that maybe in the future. I'm pretty sure I got $5,000.

201

A while ago I wrote a story about "Mr Suitcase," who has a bag full of nasty things he uses to kill people with. Spider-Legs is from the same family of monsters, together with a character from a poem I wrote, Lazy Bones Jones. I'm creating a bit of a mythology around them, but not in any sort of an organized way.

200

MAN did this one take a lot of work. It kept being like 300 words long and originally included as an opening line *"Rocket got his name from his trajectory; from an early age it was apparent he would always be heading perpendicular to everything else."* I LOVE that line, but I couldn't make it fit in there. So I put it in this note.

"Rocket" as a guy comes from tonight, when I was outside playing Big Wheel with Mr F. He rides it down our hill, as fast as he can, turning left at the bottom, and I run alongside to keep him from smacking into something or getting run over. After one ride, I said "Nice run, Rocket!"

Then I began thinking of a guy named "Rocket" who would be a daredevil like Evel Knievel used to be. I think daredevils should still be a thing. Although I guess they are: Felix Baumgartner, that other guy who jumped out of a balloon, the guy who rode the world's biggest wave. They just all don't have the pizzazz that Evel Knievel's rocket car jumping Snake Canyon has in my memory.

199

Happy Halloween, 2014!

198

November 1, 2014. 8:42 a.m., Saturday morning. I am on day two of my diet, in which I am trying to eat only 1,600 calories per day because I can't work out, really, without causing all kinds of whatever. So yesterday I think I met the goal. Today I had two cookies 'n' cream Pop Tarts for breakfast. That's ¼ of what I can eat all day. We are having Sweetie's birthday party tonight, which means everyone is expected to eat a "Whopper" from Burger King. Whoppers have 610 calories, so that's more than ½ of what's left. I've told myself I'll see if I can do this for a month.

198

November 1, 2014. 8:42 a.m., Saturday morning. I am on day two of my diet, in which I am trying to eat only 1,600 calories per day because I can't work out, really, without causing all kinds of whatever. So yesterday I think I met the goal. Today I had two cookies 'n' cream Pop Tarts for breakfast. That's ¼ of what I can eat all day. We are having Sweetie's birthday party tonight, which means everyone is expected to eat a "Whopper" from Burger King. Whoppers have 610 calories, so that's more than ½ of what's left. I've told myself I'll see if I can do this for a month.

198

It's Sweetie's birthday! And my diet ended yesterday about 11 a.m. I decided instead to try to take up walking again, exercise more. I was so *starved*. I don't know how people do it. I don't know how I once did it? When I was 24 I lost 108 pounds, by dieting and exercising. I always thought I could do it again but maybe that's the kind of thing you only do once in a lifetime.

197

Tonight on my walk with Mr F I tried to figure out if 197 was a prime number. I have a list of primes that I keep in this manuscript, just past the end of the current story I've written, but I forget to check it sometimes. I gave up trying to figure out if 197 was a prime and just walked with Mr F, listening to an audiobook (*The Shining Girls*) and feeling the unusually warm (58 degrees) night.

Then at the end of the night I sat down and sent an email to a lawyer I am trying to form a partnership with so I can leave my current job, which has gone terribly terribly south. Then I sent Sweetie a text (she's up in the boys' room waiting for them to fall asleep) with some words of inspiration and then I thought about a story in which Charley Horse ran into the sky, which I felt was a metaphor for planning on leaving my current job and starting a new one.

Then I checked the list and 197 is, after all, a prime. But I didn't care. I wanted to write about Charley and his run.

195

Tonight was as close as I have come to not writing a story per day in this series. I was so depressed and stressed out and tired and worried.

In the past week, we have gotten an extra $5,000 we didn't expect to have, and then today I got bad news about our firm's finances that make it almost certain that I will not make anywhere near the amount of money I need to this year. I have begun negotiating with another lawyer to start up a new firm, but that's still in the early stages, and we need money coming in so I can't just leave my present firm and start my own practice. I have no office, no computer, no phone, and while I'm sure I *would* get those things I need funding. Things have gotten increasingly uncomfortable at my firm and we're going to meet tomorrow morning in what I expect to be such a bad meeting that it's got me sick to my stomach. Sweetie is upset. I am upset. This is a terrible feeling.

I took Mr F for a ride before bed. During that ride, I prayed and prayed, saying over and over the three prayers I know by heart and seeking some guidance. Towards the end of the ride I began to feel a little bit better. I have some plans and some hope. I'm resolved to go to this meeting tomorrow and weather it out, for Sweetie and the kids. Things will get better.

On Labor Day in the year 2000, Sweetie and I had <u>no</u> money. None. We couldn't afford to go get groceries and had to eat what little food we had around the house. We spent that weekend in a stressful kind of stasis and that

Labor Day I went and sent an email to a blind box ad that led to my current job. Now, just over 14 years later, things are almost that bad. But we've gone through a lot, and we'll get through this, too.

I feel bad for the robot, who can't even get the solace that I can.

194

The meeting was somehow worse and not as bad as I imagined it would be. I did not quit; I did not get asked to resign as a shareholder. But it was uncomfortable nonetheless and my partner, the one with the majority control, spent the rest of the day doing things to emphasize that he is, after all, my *boss*. I spent the day imagining what it will be like when the rest of my plans come true.

I am alternating between hopeful optimism, waiting to hear back from the guy I made a business proposal to, and also having had another inquiry from someone who might form a new law firm venture with me, and fear about what might happen if things do not work out.

I tell myself things will be better. I tell myself they'll never be as bad as I imagine.

I found myself, on my ride with Mr F tonight, thinking about the story I would write. I was listening to a cover of "Modern Love" by the band Pizza!, and I thought of the premise of this story. I thought, then, what I might do when I get down to 50 or less words, what kinds of stories I would write, and I counted ahead to what day it would be when I hit 50 words. Today is November 6, 2014. 144 days from now will be March 30, 2015.

I really have no idea what my life will be like then. 144 days before today was June 15, 2014. That was before things started to go really bad at work. That was right at the outset of summer. That was day 338. The day before, June 14, we went on a road trip to Milwaukee and had a wonderful time. I was maybe a little worried about money but, overall, I expected this year to be pretty good. Had you said to me that day that near the end of the year I would be desperately unhappy at work, and looking for a new job, I would have thought you were crazy.

So who knows what March 30, 2015 will bring? Hopefully, things will be better. I feel pretty good right now.

I feel pretty good right now

193

Last night Mr Bunches had me do this: I had to copy down all the words to *There's A Wocket In My Pocket*, verbatim. We did it using red marker on a purple pad of Post-It notes. So this is based on a true story.

192

After I wrote this I got the feeling I was using "smite" or some form of it, a lot. But I've only used it four times now. Out of 75,617 words, which is how many words I've got in this book so far as of the phrase *out of 75,617 words.* Four out of 75,617 is 5.29 to the -5 power percent of the words. I was never very good with *powers* in math. I think that's 0.00005295%?

Here's how not good at math I am, sometimes: When I try to figure out how many stories I've written I get confused. 365-192 seems easy, but it's wrong, because that would mean I have 192 stories left, but since I've just written story 192, I have only 191 left, so it's actually 365-191 stories, and I've written 174 stories for 174 consecutive days.

Also today I wrote about 1/3 of my business plan to apply for a loan to start my own firm. So I've got three oars in the fire or something.

191

I wanted to write a dinosaur story, as I'm putting together a short collection of short stories and I chose dinosaurs as the theme; this is for a new project in which I gather up a couple of stories that have something in common and put them on Amazon under the heading "Some _____ Stories." So far, I've done "Some Zombie Stories," and I've actually sold a copy of it (plus given away something like 125 free ones.) I started doing that because putting the stories on my blog didn't pay, at all, and nobody ever read them or commented on them, much. So I wanted to see if this would make some money for me, and thus far it made $0.35.

The first version of this story was a more generic space story in which a guy named "Jason" fought space dinosaurs on Jupiter's moon. He challenged one to a duel, but when I wrote that I thought it was a little too much like another short story I wrote, "Meat," in which two people travel back in time to see dinosaurs, only to find that the dinos have guns and are intelligent.

So this one instead makes the same old "T.Rexs have short arms joke," but that's in keeping with my "Higgs Boson" stories. "Higgs Boson" is a character I invented to have a mock serial space story, like "Buck Rogers." In Higgs Boson stories, completely improbable events happen all the time, because that is my understanding of the Higgs Boson.

190

This started out as a different story entirely, inspired by a line from a Johnny Cash song that was playing as I started on tonight's story. Version one took a strange twist after Julia asked what the poster meant and Jeb didn't know; there was a third guy on the subway and the subway was a sort of ghost train, all of which was very interesting but which was hard to resolve in 190 words, and so I went back and redid the story as it is now, and realized about 95% of the way through that given what's been going on with my job right now this story is pretty symbolic, I guess. But I didn't start out to write it that way.

While I'm on that subject, I might as well 'fess up: story 312 is also the same sort of symbolism. It was way back then – 122 days ago! – that I first began fearing that something like what is going on now (battling with partners, looking for new work, worrying about the future) was going to happen. And I had said to Sweetie back then "We are okay," and then wrote that story as a way, I guess, of writing out my worries.

189

It wasn't until about 2/3 of the way through this story that I decided it was worth keeping. Up until then, I was always this close* to deleting it, but it won me over near the end.

    * *This close:* -**

    ** Which is pretty close.

PS: The meeting today with a potential new firm went very well and I have decided not to join them because I feel like I would be saving them, rather than the other way around. I have to save my family, and some coworkers. I can't take on 11 *new* people to save. But I am in a pretty good, if very tired, mood. During the meeting I realized just how much better off I am than many other people, including the 11 people at this firm who would welcome me like a conquering hero, which would be great but they are in such dire straits that it would be the equivalent of starting my own practice only with 11 additional workers I hadn't planned on.

188

This started out as a happier story, too. Which is weird because I'm in a good mood tonight. I spent the night playing *Inspector Gadget 2* with Mr Bunches, in which I was the bad guys trying to stop him from stealing the stuff to build the weapon? I couldn't really follow the plot. And I tried to spend some time with Mr F, to less success, and Sweetie and I got to talk a bit, and things overall are pretty swell, I think.

It's 16 days 'til Thanksgiving, and I decided to start a series of Thanksgiving stories based on the dinner. I may have done it a bit early? We'll see how it turns out.

187

This one took a while. All day long I thought about what 'stuffing' story I would write. I thought about stories in which stuffing came alive and stories about gods fighting over stuffing and stories about stuffing teddy bears with actual stuffing and when it came time, at 8:30, to sit down and write the story I still had no idea what to write about.

So I read a Wikipedia article on stuffing and learned that they really did stuff dormice in ancient Rome. Then I wrote a story in which a dormouse gets picked up by an eagle for the eagle's Thanksgiving dinner but they don't eat it right away because they're waiting for the dad to get home with the stuffing. I didn't like that, but I liked the dormouse character, so I went and read about dormice then, and wrote this story. The ending gave me some trouble. And I couldn't squeeze in the bit about how in Elizabethan times they used dormouse fat to induce sleep, probably because dormice are known to be sleepy animals, hibernating as much as 6 months a year.

So there's a lot of facts you just learned about dormice.

186

According to Wikipedia, Major General John Gaspard le Marchant of the British was a British cavalry commander who recommended draw-cutting beets as practice for using the broadsword in his book *The Rules and Regulations of the Sword Exercise of the Cavalry.*

185

Potatoes, and hence mashed potatoes, were illegal in France until 1772 or so, when Antoine-Augustin Parmentier, harkening back to the days when he was in prison in Prussia and ate nothing but potatoes, proved that the food could be a good source of nutrition for people suffering dysentery. The French remained suspicious of the food, though, so Parmentier began a series of strange efforts to allow it to gain acceptance. He gave potato bouquets to royalty and hosted dinners featuring potato dishes (with Ben Franklin as a guest at one at least).

He also planted a patch of potatoes and hired guards to 'protect' it, so people would think there was something valuable there, then instructed the guards to accept bribes and to leave at night so people could easily steal the potatoes. And hence this story!

PS: Sweetie says beets aren't a part of Thanksgiving dinner but whatever.

184

It's sort of hard to write about gravy.

183

OH MAN I love this story. I love it so much. I have re-read it three times already in the five minutes since I wrote it.

182

Well that was quite a life! Also, I hate green bean casserole but everyone else in my family loves it.

I have an interview tomorrow with a law firm that might like to hire me away for what would be a substantial raise. I'm awaiting a proposal from another firm that might want me to join *them*. I am feeling better about life these days. It's not as though everything's perfect but it's more in that direction than a week ago. And Thanksgiving is only just about a week away.

181

It's a prime number, and this is the story that came up randomly. Which is fine; it's okay to take a break from Thanksgiving stories for a day, right?

The interview, I feel, went really well.

180

The phrase "corn are horrible isolationists" gave me pause but I think it's grammatically correct. And if it's not, *POETIC LICENSE.*

Today the guy I've been talking to about setting up a practice with him confirmed that yeah we're gonna do that. At 10 a.m. he emailed me and asked if we could talk at 2 o'clock and I said sure, and for the next four hours I felt like I was having an asthma attack or something because I was for some reason sure he was going to call the deal off. But he didn't and the deal is a good one, which means that sometime in January or early February I will no longer be working at the firm where I not only have spent my last 14 ½ years, but am a part owner. And I'm not even sad. I don't think I'll miss it at all. A year ago I might have felt differently but this year has more or less been horrible at work. I no longer like most of the people I work with and I had given up even hoping that things would get better. Every day was a battle. After the call at 2 today, I went back to work—I'd ducked out to make the deal—and when I got back I felt *lighter.* You know how people say *"It felt like a weight had been lifted"?* LIKE THAT. I felt like that.

179

If this story were true, would it be *worse* or *better* than how, say, *meat* is made?

178

That's the last of the Thanksgiving stories, I decided.

I like the idea of pumpkins having aurora-like bodies that come alive only in the new moon. You don't imagine a pumpkin could be graceful, but once you picture it it's beautiful.

177

I tried a couple of different versions of this story, all of them dealing with rhinoceroses, before hitting on this one, in which I decided that unlike all the other animals I've written about in these types of stories, rhinoceroses would not have much of an inner life.

I briefly thought about looking up how rhinoceroses fight but decided I'd rather not research it. So if they don't fight like this, tough. They probably don't ask each other whether they've had enough or have beliefs about where they come from, either, in real life.

176

In *Rosencrantz & Guildenstern Are Dead,* one of the characters keeps flipping a coin, and that helps determine which world the play is taking place in. Or so I remember from 11th or 12th grade. I remember reading that play and loving it, so much so that I've never really forgotten the experience of reading the play, even though I don't remember much about the play itself. I remember the coin flipping, though. And this morning, on my way into what apparently soon will be my ex- job—I am finalizing a new deal this week, probably, HAPPY THANKGIVING! (I'm very nervous about it)—I was thinking of that coin toss and I started to think how weird it would be if you flipped a coin and came up heads like this, every time. There's no reason it couldn't. One of the things that bugs me is "the law of averages," which isn't a law at all. Because things have no memory, the 'law of averages' doesn't actually work. The coin doesn't 'remember' what its last flip was and cannot therefore adjust its next flip to account for what has happened before. And there's only an 8% chance that a coin flipped 100 times will come up heads 50 times and tails 50 times. EIGHT PERCENT.

So even though there's no reason 10,013 heads in a row couldn't happen, you'd have to admit, it'd be pretty freaky.

175

This story is true. That's what we did tonight.

Today I accepted the offer from the other lawyer. On December 9 we should finalize it. On January 15 I'm supposed to start my new career.

174

All day long I wanted to write a 'regular mouse' story. I hit on the title and then tried a bunch of different stories. In one the mouse tries to figure out a way to get more cheese. In another the mouse tried to stop the dreams but then changed his mind. I decided that the regular mouse is a practical sort that is full of good, clever ways of looking at things, so I had the parakeet be antidreams. That seems like a parakeet-y thing to be, especially one who is owned by the awful boys.

The regular mouse has now officially joined Bug God and Charley Horse as recurring characters.

173

I think this deserves to be expanded into a full-on story. This and Pirates. I kept thinking about that all day.

It's Thanksgiving, 2014! It's 9:57 p.m. I'm in the boys' room, and they're mostly asleep. It's been a long day. But a successful one: I think this was the first year everything I cooked turned out reasonably well, even the pecan pie that I thought might not work out so well.

172

Today *is* Black Friday. So I wrote a Black Friday story.

I once read about half a book a secretary at work loaned me, a true-crime story about a guy who'd decided to spend his life sailing around the South Pacific. Other people did it, too, all these people just pulling boats up to tiny islands and grilling crabs or whatever, this whole sort of hobo-sailor colony drifting around the Pacific. Then this week I listened to a podcast in which they talked about people in Africa still hunting chimpanzees, for food, with spears. It seems weird to think that not everybody wants a life filled with laptops and cell phones and McRibs. Every time I think I might want a life like that which the people in these stories have, I realize I'd last about a day before breaking, since that is exactly how long it lasted for me the last time I went camping, nearly 20 years ago. I like my luxuries and my technology.

What I like about this story is it feels like Daniel is wrong but it's hard to say why. He doesn't seem like a great guy, stealing a boat and all, but what, exactly, is his crime? Not talking more to the girl? Not asking if she's okay? Not trying to at least find his way back? That becomes more of a focus of the story than the fact that the sun has stopped coming up.

The first draft of this story had some cool lines about what the stars looked like and the fact that there was also never a visible moon anymore, but word-counts meant those had to go.

171

Time for some Xmas stories! Originally the tiger was going to eat the guy piece by piece while he talked but I thought that was a little too much like the Monty Python skit with that knight or whatever. I don't know which skit, exactly. I just know there was a skit with a knight getting chopped up or something but never dying.

170

Nothing. I don't want to say anything. But I suppose I have to. Sweetie and I had a fight tonight. I won't say what it was about. It was a fight. A bad one, one of the ones we've had maybe 2 times prior in all the time we've been together. I could barely get it together to write this story, and it's not much of a story but I had to write *something* because if I didn't then the fight would have killed this whole thing and I can't let that happen.

Four years ago, we got in an argument—not a terrible one, but an argument, they happen, not often to us but they happen even to us—at Christmas and each year I still remember it. Just like I remember when I was a kid and my parents got mad at me for something and my Mom burned my *Doonesbury* book in the fireplace. I sat and watched it burn. I've had so many happy Christmas memories. But it's the bad ones that stick around.

169

Today, I didn't go into the office. After we made up, mostly, last night, I slept terribly and then today couldn't bring myself to go into work. So I went to Panera and worked on a legal guide I'm writing, then made a conference call from my cell phone and then came home and worked from home until noon. Then Sweetie and I watched a movie, *Blue Ruin*, that we've been trying to set aside time to watch.

"This isn't our date," I said. We've been going on a date a week—carving out an hour or two for just us every week. This week's planned date is Friday, when I was going to come home for lunch.

"It isn't?" she said.

"This is just to…" I couldn't think of the word. "Unwind," I said.

168

Updates on various matters.

Each day the fight looms a little less but it's like after a thunderstorm when a tree has been knocked down in your yard and even after it's cleared away you can still stare at that bare spot and remember the fury. We laughed and ate pizza and stuff today but it's still sort of lingering around.

Our refrigerator isn't working right. We had to call a repairman to come out on Thursday—two days from now, it's Tuesday, December 2, 2014 at 8:26 p.m. as I write this—because it's not really making things cold anymore. So there's that, on top of our other money worries.

Today I had to talk to my 'partner' who it's now very apparent never was one. He seems completely unaware that I'm leaving, in 44 days. He kept making comments to me trying to goad me into saying something—saying that I'd misled a client in an email and that I didn't seem committed to 'client service' the way he was. He commented that he knew I'd been upset about not making as much money this year— my pay will go down for the fourth consecutive year, this year—and commented how I wasn't following this stupid program he's started that is just time consuming and does nothing. Rather than pick a fight, I just said "I'll work on it." He said "Maybe the fact that your bonus will be so much less this year will motivate you to do something." He said it in a really mean way, like he was trying to prove a point. He's been like that, this guy I thought was a good friend, since July, since I began demanding that he make changes because we were losing money. I began demanding reports and trying to actually improve the place and he responded by being mean and trying to undercut me. At one point, he followed me down the hall yelling that I was a "liar," and when I said he shouldn't say things like that in front of the staff he said "I'll say whatever I want."

So when he said today that thing about the motivation, I thought how next week Tuesday I will almost certainly be signing a new partnership agreement with all new people, and I just sat quietly and thought about dramatic irony. Then I left work early and came home, where I played "Sky Racers" with Mr Bunches, and we read *Pete The Cat* and we all took a drive and got a soda at McDonald's, and I read a Sesame Street "Elmo" book with Mr F, and it was a pretty good night.

Not a great one. But sometimes things don't have to be

167, 166

The reason these two are out of order is this: Last night, Mr F was using Sweetie's laptop to watch a movie in bed, and Mr Bunches wanted to use *my* laptop to watch his own video, because the iPad was 'low on power.' Mr Bunches doesn't like blank screens – they scare him terribly, seriously: he gets panicked if a television or laptop is turned *off*, and if one goes dead he starts to cry – and the iPad was at 80%, which is lower than he likes it. At 90% or below he plugs it in to charge.

So all the computers were being used, but I still had to write a story. So I wrote story 167 on my phone, sitting on the couch in the dark listening to Xmas music. But the notepad app doesn't have a word counter, so when I was done I just emailed it to myself and figured I'd edit it when the boys fell asleep. But they didn't fall asleep until after I did, so I didn't edit the story until today. I actually edited it this morning, while I was on a break from a mediation session. It was originally about 220 words and I chopped it down to the 167 and re-emailed it to myself, since I was not on 'my' laptop where I have this manuscript saved.

Then, tonight, it's my turn to sit with the boys in their room. I'm on my laptop now, which has a limited battery life. To make sure it didn't run out before I finished story 166 I wrote that story (which came in, rough draft, at only about 180 words) and then went and got story 167 off my email and pasted it in.

That all seemed more interesting in my head before I said it.

165

I really did have that idea for a tree, but I kept my wits about me and made it to the grocery store without mishap.

164

Today is "St. Nick's Day," which in our family means that everyone gets some small present or candy. The older kids each got a candy-cane shape filled with M&Ms. I got a box of candy. The boys each got a toy car, but Mr F didn't like his so we took him for hash browns at McDonald's. Sweetie gets a pedicure and a trip to Dairy Queen. Happy St. Nick's Day!

163

This one was *hard*. First off, I decided that *Pirates of the …* and *Trouble Down At The Old Mill* are not going to be prime number stories anymore; I'm going to turn those into full-length stories or novels, so I redid the primes to do stories about Bug God and Charley Horse and The Regular Mouse, plus *Raven*, on them.

I had the idea for what I wanted to do, but it cycled through Bug God writing to Santa, and then being told she couldn't because Santa was mad at him, and so on, and each of them was going too long. I really liked the idea of Bug God not being able to get presents because of Santa getting stung. One version had Bug God waiting up on Xmas Eve, and was called "The Bug God Refuses To Make Amends, Even On Xmas" but again, it went too long.

It's my night with Mr F, and Mr F wanted to lay on the couch. He was restless and crabby and I kept telling him he had to lay down and go to sleep, getting crabby myself, and finally Mr F got so upset that I took him for a ride. We drove our usual route, and on it, the idea for how to tell this story came to me, and that was that.

The thing about these stories getting shorter and shorter is that I have to get even more creative with how I tell them. When you only get 163 words, it's hard to tell a story, at all. So I had to work for this one, but I think it was worth it.

Hard to believe how much better this Sunday is than last Sunday. The feeling of sadness and anger from that fight is still around, just muted. The week was a good one, the weekend a good one, everything is going fine, but that fight is still just under the surface, it seems.

And I am four weeks, more or less, from telling my partner that I'm through. I find myself imagining that scene, which I plan to do on January 4, over and over. I get nervous, in a good way, thinking about it. The more I pore over the past 14 years in this firm, the more I think I was stupid to have stayed this long. I have been told over and over by people that I am too trusting and too nice to people I shouldn't be nice to. This is the latest example of that. I think I've been getting screwed over for too long and not standing up for myself for too long – taking a lot of stupid nonsense from people when I didn't need to.

I don't place a lot of stock in the change of calendars, from year to year or month to month. As evidenced by the fact that I started *this* project on a whim on some day in May, I tend to think not in terms of calendar dates but

162

Today, we finished our Xmas shopping. While we were out Mr F fell at school and chipped a tooth. I had to take him to the dentist after he got home, and on the way home from that my car made this terrible flapping sound that made it seem as if something was going to fly off the engine at any moment. I had to call Sweetie to come pick up Mr F, who rode with her and Mr Bunches behind me in case my car blew up on the way to the mechanics', but instead halfway there the noise stopped and my car appears fine.

We should do this every year…

161

I had all these ideas for stories shaped like things today, but I went and spent all day meeting with that firm I'm joining and it was a long day and it's 9:30 p.m. and I'm tired, so I wrote this one, quick. I'm not sure where the idea came from. I spent 10 minutes before writing it just flipping through pictures of Christmas, 2011, and feeling sad and nostalgic. I guess I came up with Horace to help squeeze out some stress. Poor Horace.

UPDATE: I told Sweetie about this story and she said I only named the snowman "Horace" because the boys have been watching "101 Dalmatians 2: Patch's London Adventure" over and over this week, and one of the bad guys is named "Horace."

She may be right.

160

So I clearly used the name "Jasper" because of Sweetie's claim.

159

I had this idea that I'd write a story in the shape of a Xmas tree. I wrote this story, and then when I thought about reshaping it into a tree, I thought "Why? What would that add to the story?" so I left it.

157

Another prime, another randomly-chosen "regular mouse" story. This one was tough to write. I had what I felt was kind of a great idea about the regular mouse seeing the moon and I went through a couple permutations of that but none of them were even *close* to being about 157 words. Then I came up with this one, which fit in there.

I realize I didn't write another Xmas story. It's only 12/13/14 as I write this, so I've got time to write more seasonal stories, but this morning I actually wrote "Other Snowmen, 3" and it was way over 157 words, but I liked it, so I used it in my collection I'm putting together, "Some Xmas Stories," and decided that would be the last new story in that collection, so I went back to other stories here.

I also realize I didn't do a note after story 158, so this sort of addresses that, too. If you want to read the thrilling end to "Other Snowmen," you'll have to get "Some Xmas Stories." It's totally worth it, I swear.

156

I feel like there is something missing from this story.

But I am very tired and my neck is very sore from falling asleep on the couch last night, with Mr F on the other couch. We spent the whole night sleeping on couches and today I have felt exhausted and have a stiff back.

And I am typing this story, and now this note, sitting in the dark dining room at the kitchen table, at 8:39 p.m. Also sitting in the dark dining room at the kitchen table is the "Play Doh Color Mixer" which has a tiny Elmo on it, and tiny Elmo says things, from time to time. So periodically coming out of the dark is a high-pitched baby talking voice telling me that I have made a bunch of friends, or asking me what my favorite color is. It startles me almost every time. So I'm going to leave the story as it is and head off to bed.

155

This boy is Mr F, sort of. I had this idea for a story about a boy who wanted to be a lion but he never told anybody because nobody ever asked him. Then I was playing with Mr F, one of the games he likes me to play, which is this: he jumps on his little trampoline and I hold his hands and help him bounce higher and higher and he laughs. Sometimes he has me 'dribble' him, pressing down on his shoulders or head like he's a basketball. Sometimes he has me lift him up like he's in a chair and I press his feet to the ceiling. I didn't do that tonight with him because my asthma is acting up, so I couldn't exert myself much.

It was while we were doing that, I thought of the rest of this story. In my head it was originally going to be a little sadder. Now I think it's only partially sad. I really think Mr F wants to fly. I like to think that the reason he doesn't tell us is a reason like this, but if he told me, I wouldn't tell him it was stupid. I'd tell him I'd help him. Mr Bunches talks all the time about what he's going to do. Tonight he told me he was going to be an astronaut first and go to the moon, then a fireman, and also a doctor. I tell him he can be all those things. I hope he can. And I hope Mr F can fly someday.

I wrote another story, once, about Mr F wanting to fly. It was called "What He Was Thinking As He Fell From The Lower Part Of The Sky (A Possibly True Story)" and made it into a video. It was about the time he fell off the counter and broke his head. We didn't even know he was hurt, at first. We heard him fall off the bathroom counter behind a closed door, and went in there. He seemed shaken up, lying on the floor. I picked him up and set him on my lap and comforted him and he seemed like he was okay. Then I put him on his feet and said let's see how you're doing and he dropped to the ground and began throwing up. 2 hours later he was in brain surgery. Three days later, he came home with a bandage around his head, seemingly none the worse for the wear.

I don't know if he was trying to fly, that time, or if he just slipped in the bathroom wrong. I don't know much about Mr F at all. I know he likes cheese puffs, and he likes to swing and to swim. I know he likes to play the piano, but not any songs you'd recognize. The rest of the things I think I know about him are probably just things I imagine about him and he can't tell me they're wrong.

153

This is the story inspired by Mr Bunches' comments last night.

I work as a lawyer, in my day job. Lawyers frequently have to schedule things in their cases, like depositions and meetings and hearings and the like. We could, if we wanted to, never schedule anything for Monday mornings, or Friday afternoons. We could take the month of December more or less off if we want to.

Lawyers never do that. They serve things at 4 o'clock Friday, and set depositions to begin in a faraway city at 8:30 on Monday morning. I am not *much* better, as I have done these things myself. In my defense, I have done them only when I think it absolutely necessary, but I have still done them.

The point is, we frequently make ourselves miserable. I realized once that we do it all wrong. We send kids to school all day long and then trap teens and twenty somethings in nothing jobs where they waste away (many of them), full of energy and desire to *do* things, and then by the time we have the money to do those things, many of us are tied down by kids, or jobs, or asthma and heart conditions.

What if we sent kids to school until they were, say, 14, and then from 14 to 30 just supported them while they traveled the world or wrote terrible poems or fell in love over and over and danced to music we hated and went skydiving and took selfies in the surf in Australia, and then at 30 people had to start to settle down, getting jobs, and helping support the next wave of kids. We'd all start all those stupid menial jobs and college when we were thirty, full of great memories and enriching experiences, and work our way up the corporate ladder by the time we were 50 or 60, and be in cushy executive jobs or semiretirement by then, with. Nothing against old people (I'm extremely unlikely to see the far side of 60) (although I once didn't think I'd see the other side of 40, and here I am more than halfway through the fourth decade!) but all the wealth and leisure of retirement is mostly wasted on 87 year olds. We all need to have led lives where we could have gone cliff-diving in Acapulco if we'd wanted to.

152

I was listening to "Jocasta" by Noah and the Whale when I started this song; it talks about putting a baby outside to be eaten by wolves, and so I wrote the first line of this story. As I went on, I sort of leaned on Shirley Jackson's "The Lottery" to flesh out the story: a weird tradition with no real purpose. When I was done I realized that I wanted that little boy in the first line to live, so I wrote the title.

My car died today, more or less. A 'battery' light came on. I called our mechanic and he said it was the alternator. So while I could've taken it to get fixed, that would've taken $600 or more from our savings; we have very very little money in savings right now, and it's looking like there won't be a very big share of profits from the firm I am leaving at the end of the year to go out and join a new one. So things will be tight.

I applied for a car loan and got accepted and I'm picking up our new car tomorrow. It's a "Smart" car and it wasn't very expensive and I like it. Maybe that's a good sign, that this was as smooth as it was. Maybe things are looking up. Financially, it would be hard to be any worse. I get a little down about it at times, and I'm counting the days until January 4, which is the day I plan on telling my partners I'm leaving them. Tomorrow, Sweetie and I are going to have dinner with my new partners and employees and finally sign those papers.

You're reading this way in the future, but keep your fingers crossed for us that things are going well then.

154

So first of all, story 154 is out of order because I only just realized tonight that I had skipped it, so rather than go back and tuck it in I thought I'd just do it this way so you future readers can see the actual order I wrote these in.

Second, this story is inspired by my grandson, whose actual name is Josiah. I was sitting down to write this story, sitting in the boys' room with Mr Bunches and Mr F slowly falling asleep, and our oldest, Josiah's mom, texted me a picture of him. It was about 9 p.m. and I texted back "Why are you up so late Josiah!" and I liked the way that sounded, so I wrote this story.

151

At the end of the day, when other kids walk back inside shedding a line of boots, socks, snowpants, jacket, mitten, hat, other mitten, snow boys wave good-bye with a curt flip of their hand and disappear off into the drifts. I was looking through my pictures for the last month and a half—473 of them—and came across one of Mr F and Mr. Bunches from the night we went sledding at their school. (Story 175) I liked it and thought I could use it for something, and so I saved it as "Snow Boys" and then decided that that would be this story.

So that night sledding has given me *two* stories.

150

Xmas shopping today with the boys, our annual guys-only trip to eat pizza and wander around the mall on the far side of town where we only go one day a year, *this* day. Mr F got sick though—just as we left the mall he threw up, so we had to drop him off at home and then Mr Bunches and I went out to finish up quick. No pizza, but Mr Bunches did get a Hot Wheel set, and now Mr F is sleeping on the couch. Hopefully we won't all have the flu for Xmas. But I'd expect nothing more from this year.

Still, the day was fun.

149

I don't know about this one. I had about 2/3 of one called "Interrupting Cow" and then I gave up on that and I quick wrote this one. I'm kind of tired. Maybe this one will grow on me but I don't blame you if you don't care for it very much.

148

I like this one a lot better than 149, although I feel like I'm still stuck mostly in traditional storytelling and that's harder and harder to do in a satisfying way in less than 150 words. I think the idea of this exercise is to break me free from regular storytelling, the way I spent a year trying to write a story for "McSweeney's," (actually only about half a year before I gave up and tried to write stories for other places, but still) and in the course of that year wrote a lot of stuff that was very different than I'd written before. So from here on out I might try to get more experimental except that experimenting for the sake of experimenting doesn't seem like a thing I want to do.

Then, too, I'm very tired. I was falling asleep on the couch tonight at about 7:30, watching nature documentaries with Mr Bunches, and yesterday I got so zoned out driving that I nearly got us in an accident. I think it's my asthma. I think it's making me so tired because I never sleep all that well at night and if I'm struggling to breathe during the day that'll wear me out. That's my theory, anyway, so I'm probably going to have to take more medications, or something.

147

That's more like the kind of story I want to be writing. I don't know why it seems so different than 148 but it does.

Today is December 23, 2014. I'm home sick from 'work.' I really am kind of sick. Mr Bunches got sick last night at 11, the second one of us to be felled by this flu or whatever. I started feeling crummy about 3 a.m., and while I haven't thrown up I can't really eat much and I feel weak and my stomach is upset. So I haven't had it as bad as the boys, and now, at 12:40 p.m. I'm feeling much better but I still am sick.

I would rather have gone to work. I was going to take Mr Bunches, and have it be his last time at the new office (although he wouldn't know that.) Then we'd have left early and gone shopping for our Xmas dinner (hors d'oeuvres, by which I mean "pizza rolls" and the like), and started our Xmas holiday – five days! – in style. Calling in sick is sort of a lame way to start off a 5-day weekend.

Then again, any real desire I had to do any real work there is gone. I am more and more angry with most of the people at my (soon to be ex-) firm. It looks more and more like I won't get any profit-sharing at the end of the year. So my pay will have been cut by 20% each year, for the last four years. I'm really looking forward to my new job. It's overshadowing the holidays. Twelve months from now, I hope things are much much better.

146, 145

It is Xmas Day, 2014. It's 2:30 in the afternoon. Sweetie is taking a nap, Mr Bunches has just gone off somewhere I don't know where, and Mr F is laying across his exercise ball that he got for Xmas (along with a swiveling office chair!) at the top of the basement stairs hoping I will forget he is doing that so he can try rolling down the stairs.

And I forgot to write a story yesterday – the first one I've missed in, like, 219? I may have mentioned before that the math of this confuses me. If I've just written story 147, for example, then I have 146 stories to go which means I have written 219, right? Whatever.

I am tired. We've all had the flu this week, the virus people call the flu. Sweetie had that *and* the actual flu, because she is an overachiever. Sweetie and I had another minor fight that I attribute to stress. It is looking more and more like there will be no year-end money at all. None. Our plan had been to go to after-Xmas sales and pick up beds for the boys; they have never had real beds, for a variety of reasons including but not limited to we haven't had that much money over the last two years.

But we had to cancel those plans for tomorrow, because of uncertainty about money. That has been my Xmas, partially: flu, taking Sweetie to the ER at 6 p.m. on the 23rd, Mr Bunches crying because the "Claw Machine" toy at the grocery store was hard to win and he didn't win and wanted to win, worrying about money, being mad at myself for trusting my partner for so long and mad at my partner for being a jerk.

Partially.

Because my Xmas has also been taking Mr Bunches for a ride in the new car to get muffins, our annual Xmas Eve tradition in the morning, and has also been *hors d'oeuvres* Xmas last night with the older kids, and presents – I got Sweetie a bunch of shirts she wanted and a blanket and she got a gift card to Victoria's Secret by accident (longer story) and I got sweatpants and a new sweater and a Bluetooth headset for my phone, and we watched *Guardians Of The Galaxy* last night late at night after the boys went to bed, and Mr F loves all his presents for the first time in 8 years, and Mr Bunches got the "Toy Story 3 Imaginext Tri-County Landfill Playset" he's wanted since October, and Sweetie and I played a tournament of *Angry Birds* and we played *Dumb Ways To Die* and it's nearly 40 degrees out, in December, in Wisconsin, and last year at this time I thought I might have a brain tumor and I don't, and I start my new job in just 18 days, and I have a book coming out from a traditional publisher next year, and I prefer to focus on those things.

That and that I just ate my *second* muffin of the day, plus we have *lots* of pizza rolls left over. So I can be upbeat!

Also, I didn't have to tell you that I missed a day. I could have totally faked it. You have to give me credit for honesty, right?

144

I guess this story has sort of a twist ending? I know that I said I don't like those but I threw this one in near the end of writing the story.

I am listening to *One More Thing: Stories And Other Stories*, by B.J. Novak, and it's really good. Some of the stories are stunning. The story I listened to today, December 26, 2014, was "Closure." I listened to it while I took Mr F for a short ride in the car we call *Pink Panther Car*, because Mr Bunches says the "Smart Car" I bought looks like the car in the movie *The Pink Panther*. In "Closure" a girl meets a guy who is breaking up with her because she needs closure, and she asks for one last kiss.

I thought to myself how there's always a last kiss in every relationship, but sometimes neither person knows it is, and sometimes both know it is, and sometimes it's just one. That's when I thought up the title to the story, and the basic premise. As I was writing it, I worried it was a bit too much like the episode of *Seinfeld* where George can't get either of his girlfriends to break up with him. That contributed a bit to my throwing in that ending.

143

Sweetie and I both agree that the cure for post-Xmas blues (I always get them, a little) is to look ahead to the next thing that you're excited about.

Today, we took the boys to the Madison library, where they have a great children's section. As we sat and watched them play with puzzles and crawl through the cubbies and sometimes even look at books Sweetie looked up at me, and asked *"We'll have money next year, won't we?"*

142

When I had my back surgery, about 10 years ago, I would lie in my bed and look out the window at the leaves, and enjoy the pattern they made against the blue sky. From time to time I take pictures of leaves against the sky, because I like the way they look, the little intricate overlappings.

I don't know what any of the trees in my yard are called, either. And I do wonder why we need a name for the rhombus. But this is nonetheless not a true story.

141

Now I have a new favorite story I've ever written.

Today, I decided that on Friday – Friday will be January 2, 2015, today being December 29, 2014 – that I will tell my partner that I am resigning and going to a new job. I made up my mind. Friday it is.

Then I found out he will likely not be in the office Friday. So, now, Monday it is.

140

Pro Tip: I wrote a draft of this, and edited down to 139 words. Then I realized today was 140. So I added the word "just" back in, right before *implodes*.

139

New Year's Eve, 2014. Thank GOD this year is ending. I spent the morning looking through pictures to remind me that some good things happened this year.

138

At my in-law's fiftieth anniversary party, Mr Bunches lost a balloon and it got caught about 50 feet up in a tree. He wanted me to climb up and get it and I, like that dad in this story, felt a bit like I could get it. But that wasn't really the inspiration for this story. The inspiration for this story was a different balloon caught in a different tree at a different park after a different party of some sort: That's at "Spider Park," where we actually went today (January 1, 2015), to play for 20 minutes. We wanted to get the boys out of the house and get some fresh air, and there was no snow, even though it was 18 degrees outside. So we went and played at the park

137

Well, who says 'missed connections' ads are only for a connection missed recently?

136

I sent out 93 emails today, notifying my clients that effective January 12, 2015, I will be a partner at a new firm. I cleaned out my office. I went for ice cream with the boys and Sweetie. Today was a good day.

135

Another fight today. TWO of them, actually. I'm so tired. I thought we were past this, past the stress, past the fighting. But it just keeps coming back. We had three in 36 hours, with yesterday now seeming like this dreamlike break in between what is becoming too common.

I know Sweetie is nervous about everything. I know that's why these fights keep happening. I don't know why knowing that doesn't help.

134

As with before, the anger and sadness of the fight fade, but they never fade away, not quite. Today, they were more superseded by events. I drove to work listening to "Politics in Space" by Kate Miller-Heidke. It had the right feel and close-enough lyrics:

> I'm not gonna state my case anymore
> 'Cause I haven't got a leg to stand on
> I'm not gonna take the leap anymore
> 'Cause I got no mat to land on
> I'm not gonna smoke that shit anymore
> It will only get me thinking
> And I better not paddle upstream anymore
> 'Cause this canoe is sinking

About a half-hour after I got there, my partner came in and said "So, something's up." I said:

"Yep. Here's my letter of resignation."

He looked at it and said he thought it would be better if I worked remotely for the rest of this week, before I start at my new firm next week. I said "Okay," and added that I wanted to wait for two of my staffers to get there so I could tell them personally.

He said he thought I should just go now. So I did. I stood up, and he held out his hand and said "Good luck." I shook his hand and said "Good luck."

Apropos of nothing, he said "That's called a handshake."

I said "I'm aware." And so 14 years of a job ended.

133

Things got a little tense in the firm breakup here on day 2. 35 of my 93 clients have already come with me, and my (now ex-)partner tried to impose restrictions on my ability to pick up their files, and made requests for things that I don't need to do.

I laughed when I read his emails, and felt like I had on seven-league boots, like I could do anything. Sweetie and I spent a lot of time together today, as I worked from home, and I think that helped us get past the latest fight. She said today that while she's still nervous about what's happening, she has hope.

Meanwhile, I'm still exhausted. I woke up this morning at 4 a.m. and couldn't get back to sleep. My eyes feel bleary, but this time it's a good exhaustion. The last year, the last couple of years, have taken a heavy toll on me. I keep thinking of awful things that have happened at my old job, things I tried to ignore or buried. I keep thinking of how last year Sweetie and I got into so many fights. The feeling is sort of like the time I had the heart attack. I had a heart attack and surgery on a Friday, and by Sunday, I felt like I'd been run over by a truck — but that the damage had occurred to an old body and this new body only had a memory of the damage. That's how I feel now: like all the things that happened last year happened to an old me, who told the new me about it but the new me never actually experienced those things.

132

Sometimes, when things are dull or sad, I think back to a happier time, saying to myself, *At this time, a [week/month/year] ago, I was....* Like I might say "At this time two weeks ago, the older kids had gone home and Sweetie was putting the boys to bed while I was wrapping the last of the presents and watching the episode of *The Office* where Michael proposed to Holly."

That was Xmas Eve.

And other times, when things are busy and hectic like this week, I look ahead, and think "Next week, at this time, I'll have finished the two trials I have and I'll have moved into my new office and things will have settled down, and so I will be able to spend that night playing cars with Mr Bunches and reading without so much worry and stress."

131

I had a trial all day today. I had Middle Daughter go with me and work at the trial, which mean that the two-hour drive (each way!) I didn't get to sit quietly in the car and listen to an audiobook. I did it to have Middle get some training for her paralegal job which was I think the right thing to do as her boss, but I still regretted losing my alone time.

Still, the trial went well. It didn't finish, so we're going back on February 6.

130

Today is my 46th birthday. I celebrated by stopping work early at my old job; I am now done with them; technically employed by them until Sunday, but I don't work weekends.

We went for pizza tonight, at Rocky Rococo's, finishing the trip that the boys and I didn't get to complete on our annual Xmas shopping trip. I got funny socks, and a t-shirt with SpongeBob and Patrick riding a cat, and sweaters and pants, and books and an Amazon gift card, and we played SkeeBall and arcade games.

This story, I suppose, seems sad, or dark, or both. But it's not, really. The power to end one's life, not exercised, is possibly the most positive choice one can make. I started writing it with the idea that the man had seven birthdays— inspired, I think, by a brief discussion of the seven sexes Kurt Vonnegut mentioned in *Slaughterhouse Five*, a passage I hadn't remembered until an associate at my old job discussed that briefly when we talked on the phone this week (she is reading the book because I recommended it to her). I had to think of what the birthdays were, and the first four came pretty easily. I'm not so crazy about the sixth. I was thinking that the natural seventh birthday would be death, but that seemed even less satisfying than becoming an old man. The idea was that each birthday was when one's whole world shifted, to create not just a new person but a new *existence*, which is why becoming an old man is probably the least satisfying one to me.

Death, I don't know: it certainly is a shift in worlds, but I think more dramatic, more life-altering, would be the world that exists for you after you choose not to die. There's a difference between just living your life, and living your life by making a deliberate choice not to end it at a given point.

There was a guy I read about once who jumped off the Golden Gate bridge and survived, and he said he changed his mind on the way down. I wonder, sometimes, what it would feel like to do that: to kill yourself – which is what that is, jumping off that bridge—and then change your mind and go back from that, surviving somehow. I'm not sure it would mean you'd be constantly cherishing every moment. I survived a heart attack and while I cherish my life, etc etc., I spend time just rewatching old TV programs or dozing on the couch. You can't live your life in a manic cycle just because you nearly died. But I think that going through something like that Golden Gate guy did must alter the way you view the world pretty drastically.

I suppose I'm feeling like that because I've ended one life pretty abruptly and begun another. Five whirlwind days and now everything will be different while still also being the same. I think I know how the guy feels, a tiny bit, and it's not sad or dark at all.

129

Usually to get down to the word count I begin by taking out any "that"s which I have, as it's a pretty unnecessary word.

But for this one I finished with 128, so I put a "that" in to hit the word count.

128

Today, I heard the phrase "what was in people's hearts." I think it was in *I'm Having So Much Fun Here Without You*, the new audiobook I started while walking on the treadmill. I thought of a witch who could change people's hearts into something else, some small object, and I decided that would be tonight's story. Then I wrote most of it, and decided it needed to be a longer story. Here is what I wrote first:

What Nanda needed to know was this: "Can you change a heart?"

In response, the witch showed her the small basement room, with 10,000 tiny jelly jars stacked in rows. Each contained a different object: a toy car. A tooth. A locket. One whole set of jars held one black jellybean apiece.

The witch explained that any jarred token could be swapped for someone's heart. Nanda thought she meant symbolically. A slight shake of the ancient woman's head told her no, it is literal.

Nanda peered into each jar, trying to think which one belonged in her mother's chest, piecing together how someone with a heart made of a wind-up music box, or a glass eye, might feel.

So after stopping that, I wrote "Details."

I start my new job for real tomorrow. I'm also supposed to have been editing my book, *Codes*, for the final edit by January 15, but I haven't even begun on that. I spent a lot of the weekend just relaxing: we took the boys to a yo-yo show, and Sweetie and I have been reading a book together. It's called *Into The Woods*, by Tana French. We decided we would start our own book club, and picked out this book to be our first one to read. Our actual first one to read was the fifth book in the series that begins with *Into The Woods*, but once we realized it was the *fifth* we went back and started the series together. Our goal is to read at least a chapter a week, and then discuss it, and then go on. Yesterday, I finally finished chapter 2, so today we read chapter 3. Then 4 and 5 and 6, too. It was that kind of day. I didn't feel very energetic. I think it's my asthma. Sweetie thinks it's just the past few weeks. She's probably right.

127

I started out writing a totally different story about a girl in Kansas, then scrapped that. I didn't know where this story was going until after I'd written the first two lines, and then added the bike tires. Even then I didn't know how it would end.

I like this one, a lot. I think *You're an idiot* makes it.

126

I had this idea to do a story about punctuation, so I went and read the Wikipedia entry on *ampersand*. That led me to the letter known as *thorn*, and written like this: Þ. *Thorn* makes, or made, as near as I can figure out, the "th" sound. It was slowly abandoned, at least from the English alphabet, in part because there was no type for it in printing presses early on. Instead, typesetters began to use "*y*" for Þ, which is why we think of stores, etc., called "*Ye Olde Shoppe*." The *ye* would've been pronounced *the*.

Thorn isn't a letter anymore. Now we use *th*, of course, and don't even remember that we once used Þ for that sound. And that led me to a story of a relationship that has crumbled, maybe?

125

Guess who saw a fox tonight?

124

The only one that I think looks like a bird is the one with the crush. They were sort of supposed to look like birds, when I first thought of this story. But then I didn't worry as much about that.

123

Friday night is date night! It's Friday, January 16 as I write this. I've just finished my first week as a partner in my new firm. The week went really well. No fights with Sweetie, no pressures, no stress. We took the boys swimming tonight, after a dinner of frozen pizza, and now Sweetie is sitting with them until they fall asleep and I'm writing and listening to Bastille's double album and writing about zombies in love.

122

I can't tell if there should be more to this story, or less.

121

This wasn't really a cowboy story, I guess. Or a God story. I didn't really have any ideas when I sat down to write, and then the phrase popped into my head but I wasn't really sure where to go with it for nearly 60 words.

In the longer, pre-editing draft of this, the man got into a gunfight with God and won that one, too, and the ending wasn't quite as sardonic. I had to go look up 'sardonic' to make sure I was using it correctly. I am.

120

I had to go to a mediation with some clients this morning. It ended just before noon. I was going to work from home the rest of the day.

When I was with my old firm, which seems a very long time ago already, I would, whenever I could over the last six months, drive down to this little nature-trail area near a pond, and park my car there to eat lunch and read a book. I used to go eat and read in the breakroom, because I thought it was important as a boss to be available to the staff in case they wanted to talk or had questions or something. Near the end, I didn't care anymore about most of the people there, so I didn't do that anymore.

Today, that pond was too far away, clear on the other side of town. I pulled off the road to a office park called "Nature's Trail Office Park" or something like that, but the driveway pulled away from the little pond there, and so I sat in a parking lot eating my pizza sandwich – that's a sandwich made by putting a slice of pizza in between two slices of bread, microwaving the whole thing for a minute, and then wrapping it up to cool off – and reading *In The Woods*, by Tana French. That's a book Sweetie and I are reading together; we have formed a book club of just the two of us.

Then I went home and worked until four. It was a good day.

119

Today, commuting to Milwaukee, I finished listening to the audiobook of *I Am Having So Much Fun Here Without You*, a book in which the main character and his wife have a terrible fight in their marriage. Their fight is caused by the main character having a 7-month affair and the wife, of course, finding out. The book was okay. But the ending contained a passage I liked so much that when I got to the office I looked it up online and emailed it to Sweetie. The passage is:

> *Expandable is exactly what a marriage is. If you refuse the possibility that bad things might happen, a marriage cannot survive. It isn't easy. Neither of us is joyful every day, but there is an equilibrium and a rightness that has returned to our lives – the sense that we are doing exactly what we are supposed to be doing, and together… There is an openness between us now that makes our coming togethers feel like the truest version of love – love in all its tenderness, its frustration, and the realization that despite its shortcomings, this place, ,with this person, is the place we're meant to be.*

118

The flaw in this story is that if he never tells anyone any of his names, how can he tell you you were right and give you fifty bucks?

117

I wrote this story while in the middle of several frequent terrible coughing attacks. I've got a bad cold that has been getting worse the last two days. I almost didn't feel like writing the story. But not only *did* I write it, I then jazzed it up a bit.

116

I know it's not really a *story*, but (a) I liked it and (b) I have a really bad cold and a fever and wasn't even going to write something today, but I did, and this was it.

*

and so on. I have missed several days in a row. Maybe four? Maybe 7? I am not sure. I'm sort of lost on how many days I have been sick now and how many days since I last wrote.

It's Thursday, January 29, 2015, and this is definitely the best I've felt in at least a week. Starting last week I thought I had just a bad cold, but the thing with me is it's almost never *just* a cold. And it wasn't this time. It was the flu, the actual flu that you get flu shots to avoid getting, only then you learn the flu shots are only effective 40% of the time and you are the other 60%, and so I ended up at the Urgent Care on Saturday morning, throwing up in the bathroom while I waited to be taken in, and secretly resenting the heavyset woman who appeared to be there for something *toe-related* and who got called before me.

By Sunday night, I was feeling better, but by Monday it was worsening again . With my asthma so bad, almost every respiratory thing I get ends up being super-serious, and this one turned the flu into bronchitis and a sinus infection and I was back at the doctor on Tuesday. I had a fever for nearly a week and most nights I didn't sleep more than an hour at a time, even with cough medicine and sleeping pills and stuff. And during all that I missed very little work, even going to court hearings, and now I am slowly back on the mend, just super-dehydrated so I am drinking water like crazy.

During that time, too, Sweetie and I had another of the ongoing argument, and then tried to fix that, too, so that we are continuing to try to fit together this new life with all these new stresses that are still stressful, even though things feel very optimistic, and meanwhile Mr F started having terrible, terrible sleepless nights where he would wake up howling in anger and need to be taken for car rides at 3 am and sleep on the couch.

So now I am very tired, and missed some days, but I'm back to it and will jump back on this horse.

It's amazing how quickly the idea almost loses steam: I'd done this every night for like 249 days, and then today when I was driving back from Milwaukee, I thought about how I might feel good enough to write a story tonight, and the fact that I'd missed some days almost killed the project for me. If it was much, much earlier, it might have done that. But 249 days in, I feel like I have to finish, even if I missed a couple of days.

115

I had this idea on the way home from work today. My phone was dying, my Kindle had no power, and the radio sucks, so I listened to music for 2 hours and thought about stories.

114

Sweetie and I have started answering something called "36 questions." They are 36 questions that you are supposed to answer on a first date and then you will fall in love. I read about them yesterday and said we should each day email the answer to the next question to each other.

Question 1, yesterday, was who would you have dinner with out of anyone in the world. Sweetie's answer was God, because then she could find out what Mr F is thinking. My answer was that I would like to have dinner with Mr Bunches and Mr F, who rarely join us for dinner, lost off in their own worlds.

#2 was whether, given the chance you would like to be famous. My answer was that I would only if I could also be rich, because I don't want all the bother of fame, just the money and the freedom that goes with it, so in the end I'd rather be rich than famous. Sweetie's answer was that she'd rather be rich, not famous.

So these stories are not meant to be symbolic, although as I periodically go re-read the various stories in here I am seeing them as metaphorical at times, even though they were almost never meant to be autobiographical or to relate to directly to my life—except for those stories which of course were meant to relate directly to my life.

113

Another set of interconnected stories that should each stand alone, as well. I've got sort of an ending in mind, maybe? There might only be one more of these.

Feeling a lot better today: I'm left, at the end of the sickness, with just a bad asthma day that left me struggling to breathe all day. That is a *good* health day, at this point.

112

I sort of remembered this one poem tonight about a mermaid on a merry-go-round, or something like that, and thought of this title, and then I thought I could do a set of stories about sort of surreal experiences based on real events. Like, as in this story, waiting for the merry-go-round. I may keep going with this for a while. And I may or may not come back to the bad weather couple. The only one left is "Snow," anyway.

111

There was an apple tree behind our house when we were growing up, and my mom always told us never to eat the apples. I always assumed it's because they were poisonous. There was also a rumor that the pond near our house was full of dangerously-toxic fish because there was (reportedly) toxic waste buried under the pond. I grew up thinking all of nature was dangerous like that.

110

I don't know, I expected more of this story when I began it. I wrote it and then took a break and went upstairs to play with Mr F, and give Mr Bunches his bath, and then I came back down and thought *oh, well, go with it for today's story.*

109

This is kind of a true story. Question 7 in the 36 questions was whether you have a premonition about how you will die. It turns out that when we were young, both Sweetie and I thought we'd die early – me, before 40, her before 30 – but here we are, in our mid-forties and going strong.

I told her, in response to the question, that I didn't think my heart or my asthma would get me, and that eventually I pictured us living on a beach, retired, watching Mr F walk around in the surf while Mr Bunches had an apartment nearby where we checked on him a couple times a day, and we sat on the porch and looked at the ocean together.

Tonight, I asked her what story I should write, and she said "Why don't you write about the beach house." So this story will one day be true.

108

Do you think she is the sky or the stars? *Discuss.*

107

Stories I didn't write tonight: one about the hare, from the tortoise and the hare, challenging something *else* to a race, or maybe entering rehab. A story about how the sun didn't come up one day because it wanted to make a change

I didn't write the first two because I thought those are sort of too easy to write. It's too easy to do a hipster take on an old story. B.J. Novak in fact did that in his book, and the story was good, but it doesn't feel like the kind of thing I want to write.

I actually *did* write the third, but I got about 100 words into it and thought "eh" and so I went and put on "Delirious Love" by Neil Diamond, and then wrote this story.

106

Today, Sweetie and I played *Would You Rather* while we took the boys for a ride. She had some pretty good ones, *like would you rather always smell like pickles, or always smell like cheese?*

105

"Apocalypse" actually comes from old words meaning "revelation." So apocalypse stories should contain revelations about something in them.

104

Originally I was going to do the world turning inside out, but then I thought of this.

103

Today, on my way to my Milwaukee office, I opted to listen to music for the ride in. While I was listening and thinking and driving, I came up with the idea for a sequel to my novel *Codes*. The sequel is going to be called The Watson Protocol, and it's going to be phenomenal. I had the whole basic plot worked out by the time I got to Milwaukee around 9:15, and I hurried into my office and ate a peanut butter & jelly bagel while I wrote the first chapter, in about 15 minutes.

The bagel was part of my lunch. I ate it because for some reason I was *starving.*

Sweetie and I haven't fought in two weeks now. ! The underlying problem that led to the fight is, somehow, still there, but we are working through it. Saturday is Valentine's Day (today is February 10, 2015), and I have a plan: Since Saturday we are taking the boys to see a juggler and then have to go to lunch with her mom and dad to celebrate Middle Daughter's boyfriend and so Valentine's won't be very romantic, I have arranged to have The Boy come over and babysit the two little ones, secretly. He's going to come at 5 o'clock and just show up and I am going to tell Sweetie that we are going out to dinner at a Mexican restaurant where we used to go eat when we were first dating.

102

I got my new glasses today. I've had tired eyes at the end of most days, and now that I'm at my new job I get vision insurance which pays 100% for things, so I went for an eye exam on Monday and the doctor said I just need reading glasses. We got a pair from Walgreen's, eleven bucks.

I have a lazy eye and when I was a kid I had eye patches and wore glasses, and I continued with glasses until I was in law school, when an eye doctor told me that glasses wouldn't make my lazy eye any better and if I didn't want to wear them I shouldn't. So it was about 20 years that I wore glasses and then about 20 that I didn't and now I've got them again, but I don't mind them so much, now.

101

Tonight, after cleaning up after dinner, I said to Sweetie, "Are you in a good mood?"

"Why?" she asked back, instantly tense.

"No, no," I said. "Nothing bad. I'm just in a good mood! It's Thursday! I wanted to know if you are in a good mood, too."

"I thought you were going to tell me something bad," she said.

"Why would I ask if you're in a good mood only to ruin it?" I asked.

"After last year, I never know what to expect," she said.

100

The surprise went off without a hitch; The Boy came over to babysit, and I had thought ahead and got presents for the boys so they wouldn't be too upset about us going out without them. Mr F got a book that played piano songs. Mr Bunches got a little Hot Wheels set. And we went out for dinner to the restaurant we used to go to, where we figured out that the last time we were there was when we went there for dinner on New Year's Eve and then saw the movie *Two Weeks Notice.* That was in 2002.

99

The two dinosaurs in this story are Mr Bunches' two favorite dinosaurs of all. He likes them because they start with "X," his favorite letter. The total amount of research that went into this was:

1.Asking Mr Bunches to name, again, his two favorite dinosaurs (I knew Xenotarsasaurus).
2.Checking the spelling for Xuanhuaceratops.
3.Checking which family of dinosaurs Xuanhuaceratops belongs in.
4.Trying to figure out when the Jurassic period lasted from.

The reason Xuanhuaceratops broke up was originally in this story, but had to be cut out for word-length reasons.
I wrote this story on Valentine's Day, 2015.

98

I was half-asleep on the couch, watching *Microcosmos* with Mr Bunches, about 7:30 tonight, when this story came to me.

97

Tonight I read a bunch of *A Softer World*, to get the feel for telling a story using as few words as possible. *A Softer World* does that brilliantly.

95

Ok, so this doesn't feel very storylike, but that's how it goes.

92

This is how I feel sometimes, like I can't remember anything, at all. I've been thinking a lot about memory lately, trying to remember how much I can remember. That sounds nonsensical, but it isn't. Tonight, Sweetie and I were talking about when we were kids, what television shows we liked, and I told her about Saturday nights, camping out with blankets in our family room, watching the *Don Kirshner's Rock Concert* show. I tried to remember which bands I saw on that show. The only one I could think of was Alice Cooper. After writing this story and this note, I went to check to see if Alice Cooper had actually been on that show. According to Wikipedia he was. So that's good.

91

Sweetie and I were talking about this the other day, when I told her that I sort of am skeptical of angels and guardian angels and people who have near-death experiences, which both my dad and her dad say they have had. Sweetie believes in guardian angels and angels, and while I kind of do, we disagree on how they might intervene. In my mind, angels and the spirits of our loved ones can intervene by getting God to pay attention; that's sort of a particularly Catholic point of view, I guess, even though I don't really think of myself as Catholic anymore. Sweetie thinks the angels directly intervene themselves.

We both agree, though, that the time Mr F got out a ground-floor window and went walking down a busy street a mile away from our house—he got out and I didn't know it for nearly 10 minutes—we agree that my Mom, who was a nurse, intervened to save his life. Mr F was found by a nurse who recognized something was wrong, not just because a 4-year-old shouldn't be walking around in his underwear on a summer morning, but because Mr F couldn't talk or respond correctly to her.

It's nice to picture my Mom, invisible, but walking beside him to make sure he didn't veer into the road and was found by someone. I don't totally disagree with Sweetie about this, I suppose.

90

I'm making a playlist for this Friday, the 27th of February, when I'm going to take a day off of work and Sweetie and I are going to spend the day together having brunch and going to the art museum and then briefly stopping back to get the boys off the bus before The Boy comes over to babysit, and then going to stay the night in the Edgewater hotel downtown, with a view of the lake. The playlist is ½ songs I like and ½ songs from Sweetie's playlists. There's not much overlap, but that's okay.

89

I have been a little down today. Sweetie confessed she has been a little down, today. We both sort of blamed it on money worries, and on Mr F not sleeping well the last three nights, including how he woke up at 2 a.m. Sunday night and I had to go downstairs and sleep on the couch with him, and in general on feeling worn out.

It's not, though, as bad as things have been. We're just ready for them to get better. We feel so *close* to them getting better and like that brass ring on the Merry-Go-Round you can't quite reach it.

I don't know if I have ever seen the brass ring on the Merry Go Round in real life. I recall the day Middle got married and we took her and her new husband and the bridal party to lunch – they wanted a small wedding with no reception – at a restaurant here in Madison that had a Merry Go Round outside it. I rode it three or four or five times with Mr F and Mr Bunches. It was a cold, rainy, gray day that was one of my favorite days.

88

I wrote this one last night – February 25, 2015 – and edited it down tonight. I did it that way because last night, my night to sit with Mr F, I couldn't write. He wanted me to sit by him on the couch, so I did. I sat and read for a while and then grew drowsy and tried to keep awake by thinking of stories. I didn't want to get off the couch to get my computer, because Mr F was getting drowsy, too, and sometimes if you interrupt him falling asleep he gets really upset and can't get back to sleep.

So I sat on the couch and thought, and finally thought about Sisyphus. I'm not sure what made me think of him, but then I thought about how if he just didn't push the boulder all the way up, it wouldn't fall back down again. And hence this story.

In the myths, Sisyphus beat the gods twice before: he tricked Hades into letting him go when he died, and then tricked Persephone, too.

The Greeks were big on futility. The Danaides were 50 women who were compelled to marry the 50 sons of their father's brother (got that?), but 49 of the 50 women killed their husbands. The 50th didn't, because her husband let her stay a virgin. As punishment for killing their husbands, the Danaides were sentenced, in Hades, to fill a leaky bathtub with water in order to wash away their sins; the bathtub would never fill, though.

The 50th one went on to found a dynasty, having been saved from her father's punishment (for disobeying his command to marry, then kill, her cousin/husband!) by Aphrodite.

86

I really like this one. Last night, late at night as Sweetie and I were laying in our hotel room, a room we'd booked about two months ago to celebrate my new job, on one of our rare nights out, I read up on some more Greek myths, trying to find inspiration, and I came across Tethys, who was one of the original Titans but is almost never remembered nowadays. She is the 'mother of rivers.' I wrote it on my phone and emailed it to myself, and then edited it tonight.

Originally this was titled "Tethys Has Been Forgotten," but I revised it a bit and then changed it to "Tethys' Tears," and then to this one.

85

This one came to me today while I took Mr F on one of the multiple car rides today. We did six car rides, and in between I had to snuggle with him a lot and tickle him, and he kept getting mad. He got into the room where we keep the old toys and my files from my old office, waiting for their new office (I don't want to take them to the Milwaukee office because I want the Milwaukee office to be a part-time office, and I need to make it clear at all times that it's not my *real* office) and he spilled some of those files. He also got my glasses and broke them. I'd been pretty careful about not letting him break them but I was exhausted by the end of the day. The boys get very upset when we are gone overnight, which is why we are almost never gone overnight. The day after we get home is always very tiring, as they act up and need a lot of reassuring.

For example, when we walked in, Mr Bunches said *"Daddy, you forgot to come home! I was crying and wanted to call you."* Happy morning! By the end of the day, I'd forgotten to keep my glasses out of reach of Mr F, who doesn't like my glasses anyway. I was putting *Toy Story* on the computer for him and when I looked up, he'd grabbed my glasses. I must have left them somewhere he could reach them. He'd twisted them around so a lens popped out.

84

That guy I sent the poem/story to said not to explain my stories, so I won't.

82

I have started my exercise program again, after all: Last week Wednesday, when I noticed that my vest for my favorite suit was tight again, I vowed to start walking 30 minutes every other day. I did it right that day, and then took Friday off from working out, but Sunday I took Mr F and Mr Bunches on a long nature walk, and then today I walked 30 minutes, covering 2 miles, and I even carried some small weights on a few of the laps. I feel pretty healthy.

81

Charley got tired of running, I guess. Good for him.

80

I've decided to start finishing up the continuing stories in here or the recurring characters – one last story for each. I'm 79 days away from the end of this set of stories. 79 days ago was December 16: I hadn't yet agreed to join my new firm, and my car had just died around there, and Sweetie and I were arguing a lot. I wonder what Me+79Days will be like?

The "Maxie Ford" is an actual tap dance step.

79

This is starting to feel like a farewell tour.

Most nights, this story-writing doesn't seem like a chore, at all. It probably should, after nearly 300 stories almost in a row, but I kind of look forward to it.

I know this one isn't so much a *story* but I suppose if you read *only* this part you'd at least have a sense of what is going on? 79-word stories are hard to write. I suppose 78 words stories will be 1/79th harder, and so on. Or does that math not work out? That would make the [1] story 364/365ths harder to write than the first, which is less than 1th harder.

PS I know *1th* isn't a measurement but that was before I used it. It's a measurement now.

78

BOY was this hard to write. Today, Mr. Bunches said something about piranhas, and asked if they lived around here. I said they lived in South America and he lived in North America, so he didn't have to worry. Mr Bunches then said piranhas were mean and sharks were nice; I think? I might have that backwards. So all day long I was thinking *piranha vs shark*, but every version of this story I tried didn't work out, until finally I hit on shark insulting piranha. Even then I had to cut the story almost in half; originally piranhas couldn't figure out if shark meant it as an insult or a compliment, which I think was needlessly complicated and also didn't make much sense, so the 78-word version is really a better story than the original 118-word story.

77

I was thinking of writing a story with the title "Parachute." But I couldn't think of a story to write with it. I read some six-word stories on a website, then some 75-word stories on another, to get a feel for stories this short. I didn't like them. So I wrote this one, instead.

I sometimes do this, at the pool: When Mr. Bunches wants me to jump in with him, I sometimes float a bit at the bottom of the pool, blurrily watching the bubbles float up and people swimming, while I look at the surface of the water and enjoy the kind of quiet that can only come from being wrapped up in something warm and sunny and soft and see-through. If someone could come up with a way to feel that way all the time (and without the holding-my-breath-part) I would love it.

76

When we were kids, my mom told us not to eat snow because animals pee on it. When the boys first began being old enough to tell *them* not to eat snow, I did at first, too, but then I thought *that's crazy, you can tell if snow is clean or not, it's probably the one thing in the world you can tell if it's okay to eat.* So I let them eat snow if they want. It's not like I think I'm the better parent, but I at least gave it some thought about why I was breaking *that* rule.

75

Tonight I looked through my pictures for inspiration. I think a picture helps me think of a short short story like this. That particular picture inspired 'escalators.' It's a picture of Mr F, lying on his back in a cart at the Target store near us. (They have escalators to get in, and I do love escalators.)

74

Today, the amount of money I've earned for my new firm exceeded the total that I've been paid by my new firm, which means that this move looks like it will be a success. I have a series of goals set for myself, and I'm reaching them, which is very good.

It's not 100% perfect—I have to build new relationships with people and I have to retrain lawyers and there's a lot of driving – but I feel like the challenge is both achievable and worth doing. That's something that was missing from my life for a long time.

I am taking fewer medicines now, and walking more. I keep thinking back not just on last year, but on the several years before that, when I was hospitalized and went through all kinds of tests for various things wrong with me, and every time someone suggested it was stress, I'd say that I couldn't be stressed out because I was essentially my own boss. But like the story of the frog boiling in water, slowly, I wonder how much stress I was really under that I just didn't realize, thinking it was part of every day life.

I still have worries, and I still have a heavy workload, but it feel like there's hope and I feel healthier and happier than I have in a long time. It's getting to be spring – today it hit 55 degrees, and it's only March 11, 2015 – and we went for a walk after I got home from the Milwaukee office a bit early. The sun was shining, the snow was almost melted, I might get my first bonus of the year (if I earn enough money I get draws against profits during the year, rather than at the end of the year). This year just feels different than last year in so many ways.

73

I have been taking pictures of food, against white papers, because it's a thing I decided to do. Tonight, I tried taking pictures of a row of French fries, but the camera was noncooperative; I had trouble focusing it. This fry was the last one in the lineup, and its black spot and already-broken-off tip gave it, when I stood it up, a sad demeanor that reminded me of a ghost, or perhaps a fish. This sort-of-blurry picture was my favorite. I looked at it and thought *aw, poor guy.*

71

I have just about finished B.J. Novak's book of short stories, which was influencing me as I wrote this one. It's really, really good. Today, listening to it on audiobook—that's really the way you should enjoy the book—I thought *this is like Shel Silverstein for adults.*

This afternoon, on the way to take the boys to the "Dolphin Pool" (so named because there is a dolphin statue that serves as a fountain there), I told Sweetie I had a feeling that this was going to be a great day. Now, at 7:34 p.m. (3/14/15) I can say, it was. Here is what I did today, more or less in order:

Got up.

Ate a PB&J pop tart, read the Internet for a while.

Played Batman action figures with Mr Bunches.

Read the Internet some more.

Spent an hour sending some marketing emails to lawyers and judges I met at a Moot Court event yesterday, and doing recommendation letters for a former employee of mine who is going to business school.

Spent an hour cleaning out The Boy's old room so we can turn it into a bedroom for Mr F if we ever get enough money to buy him a bed. (My new thing is on Saturday and again on

Sunday I am going to do at least 1 hour of chores; after 1 hour I can quit, but I have to do at least an hour. That avoids me putting off chores because I don't want to blow a whole day off doing them. Anyone can do anything for an hour, I figure.)

Drove to the St. Vincent's thrift store with the two old box springs, only to find they don't accept them as donations, so we went to dump them in the dumpster at Middle Daughter's apartment building.

Came home.

Ate lunch.

Took the boys to the swimming pool, at the end of which I had to blow-dry Mr F's underwear using the hand dryer, because he wears them under his wetsuit and I forgot to bring a spare pair.

Came home.

Read about 1/3 of my new book, *Fifty Mice.*

Played with Mr F.

Ate delivery pizza because the pizza place near us had a special where you could get a large pizza for $5.99, and even though I technically hate the owner of the corporation that owns the pizza place near us, I won't pass up a $5.99 pizza.

The pizza was $32, by the time you factor in two pizzas, breadsticks, and a cookie, and the tip. But you've got to get two pizzas so you have leftovers, because: Leftover pizza!

Cleaned up.

Took a family ride where we noticed a new fancy chocolate place in the rich folks' mall and I decided that for our weekly date Sweetie and I would go there this week.

Came home.

Wrote this story.

Isn't that a good day?

70

I saw a deer today, while I went for my walk. I walked on the nature trail where I used to jog. As I was coming towards the forest, I saw a flash of white bobbing up and down and as I grew closer, I saw that it was a deer, hopping over the reeds and heading further into the forest, away from me.

?

[Here's why I've skipped a day now] I've been with my new firm for two months now and the way I get paid is I get a salary against what I bring in. If I don't earn enough, I would owe the firm money at the end of the year. If I earn more than I am paid, I get a draw, so a bonus.

Sweetie and I had done some rough figuring and it was looking like we were maybe going to get a draw at the end of March. Not a big one, but one, anyway, which would be great. Better than we expected, and sooner. So last week I emailed the guy in the office who figures that stuff out, to ask if I was getting a draw and if so how much it might be, and he laid out the figures for me based on the way I am compensated (which is kind of a complicated formula) and the upshot is: no draw yet.

I mean, we're not doing *bad* but we're not doing *great*, either. We're doing *better* than last year, for sure, but we had sort of started thinking we were doing better than better, and thinking maybe we'd climbed out of the hole that the last year – last *few* years -- with my crappy old firm and stupid ex-partners who were taking advantage of me had left us in, with no savings and our budget stretched thin and our credit cards maxed out.

So we had to spend the night recalibrating our expectations and rethinking things, and it was a pretty sad day, overall. I got really upset. Not upset at Sweetie, not this time; we're a team. But upset because for fourteen years I trusted the guy who is now my ex-partner and for fourteen years I got taken advantage of; I helped build a firm that at one point had *millions* in revenues, and I got nowhere near my fair share of that, and in part I got screwed because while I was building my end of the practice – in two years I nearly doubled my revenues while more or less *inventing* an area of law – my "partner" was doing the opposite, hiring awful workers and letting things slide and sucking revenue out of the firm. And it hurt me, both financially and on a trust level. This was a guy who I once told Sweetie she should go talk to for advice if anything ever happened to me (as is pretty likely; it's almost a guarantee Sweetie will outlive me.) I had spent time with him for years, and thought of him as a brother, almost. Certainly better than my actual brothers. And I realized too late that he was using me and wasn't at all what he pretended to be. His success was based on luck, and hard work from others, including me. And he got *rich* off of me, and now we are going to have to wait longer to replace our *dish washer*, which broke three months ago and which we can't afford to replace yet.

So a lot hit me last night, pretty hard, because it meant that I was going to have longer to climb out of the hole I'd dug myself for the last 14 years. I supposed, somehow, that two months might be enough, but of course it was not. There's so much bitterness in me, and recrimination. I read back, sometimes, over the stories in here and I can see that – sometimes overtly, sometimes not so much – the bitterness and sadness of realizing that nearly *nothing* in the world is what you really thought it was, and that you have to start all over again.

I didn't sleep real well last night, then. I didn't feel like writing anything; I felt almost like a computer rebooting: numb and waiting for everything to re-set yet again.

I told Sweetie a while back that I feel like I, and her, were train-wreck survivors, that we couldn't stop marveling at how bad it was and how lucky we were to get out in one piece, and I realized last night that the feelings won't go away right away, and that there is a long road ahead of me. On the one hand, the 14 years I spent building that business helped because I am a pretty marketable guy: three firms, at least, were attempting to get me to join them. On the other hand, I am starting from scratch again, almost, and I am *tired*.

When I was 24 or so, I went on a crash diet and ate 1000 calories a day, and worked out an hour a day, and I lost 108 pounds in just 6 months.

Now, I am 46, and last October I realized I was gaining weight again. I had gotten down to 220 and then was back up to 240 or so. I can't exercise like I used to; I'll die of asthma or whatever I have. But I tried to go on a diet, and I was starving for 12 hours and couldn't do it.

It's hard achieving the same thing twice. Think of the feeling when you type a whole paper, or story, or whatever, and then accidentally delete it instead of saving it. You know that feeling where you have to start all over again? Multiply that by a million.

I know there are worse lives. But last night all I could think was *enough, God. Enough.*

Anyway, today I am feeling a bit better and so I will write two stories to get caught up:

69, 68

Nothing else to add. It's 8:16 p.m. on March 17, 2015. I'm going to hang out with Sweetie.

67

Tonight we had the fight again, just goddamn out of nowhere like a blow to the head, and now I was laying here in the dark waiting for Mr F to be fully asleep and I wasn't even going to write a story but Mr. F was watching a *Baby Einstein* in which Marlee Matlin appears and does sign language and this story popped into my head almost in its final form.

So I wrote it.

And I know that I, too, and not really mad at the person I am mad at but mad at God. I'm just not brave enough to actually think, or say, *Fuck you God.*

Only I just did.

66

Today, I had two client meetings and my temporary office space is a room at the State Bar for stuff like that. I so I was there from 10 to 5:30, with a break in-between where Sweetie came out and we talked, again, and I ate a bit of my lunch, and we hugged, and things got a bit better again.

I am still mad at God. Tonight at dinner I said grace, like I always do, but I only did it for Sweetie, so she wouldn't be uncomfortable.

65

I was going to try to write something about basketball, or basketball-related, because the NCAA Men's Tournament has started, and I always kind of like the tournament even though I don't watch it, but I couldn't think of anything to say so I just sort of whipped this story out.

We got a babysitter tonight, Middle Daughter, so that we could go see the movie *It Follows*, but *It Follows* didn't come to any theaters near us, so we ended up having Middle come over anyway, and we went for a drive. On the drive, we stopped to get a small Hot Wheels toy for Mr Bunches, as I'd promised him one to make up for him having to have a babysitter. So a significant part of our date was going to get a toy for Mr. Bunches because we went on a date, which seems ouroborosian.

We talked a bit on the date, and drove around and looked at houses and talked some more.

64

Today, Mr F had to go to a birthday party for a boy in his class. We went in, and the mom – a special ed teacher – showed us around her house and showed us a little trampoline in the basement where Mr F could go if he got stressed at the house, and made us feel very at home. We spent a minute or so sitting in the room where 10 kids were all playing a video game. We wandered from room to room, got offered popcorn, drank a sip of Sprite, looked in closets, sat on beds, wandered some more. After three tries to get Mr F to sit in the room where the party was, he tried to lock himself in the closet.

"Don't you want to come to the party?" I asked him.

"Go," he said. Whether he meant I should go and leave him in the closet or we, together, should go from the party, I decided that was the end of that. Any experience so bad that it makes you want to lock yourself in the closet is an experience that should end.

So we said good-bye and left. As a treat for him I took him to the playground where he swung and spun on these little seat-go-rounds they have. It was looking at the picture of him spinning, hours later, that gave me the idea for the beginning of this story.

63

Today, I went for a walk at the club. I'm trying to walk every other day, at least for 2 miles. I carry some small weights while I walk the track.

There was a class going on, women doing some sort of dance-y exercise. I didn't want to walk in front of the entire class and get the dumbbells up on the ledge where they sit by the mirror behind the instructor. I walked the track and listened to the audiobook of *The World According To Garp* and I hated the women dancing, because they were dancing and their music was loud and I couldn't go get the dumbbells, hated hated hated and then I got this crushing wave of sadness over me that felt like it would actually literally bowl me over. I finished walking but all day long I've felt sort of empty and hollow inside.

When I came home, I gave Sweetie a long hug.

??

But not for a bad reason; last night was March 23, 2015, and I got a new client who for various reasons was in town only for one night and couldn't meet until 8:30, so I went and met him from 8:30 until 10:15 and then when I came home I went up to our bedroom where Sweetie woke up thinking there was a bird in the room, and then I went to bed.

62

and this is tonight's (3/24/15) story, which I wrote in 6 minutes, flat, and kind of like. I came home from work early today, leaving my Milwaukee office at 2:30 because Sweetie said she needed a hug so I drove two hours home to give her one.

I started a new project today, a book kind of inspired by a dream. It is a book of short stories about my and Sweetie's life, in vignettes and snippets, told in the third person and anonymously. Each day when I go to my

Milwaukee office I will write another snippet from a set of six different categories. Then I will publish it, all without telling her until it is done. But each day, too, I send her a quote from that day's portion, with a scratch-off lottery ticket and a drawing

61

I wondered, after I wrote this, how many stories in here mention the apocalypse. As of today, it's 8, counting this one, that include that word.

When I first sat down to write, I came up with the title *How To Draw A Starfish* but couldn't really come up with a concept. Then I started a story called "Other Kinds Of Angels, 1" but couldn't think where to go with that. So I came up with the title *Slow Dancing To The Apocalypse*, and it was going to be about a couple getting married, but I thought it was too much like that other one where the guy watches the married couple dance, so I came up with this. Now, having thought and thought about it, I am not so sure I like this one, either. It feels a little facile for me at this point, the kind of flash story I can whip off in the five minutes it took me to write this one.

Then again, I am in a strange mood today, half sad, half happy, feeling somewhat energetic when I am around people and strangely moody and apathetic when I am alone. I feel like the kind of tired just before a runner's high, like I can't go on anymore but I need to just reach a few more steps and then I can fly.

Sweetie and I trade questions each day, kind of like the "36 questions to love" thing but we make up our own. Today I asked her what kind of playground equipment she thought her life was, and what she would like it to be. Her answer was beautiful. She seems to be doing okay, but maybe inside she's tired, too, and thinking she just has to make it to the top of the hill.

60

I was trying my hardest to write a happy story tonight. This was as good as it got. I'm in an okay mood today, I guess. I'm suspicious that Sweetie is sadder than she lets on. There is a quaver in her voice. That'd be fair, though, as I am sadder than *I* let on.

We could use a sunny day.

59

It is nearly 11 o'clock at night. We went to a movie tonight—*It Follows*, which Sweetie has been hoping and hoping would come to the theaters and finally it did, so we did a rare thing and went out on two consecutive Friday nights. The boys, both of them, are asleep on the couches, and Sweetie has just gone to bed. I am about to do the same, after rousting Mr. Bunches and Mr. F.

In the first version of this story, which was 109 words—I had to cut half!—the frog denied lying, but as I wrote and rewrote and chopped out words, I realized the frog couldn't deny being a liar. Or at least that it shouldn't.

58

I was stumped for a few minutes before coming up with that twist at the end. I know what I said about flash fiction twists but I like this one so: whatever.

57

I am not sure about my use of dialect in this one. I tried to give the frogs a bit of personality, but maybe it was too much?

56

They ended up together, after all.

55

Today I ate a sandwich of strips of lamb and swiss cheese with a bowl of Ramen noodles for dinner while Sweetie ate a bowl of Cookie Crisp cereal and a 'McGriddle.'

Today, I convinced a judge not to kick a woman out of her house for at least two more weeks.

Today, I blew bubbles with Mr. F and Mr. Bunches for 20 minutes after their baths.

Today, I confessed to Sweetie that I have been feeling more and more anxious and stressed out.

54

Before I wrote the shortest time-travel story I have ever written, I wrote this:

> *People think time-traveling would be great. Well, I'm here to tell you it is not. Let me tell you about the very first time I ever went traveling. It was a complete disaster, beginning with wiping out a few species and ending with... wait a second, I just thought of something. Now, where were we? Oh, yeah: People think time-traveling would be so great. It is.*

Then I decided that *couldn't* be the story because you can see that ending coming about a mile away, so I wrote the real shortest one.

53

Before I even had an idea for the story, I went and listened to the song and watched the video for *Pop Goes the World*, by Men Without Hats. I first heard that song when the video played on a small TV in a hotel room near Fort Knox, where we'd gone to visit my friend Fred. It was 1987, and Fred had joined the army. It was his first leave after spring break, so we piled into Bob's car and drove down there for the weekend. I don't remember anything else about that trip except the video in the hotel room, and the fact that on the way back, I got so tired that I began to hallucinate and thought there was an elephant crossing the highway. I swerved away from it and onto the shoulder and then had to let someone else drive.

52

Today we got a bunch of money in on some of my cases, which seems really good, except that on the way home from my deposition on the other side of town I was driving by this one farm where there are horses and a buffalo!

Really, a buffalo! And I was thinking about how it was good that we got some money in and then I got anxious that I wouldn't be able to keep doing it, and tried to just focus on the fact that it was sunny outside and the sky was blue and I'd just seen a buffalo and it was Friday.

51

I have been sitting here for the last sixty seconds wondering whether to write, in this note, about the picture that inspired this story, or about how looking through pictures to inspire this story I came across pictures I'd taken of a big display I'd put on the wall of my old firm to encourage people to help increase revenues to pay out bonuses – it was a big mountain, with a little mountain climbing the bigger mountain, and it was supposed to climb up as we got money in, to show when people would get bonuses – or if I should mention how thinking about that made me think about how my ex-partner had F***ed that one up, too, and how mad it made me that a business I helped grow had been so wrecked, or whether I should write about how there was a picture of me back in 2012 looking puffy and fatter, and then in 2013 looking slimmer, and then in 2014 back to puffier, or if instead I should mention how Kentucky and Wisconsin were playing in the NCAA Final Four tonight and that at the exact moment I was writing this note the score was Wisconsin 21, Kentucky 14.

I couldn't make up my mind.

50

Today, I had to talk to my dad on the phone. He's still dying of cancer, and I'm so mad at him that I can barely stand to speak to him. Not because he's dying – that's not his fault. Because he's dying and leaving all his money to his new wife of *eight years*. And because he said for the past 20 years since he got divorced that I was the only kid of his who had stuck by him and he was going to leave me all his money, and then after he got married he said he was going to leave me half.

Here is where I stand on this: anyone can do with their money what they want in their life, and I don't worry about it; I never worried whether he spent money or not, even though for twenty years he said he was going to leave me any money he had when he died. But after you are dead, your money does you no good, and so I am free to want it if I want to.

I won't go into the many ways my dad has treated me worse than my siblings over the past 46 years. I'm the only one of his kids who never stopped talking to him, and he was my best man at my wedding, and so on and so forth. And then I have to try to talk to him, on the same weekend Sweetie and I are sitting and hoping our finances will now work out and seeing how our budget looks going forward, and I've been stressed out about money for *years* now, and especially last year – and I am supposed to listen to my dad on the phone?

Here's a sample of that conversation. He asked how my student loans are. He *paid for my sister's college*, and has never offered to help me with student loans. When I told him that I'm in a program that doesn't even pay the whole *interest*, so they are just *growing*, he told me how I should start investing my money in the same mutual fund he is in, even maybe ten or twenty dollars per week, and then if I'm careful I might someday have as much as he has in that mutual fund, which he added, is *two hundred and fifty thousand dollars*.

That he is leaving to his wife, of *eight years*. And not leaving me *anything*.

I haven't seen him since last August, and I don't want to. After a lifetime of being screwed over by my family, this was the last straw. I only talked to him today because he left a message yesterday and he sounded weak and I felt pity so I called him and then regretted it anyway. I talked to him for an hour and the entire time I was seething mad and then I was depressed and in a bad mood the rest of the day.

I told Sweetie that I'm not going to talk to him on the weekends anymore. *"I'm not letting him wreck any more weekends,"* I said.

49

I tried and tried to write a story about dandelions, working through three or four different stories and scrapping them before coming up with this one.

I find it easy to write stories if I come up with a title that begins with "The Man" or "The Woman" or "The Robot" or something like that, and then follow it with something improbable.

48

I really worked at *this* one, too. I had a good idea for it, about a gremlin following you and how that might play into belief, and I toyed with it and toyed with it before settling on this. I'm torn as to whether this is the best version of the idea. It's the best I have right now. I like the pictures more than the story, maybe. The pictures help the story a lot.

This could have been called "The Boy Who Thought He Was Being Followed By A Gremlin." I suppose almost any story could be retitled that way. But I didn't have the title for this one until after I wrote it. The original title was "There Are Worse Fates, but Also There Are Better." That was too long, though, because it put the word count way too high. When I chopped off the second half I didn't like the title at all. It seemed smarmy.

That's Mr F in the pictures. He and I are alone in the house right now. Mr F fell asleep on the couch, but before we could move him upstairs, Mr Bunches woke up crying and in a panic because it's raining out. It's a light drizzle, but Mr Bunches is terrified of rain ever since the power went out during one thunderstorm. He only feels safe in a car when it's raining. So Sweetie took him for a ride.

47

I hadn't intended this to be a continuing story when I wrote "The Hundred," until I finished the hundred. Then I left a note for myself to continue it at The Forty-Seven.

Today, I was going to start getting up at 5:30 to write these. I already wake up about 5:45 every day, when

Sweetie gets up. I usually lay in bed until 6 or so before coming downstairs to sit and guard my coffee pot while the coffee brews—Mr. F will dump the pot out if I leave it untended, he doesn't allow me to have coffee, for reasons that are mysterious, as are all of Mr. F's reasons. But I forgot to set the alarm for 15 minutes earlier, and then woke up at 5:45 and decided I'd rather continue writing at night, when nobody else is around.

I've started jogging at the end of my exercise walks. Just a 10th of a mile, each time, right now, but I like it. I feel good. My asthma or whatever hasn't been too bad. I was talking with Sweetie about whether the stress of working at my old firm might not have been more of a cause than I thought. ~~As I was going through all kinds of terrible medical feelings the past few years, doctors occasionally suggested some of it might be caused by stress.~~

~~"I'm not stressed out," I'd tell them, but like the frog in boiling water, maybe I just didn't realize how hot it had gotten.~~

45

I had three hearings this week and won all of them. I have collected a lot of money on my files in April already and it's only April 10. I keep a running tally of the days since I have lost my temper or snapped at Sweetie, and it has been 11 consecutive days now that I haven't done that. I think this was a pretty good week.

44

I'm sitting in the boys' room with them. After the other night, Sweetie and I decided to get tougher on Mr F. The other night, he fell asleep on the couch and when I tried to get him up to bed he fought me and got mad and

screamed, so I let him go back down and fall to sleep again. That usually works, but this time when I re-woke him to go to bed this time at midnight, he did the same thing and I ended up sleeping on one couch while he slept on the other.

So now we make him go to his room. Last night he fell asleep in about 30 minutes while Sweetie sat in there. Tonight it's been 20 minutes and I think he's slowing down.

When we took a ride before bedtime, I was thinking of writing a story about vampires. I kept thinking the phrase *The best thing about being a vampire is* but I couldn't finish it.

I'm getting a bit better at writing these shorter stories, maybe? I haven't got a formula for it. I'm sort of right now just trying to do my own version of the comic strip *A Softer World*.

43

I don't know.

42

I was going to write a story about Geronimo, because I have been listening to the song *Geronimo* yesterday and today. Then I went and looked at some old pictures of Mr. F and Mr. Bunches from back in 2012. It seemed so long ago. Then I tried to write a story about a picture of Mr. Bunches, standing below a tree on a beach. It's one of my favorite pictures, ever:

Then I wrote this story because I was stumped on what else to write and rewriting fables with an ironic postmodern twist is a good way to get out of writer's block.

I am in a pensive, somewhat anxious mood today. For no real reason.

41

This is a true story.

40

This, too.

39

Also this one.

38

This one is not true. Except for the part about being able to buy solidified Krypton online. That's for real.

37

Both parts of that story were true. I wrote that story yesterday (April 18, 2015) but didn't put it in here until today, Sunday April 19, because yesterday Mr. F spilt milk on my laptop, which is the computer I call the "Batman" computer, because when I had to start it up and it says to name your computer I asked Mr. Bunches what to name it, and he said "Batman."

I was pretty upset at first, rushing and shutting off the computer and stuffing it into the bag of rice we keep for just such accidents. But after a few minutes I calmed down. I hadn't yelled or anything. I was just really bothered by the thought that my brand new computer might be wrecked. So I went upstairs and found Mr. F, who was in his room looking for a hanger to use as a tapper. I hugged him and said "I love *you*. It's just a computer. I love you." And I felt better, but not better enough to write a great story.

36

I wrote Note 37 on Sunday the 19th so I don't have much to add to this one. I'm of course back on my new laptop. I'm very tired, too. Last night, Mr. F didn't fall asleep until 11 o'clock, and then fought me taking him up to bed. Then he woke up at 3, and was kicking his closet wall enough to wake up and worry Mr. Bunches, so I brought us both downstairs and watched They Came Together until 5, when we fell asleep again. Then Mr. Bunches woke us up at 6.

Yesterday, too, I started a new book: it's called "https," and is a modernist story about a guy trying to invent a videogame and getting distracted by what he thinks might be a murder across the street from him. My routine right now is to work on my 'everyday thing' first at night, and then if I have more time and feel like it, to write something else for a while, based on a sort of random selection. My everyday thing right now is this book, of course. The next thing I'm supposed to write tonight is the sequel to my book *Codes*, a continuation I call *The Watson Protocol*, but I'm pretty tired. Maybe I'll only write it for a minute or two.

35

This one took me a while. I had the basic idea but had to rewrite it over and over to come up with how the story should *be*.

34

I feel like this is both predictable, and trite. I really wanted to write something related to that picture, and I wanted it not to be sad, and so I wrote this one, but I don't know. I think it's not such a great story.

So I wrote a second one:

34.2

That seems more like it, although it's back to sad.

33, 32, 31

I wrote stories 33 and 32 on another computer, while the one I usually use was in a plastic bag full of rice for 36 hours. It had gotten milk spilt on it by Mr. Bunches, the second time in 72 hours that had happened (the last was Mr. F). So I didn't do notes for those.

Today is April 24, 2015. I began the day by getting a call from a credit card company, which has been calling me because our payment is late this month. In calling me, they might have broken some consumer laws, which means I may not have to pay the credit card at all. Then I found a guy's wallet outside the parking lot and was able to get both a good feeling when I returned it to him—he was super happy, not least because the wallet had a bunch of cash in it and all his credit cards and junk—and a reward he gave me. $40. He offered me a reward, I said *"that's not necessary,"* and he said *"I insist,"* and handed me forty bucks and so I accepted. Why not? I did a nice thing and he wanted to do a nice thing. Then I had a hearing and we settled the case just prior to and we made a lot of money and my clients were happy. It was Friday and the day was going great and it was almost the weekend and I was planning a night out with Sweetie to have some time with her prior to my three-day business trip next week for a trial.

And then in the afternoon I got a decision in another case. We had lost. For unfair reasons that I disagreed with, but we had lost.

A week ago, I had three hearings. We won all three. In the past week, I have had five hearings and a court decision. We won four of them and lost two. Those two that I lost hung heavier on me than the four that I won could buoy me up. All my losses stay with me, forever. I think about them at night and when I drive in the car alone. I can barely remember the victories. I am sitting here today knowing that this morning was full of victories big and small and the afternoon was marked by one setback (and one I might be able to reverse at that), and the loss is dragging me down.

At dinner, we ordered appetizers, plus individual pizzas. We talked about which celebrities we would most want to have dinner with because they would be interesting or fun. My top choice was Ben Affleck. Sweetie's was George Clooney. We agreed that they were essentially the same thing. Then we drove downtown and around the Capitol and out past the campus where once we saw a fox, and then home.

30

I didn't lose my cool. I didn't yell or get upset or punch my knee so hard I left a bruise and my hand hurt for three days.

Not this time.

But: the fight.

Again.

Really. The same thing. The. Same. Thing. And when it died out at the end I took the boys swimming in the pool. Sweetie is sad. I am sad. There will again linger a pall over the week, slowly fading away.

It had been a pretty good day. Not a great day – there was the deodorant flushed down the toilet, the cleanup, nothing terrible but nothing too great. I had nearly dozed off this afternoon on the couch, then gone for my walk, then came home and walked right into The Fight.

It *is* the things you refuse to think about that matter the most, I think. They are the things we carry with us and will not look at, homunculi that drag us down with their spiny, oily weights, gnawing on our bones when we are not looking. We want the other things to matter: we want the happy moments and sunlight to be the important stuff. We want photo albums of people squinting into flashes at birthday parties and making bunny ears behind each other at prom. But what we are confronted with are dark corners, shadows, quick glances over our shoulder.

I had a nightmare, when I was about 15, I think: I was running through a snowy woods and a man jumped out and stabbed me in my side. I woke up, panting and sweating and scared. I had been running so long, only to be stabbed at the end. I was actually holding my side when I went to the bathroom, and I was afraid to move my hand, the dream was so real.

I can't remember huge chunks of my happy childhood, but I remember that dream like it was last night's. I sometimes hold my hand in the same place as I did that night.

All the things we would rather not think about are the things that push us around throughout our lives. We are all victims of the bullying of our pasts.

29, 28

I guess this last one isn't so much a story as just a thought? But it's hard to do a story and anyway I really wanted to use this title, which was a direct quote from Mr. Bunches. Mr. Bunches has trouble with time, and sequences, and what comes after or before or next. So yesterday – April 26, 2015- was a Sunday and Mr. Bunches was working through something, trying to figure out this week. He said *"Today is Sunday,"* and I agreed it was. Then he thought for a minute and said *"At the bottom of Sunday is Monday,"* and I agreed with that, too, even though secretly up until that point I'd always thought of evening as the 'top' of the day – like morning was at the bottom and we climbed up the day and then dropped down and started again. That's really how I thought of it.

But I thought the way he put it was even better, because if there's anything worse than a Sunday, it's a Monday. Or mostly. I don't really dislike Mondays anymore. Not this year. There've only been a few Mondays I was sort of down about. I guess that's because I like my job again.

Today is Monday. I am sitting in a hotel in Merrill, Wisconsin, on my first-ever business trip. It's to go to a trial, a three-day trial in a town that's 158 miles (I gps'd it) from my house. 2 ¾ hours. So I can't commute back and forth the way I did the last time I had a long trial a ways away; that was a 90-minute one way commute.

So I am staying in a hotel. This is the first time I had slept in a bed without Sweetie since 2011, when I was in the hospital for what at the time I thought was heart attack or lung cancer or something, but was probably just really bad asthma. I was in there five days and they never figured out what was causing me to have chest pains and difficulty breathing. Now, four years later, the same symptoms I used to go to the ER for don't really bother me as much – they have either gotten better (a bit) or I've gotten used to them (a bit). Anyway, that was the last time I slept in a bed away from Sweetie.

I can't remember the last time I went a full 24-hour period without seeing Sweetie. Tomorrow at 5:15 a.m. will be the first time since, probably we got married, I figure. Maybe longer. And it'll be at least 48, possibly 60 or more. The trial is supposed to end Wednesday.

I can remember the last time I went a whole day without seeing the boys. It was 9/4/06, the day before they were born.

I didn't realize how much I'd miss them. I drove up this morning and spent the day in court and then went and checked into my hotel. I got my suitcase in and took the suits out and set out the PB&J and chips and sodas I'd brought with me so I didn't have to go out to eat every night – expensive enough, to front the $150 for the hotel until I get reimbursed – and then realized that I was setting up to have my own life for the next two days, here in this little room with a bed and a chair and a TV I've had tuned to CNN the past 2 hours without really watching it.

Tomorrow, if the trial goes well, I'll probably go afterwards and get a souvenir for the boys and Sweetie. On Wednesday, it'll probably be late and if the jury comes back with a bad verdict, I won't want to shop around town anyway. The drive home after losing a trial is a *long* one. I don't think I'll lose, but, then, I never think I'll lose.

It's 8:03 p.m. I'm going to go read or something.

27

Yesterday, on the way up to this trial, I had the idea for a comic strip called Frog, and Rabbit. The two characters would be roundish, almost purely circle, characters that stood in the front of the strip and things would happen behind them. I even drew them last night while doodling a bit. Then today I wrote this story.

The trial I believe is going well. It's gone as well as it can, I suppose. I have been working on this case for nearly three years; I was first hired by the clients in March of 2012, when they were about to lose their house. I was at my old firm then. I've been to court with these clients several times before, helping first save their house from foreclosure and then file a bankruptcy to keep the house and now suing the lawyers who screwed up in the first place. My old partners hated this case and didn't want to keep going on it. It was supposed to go to trial last December, and my ex-partner came down, just prior to Thanksgiving, to give me the firm credit card and berate me for how much the clients owed the firm and made me promise that I would not run up fees like this on a client again. I tried not to laugh and assured him that it would no longer be a problem. The trial got postponed by defense counsel not being ready. Two weeks later I signed the agreement with my new partner.

So almost everything has gone our way in this trial. We rested today. I should be elated. Instead, I have this nagging anxiety, as though it will turn out badly. I don't know why I'm feeling that. Maybe I'm tired. I slept terribly last night. It was too hot and I was too strung out by the trial and exhaustion and being away from my home.

I went and bought some souvenirs to bring home: a couple of books for the boys, who don't care if they get something labeled "Merrill, WI" and a t-shirt from "Chips," a local burger joint the clerk said was the best burger around. The burgers were okay. The kid who waited on me came by to clean the table and saw me reading on my laptop. *"Big project?"* he asked me.

"I'm in town for a trial," I said.

"Oh yeah?" he asked. *"What kind of trial?"* So I told him. He seemed impressed, and I felt like a kind of big shot.

26

You probably guessed that the trial was why I skipped a day. We finished most of everything late last night, but the judge decided that—I have to interject to point out that for some reason my word program is processing the words in spurts. For example I just typed "for example I just typed," and then it waited until I wrote the word "typed" before printing the entire phrase "for example I just typed." Yesterday or maybe today, I'm not sure, I'm *very* tired, my Word program would not type the letters "c" or "ch," on the regular keyboard or the virtual one that comes up on the touchscreen. Today it's doing this weird burst-typing thing where I type a bunch of words and it throws up four or five at a time and it's VERY distracting. I am not in the mood to be distracted.—Anyway the judge decided that—it's still doing the burst-typing thing!—the judge decided that he would send the jury home and then we'd come back today to have the jury deliberate, which meant that I had to drive *all the way home* because I only had three days' changes of clothing. I got home at 11 and got all my stuff set to get up at 4:30 am., then slept and then got up and went back up there today.

The net result: the jury found for us, but didn't award as much as we wanted in damages. The amount, $18,400, was disappointingly low. I was so nervous all day. Then the verdict. Then I had to buck up the clients, who were also disappointed, and we have to come up with a plan to deal with their newest problem: my ex-partner, who claims they owe him money and who wants to get his hands on this award.

So much more that could be said about the trial, in which I probably gave my finest courtroom performance ever, and about the last four days in general, and about my now-planned battle with my ex-partner over the $18,400, and my clients, and "Millie The Horse," which was the name of one of my client's horses that kept coming up and we were waiting throughout the trial for a bombshell of a surprise about why opposing counsel kept bringing up Millie the Horse and then at the end it was NOTHING! He was trying in some weird way to prove they were lying because of Millie The Horse, and nobody got it.

The clients said I am like a lion in the courtroom. They want me to help them against my ex-partner. I am going to. I have already started that.

So I am back home, and taking the next three days—Friday Saturday and Sunday—off from work to relax. I am exhausted. So much more to say, and I am too tired to say it.

I think tonight's story is symbolic of what I view as my dedication. I started the case that went to trial 3 years ago. I first saved their house and now I got a verdict against their former lawyer who almost lost their house for them. Next I will help them fight my ex-partner to keep the money they just won.

I am restarting building a new business, just as I did with the last one, from the ground up.

When I got home, at 4 o'clock today, having been up for 12 hours straight and for 33 of the last 36 hours, there was a social worker here to go over aid applications to get money to help the boys with therapists and things, to see what we qualified for. We met with her for two hours, then I had to work through all the emotions of the past week with Sweetie, who also has had a rough time, and needed to also spend time with the boys. I would walk around the Earth for them, too—even if I knew they were sending me on a wild goose chase? I don't know. Symbolism is lost on me most times anyway and especially when I am exhausted.

I was so nervous about the verdict that before the jury came back I nearly threw up. Then it came back and I suddenly didn't know *what* to feel. I mean, we won. So I could celebrate. But we didn't win as much as we wanted. So I could be sad. I didn't know what to feel. I think once I get past *tired*, I will probably feel *dedication* again. But for now, it's just *tired*, and also glad to be back home and away from Room 112.

25

Too cutesy? I think it might be too cutesy.

We went to see *Avengers 2* today, as I took the day off of work. It was really good. Throughout it, I kept nearly bubbling over with emotion: I got tears in my eyes and I laughed and I was excited. I think I was just overflowing with energy and emotion still. The rest of the day was fun, too; we got drive-thru burgers from the A&W and watched some movies, and took the boys to "Tall Park," which is a park we first discovered last year, the boys and I, on a Sunday after we'd gone into my old office. I played *Plants vs. Zombies 2*, which Sweetie says I am addicted to. We talked about how it is May 1, and how this summer might actually be fun for a change.

24

This story had sort of a strange inception. Today when I went for my walk, which also includes a bit of a jog now – I am hiding from Sweetie that when I walk I also jog a bit; in April it was 1 minute per walk. In May it is 2 minutes per walk. So out of 29 minutes of walking today I jogged for 2 minutes – I had the idea that I should read more William Carlos Williams, as his poem *The Red Wheelbarrow* is one I've always liked, and I thought the remainder of the stories should sort of be like Williams' poems. To that end, I decided I should try to think up a story in its entirety, and then boil it down to the bare essence and then write that up, like a Williams poem.

This is the first of those. The 'story' behind it was my imagining a robot sent to study the sun, and falling in love with it. It tries to bring a piece of the sun back to Earth, but can't keep it going all the way home. It keeps burning out.

So that's where the *poem* came from. I had it down to 23 words, and needed a title. I couldn't think of one, so I went and read about *The Starry Night* by Van Gogh, one of my favorite paintings (and one which I'd also read about today, in a story about how Van Gogh might have been color blind and that's why his colors look weird.) A year or two ago I tried to create a giant chalk version of *The Starry Night* on our driveway, getting about 1/6 of the way through it.

I learned, in reading about it, that Van Gogh had never thought much of the painting *The Starry Night*. I learned that it showed the view out of the window of his asylum, in *Saint-Remy-de-Provence*, at night, one night when Venus was particularly bright, and that the star in the painting is Venus. I thought about how the idea that you can't bring a star back home fit the idea that Van Gogh couldn't capture in a painting the night sky that had so entranced him. He originally didn't even send the painting to be sold! So I called the story that. I know I'm not supposed to explain poems according to that guy who said I shouldn't explain poems, but tough. I explained it.

23

So technically this might be a story that *never* happened. It was inspired by a line in the song "Nothing Without Love" by Nate Ruess:

> I am nothing without love
> I'm but a ship stuck in the sand
> Some would say that I'm all alone
> But I am, I'm nothing without love

I heard that song while it was playing in the background of "Chip's" restaurant in Merrill, last week, as I was eating dinner there on night 2 of the trial. I listened to it tonight, and pictured a group of people building a ship, but taking so long to finish it that they can't ever sail it because the oceans have dried up by the time it's done, so they go somewhere else and do something else instead.

Again, I know I'm not supposed to *explain* stories, but why not?

Tomorrow I go 'back' to work. I technically only had Friday off, but it feels like a lot longer than that. I'm not too bummed out about it. I'd rather not ever have to work, but I have a good job and I get to do fun things in it.

22

So I forgot to do this one at 24, but the need to reduce the number to 22 helped me move the plot along.

Something I left out of the note on the other story: Van Gogh, and many other painters, liked to do series of paintings, figuring it helped illuminate something that might otherwise have been missed. That's why there's so many similar paintings from painters, like all the different versions of *The Scream*, maybe. By redoing something over and over, it becomes better known and possibly new truths are seen in it.

I didn't know that when I started this book, although I guessed that the process of removing one word at a time would be interesting for me, and it has been. I also didn't know it when I started the various series of stories that appear in here. But it turns out it's kind of fun to do, and it does help to work through a particular idea. A few years back I did a series of 10 short Xmas stories all at once, and I'd decided before I wrote the first word that I would definitely write 10 of them and that they would all be written in one sitting, and that's one of my favorite things I ever wrote. Then again, almost everything I ever wrote is one of my favorite things I ever wrote.

21

Eh.

A little frazzled. I have a trial tomorrow and Middle Daughter was supposed to bring the file back from the Milwaukee office and drop it off, since I was working in Madison today. She forgot, so I had to spend 45 minutes going online and reprinting all the file materials. But the boys went to bed really really early—it's 8 p.m. right now, and they're both asleep, which is good because last night they were up at 2 so I've been up for nearly 18 hours now.

This story took me about 5 minutes to right. I was wondering what to do tonight for story 21 and it popped into my head, almost fully formed.

20

I'm not sure where this one came from.

Today was … I was about to say a pretty good day, but I suppose it was not a pretty good day or a pretty bad day, or even a day that was worth noting.

Today was a day. Today was the kind of day that I suppose I will never remember if I do not write down any details. If I mention that today was day 3 of a trial involving a painter trying to sue my client for $12,000, and that I listened to *The Golden Compass* audiobook on the way to and from the trial, and that tonight I took Mr. F outside to play *Big Wheels* but he was sort of naughty, running into people's yards so I quit early and we bummed around the backyard with Mr. Bunches, and Mr. Bunches wanted to sit under the evergreen bushes that I don't trim anymore, but there was a bug there so he wanted me to help him, and Mr. F dumped over the flowerpot where we planted carrot seeds, and I looked around the backyard and could see almost the way it might be if I ever have money to actually landscape it, if I mention that we had waffles and pancakes and eggs and toast for dinner, that I ate a *Zero* bar on the ride before bed, that I finished the Ancient Egypt level of Plants vs. Zombies, 2, and we finished watching *Tropic Thunder* in our quest to watch all of the Tom Cruise movies, if I mention all of that I will someday remember this day, I suppose, but otherwise, I doubt I would because this day wasn't really worth remembering. It wasn't *not* worth it, either. Now, though, I will probably remember this day long beyond its worth.

19

I skipped two days. Of course it was because of The Fight, which happened again, with such alarming regularity, on Thursday. This time it was so bad I felt as though something quite literally died in me. My head has hurt since then and I have had this welling pit of anger and sadness in me. I cancelled our date on Friday, and rather than work from home I spent the day at the Courthouse and then the library, working on my laptop. I got so mad I screamed Thursday night, and Mr. Bunches got scared and started crying and then I felt even more awful. I couldn't hardly sleep and didn't want to sleep in our bed, although I did because I thought it would be more awful to not do that. On Friday morning I told Sweetie that we had to go to counseling and that I wouldn't talk about it, or Fight about it, anymore in the house, that I wouldn't let anything keep poisoning our house like this and wouldn't let it get so bad that I didn't want to be here or that I scared the boys again. I told her if she wanted to discuss it outside of counseling she had to email it to me. I haven't felt happy in 48 hours. I have to try to pretend that I'm okay and I can't quite do it. Tomorrow is Mother's Day and I had to take the boys to get her presents today, and I just felt numb the entire time. We took the boys to a fair at the mall tonight, a little carnival set up in the parking lot that Mr. Bunches was excited to go to. It was the saddest I've ever felt at a carnival. I can't even get angry or cry anymore. I just don't want to be *me*. And I don't entirely feel like *me*. I feel like some part of me has gone away, the part that helps keep me happy, and now where it was it's all just black tar, pulling at the rest of me. My head hurts and I feel like I can't quite breathe right. I thought maybe I was having a heart attack for a while today. Then I wondered, if I was, would I go to the hospital right away? I wasn't sure. I spent a lot of time hugging Mr. F today.

18

It's Mother's Day, May 10, 2015. I have still been feeling down, and still rundown, too. I keep reassuring Sweetie nothing is wrong. I'm not sure if she thinks things are over or not, if she's just papering over everything like I feel I am. We made her Pop Tarts for breakfast in bed, the boys gave her her presents, we played *Plants vs. Zombies 2*, we took a drive to go to a bakery that was closed so we went to Dairy Queen instead, the older kids took her to a movie and then later to dinner, and through it all I felt like I was sleepwalking. My head feels heavy. Whenever I am alone with my thoughts for even a second, I feel like I'm falling apart. This weekend was terrible. And now it's back to the workweek, and one which promises to be busy *and* in which my 15th anniversary falls, on Wednesday, and I'm taking the whole day off to spend with Sweetie on Friday. I feel tired just thinking about it.

17

I'm going to bed.

16

It's 9:06 p.m. Mr. F is having a bad night and I have volunteered to sit here with him. Tomorrow is my 15th wedding anniversary. Today was my first marriage counseling. I don't know how I feel about it. We went for an hour and talked about why we were there and then made plans to each see the doctor for an hour individually, and then I got into my car and drove to my Milwaukee office, where I spent four bewildering hours. I feel sort of numb. I've been really rundown, too, with the asthma, and I had to call the doctor and get the steroids that I only take when things are really bad.

Today after work and after dinner I took the boys outside to play water balloons. When we ran to the Dollar Store yesterday to get me a new pair of reading glasses—Mr. F had gotten hold of mine and broken them—Mr. Bunches went in and opted to buy water balloons. But it's been in the fifties yesterday and today, so I said they couldn't have a water balloon fight, but instead we filled up five balloons, each, and went outside to throw them on the driveway. The boys seemed okay with that. It seems like standing on the stairs throwing water balloons in a mock fight on a too cold day should be metaphorical of something, but, then, everything's symbolic of everything.

15

This story was inspired by a picture of Mr Bunches looking at a tiger that had come and lain right in front of him in the zoo.

Today is my 15th wedding anniversary. It is May 13, 2015, at 8;12 p.m. Today included bananas foster French toast, a walk around the neighborhood, two episodes of *Bob's Burgers*, my gleefully finding that the Court of Appeals had ruled against my old firm in a case, a note from Mr. F's teacher that he is becoming increasingly uncontrollable at recess and will have to stay indoors for a while, a talk with an expert witness about whether a bench at a pawnshop was safe enough, and seeing a buffalo and donkey grazing in a small pasture on my way home.

14

Is it a story, though? I mean, if that 'baby shoes never worn' is a story, then anything might be a story. Here's the thing about 'baby shoes,' completely aside from how Hemingway didn't write it: the story comes from *you*. "Baby shoes for sale, never worn" could be – as anyone who's ever had a baby knows – the story of how for a baby shower people gave you a billion pairs of shoes instead of what you need (diapers and money) and now the kid never even wore them. It could be a story of happy excess, a family with a strong, sturdy toddler trundling about the garage sale where his never-worn baby shoes are among the ephemera of his early childhood and his parent's lapsed lives: "Eight Track Tapes, never played, for sale." "Barbells, used sporadically, for sale." And the sun beats down on the driveway where the early morning rain is evaporating. It's going to be a humid day, and at noon dad and son pack the stuff into a box and leave it at the local Goodwill store before heading to the zoo, where dad will carry the boy on his shoulders and they will pretend the boy is an elephant for a while, laughing and still sticky from cotton candy.

13

The first version of this was more poetic, and mentioned sunlight. This one took me a while.

12

Tonight, we went for a drive and I had a "Red Velvet Oreo Shake." I lost four pounds this week, if you consider that last Saturday when I took the boys swimming I weighed myself (as I do every time I am at the club, regardless of the time of day) and I weighed over 247 pounds, but tonight when I weighed in after swimming, I weighed just over 243. I haven't been sleeping much this week. Sweetie thinks it might be the steroids I had to take for the asthma all week. I have been up until midnight, even one, the last few nights. I slept in a bit today, getting up at 7, an hour or more after everyone else. I dozed for about 45 minutes on the couch today. I don't know why I am saying all this. There's no pattern here. Mr. F is starting to fall asleep on the couch. *Under the Sea* is playing on *The Little Mermaid* on television. I have my glasses on. I am listening to "We Are Young" by fun.

11

One minute. It took *one minute* to write this. From the title to the end to editing it down from its original 13 words took *one minute*. I didn't know what I'd write at all until I wrote the title, then I wrote a sentence and deleted it and then wrote *I guess I'd better go* and the story was pretty much done.

10

This one was tougher. I had trouble fitting the story into the title, which had to be the title based on this thing I'm doing with the last 12 stories. I had this idea that a girl would fight falling in love, out of fear of what it would do to her, and related that to how we stand against gravity because to *not* do that is to give into the force that eventually will pull us into the ground, and I wrote a story that captured exactly what I wanted to say but it was 54 words long, and so I deleted it and it will be forever gone. I was going to print it here, but decided, no, that would be like cheating, at this point. It's bad enough I've used this note to explain it so much. Putting the 54-word story in for the 10-word story that *almost* gets what I wanted to explain would be so much worse.

To say love is like gravity makes it sound like a good, or bad, thing, depending on your mood. But gravity is neither good nor bad, or it is both, depending on the situation. If you are trying to blast off a rocket, or need to get up a tree to escape a wolf, or have to toss your infant out the window of a burning building, gravity can seem cruel. But if you would rather have air to breathe and a world to live in and a sun to spin around and warm you so that one morning in May you walk outside and it's bright and sunny and your sunflowers are starting to sprout and you say to your wife *It's a nice morning*, then gravity's okay I guess.

9

It's necessary I guess to get a little more creative again, with only 9 words available and one used for the title. I tried this idea a few different ways before settling on the basic words and then moving them around so that they could make a few different arrangements.

I thought I'd heard somewhere that everything we ever see or do or hear or experience our mind stores up. I don't know if that's true and I don't want to go look it up to see if it is, or more particularly to see if it isn't. I've also I think read that we don't really pay attention to things we see or do or hear anymore, after a while, because they become so familiar, and that what's really going on as we drive by the Walgreen's on our way to the grocery store is that our mind is sort of rendering the scenery by putting in what we *expect* to be there, rather than noticing what is really *there*. So as I drive to Milwaukee tomorrow, and I notice the various things on the highway, most of it is just my mind not paying attention and saying *yeah there's like a tree there or something and hey some clouds*.

I like to think that I pay more attention than that, that I notice the things around me. I look at trees on the horizon and watch for birds and try to see what's on the side of the road, but I'm probably no better than anyone else about it and I'm sleepwalking through life, too.

But the stars? I like to look at the stars. I took an astronomy class in college and when I go out at night I try to remember the constellations we learned about. I can't, hardly, remember them, but I try. I like to think that every time I've looked up at the stars, that view of the sky is stored somewhere in my mind, just there waiting to be used sometime. The sky I looked at from the hillside where we camped and drank beer and smoked the night before I had neck surgery when I was 21. The sky the way it looked when I walked home from the job at the gas station that one time. The cold sky the night I stood outside the mall smoking a cigarette and getting up the nerve to go back inside and buy the engagement ring I was going to give to Sweetie. They're all there, hoping I don't blink.

8

I kind of like this one. I think.

7

I realized tonight that most less-than-10 word stories don't have titles, at all. That makes sense. If you could write a title that's super long (as I did once, for a story, writing a 249-word title to a one-word story) you can essentially lengthen the story. So I figure it's okay to let the first word of the story be the title, right? It's not as dumb as calling something "Untitled." I hate when artists/poets, etc. leave a piece "untitled." Give it a title! At least "Sonnet #7" or "Red Bird with Lute," or something.

I am feeling a bit better today. I haven't been feeling that great the last few days—weird, stuffy headaches and fatigue. But today it's not as bad. So there's that. It's almost Memorial Day, coming early this year, in just four days. The start of summer! Today the high was only 68 degrees. It doesn't feel like summer yet. I want to take the boys to the park near us where there is a harbor with small boats and we can swim and wave at the boats as they go in and out. We did that a few years ago and it's one of my favorite memories. I am waiting until it is warm enough to do that. I feel an almost tangible pull to re-create that day. I don't know why. I drive by that park, all the time, and I think *We need to go there and play in the water and wave at the boats*, and it's all I can do to not drag the boys there on a 68-degree Thursday night in May.

6

This one I think is great.

5

This is a story, I think.

I am trying to learn not to wish.

I am trying to learn to hope without relying on hope. For years now, we have been thinking *one big break and we're okay*, one lump-sum of bonus cash, one grant of money, one big partnership check. I'm trying to break myself of that, to remember that the money I make – and it really is a lot, really – is enough and even if we might make more I should content myself with how much we make and try to build, slowly, rather than imagine the day that the big break will come and set my life up waiting for that.

And then I spend a day like today, running some errands – getting Velcro to use on the picture board we are making so Mr F can tell us when he wants French fries or to go for a ride, picking up some pink insulation to use on the windows when we install the air conditioners tomorrow, going to the bakery over on Williamson Street for a snack – and I see all the people spending money and all the plants I would put in my garden and all the improvements for my house and all the toys that Mr Bunches would love to buy – and I fight against the feeling like maybe I won't get a break, that I'll never catch up and never have that kind of freedom, never take a big vacation or have extra money.

In the midst of that, my dad called and left me a nasty message, claiming I never call him and that I am ungrateful. When I tried to call him back, I heard his stupid wife tell him *You're going to talk to him*, as though *she* cares. And then he hung up the phone. It's just as well. Might have told him that he burned all his bridges with me, years ago, and that *family* doesn't get you very far with me, not given *my* family. I might have told him that I could've used the stupid money he is leaving to his stupid second wife, who he has known *eight years* and who he married because he didn't want to live on his own after his mom and dad died. I might have told him that I was the only person in his life who ever tried to stay loyal to him and that all through this past year when I could've used his help, to start up my own law firm instead of having to leave the one I built up and join a new one that now turns out to be nowhere near as successful as I thought it was (that's a WHOLE DIFFERENT STORY that threw me for a loop this week, too, and left me thinking I've got no choice but to gear up again and find a way to just go out on my own and not keep getting saddled with these terrible partners), all this past year when he was deciding to leave his money (assuming it exists and he's not lying about that too) to his stupid new wife, he was just destroying what few ties held me to him. He stole my identity, cost me thousands in taxes, paid for my sister's college and not mine, started fights with me year after year after year (he stopped talking to me because I was best man in my brother's wedding, and stopped talking to me when I took my 15-year-old sister to Thanksgiving at his house and then to my mom's house, after they divorced, and after I told him one time that we would be to Christmas dinner after we went to see a movie, something that had become a tradition with Sweetie and me, he stopped talking to me too many times to catalog), he's been at best a middling father and at worst a terrible one, and he's left me with no emotional *or* financial reasons to care what he thinks about me anymore. Mr. Bunches got a new toy today. He got the "My Little Pony" castle or something. He's really into my little ponies. I sent a picture of him playing with the ponies to his older brothers and sisters. They said how happy he looked. I've got all the family I need.

4

The only question in my mind, all day, was what pronoun to end this story with.

3

I'm listening to this song, "Frog Round," a weird sort of techno-round I found on the Internet years ago. It goes:

> *What a queer bird*
> *The frog are*
> *When he sit he stand, almost*
> *When he walk he fly, almost*
> *He ain't got no sense hardly*
> *He ain't got no tail either hardly*

Nobody knows who wrote it. It's supposedly from Ogden Nash but it's not really. It's a weird, eerie song that I love to listen to, sometimes.

It's 7:56 p.m. Sunday, May 25, 2015. I only have two stories left in this series. It seems weird, almost sad. I was thinking yesterday that I ought to keep a diary or journal from now on, since that's what this has become only it's something more. Because I wrote this as a book, a book I planned to sell, it's like I'm writing it *to* someone, to whoever is reading this. So over the past year+, I have been talking to *you*, and I think if I keep a journal it wouldn't be the same. It would be for *me*. This has been like a long letter, intended to be sent out, not a private rumination meant to be kept away from others.

And yet it's more honest than I usually would be in public disclosures about myself. A few times I have thought that I should pull these notes out before I send it to publishers or publish it myself, because they are very private. Then I've thought, *no, that was really the point*. The point in the end was not just to write stories, but to write stories about the stories and give some insight into why I wrote the stories, and I guess I have done that.

I'm not feeling that well tonight. Very dizzy and asthma-y. I was sort of almost dozing off before we went for our nightly ride. We took the boys to the Capitol today. It felt almost a little tense at times, Sweetie and I. I have been trying to include her in what was traditionally a day for me and the boys, because I don't want her to feel left out, to have her sitting at home alone wondering what's happening to us, in every sense she could wonder that. So we're fitting her into our boys' days, and it's not always a perfect fit but we're both trying. She sat downstairs while the boys and I went up to the observation deck, for example. She said she did that because she knows we make her nervous, and it's true. So she was more a part of the trip than in the past but not a full part of it.

Walking up the narrow spiral stairs to the observation deck I got out of breath and weak-legged.

When we got home, I printed a picture of Mr. Bunches looking into the rotunda from an inner viewing area. We glued it to a map of Madison we got at the Capitol. We're going to make a collage of photos of things we do around the city this summer.

2

I am done.

It's 8:30 p.m. on Tuesday, May 26, 2015. Mr F is on his couch, complaining loudly and every few minutes I try to get him to quiet down so he will go to sleep. I've just had a peanut butter and jelly sandwich, because my stomach felt upset and I've had bad asthma all day. I was crabby and didn't get the right kind of sleep last night, or any night, for about a week. I wake up exhausted and I'm probably going to have to go back to the doctors.

I finished 2, and 1, in the same night because I already knew what I was going to write for 1, having thought about it off and on for the last 365+ days and hitting on something the other day that felt right but I let it sit until tonight when I thought *yeah that's how it ends*, and so I just wrote it. After all, I skipped some days here and there so I'm not exactly sticking to the rules.

This morning I worked some more on my business plan, finishing up the rough draft. In the afternoon I spoke to a banker about a business loan. My partner – the one who was supposed to be part of my rescue but who turned out to be a different sort of problem – is probably going to want to talk about some sort of drastic cut to our staff on Thursday, and Sweetie and I are again spending time this way:

It was 2:40 in the afternoon, and we were outside in the damp, getting-humid air that was bright and sun-shiney and fresh and wet the way only a May afternoon can be when the temperature has just hit 70 for the first time that day and the sun is making a brief appearance in between heavy rain showers. I could hear the water dripping on the leaves. I wondered if our pumpkin plants in the old wagon planter (a planter in the backyard made from the wagon I used to tow the boys in when they were littler) were sprouting. (Later I checked, they are.) Memorial Day was yesterday so we are in summer now, never mind what the calendar or the meteorologists say. The boys would be home from school soon, running off the bright yellow school bus and saying *Dad! Mom!* And high-fiving us as they ran inside to get their after-school snacks and settle in to watch a movie or play *Angry Birds*. The neighborhood was quiet.

And we were discussing how much money we would need for me to start my own firm and what we would do if my partner tries to cut my draws from their current level and again both of us were silently thinking or at least I was silently thinking *someday I will be rich*.

Someday.

Everything is different now and everything is the same. I don't think I've ever tracked myself through a year this way, marking every day with *something* to remember. I would like to say that I've never had years this dramatic before but I've had years that were way *more* dramatic, years when we went to Las Vegas on vacation or when Mr F needed emergency brain surgery after falling off our bathroom counter or when I nearly died of bee stings or when I got married or when I went to Morocco – that was the last year I detailed in any sort of ongoing manner, back in 1994. That was a far more dramatic year, me living in Washington D.C. and Morocco and crashing on my mom's couch and breaking up with my girlfriend of 2 years and making a list of things I wanted to accomplish before I turned 26 (I did them all!)

This year hasn't been like that year or like any other year. I feel like this past year, these past 365 days, have broken me apart from the inside and then pulled me together: I don't feel like I'm the same person I was, a year ago. It's like a tectonic shift inside me, like when earthquakes happen and rivers suddenly reverse course. I don't know how I'm different, yet, though. My entire life, sometimes, feels like that moment when you wake up in the morning and stretch and for just a second, even less, you don't know who or what you are and it's frightening, exhilarating, frightening.

I've liked talking to you.

1

I hope you enjoyed the book.

Now I'm going to see how everything outside of it turns out.

And More Words.

No Souls Will Burn in the Sky Tonight appeared first in "Yellow Mama", the June 2014 issue.

For story 318, I wrote an entire story and then decided not to use it. This is that story, before any editing (so it's more than 318 words):

You Are Here.

Once upon a time, you were not here.

You were one of a group of adventurers who rode horses big as elephants over mountain trails steeped in mists trailing down sad and exciting, hiding danger—witches, and angry dragons with fire in their eyes, and chasms full of crocodiles.

You were not afraid of these things. They were why you left your home, waving to your parents as they stared, solemn, wondering if you would, really, come back with gold, and a princess.

It was in the mountains, those mountains, that you found the gem, the eye peering out at you from inside the ruby-red crystal. You didn't tell anyone about the gem, the eye, the find, and just put it in your pocket, quickly, hiding it from others. That should have served as your first warning! You are not selfish. *All for one!* But you hid the gem.

And that night, after the others were asleep, around the fire, the calls of the night eagles still echoing in the canyons, you pulled the gem out, and looked at the eye staring out at you from its depths.

How did the eye get in there, you wondered. I wondered it, too!

I wondered it when I found the gem, as you did, and for me as it did for you, the gem blinked!

We both jumped, you there in your mountain, me there on the beach.

You must remember!

We jumped and we whispered *it is alive*, and we asked it how it got in there but of course the eye couldn't speak! It was just an eye. It blinked again, and we—you and I both, in our days—whispered *are you trapped*?

The eye blinked again.

How can I free you? We asked. We both imagined, genies, spirits, monsters, the lion with a thorn, gratitude… *riches.*

The eye blinked again, and teared up. For both of us!

We both wished! We both hoped, prayed, yearned for that eye to be free, with the promise that freedom would hold for us, its benefactors, its heroes.

We both arrived *here.*

It was my eye you saw, and your eye I saw.

You must remember.

You must help me discern what type of curse this is.

That wasn't the end of the story; that was just where I gave up on it and switched to a different story.

This Is Not A Metaphor, story 325, was submitted to Fabula Argentea, which passed.

———————

Here There Be Dragons was published in the June, 2014 issue of *The Olentangy Review*.

———————

Shark vs. Crocodile may seem like a total work of fiction but on August 6, 2014, the Huffington Post printed a story entitled "Crocodile vs. Shark: Only One Emerges Victorious," with photos of a crocodile forcing a small shark up onto the sand and eating it. My story was written well before that newsworthy event.

———————

Here is the story I mentioned in Note 246:

It was love at first sight: from the moment Earth saw Moon it could not let go.

Come to me Earth beckoned, but Moon would not, because Earth was falling into Sun and Moon did not want to be destroyed.

That will not happen for billions of years Earth pouted, but both knew that was immaterial: they would live billions of years.

I must have you Earth decided, and started folding in on itself over and over, becoming rocky, wrapped in itself, more solid, harder to understand but more powerful.

Moon saw the transformation, felt what Earth was doing.

No

Noooooooooooo

Moon wailed into infinity.

But Earth's rocky grasp had Moon already.

Moon was no longer *free*.

You may have captured me, but you will never see me Moon said, its last words, ever before turning its back on Earth, staring bereft out to the ever-receding horizons it could only dream of, watching others dancing wondrously away throughout creation while it was stuck here.

Earth tried everything it could to get Moon to forgive it. It flung cooling waters about in majestic waves. It grew giant thundering lizards to rage and fight for amusement. When those did not work Earth destroyed them, blasting its volcanoes and starting over. *I shall come up with something*, Earth vowed, and began teaching its newest creations all they would need to know to leave its surface someday, to go talk to Moon.

———————

Here is that partial version of *The Dragon, and The Mermaid* that I mentioned back in Note 266:

The Dragon, and The Mermaid.

"I bet," said the dragon, "That fewer people believe in me anymore than believe in you."

"Don't let it get you down," the mermaid advised.

"Oh, I don't," said the dragon. "I was just saying."

"You could make people believe in you. You know? You could, I don't know, go rampage over

one of those cities. What's the one they're all so proud of?"

"New York?" guessed the dragon.

"No. No. I think... Paris? Yeah, Paris, you could rampage over it, blow some fire, eat some people, maybe knock down some buildings with that tail."

"And then what? They hunt me until I'm dead and it's over. It doesn't seem worth it to have to die to get people to believe in you."

"Let's not get too metaphorical," said the mermaid.

"If I did that, if I made people believe in me, would you go out with me then?" The dragon tried to look both menacing and alluring.

"Yeah, I guess," the mermaid said. "Yeah, why not?"

Later, she watched from the ...

This is an alternate ending that I tried:

"And then what? They hunt me until I'm dead and it's over. It doesn't seem worth it to have to die to get people to believe in you."

"Let's not get too metaphorical," said the mermaid.

"If I did that, if I made people believe in me, would you go out with me then?" The dragon tried to look both menacing and alluring.

"If I say no, are you going to get mad and go rampaging?" the mermaid answered without answering.

The dragon blew fire, caused the little lagoon to steam up in a cloud of hot breath. "Probably not," it admitted.

A few minutes later, the dragon said "So why won'...

You can see I quit on that one before I even finished the word *won't*.

And this was the first ending I tried to work towards:

"Let's not get too metaphorical," said the mermaid.

"Lured any ships lately?"

"I don't do that anymore. It got old."

"Really? When did you quit?"

"Long time ago."

The mermaid swished her tail meditatively and then asked if the dragon wanted to go out some time.

"What, like on a date?" the dragon mulled that.

"Yeah, I guess, a date, if you wanted,"

———————

Story 281, *A Sky Too Full of Stars* was published by Daily Science Fiction on December 18, 2014. It was rated an average of 4.8 Rocket Dragons, out of 7 possible. Not bad!

This Is Not A Metaphor, story 325, was submitted to Fabula Argentea, which passed.

Here There Be Dragons was published in the June, 2014 issue of *The Olentangy Review.*

Shark vs. Crocodile may seem like a total work of fiction but on August 6, 2014, the Huffington Post printed a story entitled "Crocodile vs. Shark: Only One Emerges Victorious," with photos of a crocodile forcing a small shark up onto the sand and eating it. My story was written well before that newsworthy event.

Here is the story I mentioned in Note 246:

It was love at first sight: from the moment Earth saw Moon it could not let go.

Come to me Earth beckoned, but Moon would not, because Earth was falling into Sun and Moon did not want to be destroyed.

That will not happen for billions of years Earth pouted, but both knew that was immaterial: they would live billions of years.

I must have you Earth decided, and started folding in on itself over and over, becoming rocky, wrapped in itself, more solid, harder to understand but more powerful.

Moon saw the transformation, felt what Earth was doing.

No

Noooooooooooo

Moon wailed into infinity.

But Earth's rocky grasp had Moon already.

Moon was no longer *free.*

You may have captured me, but you will never see me Moon said, its last words, ever before turning its back on Earth, staring bereft out to the ever-receding horizons it could only dream of, watching others dancing wondrously away throughout creation while it was stuck here.

Earth tried everything it could to get Moon to forgive it. It flung cooling waters about in majestic waves. It grew giant thundering lizards to rage and fight for amusement. When those did not work Earth destroyed them, blasting its volcanoes and starting over. *I shall come up with something*, Earth vowed, and began teaching its newest creations all they would need to know to leave its surface someday, to go talk to Moon.

Here is that partial version of *The Dragon, and The Mermaid* that I mentioned back in Note 266:

The Dragon, and The Mermaid.

"I bet," said the dragon, "That fewer people believe in me anymore than believe in you."

"Don't let it get you down," the mermaid advised.

"Oh, I don't," said the dragon. "I was just saying."

"You could make people believe in you. You know? You could, I don't know, go rampage over

one of those cities. What's the one they're all so proud of?"

"New York?" guessed the dragon.

"No. No. I think... Paris? Yeah, Paris, you could rampage over it, blow some fire, eat some people, maybe knock down some buildings with that tail."

"And then what? They hunt me until I'm dead and it's over. It doesn't seem worth it to have to die to get people to believe in you."

"Let's not get too metaphorical," said the mermaid.

"If I did that, if I made people believe in me, would you go out with me then?" The dragon tried to look both menacing and alluring.

"Yeah, I guess," the mermaid said. "Yeah, why not?"

Later, she watched from the ...

This is an alternate ending that I tried:

"And then what? They hunt me until I'm dead and it's over. It doesn't seem worth it to have to die to get people to believe in you."

"Let's not get too metaphorical," said the mermaid.

"If I did that, if I made people believe in me, would you go out with me then?" The dragon tried to look both menacing and alluring.

"If I say no, are you going to get mad and go rampaging?" the mermaid answered without answering.

The dragon blew fire, caused the little lagoon to steam up in a cloud of hot breath. "Probably not," it admitted.

A few minutes later, the dragon said "So why won'...

You can see I quit on that one before I even finished the word won't.

And this was the first ending I tried to work towards:

"Let's not get too metaphorical," said the mermaid.

"Lured any ships lately?"

"I don't do that anymore. It got old."

"Really? When did you quit?"

"Long time ago."

The mermaid swished her tail meditatively and then asked if the dragon wanted to go out some time.

"What, like on a date?" the dragon mulled that.

"Yeah, I guess, a date, if you wanted,"

———————

Story 281, *A Sky Too Full of Stars* was published by Daily Science Fiction on December 18, 2014. It was rated an average of 4.8 Rocket Dragons, out of 7 possible. Not bad!